Gripping Tales of Intrigue and Suspense

SIGNET DOUBLE MYSTERIES:

TEN DAYS' WONDER

and

THE KING IS DEAD

TEN DAYS' WONDER
and
THE KING IS DEAD

by

Ellery Queen

A SIGNET BOOK
NEW AMERICAN LIBRARY
TIMES MIRROR

PUBLISHER'S NOTE

These novels are works of fiction. Names, characters, places, and incidents are either the product of the author's imagination or are used fictitiously, and any resemblance to actual persons, living or dead, events or locales is entirely coincidental.

Published by arrangement with Frederic Dannay and the late Manfred B. Lee. TEN DAYS' WONDER and THE KING IS DEAD also appeared in paperback as separate volumes published by The New American Library.

SIGNET TRADEMARK REG. U.S. PAT. OFF. AND FOREIGN COUNTRIES
REGISTERED TRADEMARK—MARCA REGISTRADA
HECHO EN CHICAGO, U.S.A.

SIGNET, SIGNET CLASSICS, MENTOR, PLUME, MERIDIAN AND NAL BOOKS
are published by The New American Library, Inc.,
1633 Broadway, New York, New York 10019

First Printing (Double Ellery Queen Edition), November, 1980

1 2 3 4 5 6 7 8 9

PRINTED IN THE UNITED STATES OF AMERICA

TEN DAYS' WONDER

Contents

Part One

NINE DAYS' WONDER

Part Two

TENTH DAY'S WONDER

Part I Nine Days' Wonder

The First Day

IN THE BEGINNING it was without form, a darkness that kept shifting like dancers. There was music beyond, tiny, cheerful, baffling, and then it would be vast, rushing on you and, as it rushed, losing its music in sounds so big you flowed through the spaces like a gnat in an air stream, and then it was past and dwindling and tiny music again and there was the darkness shifting again.

Everything swayed. He felt seasick.

That might be a sea sky up there over the Atlantic night with a shadow like a wash cloud and trembly places where stars were. And the music could be singing in the fo'c'sle or the shift of black water. He knew it was real, because when he closed his eyes the cloud and the stars blinked out, although the sway remained and so did the music. There was also the smell of fish and something with a complicated taste, like sour honey.

It was interesting because everything was a problem and having sights and sounds and smells and tastes to worry over gave him a feeling of new importance, as if before he had been nothing. It was like being born. It was like being born in a ship. You lay in the ship and the ship rocked and you rocked with it in the rocking night, looking up at the ceiling of the sky.

You could rock here forever in this pleasant timelessness if only things remained the same, but they did not. The sky was closing in and the stars were coming down and this was another puzzle, because instead of growing as they neared they shrank. Even the quality of the rocking changed: it had muscles in it now and suddenly he thought, Maybe it's not the ship that's rocking, but me.

He opened his eyes.

He was seated on something hard that gave. His knees were pressing against his chin. His hands were locked around his shins and he was rocking back and forth.

Somebody said, "It isn't a ship at all," and he was surprised because the voice was familiar and for the life of him he couldn't remember whose it was.

He looked around rather sharply.

Nobody was in the room.

Room.

It was a room.

The discovery was like a splash of seawater.

He unclasped his hands and put them down flat against something warm and grainy yet slithery to the touch. He did not like it and he raised his hands to his face. This time his palms were offended as if by mohair and he thought, I'm in a room and I need a shave but what's a shave? Then he remembered what a shave was, and he laughed. How could he possibly have had to think what a shave was?

He lowered his hands again and they felt the slithery stuff and he saw that it was a sort of blanket. At the same instant he realized that during his reflections the darkness had gone away.

He frowned. Had it ever been there at all?

Immediately he knew it had not. Immediately he knew the sky had never been, either. It's a ceiling, he thought, scowling, and a damned scabby ceiling at that. And those stars were phonies, too. Just fugitives of sun-streaks sneaking in through the tears in an exhausted window shade. Somewhere a voice was bellowing "When Irish Eyes Are Smiling." There was also sloshing water. And that smell was fish, all right, fish frying in lard. He swallowed the sour-sweet taste and he realized that the taste was also an odor and that both were in chemical combination in the air he was breathing. No wonder he felt like heaving. The air was aged, like cheese.

Like cheese with socks on, he thought, grinning. Where am I?

He was sitting up on a bed of fancy iron which had once been painted white but now was suffering from a sort of eczema, facing a slash of undecided glass. The room was comically small, with banana-colored walls. And, he thought, grinning again, the banana's peeling.

That's three times I've laughed, he thought; I must have a sense of humor. But where the hell am I?

There was a grand oval-backed chair with carving and a mumpy green horsehair seat, an X of wire holding its elegant legs together; a man with long hair who looked as if he were dying stared at him from a tilted calendar on the wall; and the back of the door poked a chipped china clotheshook at him, like a finger. A finger in a mystery, but what was the answer? Nothing was on the hook, nothing was on the chair, and the man in the picture looked as familiar as the voice which had said it wasn't a ship, only both remained just out of reach.

The man on the bed with his big knees sticking up was a dirty bum, that's what he was, a dirty bum with a beat-up face who hadn't even bothered to take his dirty clothes off, the dirty bum; he sat there wrapped in his own dirt as if he liked it. And this was a pain.

Because I'm the man on the bed and how can I be the man on the bed when I never saw the dirty bum before?

It was a sticker.

It was a sticker when you not only didn't know where you were but who you were, either.

He laughed again.

I'll flop back on this alleged mattress and go to sleep, he thought, that's what I'll do; and the next thing Howard knew he was in a ship again under a covering of stars.

When Howard awoke for the second time it was all different, no gradual being born again, no ship fantasy or any of that nonsense; but an opening of the eyes, a recognition of the foul room, of the Christ on the calendar, of the broken mirror, and he was out of the functional bed in a bound and glaring at his remembered image.

Nearly everything flashed back in place in his head: who he was, where he came from, even why he had come to New York. He remembered catching the Atlantic Stater at Slocum. He remembered trudging up the ramp from the smelter of Track 24 into the oven of Grand Central Station. He remembered phoning the Terrazzi Galleries and asking what time the doors opened for the Djerens exhibition, and the annoyed European voice saying in his ear, "The exhibition of Mynheer Djerens expired as of yesterday." And he remembered opening his eyes in this garbage can. But between the voice and the room hung a black mist.

Howard got the shakes.

He knew he was going to get them before he got them. But he didn't know they were going to be so bad. He tried to control himself. But muscle-tightening only made them worse. He went to the door with the chipped china hook.

I can't have slept very long this last time, he thought. They're still sloshing water around out there.

He opened the door.

The hall was an odorous memorial to departed feet.

The old man pushing the mop looked up.

"Hey, you," said Howard. "Where am I?"

The old man leaned against the mop and Howard saw that he had only one eye. "I was out West one time," the old man said. "I traveled in my day, cully. There was this Red Injun sitting outside a wide place in the road. Nothing for miles around, see, just this one little old shack, and a mountain back there. Kansas, I think it was—"

"More likely Oklahoma or New Mexico," said Howard, finding himself holding up the wall. That fish had been eaten, no doubt, but its corpse haunted the place tantalizingly. He'd have to eat, and soon; that's the way it always was. "What's the point? I've got to get out of here."

"This Injun, he was sitting on the dirt with his back against this shack, see—"

Suddenly the old man's eye shifted to the center of his forehead and Howard said, "Polyphemus."

"No," said the old fellow, "I didn't know his name. The thing is, right over this Red Injun's head, nailed to the wall, was a sign on it with great big red sort of lettering. And what do you think it says?"

"What?" said Howard.

"Hotel Waldorf," said the old fellow triumphantly.

"Thanks a lot," said Howard. "That really sets me up, old-timer. Now where the hell am I?"

"Where the hell would you be?" snarled the old man. "You're in a flophouse, my friend, a flophouse on the Bowery, which was good enough for Steve Brody and Tim Sullivan but it's too good for the likes of you, you dirty bum."

The slop pail flew. It took off like a bird. Then it landed on its side with a musical splash.

The old man quivered as if Howard had kicked, not the pail, but him. Standing there in the gray suds, he looked about to cry.

"Give me that mop," said Howard. "I'll clean it up."

"You dirty bum!"

Howard went back into the room.

He sat down on the bed and cupped his palms over his mouth and nose, exhaling hard, because he was hoping hard.

But he hadn't been drinking, after all.

His hands dropped.

His hands dropped and there was blood all over them. Blood all over his hands.

Howard tore at his clothes. His fawn gabardine was ripped and wrinkled, grease-smeared, stiff with filth. He reeked like the pens on Jorking's farm beyond Twin Hills. As a boy he had taken the long way round to Slocum Township just to avoid Jorking's pigs. But now it didn't matter; it was even pleasant, because it wasn't what you were looking for.

He searched himself like a louse-ridden monkey.

And suddenly he found it. A big, brown-black clot. Part of the clot was on his lapel. The other part was on his shirt. The clot was making the shirt stick to the suit. He tore them apart.

The raw edge of the clot was fibrous.

He jumped off the bed and ran over to the slice of mirror. His right eye resembled an old avocado pit. There was a scarlet trench across the bridge of his nose. The left side of his lower lip was blown up like a piece of bubble gum. And his left ear was a caricature in purple.

He had picked a fight!

Or had he?

And he had lost.

Or had he won?

Or had he won and lost, too?

He held his shaky hands up to his functioning eye and peered at them. The knuckles of both were gashed, scraped, oversize. The blood had run into the blond hairs, making them stand up stiff, like mascaraed eyelashes.

But that's my own blood.

He turned his hands palms up and relief washed over him in a wave.

There was no blood on the palms.

Maybe I didn't kill anybody after all, he thought gleefully.

But his glee dribbled away. There was that other blood. On his suit and shirt. Maybe it wasn't his. Maybe it was someone else's. Maybe this time it had happened.

Maybe . . . !

This is going to push me over, he thought. If I keep thinking about it, by God I'll go right over.

The pain in his hands.

He went through his pockets slowly. He had left home with over two hundred dollars. The inventory was perfunctory; he had no real hope of finding anything and he was not disappointed. His money was gone. So was his watch, with the miniature gold sculptor's mallet his father had given him to wear as a fob the year he went to France. So was the gold fountain pen Sally had given him last year for his birthday. Rolled. Maybe after he'd checked into this opium den. It sounded plausible; they'd never have given him a room without payment in advance.

Howard tried to conjure up "desk clerk," "lobby," "Bowery"—how it had all looked the night before.

Night before. Or two nights before. Or two weeks before. The last time it had taken six days. Once it had been for a mere couple of hours. He never knew until afterwards because the thing was like a streak of dry rot in Time, unmeasurable except by what surrounded it.

Howard went drearily to the door again.

"What's the date?"

The old man was on his knees in the slop, soaking it up with his mop.

"I said what's the date."

The old man was still offended. He wrung the mop out over the pail stubbornly.

Howard heard his own teeth grinding. *"What is the date?"*

The old man spat. "You get tough, brother, I'll call Bagley. He'll fix your wagon. He'll fix it." Then he must have seen something in Howard's good eye, because he whined, "It's the day after Labor Day," and he picked up the pail and fled.

Tuesday after the first Monday in September.

Howard hurried back into the room and over to the calendar.

The year on it was 1937.

Howard scratched his head and laughed. Cast away, that's what I am. They'll find my bones on the bottom of the sea.

The Log!

Howard began to look for it, frantically.

He had started The Log immediately after his first baffling cruise through time-space. Making a nightly report to himself enabled him to fix the conscious part of his existence, it provided a substantial deck for his feet from which to look back over those black voyages. But it was a curious log. It recorded only the events, as it were, on shore. For the intervals he passed on the timeless sea the pages stood smooth and blank.

His diary was a collection of fat black pocket notebooks. As he filled one he put it away in his writing desk at home. But he always carried the current one.

If they'd lifted that, too—!

But he found it in the outside breast pocket of his jacket, under the Irish linen handkerchief.

The final entry told him that this latest voyage had lasted nineteen days.

He found himself staring through the dirty window. Three stories above the street.

Enough.

But suppose I just break my leg?

He plunged out into the hall.

Ellery Queen said he wouldn't listen to a word until later because a story told under stress of pain and hunger and exhaustion, while it might interest poets and priests, could only prove a waste of time to a man of facts. So pure selfishness demanded that he strip Howard, toss him into a hot tub, scrape off his beard, doctor his wounds, provide him with clean clothing, and push a breakfast into him consisting of a large glass of tomato juice mixed with Worcestershire and Tabasco, a small steak, seven pieces of hot buttered toast, and three cups of black coffee.

"Now," said Ellery cheerfully, pouring the third cup. "I recognize you. And now you can probably think with at least a primitive efficiency. Well, Howard, when I last saw you, you were bashing marble. What have you done—graduated to flesh?"

"You examined my clothes."

Ellery grinned. "You were a long time in that tub."

"I was long time walking up here from the Bowery."

"Broke?"

"You know I am. You looked through my pockets."

"Naturally. How's your father, Howard?"

"All right." Then Howard looked startled and pushed away from the table. "Ellery, may I use your phone?"

Ellery watched him go into the study. The door didn't quite close after him and Ellery was reluctant to make a point of closing it. Apparently Howard was putting through a long-distance call, because for some time there was no sound from beyond the door.

Ellery reached for his after-breakfast pipe and reviewed what he knew of Howard Van Horn.

It wasn't much and what there was of it lay darkly behind a war, an ocean, and a decade. They had met on the *terrasse* of the café at the corner where the Rue de la Huchette meets the Boulevard St. Michel. This was prewar Paris: Paris of the Cagoulards and the *populaires;* of the incredible Exposition, when Nazis with elaborate cameras and guidebooks infested the Right Bank, shouldering their way *Uebermensch*-wise through pale refugees from Vienna and Prague, going to view Picasso's mural, *Guernica,* with every appearance of tourist passion; Paris of the raging Spanish argument, while across the Pyrenees Madrid lay dying of nonintervention. A decaying Paris, and Ellery was there looking for a man known as Hansel, which is another and dated story and therefore will probably never be told. But since Hansel was a Nazi, and few Nazis were believed to come to the Rue de la Huchette, that was where Ellery looked for him.

And that was where he found Howard.

Howard had been living on the Left Bank for some time, and Howard was unhappy. The Rue de la Huchette did not share the confidence of other Parisian quarters in the impregnability of the Maginot Line; there were disturbing political atmospheres; it was all upsetting to a young American who had come abroad to study sculpture and whose head was full of Rodin, Bourdelle, neoclassicism, and the purity of Greek line. Ellery recalled that he had felt rather sorry for Howard; and because a man who is watching the world go by is less conspicuous if he is two, he permitted Howard to share his *terrasse* table. For three weeks they saw a great deal of each other; until one day Hansel came strolling out of fourteenth century France, which is the Rue St. Séverin, into Ellery's arms, and that was the end of Howard.

In the study Howard was saying, "But, Father, I'm okay. I wouldn't lie to you, you mug." And then Howard laughed and said, "Call off the dogs. I'll be home right off."

In those three weeks Howard had spoken at length and with terrible adoration of his father. Ellery had gathered the impression that the elder Van Horn was a great iron-chested figure, hero-sized, a man of force, dignity, humanity, brilliance, compassion, and generosity —a veritable father-image; and this had amused the great man, because when Howard took him to his impressive *pension* studio, Ellery saw that it was thronged with sculptures, worked directly in the stone on a solid geometric basis, of such looming deities of maleness as Zeus, Moses, and Adam. It had seemed significant at the time that Howard did not once mention his mother.

"No, I'm with Ellery Queen," Howard was saying. "You remember, Father—that wonderful guy I met in Paris before the war . . . Yes, Queen . . . Yes, the same one." And, grimly: "I decided to look him up."

During that Parisian idyl, Howard had struck Ellery

as rather pitifully provincial. He came from New England—Ellery never did learn from just where in New England; but it was not far, he had gathered, from New York. Apparently the Van Horns lived in one of the town's great houses: Howard, his father, and his father's brother; no women were mentioned, and Ellery supposed that Howard's mother had been dead for many years. His boyhood had been surrounded by a high wall of tutors and governesses; he learned a great deal of the world through the eyes of paid adults, which is to say, he learned nothing. His only contact with reality was the town he lived in. It was not wonderful, then, that in Paris Howard should have been uneasy, bewildered, and resentful. He was too far from Main Street . . . and, Ellery suspected, from papa.

Ellery remembered thinking that Howard would have interested a psychiatrist. He was structurally the big-boned, muscular, rugged, bony-headed, square-jawed, thick-skinned man of action—bold, adventurous and masterful, the typical hero of popular fiction. Yet, caught up in the ferment of Europe at the most tempestuous moment in its history, he kept stealing wistful glances, as it were, over his big shoulder at fireside and father an ocean away. The father creates the son in his own image, Ellery had thought, but not always with the expected result.

Ellery had got the feeling that Howard was in Europe not because he wanted to be but because Diedrich Van Horn expected him to be. Howard would have been far happier, Ellery knew, in a Boston fine arts class or, as the town's sole authority in such matters, acting as consultant to the Mayor's Planning Committee on the propriety of allowing that foreign sculptor to go ahead with those undraped females planned for the pediment of the proposed Civic Recreation Center. Ellery had thought with a grin that Howard would have made the perfect adviser in such a situation, for he invariably blushed when they passed the *clandestin* at the corner of the Rue de la Huchette and the Rue Zacharie, and he had once summarized his feelings about Europe by pointing earnestly to the *Poste de Police* across the street from it and bursting out: "I'm no prude, Ellery, but by God that's going too far, that's pure decadence!" Ellery recalled thinking at the time that Howard could not have been too familiar with the sociological facts of life as it was lived in his own home town. He had often thought since of Howard hacking soberly away at his father's image in that splendid Left Bank studio, an overgrown and troubled young soul. He had been very fond of Howard.

"But that's silly, Father. You tell Sally she's not to worry about me. At all."

But all this had been ten years ago. Another Sculptor had been at work on Howard's physiognomy in the intervening decade, and Ellery was not thinking of the unknown artist who had given it such an expert going-over with his fists. There were secretive corners to Howard's mouth now and an older, warier glint in his undamaged eye. Things had happened to young Van Horn since their last meeting. He would not be abashed by a bordel now; and there was a note in his voice as he spoke to his father which Ellery had not heard ten years before.

Ellery experienced a sudden very odd feeling.

But before he could examine it, Howard came out of the study.

"Father had all the cops in the East out looking for me," grinned Howard. "Doesn't speak very well for Inspector Queen's profession."

"The East is a big place, Howard."

Howard sat down and began to examine his bandaged hands.

"What was it?" asked Ellery. "The war?"

"War?" Howard looked up, really surprised.

"You're so obviously suffering from a painful—and I should think a chronic—experience. It wasn't the war?"

"I wasn't even in it."

Ellery smiled. "Well, I've given you your opening."

"Oh. Yes." Howard scowled, jiggled his right foot. "I don't know why I should think you'd be interested in my troubles."

"Let's assume I am."

Ellery watched him struggle with himself.

"Come on," he said. "Get it off your chest."

Howard blurted: "Ellery, two and a half hours ago I was going to jump out of a window."

"I see," said Ellery, "you changed your mind."

Howard went slowly red. "I'm not lying!"

"And I'm not the least bit interested in dramatics." Ellery knocked out his pipe.

Everything in Howard's battered face tightened and blued.

"Howard," said Ellery, "I don't know of anyone who hasn't toyed with the notion of committing suicide at one time or other. But you'll notice that most of us are still around." Howard glared at him. "You think I'm one hell of a confidant. But Howard, you started the wrong way. Suicide isn't your problem. Don't try to impress me." Howard's glance wavered, and Ellery chuckled. "I like you, you ape. I liked you ten years ago when I thought you were a fine kid who'd been thoroughly screwed up by a dominating and overindulgent father—and stop making with the jaw, Howard, I'm not talking your father down; what I just said is true of most American fathers—what differences exist are only in degree, varying according to the individual.

"I say I liked you then, when you were a damp-muzzled pup, and I like you now, when you're obviously a full-grown dog. You're in trouble, you've come to me, and I'll help all I can. But I can't do a thing if you strike attitudes. Heroics are going to get in the way. Now have I wounded you to the soul?"

"Damn you."

They both laughed, and Ellery said briskly, "Wait till I reload my pipe."

Early on the morning of September 1, 1939, Nazi warplanes roared over Warsaw. Before the day was out the Republic of France had decreed general mobilization and martial law. Before the week was out Howard was homeward bound.

"I was glad of the excuse," Howard confessed. "I'd had a bellyful of France, refugees, Hitler, Mussolini, the Café St. Michel, and myself. I wanted to crawl under the comforter in my own little bed and sleep for twenty years. I was even sick of sculpture; when I got home I chucked my chisel away.

"Father came through, as usual. He didn't ask any questions, and he didn't throw anything up to me. He let me work it out alone."

But Howard had not worked it out. His bed was not the slumbrous womb he had looked forward to; Main Street unaccountably seemed more foreign than the Rue du Chat Qui Pêche; he found himself reading newspapers and news magazines and listening to the radio report Europe's agony; he began to avoid mirrors. And he discovered that he resented violently some of his uncle's isolationist observations. There were quarrels at the Van Horn dinner table, with Howard's father the rather troubled mediator.

"Uncle?" said Ellery.

"My Uncle Wolfert. Father's brother. He's something of a character," said Howard, and he let it go at that.

And then Howard sailed on his first cruise on the black sea.

"It happened the night Father married," said Howard. "It was a surprise to all of us—I mean the marriage; I remember Uncle Wolf making a typical snide remark about old fools in their second childhood. But Father wasn't so old, and he'd fallen in love with somebody pretty wonderful—he hadn't made any mistake.

"Anyway, he married Sally and they left for their honeymoon and that same night I was standing in front of my bureau mirror ripping off my tie—undressing to hit the hay—when the next thing I knew I was choking over a piece of fly-specked blueberry pie in a truckmen's diner four-hundred-odd miles away."

Ellery very carefully put a match to his pipe again. "Teleportation?" he grinned.

"I'm not kidding you. It was the next thing I knew."

"How long a time had elapsed?"

"Five and a half days."

Ellery puffed. "Damn this pipe."

"Ellery, I had no recollection of a thing. One minute I was taking off my tie in my own bedroom, the next minute I was sitting on a stool in a diner over a hundred miles away. How I'd got there, what I'd done for almost six days, what I'd eaten, where I'd slept, whom I talked to, what I said—nothing. A blank. I had no sensation of the passage of time. I might just as well have died, been buried, and been resurrected."

"That's better," said Ellery to his pipe. "Oh, yes. Unsettling, Howard, but not uncommon. Amnesia."

"Sure," said Howard with a grin. "Amnesia. Just a word. Did you ever have it?"

"Go on."

Three weeks later it happened again.

"The first time nobody knew about it. Uncle Wolfert didn't give a damn where I was or how long I stayed away, and Father was off on his honeymoon. But the second time Father and Sally were back home. I was gone twenty-six hours before they found me, and I didn't snap out of it for another eight. They had to tell me what happened. I came to thinking I'd just stepped out of my shower. But it was a full day and a half later."

"And the doctors?"

"Naturally Father had every doctor he could lay his

hands on. They couldn't find a thing wrong with me. Brother Queen, I was scared, and no fooling."

"Of course you were."

Howard lit a cigaret, slowly. "Thanks. But I mean scared." He frowned as he blew out the match. "I can't describe . . ."

"You felt as if all the normal rules were suspended. But only for you."

"That's it. All of a sudden I felt absolutely alone. Sort of—sort of fourth-dimensional stuff."

Ellery smiled. "Let's get off the auto-analysis. The attacks kept recurring?"

"Right up to and through the war. When Pearl Harbor was blasted, I was almost relieved. To get into uniform, get going, do things . . . I don't know, it looked like a possible answer. Only . . . they wouldn't take me."

"Oh?"

"Turned down, Ellery. By the Army, the Navy, the Air Force, the Marine Corps, and the Merchant Marine—in that order. I guess they didn't have much use for a guy who staged his own private blackouts at the most unpredictable times." Howard's puffed lip curled. "I was one of Uncle Sam's pet four-effs."

"So you had to stay home."

"And it was rugged. People in town gave me an awful lot of queer looks. And the boys home on leave sort of avoided me. I guess they all thought because I was the son of . . . Anyway, I fought the war working on the night shift at a big aircraft plant up home. Half-days I messed around with clay and stone in my studio at the house. I didn't show myself much. It was too tough trying to shrink up so I wouldn't be noticed."

Ellery glanced over the powerful body sprawled in the armchair, and he nodded.

"All right," he said crisply. "Now let's have some details. Tell me everything you know about these amnesia attacks."

"They're periodic and sporadic. Never any warning, although one doctor claimed that they seemed to occur when I've been unusually excited, or upset. Sometimes the blackout lasts only a couple of hours, sometimes three or four weeks. I snap out of them in all sorts of places—at home, in Boston, in New York, once in Providence. Other times on a dirt road in the middle of nowhere. Or any old place. I never have the faintest recollection of where I've been or what I've done."

"Howard." Ellery's tone was casual. "Did you ever come to on a bridge?"

"On a bridge?"

"Yes."

It seemed to Ellery that Howard's tone was as deliberately casual as his own.

"I did once, at that. Why?"

"What were you doing when you became conscious of yourself? I mean on the bridge."

"What was I," Howard hesitated, "doing?"

"That's right."

"Why . . ."

"You were about to jump off, weren't you?"

Howard stared at him. "How the hell did you know that? I never even told that to the doctors!"

"The suicide pattern suggests itself strongly. Any other such episodes? I mean waking up to find yourself about to take your own life?"

"Two other times," said Howard tightly. "Once I was in a canoe on a lake; I came to as I hit the water. The other time I was just about to step off a chair in a hotel room. There was a rope around my neck."

"And this going-to-jump-out-of-window business this morning?"

"No, that was conscious." Howard jumped up. "Ellery—"

"No. Wait. Sit down." Howard sat down. "What do the doctors say?"

"Well, I'm perfectly sound organically. There's no medical history that would account for the attacks—epilepsy, or anything like that."

"Have they put you under?"

"Hypnosis? I think they have. You know, Ellery, they've got a cute trick of hypnotizing you and then, before they bring you out of it, they'll order you not to remember having been put under—to wake up thinking you'd simply fallen asleep." Howard grinned grimly. "I have an idea I'm not a very hypnotic subject. I'm sure it hasn't happened more than once or twice, and then unsatisfactorily. I don't co-operate."

"They haven't offered anything constructive?"

"There's been a lot of learned talk, and I suppose some of it means something, but they certainly haven't been able to stop the attacks. The last psychiatrist Father sicked onto me suggested that I may be suffering from hyperinsulinism."

"Hyper-what?"

"Hyperinsulinism."

"Never heard of it."

Howard shrugged. "The way it was explained to me, it's the exact opposite of the condition that causes diabetes. When the pancreas or whatever it is doesn't manufacture—the M.D. used the word 'elaborate'—enough insulin, you have diabetes. When it elaborates too much insulin, you have the big fancy word and it can cause, among other things, amnesia.

"Well, maybe that's it and maybe it isn't. They're not sure."

"You must have been given sugar-tolerance tests?"

"Inconclusive. Sometimes I reacted normally, sometimes I didn't. The truth is, Ellery, they just don't know. They say they could find out all right if I'd really co-operate, but what do they expect? A piece of my soul?"

Howard glared at the rug.

And Ellery was silent.

"They admit it's perfectly possible for me to have periodic, temporary attacks of amnesia and still be organically and functionally okay. Helps, doesn't it?" Howard squirmed in the armchair, rubbing the back of his neck. "I don't give a damn any more what the doctors say, Ellery. All I know is, if I don't stop walking into these black holes, I'll . . ." He sprang to his feet. Then he walked over to the window and stared out at Eighty-seventh Street. "Can you help me?" he said, without turning around.

"I don't know."

Howard whirled. He was very pale. "Somebody's got to help me!"

"What makes you think I can help?"

"What?"

"Howard, I'm not a doctor."

"I'm fed up with doctors!"

"They'll locate the cause eventually."

"And what am I supposed to do in the meantime? Go off my trolley? I tell you I'm close to it right now!"

"Sit down, Howard, sit down."

"Ellery, you've got to help me. I'm desperate. Come home with me!"

"Come home with you?"

"Yes!"

"Why?"

"I want you near me when the next one comes. I want you to watch me, Ellery. See what I do. Where I go. Maybe I'm leading a . . ."

"Double life?"
"Yes!"
Ellery rose and went to the fireplace to knock out his pipe again.
And he said: "Howard, come clean."
"What?"
"I said come clean."
"What do you mean?"
Ellery glanced at him sidewise. "You're holding something out on me."
"Why, I'm doing nothing of the sort."
"Yes. You won't co-operate with the only people who can really help you find a cause—and consequently a cure—for this condition, the doctors. You're not an 'easy' subject for diagnosis or treatment. You admit you've told me things you haven't told any of the medical men. Why me, Howard? We met ten years ago—for three weeks. Why me?"
Howard did not answer.
"I'll tell you why. Because," said Ellery, straightening, "I'm an amateur snoop, Howard, and you think you've committed a crime during one of your blackouts. Perhaps more than one crime. Perhaps one in each episode."
"No, I—"
"That's why you won't help the doctors, Howard. You're afraid of what they might find out."
"No!"
"Yes," said Ellery.
Howard's shoulders drooped. He turned around and put his bandaged hands in the pockets of the jacket Ellery had given him and he said, in a hopeless sort of way, "All right. I suppose that's what's behind it."
"Good! Now we have a basis for discussion. Any concrete reason for your suspicion?"
"No."
"I think you have."
Howard suddenly laughed. He withdrew his hands and held them up. "You saw them when I got here. That's the way they were when I came to in that flophouse this morning. You saw my coat, my shirt."
"Oh, is that it? Why, Howard, you were in a fight."
"Yes, but what happened?" Howard's voice rose. "It's not being sure that's getting me down, Ellery. Not knowing. I've got to know! That's why I wish you'd come home with me."
Ellery took a little walk around the room, sucking on his empty pipe.

Howard watched him, uneasily.

"Are you considering it?" Howard asked.

"I'm considering," said Ellery, stopping to lean against the mantelpiece, "the possibility that you're still holding something back."

"What's the matter with you?" cried Howard. "I'm not!"

"Sure, Howard? Sure you're telling me everything?"

"My God in His sweet heaven, man," shouted Howard, "what do you want me to do—take my skin off?"

"Why the heat?"

"You're calling me a liar!"

"Aren't you?"

This time Howard did not shout. He ran over to the armchair and flung himself into it, angrily.

But Ellery persisted: "Aren't you, Howard?"

"Not really." Howard's tone was unexpectedly calm. "Naturally, we girls have our secrets. I mean secrets." He even smiled. "But Ellery, I've told you every damned thing I know about the amnesia. You can take it or leave it."

"At this point," said Ellery, "I'm inclined to leave it."

"Please."

Ellery looked at him quickly. He was sitting on the very edge of the armchair, grasping the arms, not smiling now, not angry, not calm—not any of the things he had done and been for the half-hour past.

"There are some things I can't tell, Ellery. If you knew, you'd understand why. Nobody could. They involve—" Howard stopped and slowly got up. "I'm sorry I've bothered you. I'll send these duds back as soon as I get home. Would you stake me to the fare? I haven't a dime."

"Howard."

"What?"

Ellery went over and put his arm around Howard's shoulders. "If I'm to help I've got to dig. I'll come up."

Howard telephoned home again to tell the elder Van Horn that Ellery was coming up for a visit in a couple of days.

"I thought you'd whoop," Ellery heard Howard say with a laugh. "No, I don't know for how long, Father; I imagine for as long as Laura can keep him interested in her cooking."

When he came out of the study, Ellery said to him:

"I'd leave with you now, Howard, but it's going to take me a day or so to get away."

"Sure. Naturally." Howard was feeling good; he was almost bouncing.

"Also, I'm writing a novel . . ."

"Bring it with you!"

"I'll have to. I'm committed by contract to deliver the manuscript by a certain date, and I'm behind schedule now."

"I suppose I ought to feel like a skunk, Ellery—"

"Learn to have the courage of your emotions," chuckled Ellery. "Can you provide a typewriter in decent working order?"

"Everything you'll need, and the best quality. What's more, you can have the guest house. You'll have privacy there, yet you'll be near me—it's only a few yards from the main house."

"Sounds good. Oh, and by the way, Howard. It won't be necessary to tell your family why I'm coming up. I'd prefer an atmosphere as free from tensions as possible."

"It's going to be pretty tough fooling the old gent. He just said to me on the phone, 'Well, it's about time you decided to hire a bodyguard.' He was kidding, but Father's shrewd, Ellery. I'll bet he's figured out already why you're coming."

"Just the same, don't say any more about it than you can help."

"I could tell them you had to finish your novel and I offered you a chance to do it far from the madding crowd." Howard's good eye clouded over. "Ellery, this may take a long time. May be months before the next attack—"

"Or never," said Ellery. "Hasn't that ever occurred to you, my fine Denmarkian friend? The episodes may stop as suddenly as they started." Howard grinned, but he looked unconvinced. "Say, how about your putting up with Dad and me here at the apartment until I can get away?"

"Meaning you're worried about how I'll get home."

"No," said Ellery. "I mean yes."

"Thanks, but I'd better be getting back today, Ellery. They've been frantic."

"Of course. — You're sure you'll be all right."

"Positive. I've never had two attacks less than three weeks apart."

Ellery gave Howard some money and walked him downstairs to the street.

They were shaking hands before the open door of the taxi when Ellery suddenly exclaimed: "But Howard, where the devil do I go?"

"What do you mean?"

"I haven't the remotest idea where you live!"

Howard looked startled. "Didn't I tell you?"

"Never!"

"Give me a piece of paper. No, wait, I've got a notebook—did I transfer all my things to your suit? Yes, here."

Howard tore a page out of a fat black notebook, scribbled on it, and was gone.

Ellery watched the taxi until it turned the corner.

Then he went back upstairs, thoughtfully, the piece of paper still in his hand.

Howard's already committed a crime, he thought. *It's not the "possible" crime of his amnesic state that he dreads. It's a remembered crime, committed in his conscious state. This crime, and the circumstances surrounding it, are the "things" Howard can't "tell"—the "secrets" which, in all conscious sincerity, he protests are irrelevant to his emotional problem. But it's the guilt feeling involving precisely that crime that's sent him desperately to me. Psychologically, Howard is seeking punishment for it.*

What was the crime?

That was the first question to be answered.

And the answer could only lie in Howard's home, in . . .

Ellery glanced at the sheet of paper Howard had scribbled on.

He very nearly dropped it.

The address Howard had written was:

Van Horn
North Hill Drive
Wrightsville

Wrightsville!

The squatty little railroad station in Low Village. Steep square-cobbled streets. The round Square, its ancient horse trough supporting the bird-stippled bronze of Founder Jezreel Wright. The Hollis Hotel, the High Village Pharmacy-that-used-to-be, Sol Gowdy's Men's Shop, the Bon Ton Department Store, William Ketcham—Insurance, the three gilt balls above the shop front of J. P. Simpson, the elegant Wrightsville National Bank, *John F. Wright, Pres.*

Wheel-spoke avenues . . . State Street, red-brick Town Hall, the Carnegie Library and Miss Aikin, the tall obsequious elms. Lower Main, the *Wrightsville Record* building with the presses on display beyond the plate-glass windows, old Phinny Baker, Pettigrew's real estate office, Al Brown's Ice Cream Parlor, The Bijou Theater and Manager Louie Cahan . . .

Hill Drive and Twin Hill Cemetery and Wrightsville Junction three miles down the line and Slocum Township and *The Hot Spot* on Route 16 and the smithy with the neon sign and the distant peaks of the Mahoganies.

Old scenes flashed across his memory as he sank frowning into the worn leather armchair Howard had just vacated.

Wrightsville . . .

Where had Howard Van Horn been while Ellery observed the tragedy of Jim and Nora Haight develop?[1] That had been early in the war, when Howard was living at home, by his own admission, working in an aircraft factory. Why, during Ellery's revisit to Wrightsville not long after the war, in the case involving Captain Davy Fox, hadn't he run across Howard's trail then?[2] True, Ellery had mixed with few Wrightsvillians during that investigation. But on his first visit, on the Haight business, he had received a great deal of local publicity; Hermione Wright had seen to that. Howard couldn't possibly have remained ignorant of his presence in town. And North Hill Drive was a mere extension of Hill Drive, where the Wrights and the Haights lived and where Ellery had occupied, first the Haight cottage, then a guest room in the Wright house next door—perhaps ten minutes from the Van Horn place by car, certainly no longer. Now that Ellery thought of it, the very name "Van Horn" had a Wrightsville ring. He was sure he had heard old John F. mention Diedrich Van Horn on several occasions as being one of the *points d'appui* of the town, a civic-minded, philanthropic millionaire; and so, he seemed to recall, had Judge Eli Martin characterized him. Howard's father could not have been one of the Wright-Martin-Willoughby set or Ellery would have met him; but that

[1] *Calamity Town*, by Ellery Queen; Little, Brown & Co., 1942; Pocket Book No. 2283.

[2] *The Murderer Is a Fox*, by Ellery Queen; Little, Brown & Co., 1945; Pocket Book No. 2517.

was understandable—they constituted the traditional society of Wrightsville. So the Van Horns must be of the industrial element, the tycoons, the Mitsubishis of the community—the Country Club crowd, between the traditional caste and for whom the fence was unscalable. Still, Howard must have known that Ellery was living in town; and since he had not come forward, it seemed clear that he had deliberately avoided his old acquaintance of the Rue de la Huchette. Why?

Ellery was not seriously disturbed by the question. Howard was newly in the grip of his malady in those days. Probably he had been too frightened to face the ordeal of renewing their acquaintanceship. Or very likely he had been immobilized by feelings of guilt still buried deep.

Ellery refilled his pipe. What really bothered him was that he was Wrightsville-bound on a case for the third time. It was a disheartening coincidence. Ellery disliked coincidences. They made him uneasy. And the longer he thought about it, the uneasier he became.

If I were superstitious, he thought, I'd say it was Fate.

Strangely enough, in each of the previous Wrightsville investigations, circumstances had nudged him into the same unsatisfying speculations. He wondered, as he had wondered before, if there might not be a pattern in all this, a pattern too large to be discerned by the human eye. Certainly it was odd that, while he had brought the Haight and Fox cases to successful solutions, the nature of each had compelled him to suppress the truth, so that the world outside regarded his Wrightsville ventures as among his more conspicuous failures.

And now this Van Horn business . . .

Damn Wrightsville and all its works!

Ellery thrust Howard's address into a pocket of his smoking jacket and loaded his pipe irritably.

But then he caught himself wondering what had ever happened to Alberta Manaskas and if Emmy DuPré would invite him this time to discuss the Arts in the coolth of the evening, and he grinned.

The Second Day

As THE TRAIN scuttled away toward Slocum Ellery thought, It isn't so different.

There weren't so many horse droppings in the gravel and some of the stoop-shouldered frame houses around the station had disappeared; the latticework of a block of stores going up made an unfamiliar arabesque in the old fresco; the smithy with the neon sign was now a garage with a neon sign; Phil's Diner, which had been a reconditioned castoff of the Wrightsville Traction Company, was a grand new thing of blue-awninged chrome. But through the open doorway of the stationmaster's office the bald dome of Gabby Warrum shone in welcome; it seemed as if the same dusty-footed, blue-jeaned urchin sat on the same rusty hand truck under the station eaves chewing the same bubble gum and staring with the same relentless vacancy; and the surrounding countryside had not changed in contour, only in coloration, for this was Wrightsville putting on its war paint for the Indian summer.

There were the same fields, the same hills, the same sky.

Ellery caught himself breathing.

That was the sweet thing about Wrightsville, he thought, setting his suitcase down on the platform and looking around for Howard. It struck even the passer-by as home. It was easy to understand why Howard in Paris ten years before had seem provincial. Whether like Linda Fox you liked Wrightsville, or like Lola Wright you loathed it, if you had been born here and raised here you took Wrightsville with you to the fourth corner and the seventh sea.

Where's Howard?

Ellery wandered to the east end of the platform. From here he could see up Upper Whistling Avenue, which ambled through Low Village to within one square of the Square and then turned elegant and marched sedately into the land of milk and honey, even unto the place of the Canaanite. He wondered if Miss Sally's Tea Roome in town was still serving pineapple marshmallow nut mousses to the Wrightsville *bon ton;* if you could still smell the delectable olio of pepper, kerosene, coffee beans, rubber boots, vinegar and cheese in Sidney Gotch's General Store; if at Danceland in the Grove on Saturday nights care-worn mothers still beat the brush seeking their young; if . . .

"Mr. Queen?"

Ellery turned around to find a terrifying station wagon beside him with a smiling girl behind its wheel.

Someone he'd once met in Wrightsville, no doubt. She had a vaguely familiar look.

But then he saw D. VAN HORN gilt-lettered on the door.

Howard hadn't mentioned a sister, damn him! And a pretty one, at that.

"Miss Van Horn?"

The girl looked surprised. "I ought to feel crushed. Didn't Howard mention me?"

"If he did," quoth Mr. Queen gallantly, "I was out to lunch. Why didn't he say he had a beautiful sister?"

"Sister." She threw back her head and laughed. "I'm not Howard's *sister*, Mr. Queen. I'm his mother."

"Beg pardon?"

"Well . . . his stepmother."

"You're *Mrs.* Van Horn?" exclaimed Ellery.

"It's the family joke." She looked mischievous. "And I've been in awe of you so long, Mr. Queen, I just couldn't resist cutting you down to my size."

"In awe of *me?*"

"Howard said you were nice. Don't you know you're a famous personality, Mr. Queen? Diedrich's got all your books—my husband thinks you're the greatest mystery writer in the world—but I've had a secret crush on you for years. I once saw you in Low Village driving through with Patricia Wright in her convertible, and I thought she was the luckiest girl in America. Mr. Queen, is that your suitcase over there?"

It was an agreeable start to any case, and Ellery hopped in beside Sally Van Horn feeling very important, very male, and absurdly envious of Diedrich Van Horn.

As they drove away from the station, Sally said: "Howard was so miserable at the prospect of driving into town with his face all mashed up that I made him stay home. I'm sorry now I didn't make him come! Imagine not even mentioning me."

"Simple justice compels me to exonerate the knave," said Ellery. "Howard mentioned you emphatically. It's just that I wasn't quite prepared—"

"To find me so young?"

"Er, something like that."

"It throws most people. I suppose it's because marrying Dieds gave me a son older than I am! You don't know my husband, do you?"

"Never had the pleasure."

"You don't think of Dieds in terms of *years*. He's immense and powerful and so wonderfully young. And,"

Sally added with the lightest touch of defiance, "handsome."

"I'm sure of that. Howard's disgustingly like a Greek god himself."

"Oh, there's no resemblance between them at all. They're built along the same lines, but Dieds is black and ugly as an old butternut."

"You just said he was handsome."

"He is. When I want to make him mad I tell him he's the *ugliest* handsome man I ever saw."

"There seems," chuckled Ellery, "to be a slight paradox involved."

"That's what Diedrich says. So then I tell him he's the handsomest ugly man I ever saw, and he beams again."

Ellery liked her. It was not hard to grasp how a man of solidity and character, as he judged Diedrich Van Horn to be, could have fallen in love with her. Although he took Sally to be twenty-eight or twenty-nine, she had the look, the figure, the laugh, the glow of eighteen. At Van Horn's age, and with a vigor probably untapped through many years of loneliness, this could be an irresistible magnet. But Howard's father, from all reports, was also a man of seasoned horse sense; Sally's youth might pull him emotionally, but he would want—and know he wanted—more in a wife than a companion of his bed. Ellery saw how Sally might have seemed to satisfy this want, too. Her look was also gracious, her figure was rich as well as young, her laugh had wisdom, her glow a promise of fire. She was intelligent and, for all her warm, quick friendliness, Ellery felt a certain reserve under the surface. Her frankness was natural and charming, like a child's; and yet her smile seemed old and sad. In fact, Ellery thought as they chatted, Sally's smile was the most provocative thing about her, the supreme contradiction in a personality that appealed by contradiction. He wondered again where he had seen her before, and when . . . The more he studied her, as she drove along, talking pleasantly and unaffectedly, the more he was able to understand how Van Horn could have abdicated his bachelordom without a regret.

"Mr. Queen?" She was looking at him.

"Sorry," said Ellery quickly. "I'm afraid I didn't catch that last."

"You've been looking at Wrightsville and probably wishing I'd stop twittering in your ear."

Ellery stared. "We're on Hill Drive!" he exclaimed.

"How on earth did we get here so fast? Didn't we drive through town?"

"Of course we did. Where were you? Oh, I know. You were thinking of your novel."

"Heaven forbid," said Ellery. "I was thinking of you."

"Of me? Oh, dear. Howard didn't warn me about *that* part of you."

"I was thinking that Mr. Van Horn is undoubtedly the most envied husband in Wrightsville."

She glanced at him swiftly. "What a nice thing to say."

"I mean it."

Her glance went back to the road and he noticed that her cheek was growing pink. "Thank you . . . I don't always feel myself adequate."

"Part of your charm."

"No, seriously."

"I said it seriously."

"You did?" She was astonished.

Ellery liked her very much.

"Before we get to the house, Mr. Queen—"

"Ellery," said Ellery, "is the preferred term."

The pink deepened, and he thought she was uncomfortable.

"Of course," Ellery went on, "you can keep on calling me Mr. Queen, but I'm going to tell your husband the very first thing that I've fallen in love with you. Yes! And then I'm going to bury myself in that guest house Howard waved before my nose and work like mad substituting literature for life . . . What were you about to say, Sally?"

He wondered as he grinned at her which nerve he had touched. She was thoroughly upset; he thought for a silly moment that she was going to burst into tears.

"I'm sorry, Mrs. Van Horn," said Ellery, touching her hand. "I'm really sorry. Forgive me."

"Don't you dare," said Sally in an angry voice. "It's just me. I've got an inferiority complex a mile long. And you're very clever"—Sally hesitated, then she laughed—"Ellery."

So he laughed, too.

"You were digging."

"Shamelessly. Can't help it, Sally. Second nature. I have the soul of Peeping Tom."

"You suspect something about me."

"No, no. Just jabbing in the dark."

"And?"

Ellery said cheerfully: "I'll let you tell me, Sally."

That odd smile again. But then it faded out. "Maybe I will." And after another moment: "I have the queerest feeling I could tell you things that . . ." She broke off abruptly. He said nothing. Finally, in an altogether different tone, Sally said: "What I began to say was . . . I wanted to talk to you about Howard before we reach home."

"About Howard?"

"I suppose he's told you—"

"About his attacks of amnesia?" said Ellery pleasantly. "Yes, he did mention them."

"I wondered whether he had." She stared straight ahead as the station wagon began to climb. "Naturally, Howard's father and I don't talk about it much. To Howard, I mean . . . Ellery, we're scared to death."

"Amnesia is commoner than people realize."

"You must have had gobs of experience with odd things like that. Ellery, do you think it's anything to—well, worry about? I mean . . . really?"

"Of course, amnesia isn't normal and the cause should be ascertained—"

"We've tried and tried." Her distress was quick and she made no attempt to hide it. "But the doctors all say he's an antagonistic subject—"

"So I gathered. He'll snap out of it, Sally. Many amnesia cases do. Well, for heaven's sake, there's the Wright place!"

"What? Oh. Does it bring back memories?"

"In droves. Sally, how are the Wrights?"

"We don't see much of them—they're the Hill crowd. You know, I suppose, that old Mr. Wright is dead?"

"John F.? Yes. I was awfully fond of him. Simply have to look up Hermione Wright while I'm here . . ."

Somehow, the subject of Howard's amnesia failed to come up again.

Ellery had expected opulence, but in the Wrightsville manner, which is homely and rooted in the past. So he was completely unprepared for what he found.

The station wagon turned off North Hill Drive between two monoliths of Vermont marble to glide over a tailored private drive lined with spaced Italian cypresses, the most beautiful English yews Ellery had ever seen, and a parade of multicolored shrubs which even to his unhorticultural eye looked more like the rarer products of a rich man's nursery than the random efforts of

Nature. The drive took a spiral rising course, past rock gardens and terraces, and it came to an end under the porte-cochere of a great modern house at the very top of the hill.

To the south lay the town, hugging the floor of the valley from which they had just come, a cluster of toy buildings dribbling squiffs of smoke. To the north crouched the Mahoganies. Westward, and beyond the town to the south, stretched the broad farmlands which give Wrightsville its rural complexion.

Sally switched off the ignition. "How splendid it all is."

"What?" asked Ellery. She was full of surprises.

"That's what you were just thinking. How tremendously splendid."

"Well, it is," grinned Ellery.

"Too much so."

"I didn't say that."

"I'm saying it." Again she was smiling that odd smile. "And we're both right. It is. Too much so, I mean. Oh, not that it's vulgar. It's like Dieds himself. Everything in perfect taste—but gigantic. Dieds never does things normal size."

"It's one of the most beautiful places I've ever seen," Ellery said truthfully.

"He built it for me, Ellery."

He looked at her. "Then it's not one bit too tremendously splendid."

"You're a love," she said, laughing. "Actually, it shrinks as you live in it."

"Or you expand."

"Maybe, I never told Dieds how scared I was, how lost I felt in it at first. You see, I came originally from Low Village."

Van Horn had built this magnificence for her and she came from Low Village . . .

Low Village was where the factories were. There were a few blocks of misshapen brick houses in Low Village; but most of the dwellings were rotted frame, pinched and mean, with broken porches. Occasionally one saw a house with a clean face and dainty underpinning; but only occasionally. Through Low Village ran Willow River, a narrow saffron-charged ditch fed by the refuse of the factories. The "foreigners" lived in Low Village: the Poles, the French Canadians, the Italians, the six Jewish families, the nine Negro families. Here were the whore houses and the 60-watt storefront gin mills; and on Saturday nights Wrightsville's radio cars patrolled its cobbled crooked streets restlessly.

"I was born on Polly Street," Sally said with that funny smile.

"Lucky Polly Street." Polly Street!

"You're such a dear. Oh, here's Howard."

Howard came bounding up to crush Ellery's hand and seize his suitcase. "Thought you'd never get here. What did you do, Sally, kidnap him?"

"It was the other way around," said Ellery. "Howard, I'm just mad about her."

"And I about him, How."

"Say, is this a thing already? Sal, Laura's in a tizzy about the dinner. It seems the mushrooms didn't come with the order—"

"Oh, dear, that's a catastrophe. Ellery, excuse me. How'll take you over to the guest house. I saw to everything myself, but if you want something you can't find there's an intercom in the sitting room there; it connects with the kitchen in the main house. Oh, I've got to run!"

Ellery was disturbed by Howard's appearance. He had last seen Howard on Tuesday. This was only Thursday, and Howard looked years older. There was a muddy trench under his undamaged eye, his mouth was crimped with tension, and in the bright afternoon his skin looked yellow-gray.

"Did Sally explain why I didn't meet the train?"

"Don't apologize, Howard. You were inspired."

"You really like Sal."

"Crazy about her."

"It's right here, Ellery."

The guest house was a field-stone gem in a setting of purple beeches, separated from the terrace of the main house by a circular swimming pool with a broad marble apron on which stood deck chairs and umbrella tables and a portable bar.

"You can set your typewriter up on the edge of the pool and jump in between adjectives," said Howard, "or if you want real privacy . . . Come take a look."

It was a two-room-and-bath house, done in rustic lodge style, with big fireplaces, massive hickory furniture, white goat rugs, and monk's cloth hangings. In the sitting room stood the handsomest desk Ellery had ever laid eyes on, an emperor's affair of hickory and cowhide, with a deep-bottomed swivel chair to match.

"My desk," said Howard. "I had it hauled down from my rooms at the other house."

"Howard, you overwhelm me."

"Hell, I never use it." Howard went to the far wall. "But this is what I wanted to show you." He drew the hanging which covered the wall. And there was no wall. It was one great window.

Far below, with a green shag rug between, lay Wrightsville.

"I see what you mean," murmured Ellery, sinking into the swivel chair.

"Think you can write here?"

"It'll be tough." Howard laughed, and Ellery went on casually, "Everything's all right, Howard?"

"All right? Sure."

"Don't get coy with me. No recurrence?"

Howard straightened a stag head which needed no straightening. "Why do you ask? I told you I never—"

"I thought you were looking a little brown around the edges."

"Probably a reaction from that beating." Howard turned busily. "Now the bedroom's in there. Stall shower in the bathroom. Here's a standard typewriter, portable's in the corner there, and you'll find paper, pencils, carbons, Scotch . . ."

"You'll spoil me permanently for the Spartan life of Eighty-seventh Street. Howard, this is magnificent. Really it is."

"Father designed this shack himself."

"A great man, sight unseen."

"The best," said Howard nervously. "You'll meet him at dinner."

"I'm looking forward to it."

"You don't know how he wants to meet you. Well . . ."

"Don't walk out on me, you ape."

"Oh, you'll be wanting to sluice down, maybe rest up a bit. Come on back to the house when you feel like it and I'll show you around."

And Howard was gone.

For some time Ellery teetered gently in the swivel chair.

Something had gone wrong between Tuesday and today. Very wrong indeed. And Howard didn't want him to know.

Ellery wondered if Sally Van Horn knew.

He decided that she did.

He was not surprised when he found, not Howard,

but Sally waiting for him in the living room of the main house.

Sally had already changed. She was wearing a Vogueish black dinner dress with a swirl of black chiffon over an extreme *décolletage*—Contradiction again, he thought, in its most attractive form.

"Oh, I know," she said, coloring. "It's indecent, isn't it?"

"I'm torn between admiration and contrition," Ellery exclaimed. "Was I to dress for dinner? Howard didn't mention it. As a matter of fact, I didn't bring dinner clothes with me."

"Dieds will fall on your neck. He hates dinner clothes. And Howard never dresses if he can help it. I only put this on because it's new and I wanted to impress you."

"I'm impressed. Believe me!" Sally laughed. "But what does your husband think?"

"Dieds? Heavens, he had it made for me."

"A great man," said Ellery reverently, and Sally laughed again, enabling him to go on without seeming to make a point of the question, "Where's Howard?"

"Up in his studio." Sally made a face. "How's in one of his moods, and when he gets that way I send him upstairs to his own quarters like the spoiled brat he is. He has the whole top floor and he can grouse there to his heart's content." She added lightly, "I'm afraid you're going to have to overlook a great deal in Howard's behavior."

"Nonsense. My own isn't recommended by Emily Post, especially when I'm working. You'll probably ask me to leave in three days. Anyway, I'm grateful. It gives me the opportunity to monopolize you."

He said it deliberately, looking her over with his admiration showing.

He had felt from the moment of their meeting at the station that Sally was an important factor in Howard's problem. Howard was emotionally involved with his father. The sudden intrusion of this desirable woman between them, monopolizing the father's interest and affections, had reacted traumatically on the son. It seemed significant that Howard's first attack of amnesia, according to his own story, had occurred on his father's wedding night. Ellery had watched very closely for signs of tension between Howard and Sally in the few moments of their meeting under the porte-cochere, and he had seen them. Howard's exaggerated spirits, his ultra-casual manner of speaking to Sally before Ellery—and his avoidance of ocular contact—were clearly defensive expressions of an inner conflict. Sally, being a woman, had been more circumspect, but Ellery had no doubt that she was aware of Howard's feelings about her. *Against her.* It suggested to Ellery that if she were a woman of a certain sort she might seek relief in a completely uninvolved male object. Was she that sort?

So he looked her over obviously.

But Sally said: "Monopolize me? Oh, dear, I'm afraid it wouldn't be for long," and smiled.

"Afraid?" murmured Ellery, smiling back.

She said levelly: "Dieds just got home. He's upstairs brushing up, excited as he can be. Would you like a cocktail now, Ellery?"

It was an invitation to refuse. So Ellery said: "Thanks, but I'll wait for Mr. Van Horn. What a wonderful room!"

"Do you really like it? Suppose I show you around until my husband comes down."

"Love it."

Ellery liked Sally very much indeed.

The room *was* wonderful. They all were. Great rooms designed for lordly living and furnished in heroic taste by someone who loved the richness of natural woods and had a dramatic feeling for the sweep of a wall, the breadth of a fireplace, the juxtaposition of simple colors, the affinity of a window for what grew beyond . . . rooms for giants. But what Ellery found even more wonderful was their mistress. The Low Village girl moved through this splendor splendidly. As if she had been born to it.

Ellery knew Polly Street. Patricia Bradford had given him a sampling of its sour poverty during his first visit to Wrightsville, when she was still Patty Wright the sweater girl, his sociological guide to her town. Polly Street was the meanest slum in Low Village, a butchered alley of grim cold-water flats and work-stupefied factory hands. Its men were silent and beaten, its women defeminized, its adolescents hard-eyed, its babies dirty and undernourished.

And Sally came from Polly Street! Either Diedrich Van Horn was a sculptor himself, molding flesh and spirit as his son molded clay; or this girl was a chameleon, taking on the color of her surroundings by some mysterious natural process. Ellery had seen Hermione Wright walk into a room and diminish it by her grandeur; but

Hermione was a lout's wench compared with Sally for sheer functional association.

And then Diedrich Van Horn came quickly down the staircase with outstretched hand and a "Hello!" that caromed off the handhewn beams.

His son followed him, shuffling.

In an instant the son, the wife, the house grouped themselves around Van Horn, reshaped, reproportioned, integrated.

He was an extraordinary man in every way. Everything about him was oversize—his body, his speech, his gestures. The great room was no longer too great; he filled it, it had been built to his measure.

Van Horn was a tall man, but not so tall as he seemed. His shoulders were actually no broader than Howard's or Ellery's, but because of their enormous thickness he made the young men look like boys. His hands were vast: muscular, wide-heeled, two heavy tools; and Ellery suddenly remembered a remark of Howard's on the *terrasse* of the Café St. Michel about his father's beginnings as a day laborer. But it was the elder Van Horn's head which fascinated Ellery. It was large and bony, of angular contour and powerful brow. The face beneath was at once the ugliest and the most attractive male face Ellery had ever seen; it struck him that Sally's remark about it had been, not a conversational whimsy, but the exact truth. What made it seem so ugly was not so much the homeliness of its individual features as their composite prominence. Nose, jaw, mouth, ears, cheekbones—all were too large. His skin was coarse and dark. In this disproportioned, unlovely composition were set two remarkable eyes, of such size, depth, brilliance, and beauty they illuminated the darkness in which they lay and transformed the whole into something singularly harmonious and pleasing.

Van Horn's voice was as big as his body, deep and sexual. And he spoke with his body as well as with his voice, not disconnectedly but in unconscious rhythm, so that one was drawn and held; it was impossible to escape him.

Shaking hands with Ellery, putting a long arm quickly around his wife, pouring cocktails, telling Howard to touch off the fire, sitting down in the biggest chair and hooking his leg over one arm—whatever Diedrich Van Horn did, whatever he said, were important and unavoidable. Simply, the master was in his house; he made no point of it—he was the point.

Seeing him in the flesh, in relation to his son and his wife, what they were became inevitable. Anything Van Horn turned his vitality upon would eventually be absorbed by it. His son would worship and emulate and, unable to resolve his worship or rival his object, would become . . . Howard. As for his wife, Van Horn would create her love out of his, and he would preserve it by engulfing it. Those he loved attached themselves to him helplessly. They moved when he moved; they were part of his will. He reminded Ellery of the demigods of mythology, and Ellery uttered a voiceless apology to Howard for having been merely amused in Howard's *pension* studio ten years before. Howard had not been romanticizing when he had chiseled Zeus in his father's image; unconsciously, he had been sculpturing a portrait. Ellery wondered if Diedrich had the gods' vices as well as their virtues. Whatever his vices might be, they would be anything but trivial; this man was quite above pettiness. He would be just, logical, and immovable.

And Sally had been right; you didn't think of him in terms of years. Van Horn must be over sixty, Ellery thought, but he was like an Indian—you felt that his coarse black hair would neither thin or gray, that he would never stoop or falter; you could think of him only as a force, prime and unchanging. And he would die only through some other force, like lightning.

The talk was all about Ellery's novel, which was flattering but advanced nothing.

So at the first opportunity Ellery said: "Oh, by the way. Howard told me the other day about these amnesia attacks and how they've absolutely baffled him. Personally, I don't think they're alarming, but I was wondering, Mr. Van Horn, if you had any idea what causes them."

"I wish I had." Diedrich put his big hand briefly on his son's knee. "But this boy is a hard customer, Mr. Queen."

"You mean I'm like you," said Howard.

Diedrich laughed.

"I've told Ellery how unco-operative he's been with the doctors," said Sally to her husband.

"If he were a little younger, I'd whale the tar out of him," growled Van Horn. "Dearest, I should think Mr. Queen is starved. I know I am. Isn't dinner ready?"

"Oh, yes, Dieds. I was waiting for Wolfert."

"Didn't I tell you? I'm sorry, darling. Wolf is going to be late. We won't wait for him."

Sally excused herself quickly and Diedrich turned to Ellery.

"My brother has the bad habit of all bachelors. He never gives a thought to the feelings of the cook."

"Not to mention the family," remarked Howard.

"Howard and his uncle don't get along very well," chuckled Diedrich. "As I've told my son, he doesn't understand Wolfert. Wolfert is conservative—"

"Reactionary," corrected Howard.

"Careful with money—"

"Stingy as hell."

"Admittedly a hard man to beat in a business deal, but that's no crime—"

"It is the way Uncle Wolfert does it, Father."

"Son, Wolf's a perfectionist—"

"Slave driver!"

"Will you let me finish?" said Diedrich indulgently. "My brother is the kind of man, Mr. Queen, who expects instant obedience from people, but on the other hand he drives himself harder than anyone under him—"

"He doesn't make thirty-two bucks a week," said Howard. "He has something to drive himself for."

"Howard, he's done a lot for us, running the plants. Let's not be ungrateful."

"Father, you know perfectly well that if you didn't sit on him he'd institute the speed-up system, hire labor spies, abolish seniority, fire anyone with guts enough to talk back to him—"

"Why, Howard," said Ellery. "Social consciousness? You've changed since the Rue de la Huchette."

Howard snarled something, and they all laughed.

"My point is that my brother's essentially an unhappy man, Mr. Queen," Diedrich went on. "I understand him; I can't expect this pup to. Wolfert's a bundle of fears and frustrations. Afraid of living. That's what I've always tried to teach Howard: Look trouble in the eye. Don't let things fester. Do something about them. Which reminds me—if I'm to keep from wasting away I'd better do something about this dinner situation. Sally!"

Sally came in with a handsome plastic apron over her gown and her cheeks round with laughter. "It's Laura, Dieds. She's gone on strike."

"The mushrooms," exclaimed Howard. "By God, the

mushrooms—and Laura's a fan of yours, Ellery. This is a crisis."

"What about the mushrooms?" demanded Dietrich.

"I thought I had it all straightened out this afternoon, darling, but now she says she *won't* serve her steak without mushroom sauce to Mr. Queen, and the mushrooms didn't come—"

"Hang the mushrooms, Sally!" roared Diedrich. "I'll fix that steak myself!"

"You'll sit here and pour another cocktail," said Sally, kissing her husband on the top of his head. "Steak is expensive."

"Strikebreaker," said Howard.

Sally gave him a look on her way out.

The dinner got on Ellery's nerves; and this was baffling, because it was a tasty, nourishing, and excellently served dinner in a dining room whose prodigious fireplace spoke of charcoal fires and spits in the royal manner, with a great china service designed by a gourmet to preactivate the taste buds and handmade silver utensils forged by a Vulcan of the art. Diedrich mixed his own salad in a colossal wooden bowl which could only have been hollowed out of the heart of a sequoia tree; and for dessert there was an unbelievable something which Sally called an "Australian tart"—surely the great-grandmother of all tarts, Ellery thought innocently, since it was as vast as the centerpiece and every bite an orgy. And the talk was animated.

Still, there was an undercurrent.

There shouldn't have been. The talk was as nourishing as the food. Ellery learned a great deal about the Van Horns' beginnings. The brothers, Diedrich and Wolfert, had come to Wrightsville as boys, forty-nine years before. Their father had been a hell's-fire-and-brimstone evangelist who traveled from town to town calling down eternal damnation upon sinners.

"He meant it, too," chuckled Diedrich. "I remember how scared Wolf and I used to be when he really got going. Pa had eyes that I swear turned red when he was bellowing and a long black beard that was always beaded with spit. He used to beat the hell out of us—spare-the-rod business. He got a lot more fun out of the Old Testament than the New; I've always thought of him as Jeremiah, or old John Brown, which isn't fair to either of 'em, I guess. Pa believed in a God you could see and feel—ESPECIALLY FEEL. It wasn't till I grew up that I realized my father had created God in his own image."

Wrightsville was merely a way station on the evangelist's road to salvation, but "He's still here," said Diedrich. "Buried in Twin Hill Cemetery. He dropped dead of apoplexy during a Low Village prayer meeting."

Evangelist Van Horn's family remained in Wrightsville.

It took an unusual man, thought Ellery, to rise from Low Village to the crest of North Hill Drive and to go back to Low Village for his wife.

And why did Howard have so little to say?

"We were pretty darned near the poorest folks in town. Wolf got a job in Amos Bluefield's feed store. I couldn't take Amos or the indoors. I went to work with a road gang."

Sally was pouring from the silver coffee pot very carefully. It certainly wasn't her husband's autobiography that was troubling her; there was unmistakable evidence of her pride in Diedrich. It was Howard, halfway down the field-long board. Sally was feeling Howard's half-smile silence as he played tricks with his dessert fork and pretended to listen to his father.

"One thing led to another. Wolf was ambitious. He studied nights, correspondence courses in bookkeeping, business administration, finance. I was ambitious, too, but in a different way. I had to get out among people. I learned about the other things from books—read every chance I got. Still do. But it's a funny thing, Mr. Queen: Aside from technical books, I never found a syllable outside of my father's Bible, Shakespeare, and certain studies of the human mind that I could apply to my own life. What good is learning something if it doesn't help you live?"

"It's a fairly well-debated question," laughed Ellery. "Apparently, Mr. Van Horn, you agree with Goldsmith that books teach us very little of the world. And with Disraeli, who called books the curse of the human race and the invention of printing the greatest misfortune that ever befell man."

"Dieds doesn't really believe what he's saying," said Sally.

"But I do, dear," protested her husband.

"Blah. I wouldn't be here, sitting at this table, if not for books."

"Take that," murmured Howard.

Sally said: "Why, How, are you still with us? Let me refill your cup."

Ellery wished they would stop.

"I had my own road-construction company at twenty-four. At twenty-eight I owned a couple of pieces of Lower Main property and I'd bought out old man Lloyd's—he was Frank Lloyd's grandfather—lumberyard. Wolfert was plugging away in a Boston brokerage house by then. The World War came along and I spent seventeen months in France. Mostly mud, as I recall it, and cooties. Wolf wasn't in it—"

"He wouldn't be," said Howard, with the bitterness of a man who hadn't been, either.

"Your uncle was exempted because of a weak chest, Son."

"I notice it hasn't bothered him since."

"Anyway, Mr. Queen, my brother came up from Boston to run things for me during my hitch overseas, and—"

"Big of him," commented Howard.

"Howard," said his father.

"Sorry. But you did come back to find that he'd pulled a few miracles by way of lumber contracts for the army."

"That'll be enough, Son," Diedrich said it pleasantly enough, but Howard drew his lips in and said no more. "But Wolf *had* done pretty well, Mr. Queen, and after that we naturally stuck together. We went bust in the '29 crash together and we built it up again together. This time it stuck, and here we are."

Ellery gathered that "here" was a rhetorical allusion both to the eagle's nest on North Hill Drive and what he had come to suspect was Van Horn's dictatorship among Wrightsville plutocracy. And as the big man went on, from casual references Ellery found his suspicion strengthened. Apparently the Van Horns owned lumberyards, sawmills, machine shops, the jute mill, the paper mill in Slocum, and a dozen other plants scattered over the county, besides controlling interests in Wrightsville Power & Light and the Wrightsville National Bank—this last a development of John F.'s death. And Diedrich had recently bought up Frank Lloyd's *Record*, modernized it, liberalized it, and it was already a fighting power in state politics. The great upsurge in the Van Horn's fortunes seemed to have come just before, during, and since World War II.

It was all factual, unstudied, and inoffensive, and

Ellery was just beginning to relax when, suddenly, Wolfert Van Horn came in.

Wolfert was a one-dimensional projection of his brother.

He was as tall as Diedrich, and his features were as ugly and as overlarge, but where Diedrich had breadth and thickness Wolfert was a thin crooked line. He seemed all length and no substance. There was no blood in him, no heat, no grandeur. If his brother was a sculpture, Wolfert was a scratch-pen caricature.

He came into the dining room with a sort of swoop, like a starving bird alighting on carrion. And he fixed Ellery with a frigid, avian glance.

This man gave off acerbity as Diedrich gave off sweet, warm strength. But even this was given stingily; Ellery had the ridiculous feeling that he had been granted one glimpse into hell, and then the man's elongated face split in what he intended as a smile and was instead a contortion of foxy lips and horsy dentures. He offered a hand, too, and it was all bones.

"So this is our Howard's famous friend," said Wolfert. His voice had a thin, acid bite. The way he said "our Howard" soured any hope of a *rapprochement* between them; his "famous" was a sneer, and "friend" an obscenity.

Unhappy and frustrated—yes, thought Ellery; and dangerous, too. Wolfert resented Diedrich's son; he resented Diedrich's wife; one felt he resented Diedrich. But it was interesting to observe how differently he expressed his various resentments. Howard he ignored; Sally he patronized; toward Diedrich he deferred. It was as if he despised his nephew, was jealous of his sister-in-law, and feared and hated his brother.

Also, he was a boor. He did not apologize to Sally for being late to her dinner; he ate bestially, with his elbows planted challengingly on the table; and he addressed himself exclusively to Diedrich, as if they had been alone.

"Well, you got yourself into it, Diedrich. Now I suppose you'll ask me to get you out."

"Into what, Wolfert?"

"That Art Museum business."

"Mrs. Mackenzie called?" Diedrich's eyes began to sparkle.

"After you left."

"They've accepted my offer!"

His brother grunted.

"Art Museum?" Ellery said. "When did Wrightsville acquire an Art Museum, Mr. Van Horn?"

"We haven't, yet." Diedrich was beaming. Wolfert's skeletal wrists continued to fly about.

"It's been quite a thing," Howard remarked suddenly. "Going on for months, Ellery. A group of the old biddies—Mrs. Martin, Mrs. Mackenzie, and especially—"

"Don't tell me," grinned Ellery. "And especially Emmeline DuPré."

"Say! You know the unphysical culturist of our fair city?"

"I have had that honor, Howard—numerously."

"Then you know what I mean. They're a Committee, capital C, and they rammed a Resolution, capital R, through the Selectmen, and everything was all set for Wrightsville to become the capital of all the County's Culture, capital C again, only they forgot art museums take lettuce and lots of it."

"They've had a horrible time trying to raise funds." Sally was looking at her husband in an anxious way.

Diedrich kept beaming, and Wolfert kept stuffing himself.

"But, Father," Howard sounded puzzled. "How the devil are you mixed up in it?"

"I thought," said Sally, "you'd made your contribution, Dieds."

Diedrich merely chuckled.

"Oh, come *on,* darling. You've done something heroic again!"

"I'll tell you what he's done," said Wolfert in a chewy voice. "He's guaranteed to make good the deficit."

Howard stared at his father. "Why, they're hundreds of thousands of dollars short."

"Four hundred and eighty-seven thousand," snapped Wolfert Van Horn. He threw down his fork.

"They came to me yesterday," Diedrich said placatively. "Told me the fund-raising campaign was a bust. I offered to make up the deficit on one condition."

"Dieds, you didn't tell me a thing about this," wailed Sally.

"I wanted to save it, dear. And besides, I had no particular reason to think they'd accept my terms."

"What terms, Father?"

"Remember, Howard, when the Museum was first suggested? You said you thought an appropriate architectural plan would be to run a pediment or frieze or whatever you call it across the entire face of the building in which there'd be life-size statues of the classical gods."

"Did I say that? I don't remember."

"Well, I do, Son. So . . . that was my condition. That, and the proviso that the sculptor of those statues must be the artist who signs his stuff 'H. H. Van Horn.' "

"Oh, *Dieds,*" breathed Sally.

Wolfert got up, belched, and left the room.

Howard was extremely pale.

"Of course," drawled his father, "if you don't want the commission, Son . . ."

"Want it." He was whispering.

"Or if you think you're not qualified—"

"Oh, I can do it!" said Howard. "I can do it!"

"Then I'll send Mrs. Mackenzie a certified check tomorrow."

Howard was shaking. Sally poured a fresh cup of coffee for him.

"I mean I think I can do it . . ."

"Now don't start that silliness, Howard," said Sally quickly. "What exactly would you sculpt? What gods would you plan on?"

"Well . . . the sky god, Jupiter . . ." Howard looked around; he was still dazed. "Anybody got a pencil?"

Two pencils clattered before him.

He began sketching on the cloth.

"Juno, queen of heaven—"

"There'd be Apollo, wouldn't there?" said Diedrich solemnly. "The sun god?"

"And Neptune," cried Sally. "God of the sea."

"Not to mention Pluto, god of the Lower World," said Ellery, "Diana of the chase, martial Mars, bucolic Pan—"

"Venus—Vulcan—Minerva—"

Howard stopped, looking at his father. Then he got up. Then he sat down. Then he got up again and ran out of the dining room.

Sally said, "Oh, Dieds, you fool, you've got me b-blubbing," and she ran around the table to kiss her husband.

"I know what you're thinking, Mr. Queen," said Diedrich, holding his wife's hands.

"I'm thinking," smiled Ellery, "that you ought to apply for a medical license."

"Kind of expensive medicine," chuckled Van Horn.

"Yes, but Dieds, I know it's going to work!" said Sally in a muffled voice. "Did you see Howard's face?"

"Did you see Wolfert's face?" And the big man threw back his head and roared.

While Sally went upstairs after Howard, Diedrich took Ellery into his study.

"I want you to see my library, Mr. Queen. Incidentally, whatever you can use in here, I mean in writing your novel—"

"That's very kind of you, Mr. Van Horn."

Ellery wandered about this kingly study, a cigar in his teeth and a brandy in his hand, looking. From the depths of a huge leather chair his host quizzically watched him.

"For a man who's found so little in books," remarked Ellery, "you've certainly done a lot of hunting."

The great shelves displayed a magnificent collection of first editions and special bindings. The titles were orthodox.

"You have some extremely valuable items here," murmured Ellery.

"A typical rich man's library, eh?" said his host dryly.

"Not at all. There are too few uncut pages."

"Sally's cut most of them."

"Oh? And, by the way, Mr. Van Horn, I promised your wife this afternoon that I'd tell you I'm completely in love with her."

Diedrich grinned. "Come right in."

"I gather it's a common complaint."

"There's something about Sally," said Diedrich thoughtfully. "Only sensitive men see it—Here, let me refill your glass."

But Ellery was staring at one of the shelves.

"I told you I was a fan of yours," said Diedrich Van Horn.

"Mr. Van Horn, I'm thrown. You have them all."

"And these I've read."

"Well! There's hardly anything an author won't do to repay this sort of kindness. Anybody I can murder for you?"

"I'll tell you a secret, Mr. Queen," said his host. "When Howard told me he'd asked you up here—and to work on a novel—I was as excited as a kid. I've read every book you ever wrote, I've followed your career in the papers, and the greatest regret of my life was that during your two visits to Wrightsville I couldn't get to meet you. The first time—when you stayed with the Wrights—I was in Washington most of the time hunting war contracts. The second time—when you were here on that Fox business—I was in Washington again, this time by request of—well, it doesn't matter. But if that's not patriotism, I don't know what is."

"And if this isn't flattery—"

"Not a bit of it. Ask Sally. And incidentally," smiled Diedrich, "you may have fooled Wrightsville in both those cases, but you didn't fool me."

"Fool you?"

"I followed the Haight and Fox cases pretty closely."

"I failed in both of them."

"Did you?"

Diedrich grinned at Ellery. Ellery grinned back.

"I'm afraid I did."

"Not a chance. I told you, I'm a Queen expert. Shall I tell you what you did?"

"I've told *you.*"

"I hesitate to call my honored guest a cockeyed liar," chuckled Diedrich, "but you solved the murder of Rosemary Haight—and it wasn't young Jim, even though he did pull that fool stunt of making a break at Nora's funeral and running that newspaper woman's car—what was her name?—off the road in his escape. You were protecting somebody, Mr. Queen. You took the rap."

"That wouldn't give me a very good character, would it?"

"Depends. On whom you were protecting. And why. The mere fact that you did a thing like that—you being what you are—is a clue."

"Clue to what, Mr. Van Horn?"

"I don't know. I've beaten my brains out about it for years. Mysteries bother me. I guess that's why I'm such a sucker for them."

"You have my type of mind," remarked Ellery. "Labyrinthine. But go on."

"Well, I'd bet a whole lot that Jessica Fox didn't commit suicide, either. She was murdered, Mr. Queen, and you proved it, and what's more you proved who murdered her . . . I *think* . . . and you withheld the truth about that, too, for I suppose the same reason."

"Mr. Van Horn, you should have been a writer."

"What I don't get in the Fox case—what I didn't get in the Haight case, for that matter—is where the truth *might* lie. I know all the people involved in both cases, and I'd swear none of 'em's the criminal type."

"Doesn't that answer your question? Things were what they seemed and I failed to establish otherwise."

Diedrich was looking at him through the smoke of his cigar. Ellery looked back, politely. Then Diedrich laughed.

"You win. I won't ask you to violate any confidences. But I did want to establish my right to be known as the number one Queen fan of Wrightsville."

"I won't even react to that one," murmured Ellery, "on advice of counsel."

Diedrich nodded with enjoyment, pulling on his cigar. "Oh, and just to reassure you, you're not going to be pestered while you're here. I want you to use this house as if it were your own. Please don't stand on the slightest ceremony. If you don't feel like eating with us at any time, just tell Sally and she'll have Laura or Eileen serve you in the guest house. We have four cars and you're welcome to use any one of them if you feel like getting away from us, or running over to the public library, or just running."

"This is really handsome of you, Mr. Van Horn."

"Selfish. I want to be able to brag that your book was written on Van Horn property. And if we bother you, Mr. Queen, it'll be a bad book and then I shan't have so much to brag about. D'ye see?"

While Ellery was laughing, Sally came in, straight-arming a sheepish Howard before her. Howard was loaded down with reference books and his bruised face was alive again.

For the remainder of the evening they sat listening to his enthusiastic plans for recreating the gods of ancient Rome.

It was after midnight when Ellery left the main house to return to the cottage.

Howard walked him out to the terrace, and they had a few minutes alone together.

The moon was being coy and beyond the terrace lay overlapping darknesses. But someone had turned the lights on in the guest house and it poked fingers into the garden like a woman exploring her hair. A breeze played on the invisible trees and overhead the stars stirred, as if they were cold.

They stood side by side smoking cigarets in silence.

Finally Howard said: "Ellery, what do you think?"

"About what, Howard?"

"About this Art Museum deal."

"What do I think?"

"You don't go for paternalism, do you?"

"Paternalism?"

"Father buying me a museum to make sculptures for."

"That's bothering you?"

"Yes!"

"Howard." Ellery paused to grope for the right words; talking to Howard called for a diplomat's tact. "Cellini's saltcellar was made possible by Francis the First. In a very real sense Pope Julius was every bit as important to the Sistine ceiling, the *Moses* in Vincoli, and the *Slaves* at the Louvre, as Michelangelo. Shakespeare had his Southhampton, Beethoven his Count Waldstein, van Gogh his brother Théo."

"You put me in distinguished company." Howard stared into the gardens. "Maybe it's because he's my father."

"Etymologically, *patron* and *father* come from the same womb."

"Don't be cute. You know what I mean."

"Do you feel," asked Ellery, "that if you weren't Diedrich Van Horn's son, you wouldn't get this commission?"

"That's it. It would be put on the usual competitive basis—"

"Howard. I saw enough of your work in Paris to tell me you have considerable talent. In ten years you can't help having grown as an artist. But let's assume you're no good—no good at all. As long as we're discussing this frankly . . . What's wrong with the patronage system in art is that too often the creation of the art work depends on the whim of the patron. But when the whim is there, a positive good results."

"You mean if my sculpture is good."

"Even if your sculpture is not so good. Hasn't it occurred to you that unless you do those statues, your father won't come across with those fantastic funds necessary to make the Art Museum a reality? It's brutal, certainly; but we live in a brutal world. You're making it possible for Wrightsville to acquire an important cultural institution. That's something to work for. I hope it doesn't sound stuffy, Howard, but the fact is your job is to do the finest sculpture you're capable of—not so much for your own sake or your father's as for the sake of the community. And if you should pull off a really bang-up job, why, the fact that you're home talent will give the project an added and very strong local appeal."

Howard was silent.

Ellery lit another cigaret, fervently hoping his argument sounded more convincing than it felt.

Finally, Howard laughed. "There's a flaw in that somewhere, but I'm damned if I can find it. It sounds good, anyway. I'll try to keep it in mind." And then he said, in a different way, "Thanks, Ellery."

He turned to go into the house.

"Howard."

"What?"

"How are you feeling?"

Howard stood there. Then he turned back, patting his swollen eye. "I'm just beginning to appreciate how smart my old man is. This Art Museum business drove all that out of my head! I'm feeling fine."

"Still want me to hang around?"

"You're not thinking of leaving!"

"I simply wanted to find out how you feel about it."

"For God's sake, stay!"

"Of course. Incidentally, there are certain disadvantages to the housing arrangement. You on the top floor of the main house, me over there at the cottage."

"You mean in case I get another attack?"

"Yes."

"Why not bunk with me? I have the whole top floor—"

"Then I wouldn't have the privacy I need for that blamed novel, Howard. I'll be doing a lot of night work. Wish I didn't have that contract commitment . . . Do the attacks often come in the middle of the night?"

"No. As a matter of fact, I can't recall a single one coming on while I was asleep."

"Then my job is not to turn in myself until you're snoring. That simplifies it. During the day I'll work where I can keep an eye on the front door here. At night I won't go to bed until I'm reasonably certain you're in dreamland. Is that your bedroom? Where the light is, up on the top floor?"

"No, that's the big window of my studio. My bedroom is to the right of that. It's dark now."

Ellery nodded. "Go to bed."

But Howard did not move. He was slightly turned away and his face was in shadow.

"Something else on your mind, Howard?"

Howard stirred, but no sound came from him.

"Then hit the sack, slug. Don't you know I can't until you do?"

"Good night," said Howard in a very odd voice.

"Good night, Howard."

Ellery waited until the front door closed. Then he crossed the terrace and slowly made his way around the star-specked pool to the cottage.

He turned off the lights in the cottage, came out to sit down on the porch. He sat smoking his pipe in the dark.

Apparently Diedrich and Sally had gone to bed: the second floor of the main house showed no lights. And after a moment the light in Howard's studio went out. Another moment, and a window to the right lit up. Five minutes later that window, too, darkened. So Howard had turned in.

Ellery sat there for a long time. Howard would not fall asleep easily.

What was bothering Howard today, tonight? It wasn't the amnesia. It was something new, or a fresh development of something old; something which had occurred in the last two days. Whom did it involve? Diedrich? Sally? Wolfert? Or someone Ellery had not met?

The strain between Howard and Sally might be part of it. But there were other stresses. Between Howard and his unlovely uncle. Or the older stress, the stress of love, between Howard and his father.

The dark big house faced him imperturbably.

Dark and big.

It was a big house to hate in. Or to love in.

It came suddenly to Ellery that this was something reexperienced, this sitting in the Wrightsville night puzzling over a problem in Wrightsville relationships. The night he had rocked on the porch of the Haight cottage after Lola and Patty Wright had gone . . . the night he had sat in the slide swing on the porch of Talbot Fox's house . . . both down the Hill there, somewhere in the darker darkness. But he'd had his teeth into something then. This . . . this was like trying to take a bite out of the darkness itself.

Maybe there was nothing. Maybe there was just Howard's amnesia, for clear and unmysterious cause. And all the rest imagination.

Ellery was about to knock out his pipe and go in to bed when his hand stopped in mid-air and every muscle stiffened with alarm.

Something had moved out there.

His eyes had become accustomed to the darkness and he could make out degrees of it. It had dimensions now, gray spots and dappled spots, jigsaw pieces of the night.

Something had moved in that lighter fragment, in the gardens beyond the pool, just short of the ghostly blue spruce.

He was positive no one had come out of the house. So it could not be Howard. It must have been someone there all the time—all the time he and Howard had stood on the terrace talking, all the time he had sat here alone before the cottage, smoking and thinking.

He strained, squinting, trying to get through the shadows.

He remembered now that there was a marble garden seat on that spot.

With this he tried to take apart the darkness. But the more he looked, the less he saw.

He was about to call out when a shower of light fell on the pool and the garden. The cloud had backed away from the moon.

Something was on the garden seat. A great lump of a thing that spilled over to the ground.

As his eyes readjusted themselves, he saw what it was.

It was a figure draped in cloths, or a cloak; a female figure, to judge from the fullness around the legs.

It was still now.

For a moment he recognized it. It was Saint-Gaudens's sculpture of *Death*. The seated female with swathing garments, even her head covered and a face in darkness with one arm showing, the hand supporting the chin.

But then the resemblance dissolved in shifting draperies as the moonlight struck life from the stone. And the figure, incredibly, rose, and it became an old, a very old, woman.

She was so old that her back described the semicircle of an angry cat. She began to move, and her movements were secretive, with something ancient in them.

And as she inched along, hovering over the earth, sounds came out of her. They were thin, faint sounds, with the haunting quality of whispers drifting on the wind.

"Yea, though I walk through the valley of the shadow of death . . ."

And then she vanished.

Utterly.

One moment she was there. The next she was not.

Ellery actually rubbed his eyes. But when he looked

again, there was still nothing to be seen. And then another cloud concealed the moon.

He cried out: "Who is that?"

Nothing answered.

A trick of the night. There'd been nothing there. And the words he had "heard" had been the echo of some racial memory in his brain. Talk of sculpture . . . the still deathly blackness of the house . . . concentrated thought . . . self-hypnosis . . .

Because he was Ellery, he felt his way around the pool toward the now-invisible garden seat.

He placed his hand on it, palm down.

The stone was warm.

Ellery went back to the cottage, put the light on, rummaged in his suitcase, found his flashlight, and returned quickly to the garden.

He found the bush she had stepped behind an instant before the moon went out.

But nothing else.

She was gone, and there was no answer anywhere. He searched the grounds for a half hour.

The Third Day

SALLY'S VOICE WAS so taut with tension that he thought Howard had had another attack.

"Ellery! Are you up?"

"Sally. Something wrong? Howard?"

"Heavens, no. I took the liberty of walking in. I hope you don't mind." Her laugh was pitched too high. "I've brought you your breakfast."

He washed quickly and when he came out into the living room in his robe he found Sally striding up and down, smoking a cigaret jerkily. She threw it immediately into the fireplace, snatched the lid off a large silver tray.

"Sally, you're a darling. But this wasn't at all necessary."

"If you're anything like Dieds and Howard, you like a hot breakfast the first thing. Coffee?"

She was very nervous. She kept chattering.

"I know I'm awful to do this. Your first morning here. But I didn't think you'd mind. Dieds has been gone for hours, and Wolfert. I thought if you didn't mind wasting your time sleeping so late, you wouldn't mind my barging in on you with coffee and ham and eggs and toast. I know how anxious you must be to get to your novel. I promise I shan't make this a habit. After all, Dieds did lay the law down about your not being disturbed and I'm a dutiful wife . . ."

Her hands were trembling.

"It's all right, Sally. I wouldn't have made a start for hours. You don't know how many things a writer has to do before he can recapture the slimy thread of his story. Like cleaning his fingernails, reading the morning newspaper . . ."

"That makes me feel better." She tried to smile.

"Have a cup of this coffee. It'll make you feel better still."

She accepted the second cup which had been on the tray. He had noticed its presence at once.

"I was hoping you'd ask me, Ellery." Too light.

"Sally, what's the matter?"

"I was hoping you'd ask me that, too."

She set her cup down; her hands were really shaking badly. Ellery lit a cigaret and got up and walked around the table and put the cigaret between her lips.

"Lean back. Close your eyes, if you'd like."

"No. Not here."

"Then where?"

"Anywhere but here."

"If you'll wait till I dress—"

Her face was haggard; something hurt. "Ellery, I don't want to take you away from your work. It isn't right."

"You wait, Sally."

"I wouldn't have dreamed of doing this if—"

"Now stop it. I'll be out in three minutes."

Howard said from the doorway: "So you went to him after all."

Sally twisted in the chair, her hand on the back. She was so pale Ellery thought she was going to faint.

Howard's cheeks were gray.

Ellery said calmly, "Whatever it is, Howard, I'd say offhand Sally was right to come to me, and you're wrong to try to hold her back."

The swollen part of Howard's lower lip gave his mouth a bitter twist.

"Okay, Ellery. Get your clothes on."

When Ellery came out of the cottage, he saw a new convertible drawn up under the porte-cochere of the main house. Sally was at the wheel. Howard was just stowing a hamper away.

Ellery walked over to them. Sally was wearing a deer-brown suède suit and she had bound her hair with a silk scarf, turban-fashion; she had made up rather heavily; her cheeks had color.

She avoided his eyes.

Howard seemed most particular about the hamper. He didn't look up until Ellery was seated beside Sally. Then he squeezed in beside Ellery and Sally started the car.

"What's the hamper for?" Ellery asked cheerfully.

"I had Laura put up a picnic lunch," said Sally, very busy shifting gears.

Howard laughed. "Why don't you tell him why? It's so if anybody calls up, the help can say we've gone on a picnic. See?"

"Yes," said Sally in a very low voice, "I'm getting quite clever at this."

She took the curves of the winding drive angrily. At the exit to North Hill Drive she turned left.

"Where are we going, Sally? I've never been in this direction."

"I thought we'd run up to Quetonokis Lake. It's in the foothills of the Mahoganies there."

"Good place for a picnic," commented Howard.

Sally looked at him then, and he flushed.

"I've taken along some coats," he said gruffly. "It's kind of chilly up there this time of year."

And after that there was no conversation whatever, and Ellery was grateful.

Under ordinary circumstances the drive north would have been a jaunt.

The country between Wrightsville and the Mahoganies has flexible contours—a hilly land with life of its own, stone fences running and little crooked bridges named Sheep Run and Indian Wash and McComber's Creek rattling over moving water and the heave of green, clover-flecked, overlapping meadowlands, like deep-sea swells, in which schools of cows shift placidly, feeding. Here are the great dairies of the state; Ellery saw hospital-like barns, the flash of stainless steel vats, slow herds grazing, all the way up to the foothills.

And the road was a clean wake foaming toward the mountains.

But they darkened this road with their cargo of secrets; it was a sinful cargo, piratical and contraband, of that Ellery had no doubt.

The character of the country changed as the convertible

climbed. Scrub pine appeared, outcroppings of granite. The cows became sheep. Then the sheep disappeared, and the fences, and there were lone stands of trees, and then clumps, and then patches of woods, and finally a great and continuing forest. The sky was nearer here, a cold clear blue, like a different sea, with clouds sailing it swiftly. And the air was sharp; it had teeth.

They rolled through the woods past immense dark glens where the sun never came under great pine and spruce and hemlock, and everywhere were the granite bones of the mountain. A giant country; and it made Ellery think of Diedrich and he wondered if some relentless harmony of subject and mood had not made Sally choose this place for her confession.

And there was Quetonokis Lake, a blue wound in the mountain's flank, stanched by its green hair, and lying quietly.

Sally ran the car up to a moss-sprayed boulder on the lake's edge, turned off the ignition.

There was laurel all about, sumac, and the spicy breath of pine. Birds flew off, settled on a log in the lake. They poised for flight.

Ellery said: "Well?" and they rose.

He offered a cigaret to Sally but she shook her head; her gloved hands were still on the wheel, gripping it. Ellery glanced at Howard; but Howard stared at the lake.

"Well?" said Ellery again. He put the cigarets back into his pocket.

"Ellery." It came out crookedly, and Sally wet her lips to try again. "I want you to know this is all my doing. Howard was dead against it. We've been arguing in corners and in snatches for two days. Ever since Wednesday, Ellery."

"Tell me about it."

"Now that we're here I don't know how to begin." She was not looking at Howard, but she stopped and waited.

Howard said nothing.

"Howard. May I tell Ellery about . . . you? First?"

Ellery could feel the wood in Howard. His body was as rigid as the trees. And suddenly it came to Ellery that what he was about to hear was at least one root of Howard's great trouble. Perhaps the biggest root, the root that plunged deepest into his neurosis.

Sally began to cry.

Howard slumped in the leather seat and his lips loosened under the pull of his misery. "Don't do that, Sally. I'll tell him myself. Just don't do that!"

"I'm sorry." Sally fumbled in her bag for a handkerchief. She said, muffled: "It won't happen again."

And Howard turned to Ellery and said, quickly, as if to get it over with: "I'm not Diedrich's son."

"No one knows it outside our family," Howard said. "Father told Sally when they got married. But Sally's the only outsider." His lip curled. "Except me, of course."

"Who are you?" asked Ellery, as if it were the most ordinary question in the world.

"I don't know. Nobody knows."

"Foundling?"

"Corny, isn't it? It's supposed to have gone out with Horatio Alger. But it's still happening. I'm it. And let me tell you something: When it happens to you, it's the most wonderfully new thing in the world. It never happened before to anybody. And you pray to God it'll never happen to anybody again."

This was said matter-of-factly, almost impatiently, as if it were the least important of the elements of the problem. By which Ellery knew that it was the most deeply imbedded.

"I was an infant. Only a few days old. In the traditional way I was left on the Van Horn doorstep, in a cheap clothesbasket. There was a piece of paper pinned to my blanket with the date of my birth on it—just the birth date, no other message. The basket's up in the attic somewhere; Father won't part with it." Howard laughed.

Sally said: "It's such a tiny basket."

Howard laughed.

"And there was no clue?" Ellery asked.

"No."

"How about the basket, the blanket, the piece of paper?"

"The basket and the blanket were of very cheap quality—standard stuff, Father says; he found that they were sold everywhere in town. The paper was just a piece torn off a sack."

"Was your father married?"

"He was a bachelor. He didn't marry till he married Sally, a few years ago . . . It was just before the First War," Howard said, looking at the birds, who had settled back on the log again. "How Father finagled it I don't know, but he managed somehow to get a court order of adoption—I guess they weren't as strict about adoptions in those days. He got a first-class nurse to take care of me; I suppose that helped. Anyway, he gave me the name of

Howard Hendrik Van Horn—Howard after his father, the old fire-eater, and Hendrik after his grandfather. And then the War came along and he got Wolfert down from Boston and went off.

"Wolfert wasn't very nice to me," said Howard with another laugh. "I seem to remember him walloping me all over the place, and the nurse crying and arguing with him. She stuck only till Father got back from the trenches. After that, there was another nurse. Old Nanny. Her name was Gert, but I always called her Nanny. Original, wasn't I? She died six years ago . . . Of course, there were tutors afterward, when Father got more prosperous. All I can remember are giants, lots of giants. Their big faces came and went.

"I didn't know I was somebody else till I was five. Dear Uncle Wolf told me."

Howard paused. He took out a handkerchief and wiped the back of his neck and then he put the handkerchief away and went on.

"I asked Father that night what it meant, if he was going to send me away, and he picked me up and kissed me and I guess he explained it all to me and reassured me, but for years afterward I went around afraid somebody would come and take me away. Every time I saw a strange face coming I'd hide.

"But I'm getting away from the point. There was a big row that night between Father and Uncle Wolfert. About Wolfert's having told me I'd come in a basket out of nowhere and that Father wasn't my father. I was supposed to be in bed asleep, but I remember hearing angry voices and creeping down the stairs and sneaking a look through a pair of . . . portieres, I guess they were. Father was madder than I've ever seen him since. He was yelling that he'd intended to tell me himself, when I was a few years older, that it was his job and he'd have known how to do it right, and what did Wolfert mean by scaring the hell out of me when his back was turned? Uncle Wolfert said something—something pretty nasty, I guess—because Father's face got like a rock and he made a fist . . . you know how big his hand is, but it looked to me then like one of those old Civil War cannon balls piled up at the Soldier's Monument in Pine Grove . . . made a fist and hit Wolfert with it smack in the mouth."

Howard laughed once more.

"I can see Wolfert's head snapping back on his skinny neck and a flock of teeth spraying out of his mouth, the way they used to do it in the slapstick comedies in the movies when I was a kid, only these were real teeth. His jaw was broken and he was in the hospital for six weeks; they thought for a while an important nerve or vertebra or something in his neck had been injured and that he'd be paralyzed for life or die. It wasn't and he didn't, but Father's never hit anybody since."

And so Diedrich was carrying his own burden of guilt around, which his brother had doubtless been exploiting for twenty-five years. But this was relatively trivial; even the strong carry such guilt feelings with them; the important part of the story was Howard's part, and what it explained about his neurosis. The powerful attachment between Howard and Diedrich had been born out of Howard's fears concerning his origin, fears bred by Wolfert and fixed in Howard's unconscious mind traumatically by the violence of the whole episode. Knowing he was not Diedrich's child, and not knowing whose child he was, Howard clung to Diedrich and made of him the colossal father-image he was later to hammer out of stone, the symbol of his security and the bridge between him and the hostile world. So that when Sally came along, and the father married her . . .

"The only reason any of this is important," Howard was saying earnestly, "is that, if you're to understand what happened later, and the spot we're in, you've got to know what Father means to me, Ellery."

"I think I know," said Ellery, "what your father means to you."

"You can't possibly. Everything I am, everything I have, I owe to him. Even my name! He took me in. He provided the finest of care, at times when it meant real sacrifices. And always with his brother needling him and telling him what a sucker he was. He gave me an education. He's encouraged my yen to be a sculptor, from the time when I messed around with those kid modeling-clay sets. He sent me abroad. He took me back in. He's made it possible for me to continue my work without economic pressure. I'm one of his three heirs. And he's never once thrown anything up to me, about my failure to produce anything recognizably successful, about my laziness at times . . . anything. You yourself saw what he did last night—bought me a museum—so I'd have a practical immediate outlet for whatever talent I possess. If I were Judas I couldn't hurt him or let him down. I mean, I wouldn't want to. He's my reason for being. I owe him everything."

"Don't you mean, Howard," said Ellery with a smile, "that he's acted exactly like what he is—your father?"

Howard said angrily: "I didn't expect you to understand it," and he jumped out of the car, walked over to the boulder, and sat down on the moss to kick at a stone, miss it, pick it up, flip it at the log.

The birds rose again.

"That's Howard's part of the story," said Sally. "Now let me tell you mine."

Ellery moved over in the seat and Sally turned around and tucked her legs under her. This time she accepted a cigaret. She smoked for a moment, her left arm resting on the wheel. It was as if she were groping for the sesame word. Howard glanced over at her, and then he glanced away.

"My name was Sara Mason," she began hesitantly. "Sara without the *h*. Mama was very particular about that. She'd seen it spelled that way in the *Record* and she thought it had elegance . . . It's Dieds who started calling me Sally," she smiled faintly, "among other things.

"My father worked in the jute mill. Jute and shoddy. I don't know if you know what a jute mill can be like. Before Dieds bought it it was a hellhole. Dieds made it into something decent. It's very successful now—the jute's used for so many things, even goes into phonograph records, I think—or is it the shoddy? I never can remember. Anyway, Dieds took the whole place over and reorganized it. One of the first things he did was to fire my father."

Sally looked up. "Papa was just no good. The job he had in the mill was one that's usually given to girls—unskilled, not very hard. But he couldn't make good at that, either. He'd been everything—he'd had a pretty good education—and he'd been a failure at everything. He drank, and when he drank he'd beat up Mom. He never beat me—he didn't get the chance. I learned very early how to stay out of his way." She smiled the same faint smile. "I'm the prize example of Darwin's theory. I had a raft of sisters and brothers, but I'm the only one who survived. The others died in infancy and early childhood. I imagine I'd have died, too, if Papa hadn't died first. And Mom."

"Oh," said Ellery.

"They died a few months after Papa lost his job at the mill. He never did get another job. One morning he was found in Willow River. They said he'd blundered in the night before, drunk, and just drowned. Two days later, Mama was taken to Wrightsville Hospital to be delivered of her umpteenth baby, prematurely. The baby was born dead and Mom died, too. I was nine years old."

It was a typical Polly Street case history, Ellery reflected. But he was beginning to be puzzled. In none of this was the germ of the Sally beside him. Sociologically, there are few miracles. How had grubby little Sara Mason become Sally Van Horn?

She smiled again. "It's really no mystery, Ellery."

"You're a very annoying female," snapped Ellery. "Well, how?"

"Dieds. I was a minor, penniless, the only relatives I had were one in New Jersey, a cousin of Mom's, and the other in Cincinnati, a brother of Papa's; and they didn't want me. Well, they were both very poor, with large families; I can't blame them. I was headed for the Slocum Orphanage as a ward of the County when Dieds heard about me. He was a trustee of the hospital and he was told about Mom's dying and leaving a brat . . .

"He'd never seen me. But when he found out who I was—the orphan of Matt Mason, whom he'd fired . . . I used to ask him why he bothered. Dieds would always laugh and say it was love at first sight. His first sight of me was the day he came to see me at Mrs. Plaskow's house on Polly Street; she was the neighbor who took me in. I can still see Mrs. Plaskow, a big, stout, motherly woman with gold-rimmed eyeglasses. It was a Friday night and Mrs. Plaskow was lighting candles—they were Jews, and I remember she explained to me that the Jews lit candles on Friday nights because sundown Friday was the beginning of the Jewish sabbath and had been for thousands of years—and I remember being terribly impressed when there was a knock at the door and little Philly Plaskow opened it and there was this huge man looking around at the candles and at the kids and saying, 'Which one is the little girl whose mother died?' Love at first sight!" Sally smiled again, a little secretively. "I was a dirty, frightened brat with skinny arms and legs and a chest you could have played chopsticks on. I was so frightened I fought back. An alley cat." This time she laughed. "I think that's what did it. He tried to take me on his lap and I battled him off—scratched his face, kicked his shins—while Mrs. Plaskow started to cry and the Plaskow kids all danced around screaming at me . . ." Her expression changed. "I remember how strong he was, how big and warm and wonderful-smelling . . . smelling even more wonderful than the fresh-baked bread on the kitchen table. And I found myself shrieking and wetting his tie while he kept stroking my hair and talking quietly to me. Dieds is a fighter himself. He goes for fighters."

Howard got up and came over to the car and said hoarsely: "Let's get on with this, shall we?"

"Yes, Howard," said Sally; and then she said: "Well, he made an arrangement with the County authorities. He set up a fund for me—I don't have to go into the details. I was brought up in private schools, with kind and understanding and progressive people, the right private schools. On Dieds's money. They were schools in other states. Eventually I went to Sarah Lawrence. Abroad. I'd become interested in sociology." She said lightly: "I have a couple of degrees, and I did some rather interesting work in New York and Chicago. But I always wanted to come back to Wrightsville and work here—"

"In Polly Street."

"In all the Polly Streets. And that's what I did. I'm still doing it, in fact. We have staffs of experienced people now, day schools, clinics, a complete social service program. Chiefly on Dieds's money. Naturally, I saw a great deal of him . . ."

"He must have been very proud of you," murmured Ellery.

"I suppose it started out that way, but . . . then he fell in love with me.

"I don't think I can quite describe how I felt when he told me. Dieds had always corresponded with me. He'd made flying trips to see me when I was at school. I'd never thought of him as a father . . . more like a big strong protecting angel of a very masculine type. Would it sound awfully silly if I said, 'like a god'?"

"No," said Ellery.

"I'd kept every letter he ever wrote me. I had snapshots of him tucked away in hiding places. At Christmas I'd get enormous boxes of the most wonderful things. On my birthday there was always something exquisite—Dieds has fantastically good taste, almost a woman's sense of the unusual. And at Easter, gobs and gobs of flowers. He was everything to me, everything that was good, kind, strong, and oh, a comfort, a place to put your head when you were lonely. Even when he wasn't there.

"And I'd got to know other things about him: that only a year or so after he'd established that big fund that was to care for me and educate me, for instance, he went broke. In the 1929 market collapse. It wasn't an irrevocable trust; he could have taken the money and used it—

heaven knows he needed it. But he wouldn't touch it. Things like that.

"When he asked me to marry him, my heart flopped right up into my mouth. I got actually dizzy. It was too much. Too terribly much. There was so much . . . much feeling in me that I felt I couldn't stand it. Physically. All the years of adoring, of worshiping, and now this."

Sally stopped and then she said, very low: "I said yes and cried for two hours in his arms."

Suddenly she looked into Ellery's eyes.

"You've got to realize, really understand, that Diedrich created me. Whatever I am, he shaped with his hands. It wasn't just money and opportunities. He took a creative interest in my progress. He directed my schooling. His letters were wise and adult and terribly right. He was my friend and my teacher and my confessor, chiefly by remote control, but the lessons sank in somehow that way, maybe more than they'd have done if I'd seen him frequently. He was so vital to me that in my own letters to him I told him things other girls hesitate to tell their own mothers. I never found Dieds wanting. He was always there with just the right word, the right touch, the right gesture.

"If not for Dieds," said Sally, "I'd be a Low Village slattern married to a struggling factory hand trying to bring up a brood of undernourished kids—uneducated, ignorant, dried up, full of pain, and without hope."

She shivered suddenly, and Howard reached into the back of the car, fished out a camel's-hair coat, and came quickly around to put the coat about Sally's shoulders. He let his hand remain on her shoulder and to Ellery's amazement her hand came up and rested on his, tightening, tensing the leather across her knuckles.

"And then," said Sally, looking steadily into Ellery's eyes, "and then I fell in love with Howard and Howard fell in love with me."

The phrase, *They're in love,* kept repeating itself stupidly in his head.

But then order came, and things dropped magically into place, and Ellery was astounded only by his own blindness. He had been wholly unprepared for this because he had been so sure he understood the nature of Howard's neurosis. His analysis had convinced him that Howard hated Sally, hated her because she had stolen Howard's father-image. What he had failed to take into account, obviously, was the cunning and complex logic of the unconscious process. He saw now that *it was precisely be-*

cause Howard hated Sally that he had fallen in love with her. She had come between him and his father. By falling in love with her, he took her away from his father —*not in order to have Sally, but to regain Diedrich.* To regain Diedrich, and possibly to punish him.

Ellery knew that Howard and Sally knew nothing of this. Consciously, Howard loved; consciously, he suffered the torments of the guilt which was the consequence of his love. It was probably because of this guilt that Howard had concealed, concealed; concealed his relationship with his father's wife even as he begged Ellery to come to Wrightsville to help him; tried to conceal it again when Sally herself wanted to come to Ellery with the truth. If not for Sally, Howard would never have come.

That's the way it looks to me, Ellery thought, *and it makes sense, but this is over my depth; I can't fish in these waters, I haven't the equipment. I must try to get Howard receptive to a first-class psychiatrist, lead him there by the hand, and then go home and forget the whole involved business. I mustn't tamper, I mustn't tamper, I may do Howard serious injury.*

Sally's was a different, simpler case. She loved Howard, not as a roundabout means to an antipathetic emotional end, but for himself. Or perhaps despite himself. But if her case was simpler, the remedy there was even more difficult. Happiness with Howard was out of the question; his love was spurious; with the accomplishment of its object the counterfeit would reveal itself for what it was. And yet . . . How far had it gone?

Ellery asked: "How far has this gone?"

He was angry.

Howard said: "Too far."

"I'll tell it, Howard," said Sally.

Howard said again: "Too far," and he sounded hysterical.

"We'll both tell it," said Sally quietly.

His lips worked and he half turned away.

"But I'll start, Howard. Ellery, it happened this past April. Dieds had flown down to New York to see his lawyers about something, on business . . ."

Sally had found herself irritatingly restless. Diedrich would be gone for several days. There was work she might have done in Low Village, but unaccountably she found no taste for it that day. And they really wouldn't miss her . . .

On impulse Sally had decided to jump into her car and drive up to the Van Horn lodge.

The lodge was higher in the Mahoganies, near Lake Pharisee, in summer a favorite vacation ground for the well-to-do. But in April it was deserted. There would be no deliveries, but food supplies were kept in the lodge the year round, stored in quick-freeze lockers. She could stop on the way and buy bread and milk for a couple of days. It would be cold, but there was always a mountain of cut firewood; and the fireplaces were wonderful.

"I'd felt the need to be alone. Wolfert was always grim company. Howard was . . . Well, I wanted to get off by myself. I told them I was driving into Boston to do some shopping. I didn't want anyone to know where I was going. Laura and Eileen were there to take care of them . . ."

Sally had driven off, fast.

Howard said huskily: "I saw Sally leave. I'd been messing around in the studio, but . . . Well, Father's going away, and Sally's leaving me alone with Wolfert . . . I felt I had to get away, too. I suddenly thought," Howard said, "of the lodge."

Sally had just carried an armful of firewood into the lodge when Howard filled the doorway. Around them was the silence of the woods. They had stared at each other for a long, long time. Then Howard had crossed the room, and Sally had dropped the logs, and he had taken her in his arms.

"I don't remember what possessed me," Howard mumbled. "How it happened. What I was thinking. If I was thinking anything at all. All I knew was that she was there, and I was there, and that I had to put my arms around her. But when I did, I knew I loved her. I'd loved her for years, I just knew that."

Did you, Howard?

"I knew it was Fate that took me to the lodge when I thought all the time she was on the road to Boston."

Not Fate, Howard.

Sally said: "I was sick," and she was sick as she said it. "I was sick and I was well, too, more alive than I'd ever been in my lifetime. Everything was spinning around, the cabin, the mountain, the world. I closed my eyes and thought, 'I've known this for years. For years.' I knew then that I'd never loved Diedrich, not really, not the way I loved Howard. I'd mistaken gratitude, tremendous feelings of indebtedness, hero worship, for love. I knew it then, in Howard's arms, for the first time. I was frightened, and I was happy. I wanted to die, and I wanted to live."

"And so," said Ellery dryly, "you lived."

"Don't blame her!" cried Howard. "It was my fault. When I saw her I should have turned and run like a rabbit. I made the break. I wore her down. I was the one who made the love, who kissed her eyes, stopped her mouth, carried her into the bedroom."

Now we show the wound, now we pour salt on it.

"He's been punishing himself like that ever since it happened. It's no use, Howard." Sally's voice was very steady. "It's never just one; it's two. I loved you and I allowed myself to be carried away by you, because for the moment it was right. Right, Howard! Only for the moment, but for the moment it was right. For the rest of time . . . . Ellery, there's no justification for it; but that's what happened. People should be stronger than Howard and I were able to be. I think we were both caught off guard; there *are* times when you are, no matter what defenses you've built up beforehand. And it wasn't a momentary thing, a bad thing in itself. I did love him; he did love me." She said: "We still love each other."

Oh, Sally.

"It was completely irrational. We didn't think; we felt. We stayed in the lodge overnight. The next morning we saw it as it was."

"We had two choices," muttered Howard. "To tell Father or not to tell Father. But we hadn't talked long before we saw that we didn't have two choices at all. We had only one choice—and that's no choice."

"We couldn't tell him." Sally clutched Ellery's arm. "Ellery, do you see that?" she cried. "We couldn't tell Dieds. Oh, I know what he'd have done if we'd told him. Being Dieds, he'd have given me a divorce, he'd have offered to settle a fortune on me, he wouldn't have uttered a single word of complaint or anger; he'd have been . . . Dieds. But Ellery, he'd have died inside. Do you see that? No, you can't. You can't know what he's built up around me. It's not just a house. It's a way of living, it's the rest of his life. He's a one-woman man, Ellery. Dieds never loved a woman before me; he'll never love another. I'm not saying that boastfully; it really has nothing to do with me, what I am, what I've done or not done. It's *Dieds.* He's chosen me as his center and he's revolved his whole reason for being about me. If we'd told him, it would have been a death sentence. Slow murder."

"It's a pity," began Ellery, "that—"

"I know. That I didn't think of all that the day before. I can only say . . . I didn't. Till it was too late."

Ellery nodded. "Very well, you didn't. It happened, and you two decided to keep it from him. Then?"

"There's more to it than that," said Howard. "There's what we owe him. It would have been bad enough if I'd been his real son and he'd met Sally under normal circumstances, when she was an adult, and married her. But—"

"But you felt that he'd created you where without him you'd have been nothing, and Sally felt the same way," said Ellery, "and I quite understand all that. But what I want to know is: What did you do about it? Because it's obvious you did do something about it, and what you did only made a worse mess. What was it?"

Sally bit her lip, deeply.

"What was it?"

She looked up suddenly. "We decided then and there that it was over. That it must never be revived. We must try to forget it. But whether we forgot it or not, it must never under any circumstances happen again. And above all, Diedrich must never know.

"It's never happened again," Sally said, "and Dieds doesn't know. We buried it. Only . . ." She stopped.

"Say it!" Howard's shout rang over the lake, startling birds everywhere; they rose in clouds, wheeling away and up and disappearing.

For a moment Ellery thought something disastrous was going to happen.

But the color of convulsion faded out of Howard's face and he thrust his hands into his pockets, shivering.

When he spoke, Ellery could hardly hear him.

"It worked for a week. Then . . . It was being in the same house with her did it. Eating at the same table. Having to put on an act twelve hours a day . . ."

You could have gone away.

"I wrote Sally a letter."

"Oh, no." *Oh, no!*

"A note. I couldn't talk to her. I had to talk to somebody. I mean . . . I had to say it. I said it on paper." Howard suddenly choked up.

Ellery shaded his eyes.

"He wrote me four letters in all," said Sally. She sounded small and faraway. "They were love letters. I'd find them in my room, under my pillow. Or in the make-up drawer of my vanity. They were love letters and from any one of them a child could have told what had happened between us that day and night at the lodge . . . I'm not telling the exact truth. They were franker than that. They told everything. In detail."

"I was crazy," said Howard hoarsely.

"And of course," said Ellery to Sally, "you burned them."

"I didn't."

Ellery vaulted from the car. He was so angry he wanted to walk back through the woods, down the white road, past the sheep and cows and bridges and fences the forty-five miles back to Wrightsville, to pick up his things and head for the station and take a train back to New York and sweet sanity.

But after a moment he walked back to the car.

"I'm sorry. You didn't burn them. Just what did you do with them, Sally?"

"I loved him!"

"What did you do with them?"

"I couldn't! They were everything I had!"

"What did you do with them?"

She twisted her fingers. "I had an old japanned box. I'd had it for years, since my school days. I'd bought it in an antique shop somewhere because it had a false bottom and I could keep my secret best picture of—"

"Of Diedrich."

"Of Diedrich." Her fingers became still. "I'd never told anyone about the false bottom, not even Dieds. I thought it would sound too silly. I kept jewelry in the box proper. Well, I put the four letters in the false bottom. I thought they'd be safe there."

"What happened?"

"After the fourth letter I came to my senses. I told Howard he must never write another. He never did. Then . . . a little over three months ago . . . it was in June . . ."

"We had a robbery at our house," laughed Howard. "A little old robbery."

"A thief broke into my bedroom," Sally whispered, "one day when I was at the hairdresser's in town, and he stole the japanned box."

Ellery touched his eyelids with his two forefingers. His eyes felt hot and grainy.

"The box was jammed with expensive jewelry—things Dieds had given me. I knew that's what the thief had been after, and he'd simply picked up the whole box and made off with it, not knowing there was something in the false bottom I'd have given every diamond and emerald in the box to get back. And burn."

Ellery said nothing. He leaned on the car.

"Of course, Dieds had to be told."

"He called in Chief of Police Dakin," Howard said, "and Dakin . . ."

"Dakin." *That shrewd Yankee, Dakin.*

". . . and Dakin after weeks and weeks managed to round up all the missing jewelry. In various pawnshops—in Philadelphia, Boston, New York, Newark—a piece here, a piece there. But there were all sorts of conflicting descriptions of the thief—he was never caught. Father said we were," Howard laughed again, "lucky."

"He didn't know how Howard and I waited, waited, for that japanned box to turn up," said Sally tensely. "But it didn't, it didn't. Howard kept saying the thief had thrown it away as being of no value. It sounded reasonable. But . . . suppose he hadn't? Suppose he'd found the false bottom?"

A cluster of swollen clouds swam up over the lake. They had dark hearts and they looked against the sky like great microbes viewed against a blue field in a microscope. The lake swiftly darkened and some drops of cold rain fell, stippling the water. Ellery reached for a coat and thought irrelevantly of the hamper.

"It was worrying about those letters that brought on this last amnesia attack," Howard muttered. "I'm sure of it. The weeks passed and the box didn't turn up and everything seemed all right and all the time I felt as if I were being eaten through by acid inside. The day I went into New York for the Djerens exhibition I was just looking for something to take my mind off things. I didn't give a damn about Djerens; I don't like his work—he's like Brancusi, and Archipenko, and I'm strictly a neoclassical boy. But he was an escape. You know what happened.

"It's a funny thing that I snapped before the blow fell, and since I've been all right."

"Let's stick to the line," said Ellery tiredly. "I take it the thief's got in touch with you. Was it Wednesday?"

It must have been Wednesday; he recalled thinking that something serious had happened on the day before his arrival.

"Wednesday." Sally was frowning. "Yes, Wednesday, the day after Howard saw you in New York. I got a phone call—"

"*You* got a phone call. You mean the caller asked for you? By name?"

"Yes. Eileen answered and then said some man wanted to talk to me, and—"

"Man?"

"Eileen said it was a man. But when I got on the phone I wasn't sure. It might have been a woman with a deep voice. It had a funny sound. Hoarse, whispery."

"Disguised. And how much did this man-woman ask for the return of the letters, Sally?"

"Twenty-five thousand dollars."

"Cheap."

"Cheap!" Howard glared at him.

"I imagine your father would pay a lot more than that, Howard, to keep those letters from being published. Don't you?"

Howard did not reply.

"That's what he—or she—said," said Sally drearily. "He said he'd give me a couple of days to raise the money and that he'd phone again with instructions about how to get it to him. He said if I refused, or tried to double-cross him, he'd sell the letters to Diedrich. For a lot more."

"And what did you say to that, Sally?"

"I could hardly talk. I thought I was going to be stupid and faint. But I managed to hold on to myself, and I said I'd try to raise the money. And then he hung up. Or she."

"The blackmailer called again?"

"This morning.'"

"Oh," said Ellery. Then he said: "Who answered the phone this time?"

"I did. I was alone."

The rain was falling hard now on the lake, and Howard said peevishly, "You'd better put the top up, Sally." But Sally said, "Not much is coming through the trees; it's just a shower," and then she looked at Ellery and said, "Howard had gone into town this morning to get a copy of the architect's Museum plans—he'd driven in just after Dieds and Wolfert. I . . . had to wait until How got back. Then we . . . talked and then I brought you your breakfast."

"What instructions were you given this morning, Sally?"

"I didn't have to bring the money myself. I could send a representative. But only one person was to come. If I told the police, or tried to have somebody watch the meeting, he'd know, he said; he wouldn't show up, the deal would be off, he'd contact Dieds at his office."

"Where is this meeting to take place, and when?"

"In Room 1010 at the Hollis Hotel—"

"Oh, yes," murmured Ellery. "And that's the top floor."

"—tomorrow, Saturday, at two P.M. Whoever brings

the money will find the door to 1010 unlocked; he said to walk right in and wait there for further instructions."

And now they were both looking at him with such a concentration of anxieties that he turned aside again. He walked to the edge of the lake. The rain had stopped; the clouds had marvelously vanished; the birds were back; there was a fresh wet feel to the air.

Ellery came back.

"I take it you're intending to pay."

Sally looked bewildered.

"Intending to pay?" growled Howard. "You don't seem to get it, Ellery."

"I get it. I also have a thorough acquaintance with blackmail and blackmailers."

"But what else can we do?" cried Sally. "If we don't pay, he'll take the letters to Diedrich!"

"You've quite made up your minds that you'll do anything to keep Diedrich from finding out?" They didn't answer. Ellery sighed. "That's the diabolical thing about blackmail, isn't it? Sally, do you have the twenty-five thousand?"

"I have it." Howard reached inside his tweed jacket and took out a long, very fat, plain manila envelope. And he held it out to Ellery.

"Me?" said Ellery in a perfectly flat voice.

Sally whispered, "Howard won't let me go, and I don't think he ought to go—it'll be a great nervous strain and he might pull another amnesia attack in the middle of it. Then we'd be in the soup for fair. And besides, we're both so well known in town, Ellery. If we were noticed . . ."

"You want me to act as your intermediary tomorrow."

"Would you?"

It came out in a little exhausted puff, like the last gasp of a deflating balloon. There was nothing left in her, not anger or guilt or shame or even despair.

It hardly matters how this turns out. She'll never be the same. It's all over for her. From now on it's Diedrich, first and last. And he'll never know, and after a while she may even be happy with him after a fashion.

And Howard, you've lost. You've lost what you don't even know you've been trying to win.

"What did I tell you?" cried Howard. "This was all for nothing, Sal. You couldn't expect Ellery to do it. Especially Ellery. I'll simply have to do it myself."

Ellery took the envelope from him. It was unsealed; there was a rubber band around it. He removed the band

and looked inside. The envelope was filled with sharp new bills, five-hundred-dollar bills. He glanced at Howard inquiringly.

"The exact amount. Fifty five-hundreds."

"Sally, didn't he say anything about having the money in small denominations?"

"He didn't say."

"What difference does it make?" snarled Howard. "He knows we'd never try to trace the bills. Or catch him. All he'd have to do is talk."

"Dieds would never believe him!" She hurled it at Howard. And then she was silent again.

Ellery put the rubber band back around the envelope.

"Let me have it," said Howard.

But Ellery was stowing the envelope away. "I'll need it tomorrow, won't I?"

Sally's lips were parted. "You'll *do* it?"

"On one condition."

"Oh." She braced herself. "What, Ellery?"

"That you crack open that hamper before I starve to death."

Ellery solved a difficult problem in histrionics by pleading "the novel" as an excuse for not appearing at the dinner table. He had already lost the better part of a day, he explained, and if he was to honor his commitment, authors being notoriously honorable about commitments to publishers, he would have to push along. He managed to convey, by the delicate edge on his tone—he did not pronounce the words themselves—that his schedule would be further impaired by a certain nonliterary pursuit on the morrow.

This was all deliberate; Ellery felt a desperate need for solitude. If Sally suspected his real reason, she gave no sign; as for Howard, all the way back to North Hill Drive he dozed. Sleep, Ellery recalled, was another form of death.

Back at the cottage, with the door closed, Ellery flung himself on the ottoman before the picture window and communed with Wrightsville. Let Howard face his father; let Sally face her husband. But then he reflected that both had had plenty of practice; apparently they were good at it.

Ellery felt especially badly about Sally's role in this unpleasantness, and he wondered just what his feeling comprised. Largely disappointment, he decided: she had betrayed his estimate of her. He recognized that in this feeling there was a large content of pique; she had bruised his self-esteem. He had thought Sally an unusual woman; he had erred; she was simply a woman. The Sally he had thought she was might conceivably have surrendered herself in the excitement of discovering that she loved, not her husband, but another man; but the other man could not have been a Howard. (It occurred to him that the other man *might* have been an Ellery; but this thought he dismissed at once as illogical, unscientific, and unworthy.)

It struck Ellery that he didn't think much of Howard Van Horn, neurosis or no neurosis.

Since this brought him to Howard, his thoughts turned in natural sequence to the fat envelope in his breast pocket; and this led him to consider the nature and identity of the thief-blackmailer he was to meet the next day. But wherever his brain turned, it was confronted by an unanswerable question.

Ellery awoke to find that he had been asleep. The sky over Wrightsville was darkening; popcorn lights were jumping up in the valley below; as he turned over on the ottoman he saw windows in the main house materialize.

He didn't feel well. There were the tangled Van Horns, and there was his frowning briefcase. No, he didn't feel well.

Ellery got off the ottoman, groaning, fumbled for the switch of the desk lamp. The great acreage of the desk repelled him.

But when he had opened the case, removed the typewriter's shroud, flexed his fingers, rubbed his chin, reamed his ear, and gone through all the other traditional preparations the punctilio of his craft prescribed, he found that, *mirabile dictu,* work could be fun.

Ellery discovered himself in that rarest of auctorial phenomena, the writing mood. His brain felt greased, his fingers mighty.

The machine jumped, rattled, and raced.

At some indeterminate point in timelessness a buzzer buzzed. But he ignored it, and later he realized it had stopped. The worshipful Laura, no doubt, beckoning from the kitchen of the main house. Food? No, no.

And he worked on.

"Mr. Queen."

There was an insistence in the voice which made Ellery recall that it had actually repeated his name two or three times.

He looked around.

The door stood open and in the doorway stood Diedrich Van Horn.

In a flash it all came back to him: the drive north, the woods, the lake, the tale of the adulterers, the blackmailer, the envelope in his pocket.

"May I come in?"

Had something happened? Did Diedrich know?

Ellery raised himself from the swivel chair stiffly, but smiling.

"Please do."

"How are you tonight?"

"Stiff."

Howard's father closed the door, rather pointedly, Ellery noticed with alarm. But when he turned around, he was smiling, too.

"I knocked for two minutes and called out to you several times, but you didn't hear me."

"I'm so sorry. Won't you sit down?"

"I'm interrupting."

"I'm all gratitude, believe me!"

Diedrich laughed. "I often wonder how you fellows manage it, this sitting on your bottom hour after hour punching out words. It would drive me crazy."

"What time is it, anyway, Mr. Van Horn?"

"After eleven."

"My God."

"And you haven't had your dinner. Laura was practically in tears. We caught her trying to reach you over the intercom and threatened to tell you she got all your books from the public library. I don't know that Laura got the point, but she stopped trying to bother you."

Diedrich was nervous. He was nervous and worried. Ellery didn't like it.

"Sit down, sit down, Mr. Van Horn."

"You're sure I'm not . . . ?"

"I was going to stop soon anyway."

"I feel like a fool," said the big man, lowering himself into the big chair. "Telling everybody to let you alone, and then—" He stopped. Then he said abruptly, "See here, Mr. Queen, there's something I've got to talk to you about."

Here it comes.

"I left for the office this morning before you were up. I'd have spoken to you before I left if . . . Later I did phone, but Eileen told me you and Sally and Howard had gone off on a picnic. Then this evening I didn't want to disturb you." He took out a handkerchief and passed it over his face. "But I couldn't go to bed without talking to you."

"What's the trouble, Mr. Van Horn?"

"About three months ago we had a burglary . . ."

Ellery yearned for West Eighty-seventh Street, where adultery was only a word in the dictionary and the caged antics of nice people trapped by their relationships were confined to his filing cabinet.

"Burglary?" said Ellery, surprised. At least he hoped it sounded surprised.

"Yes. Some second-story man broke into my wife's bedroom and got away with her jewel box."

Diedrich was sweating—a luxury, Ellery thought enviously, he could afford. He thinks I don't know a thing about this and it's hard for him to talk about it.

"Not really. Was the box ever recovered?"

Neatly put, Mr. Q. Now if I can control my own sudoriferous glands . . .

"The box? Oh, the jewels. Yes, Sally's jewels were recovered piecemeal in various pawnshops around the East—the box, of course, wasn't. Probably thrown away. It wasn't valuable—an old thing Sally'd picked up in her school days. It's not that, Mr. Queen." Diedrich swabbed himself again.

"Well!" Ellery lit a cigaret and blew the match out briskly. "That's the kind of burglary story I enjoy hearing, Mr. Van Horn. No harm done, and—"

"But the thief was never found, Mr. Queen."

"Oh?"

"No." Diedrich clasped his big hands. "They were never able to lay their hands on the fellow, or even get a good idea of what he looked like."

Doesn't matter what he says from now on, Ellery thought joyfully. And he seated himself in the swivel chair, feeling better than he'd felt all day.

"Sometimes works out that way. Three months ago, Mr. Van Horn? I've known thieves to be caught after ten years."

"It's not that, either." The big man unclasped his hands, clasped them again. "Last night . . ."

Last night?

Ellery felt the slightest chill.

"Last night there was another robbery."

Last night there was another robbery.

"There was? But this morning no one said—"

"I didn't mention it to anyone, Mr. Queen."

Refocus. But slowly.

"I'm sorry you didn't tell me about this this morning, Mr. Van Horn. You should have booted me out of bed."

"This morning I wasn't entirely sure I wanted you to know." Diedrich's skin was gray under the bronze. He kept clasping and unclasping his great hands. Suddenly he jumped up. "I'm going about this like a woman! I've faced unpleasant facts before."

Unpleasant facts.

"I was the first one up this morning. Rather earlier than usual. I thought I wouldn't bother Laura about breakfast, that I'd have a bite in town. I went into my study to get some contracts on my desk and . . . there it was."

"There what was?"

"One of the French doors—they lead to the south terrace—was broken. The thief had broken the pane nearest the knob, slipped his hand through, and turned the key."

"The usual technique," Ellery nodded. "What was stolen?"

"My wall safe had been opened."

"I'll have a look at it."

"You won't find any signs of violence," said Diedrich very quietly.

"What do you mean?"

"The safe was opened by someone who knew the combination. I'd never even have looked inside if I hadn't found evidence that someone had broken into the study during the night."

"Combinations can be worked out, Mr. Van Horn—"

"My safe is practically burglarproof," said Van Horn grimly. "After the June robbery I had a new one installed. It's most unlikely that I was burglarized by a Jimmy Valentine, Mr. Queen. I tell you the thief last night knew that combination."

"What was stolen?" Ellery asked again.

"I'm accustomed to keeping a large amount of cash in the safe for business reasons. The cash is missing."

Cash . . .

"Nothing else?"

"Nothing else."

"Is it generally known that you keep a lot of money in your study safe, Mr. Van Horn?"

"Not generally." Diedrich's lips were twisted. "Not even the help. Just my family."

"I see . . . How much was taken?"

"Twenty-five thousand dollars."

Ellery got up and walked around the desk to stare into the darkness over Wrightsville.

"Who knows the safe combination?"

"Besides myself? My brother. Howard. Sally."

"Well." Ellery turned around. "You learn early in this deplorable business not to jump to conclusions, Mr. Van Horn. What happened to the broken glass?"

"I picked up the pieces and threw them away before anyone came downstairs. The terrace floor was covered with 'em."

The terrace floor.

"The *terrace* floor?"

"The terrace floor."

Something in the way Diedrich repeated the phrase made Ellery feel very sorry for him.

"*Outside* the French door, Mr. Queen. You needn't look blank. I saw the significance of that this morning." The big man's voice rose. "I'm not a fool. That's why I threw away the glass—that's why I didn't phone the police. To be lying outside the door, the pane had to be broken from inside. Inside the study. Inside my home, Mr. Queen. This was an inside job amateurishly made to look like an outside job. I knew that this morning."

Ellery came back around the desk to drop into the swivel chair and teeter, whistling softly a tune which, even had his host been able to hear it, would not have cheered him. But Diedrich was paying no attention. He was striding up and down with the angry energy of a strong man who finds nothing to vent his strength on.

"If one of my family," Diedrich Van Horn cried, "needed twenty-five thousand dollars so desperately, why in God's name didn't he come to me? They all know—they must know—that I'd never refuse them anything. Certainly not *money*. I don't care what they've done, what trouble they're in!"

Ellery drummed in time to his whistle, staring out the window. *You'd care about this, I'm afraid.*

"I can't understand it. I waited tonight, at the dinner table, and afterward, for one of them to give me some sign. Anything. A word, a look."

Then you don't really think it's your brother. Wolfert shares your working day. You must have seen him today at your office. You don't think it's Wolfert.

"But nothing. Oh, there was a strain, I felt that, but they all seemed to share it." Diedrich stopped pacing. "Mr. Queen," he said in a hard voice.

Ellery turned to face him.

"One of them doesn't trust me. I don't know if you can understand how hard that hits me. If it were anything but that . . . I don't know how to say it. I could talk. I could ask. I could even plead. Four times tonight I tried to bring it up. But I found I couldn't. Something tied up my tongue. And then there was something else."

Ellery waited.

"The feeling that . . . whichever one it was wouldn't want anyone else to know. It must be something pretty bad. See here." The ugly face was rock. "My job is to find out which one took that money. Not for the money—I'd gladly forget five times that amount. But I've got to find out which member of my family is in serious trouble. Once I know, it will be easier to find out what the trouble is. Then I'll fix it. I don't want to ask questions now. I don't want . . ." He hesitated, then went on determinedly, "I don't want lies. If I have the truth, I can handle it. Whatever it is. Mr. Queen, will you find out for me—confidentially?"

Ellery said at once, "I'll try, Mr. Van Horn, of course," disliking the game. But Diedrich mustn't know he knew; he simply mustn't know. Hesitation might have made him suspicious.

He could see his host's relief. Diedrich dried his cheeks, his chin, his forehead, with the damp handkerchief. He even smiled a little.

"You don't know how I've dreaded this."

"Naturally. Tell me, Mr. Van Horn: this twenty-five thousand dollars. How was the sum composed? What denominations?"

"They were all five-hundred-dollar bills."

Ellery said slowly: "Fifty five-hundreds. And did you happen to keep a record of the serial numbers?"

"The list is in my desk in the study."

"I'd better take it."

While Diedrich Van Horn opened the top drawer of his desk, Mr. Queen did his best to impersonate a detective searching for clues. He examined the French door, he looked carefully at the wall safe, he scanned the rug closely on a line between the door and the safe; he even stepped out onto the south terrace. When he returned, Diedrich handed him a piece of paper bearing a *Wrightsville National Bank* imprint. Ellery put it in his pocket, behind the envelope containing the twenty-five thousand dollars Howard had given him in the afternoon.

"Anything?" Diedrich asked anxiously.

Ellery shook his head. "I'm afraid normal procedures won't help us in this case, Mr. Van Horn. I could send for my fingerprint kit, or borrow one from Chief Dakin—no, that wouldn't be wise, would it? But frankly, even if your own prints haven't messed up the prints of . . . I mean, finding prints wouldn't necessarily mean anything. Not in an inside job. What's that?"

"What, Mr. Queen?"

Diedrich had not yet shut the desk drawer. The lamplight touched off a glittering object in the drawer.

"Oh, that's mine. I bought it right after the June business."

Ellery picked it up. It was a Smith & Wesson .38 safety hammerless, a snubnosed revolver finished in nickel. Its five chambers were loaded. He laid it back in the drawer.

"Nice gun."

"Yes." Diedrich sounded a bit remote. "It was sold to me as the ideal weapon for 'home defense.'" Ellery regretted his remark. "And speaking of the June robbery—"

"You suspect that wasn't an outside affair, either?"

"What do *you* think, Mr. Queen?"

It was difficult to evade this man.

"Any specific reason for thinking so? Like the glass falling on the wrong side in last night's business?"

"No. At that time, of course, I had no idea . . . Chief Dakin told me there were no clues. If he'd had reason to suspect it was an inside job, I'm sure he'd have told me so."

"Yes," said Ellery, "Dakin is devoted to the great god Fact."

"But now I'm convinced the two incidents are tied up. The jewelry is valuable. It was pawned. Money again." Diedrich smiled. "And I'd always considered myself a pretty freehanded bird. Shows how easy it is to kid yourself, Mr. Queen. Well, I'm going to bed. I have a big day tomorrow."

And so have I, thought Ellery, so have I.

"Good night, Mr. Queen."

"Good night, sir."

"If you should find out anything—"

"Of course."

"Don't tell . . . the one that's involved. Come to me."

"I understand. Oh, Mr. Van Horn."

"Yes, Mr. Queen."

"If you should hear a prowler down here, don't be alarmed. It'll only be your house guest, raiding the icebox."

Diedrich grinned and went out, waving in a wide and friendly gesture.

Ellery felt very sorry for him indeed.

And for himself.

Laura had left him a feast. Under other circumstances, and in view of the fact that he hadn't eaten since early afternoon, Ellery would have blessed her with each mouthful. As it was, he had little appetite. He tormented the roast beef and the salad just long enough to give Van Horn time to fall asleep. Then, with a coffee cup in his hand, he returned quietly to the study.

He seated himself in the chair behind his host's desk and swiveled about so that his back was to the door. Then he took the fat manila envelope from his pocket and quickly flipped through its contents. He saw at once that the bills were in numerical sequence; they had come from the Treasury Department by a direct route. He returned the bills to the envelope and the envelope to his pocket. Then he dug out the slip of paper Diedrich had given him.

The bills in his pocket were the bills which had been taken from Van Horn's safe the night before.

There had been no doubt of this in Ellery's mind from the moment his host had broached the burglary. The fact had merely called for certification.

Now there was that other matter to attend to.

"You may come in now, Howard," Ellery said.

Howard came in, blinking.

"Shut the door, will you?" He obeyed in silence. He was in pajamas and dressing gown, and he wore moccasin-like slippers over bare feet. "You know, you're really not very good at this sort of thing, Howard. How much did you hear?"

"The whole thing."

"And you waited for me to come back to the study, to see what I would do."

Howard sat down on the edge of his father's leather armchair, his big hands clenched on his knees. "Ellery—"

"Spare me the explanations, Howard. You stole that money from your father's safe last night, and it's in my pocket right now. Howard," said Ellery, leaning forward, "I wonder if you quite realize the position you've forced me into."

"Ellery, I was frantic." Ellery could scarcely hear him. "I don't have that kind of money. And the money had to be got somewhere."

"Why didn't you tell me you'd taken it from your father's safe?"

"I didn't want Sally to know."

"Oh, Sally doesn't know."

"No. I couldn't tell you up at the lake, or on the drive back. She was with us."

"You could have told me this afternoon or evening, when I was alone in the cottage."

"I didn't want to interrupt your work." Howard suddenly looked up. "No, that's not the reason. I was scared to."

"Afraid I'd renege on tomorrow?"

"It's not just that . . . Ellery, it's the first time in my life I've ever done anything like this. And to have to do it to the old man . . ." Howard rose, heavily. "The money's got to be paid. I don't expect you to believe me, but it really isn't for my sake. Or even for Sally's. I'm not as much of a coward as you think. I could tell Father tonight—right now—man to man. I could tell him and say I wanted him to divorce Sally and that I'd marry her, and if he hit me I could pick myself up from the floor and say it again."

I believe you could, Howard. And even get a sort of pleasure from it.

"But it's Father who needs the protection in this. He mustn't get those letters. They'd kill him. He can stand the loss of twenty-five thousand measly dollars—he has millions—but the letters would kill him, Ellery. If I could have invented a reason, a phony reason that would stand up, for needing that much cash I'd have asked Father for it right out. But I knew I'd have to back it up—he doesn't fool easily—and I couldn't back it up. So I took it from the safe."

"And suppose he finds out that you're the thief?"

"I'll have to cross that one when I come to it. But there's no reason why he should find out."

"He knows now it's you or Sally."

Howard looked baffled. He said angrily: "My own stupidity. I'll just have to figure out something."

Poor Howard.

"Ellery, I've dragged you into a nasty mess and I'm damned sorry. Give me the money and I'll go to the Hollis myself tomorrow. And you can stay here, or leave—whichever you think best—and I won't drag you into this any more."

He came up to the desk and held out his hand.

But Ellery said: "What else don't I know, Howard?"

"Nothing. There's nothing else."

"What about the burglary in June, Howard?"
"I didn't do that!"
Ellery looked up at him for a long time.
Howard glared back.
"Who did, Howard?"
"How should I know? Some crook or other. Father's wrong about that, Ellery. It was an outside thief. The whole thing came about accidentally. The thief lifted some jewelry and found the box had value, too. Ellery, give me the damned envelope and clear out of this!"
Ellery sighed. "Go to bed, Howard. I'll see it through."

Ellery walked back to the cottage with dragging feet. He was tired, and the envelope in his pocket weighed a great deal.
He crossed the north terrace, felt his way around the pool.
I can't even afford to fall in and drown, he thought. They'd find the money on me.
And then he bumped into the stone garden seat.
A pain shot through him, not entirely from his kneecap.
The stone seat!
The old woman he had seen sitting here last night.
He had completely forgotten about the old woman.

The Fourth Day

ON SATURDAY AFTERNOONS Wrightsville takes on a mercantile air. The goose of commerce hangs high. High Village shops are full, cash registers jump and cry out hour after hour, the Square and Lower Main are jammed, the Bijou Theater's queue stretches from the box office almost to the doors of Logan's Market at the corner of Slocum and Washington, the parking lot in Jezreel Lane raises its fee to thirty-five cents, and all over town—on Lower Main, on Upper Whistling, on State, in the Square, on Slocum, on Washington—one sees faces usually absent during the week: walnut-skinned farmers in stiff store pants from the back country, kids with stiff shoes on, stout ladies in stiff gingham, wearing hats. Model T's rub fenders with jeeps everywhere; and the public parking area on the rim of the Square, surrounding the statue of Founder Wright, forms a cordon of Detroit steel through which pedestrians find it impossible to squeeze. It is all quite different from Thursday evening, which is Band Concert Night and centers around Memorial Park on State Street, near Town Hall. Band Concert Night brings out principally the Low Village contingent and the youth of all sectors. Staring boys in their big brothers' khaki blouses line the edge of the walks and nervous girls parade before them in pairs, trios, and quartets, while the American Legion Band in silver helmets plays Sousa marches sternly in the concentrated headlights of the cars parked in military formation across the street. Thursday is more a field night for popcorn paladins and hotdog hidalgos than for the merchants dispensing their wares under a leasehold.

But Saturday is solid.

It is on Saturday afternoons that the *haut monde* descend into High Village for those quintessential gatherings at which the cultural, civic, and political health of the community is kept under unflagging observation. (Organizationally speaking, this is not industry's day. Business pursues its less selfish affairs on Mondays, which is logical, Saturday retail business being brisk and Monday retail business being sluggish. That is why you will find the Wrightsville Retail Merchants Assn. meeting for pork chops, julienne potatoes, and the Sales Tax at the Hollis Hotel each Monday at noon. The Chamber of Commerce congregates at the Kelton for baked ham, candied sweets, and the American Way on Thursdays; and Rotary assembles at Upham House for Ma Upham's fried chicken, hot biscuits, boysenberry jam, and the Menace of Communism on Wednesdays.) Each Saturday afternoon the ladies of Hill Drive and Skytop Road and Twin Hill-in-the-Beeches fill the ballrooms of the Hollis and the Kelton with their grim twitterings—that is to say, those ladies who must attend the luncheon meetings of the Civic Forum Committee, the Wrightsville Robert Browning Society, the Wrightsville Ladies' Aid, the Wrightsville Civic Betterment Club, the Wrightsville Interracial Tolerance League and such because they cannot crash the more select gatherings of the D.A.R., the New England Genealogical Society, the Wrightsville Women's Christian Temperance Union, and the Wrightsville Republican Women's Club in the Paul Revere Room and the other Early American banquet halls of Upham House. Not all these functions are held simultaneously, of course; the ladies have worked out an efficient stagger plan which permits the spryer among them to attend two, and even three, luncheons on the same day, which explains why the ballroom menus on Saturdays at all three hostelries are so leafy and the desserts so fruity. Nevertheless, husbands have been known to complain of their Spartan Sunday dinners; and at least two enterprising young lady dieticians have moved to Wrightsville, one from Bangor and the other from Worcester, and made a very good thing out of it.

In all this ferment of commerce, culture, civics, and pure yeasty mass, offenses against man seem as distant as Port Said. In fact, the last thing you would think of on a Saturday afternoon in Wrightsville is that peculiarly nasty aberration of individual behavior known as blackmail; which is undoubtedly why the blackmailer, Ellery glumly reflected, selected today for his rendezvous with twenty-five thousand of Diedrich Van Horn's dollars.

Ellery parked Howard's proletarian roadster halfway down the winding hill approach to High Village which is Upper Dade Street. He got out, touched his breast pocket, and then strolled down the hill toward the Square. He had purposely selected Upper Dade, for on Saturday afternoons Upper Dade plays host to the traffic overflow from the center of town and a man bent on anonymity can lose himself there without trying. Still, Ellery was surprised at what he found. Upper Dade Street was almost unrecognizable. A gigantic housing development in leprous brick had appeared since his last visit to Wrightsville, on the very site where gray frame, ivy-grown houses had stood for seventy-five years and longer. It was flanked by brisk and glittering new stores. There was a great used-car lot where the coal yard had sprawled, filled with rank after rank of gleaming cars which, if they had been truly used, had been driven by spirits of air over ethereal roads for exactly the wink of a hummingbird's wing.

Ah, Wrightsville!

Ellery grew glummer. Strolling along under the metal banners of Upper Dade's invading tradesmen, his face lighted variously by orange, white, blue, gold, and green neon rays—must they pit their garish little scene against God Himself in the person of His sun?—Ellery reflected that this was far from the Wrightsville of his tenderest memories.

Small wonder, blackmail.

But when he rounded the curve at the bottom of the hill, his step quickened. He was home again.

Here was the honest old Square, which was round, with the hub of Founder Jezreel Wright's bronze dripping bird droppings from his crusty nose into the verdigrised horse trough at his feet; there the spokes of State Street, Lower Main, Washington, Lincoln, and Upper Dade, each with its altered Wrightsville character, perhaps, but nonetheless in some mysterious way beckoning the prodigal home from the sinful cities. Up State Street, that broadest of spokes, might be seen Town Hall, and beyond Town Hall Memorial Park; the Carnegie Library (was Dolores Aikin still there, presiding over the stuffed owl and the fierce eviscerated eagle?); and the "new" County Court House, which was already old. Lower Main: the Bijou, the post office, the *Record* office, the shops. Washington: Logan's, Upham House, the Professional Bldg., Andy Birobatyan's. Lincoln and the feed stores and stables and the Volunteer Fire Department. But it was the Square itself which gave them life, as the mother the chicks.

Here was John F.'s bank, no longer John F.'s, but Diedrich Van H.'s; but the building was the same, and there is steadfastness in buildings. And here was the very old Bluefield store, and J. P. Simpson's pawnshop (Loan Office), and Sol Gowdy's Men Shop, and the Bon Ton Department Store, and Dunc MacLean—Fine Liquors; and the sad land change, alas, of the High Village Pharmacy, now but a link in a chain drug store, and of William Ketcham—Insurance, now the Atomic War Surplus Outlet Store.

And, dominant, the marquee of the Hollis Hotel.

Ellery glanced at his wrist watch: 1:58.

He entered the Hollis lobby unhurriedly.

Civic fervor was in full cry. From the Grand Ballroom came a mighty music of culture and cutlery. The lobby seethed. Bellboys raced. The desk bell clanged. The house phones leaped. At the newstand and cigar counter Mark Doodle's son, Grover, a portly Grover now, dispensed news and tobacco with furious geniality.

Ellery crossed the lobby at a pace calculated to attract no eye, however idle. He adjusted himself to the tempo of the crowd, moving with it, neither faster nor slower. His manner and expression, a blend of abstracted positiveness and pleasant curiosity, suggested to Wrightsvillians that he was a Wrightsvillian and to strangers that he was a stranger. And he waited for the second of the three elevators, so that he might be pushed in with a large group. Inside, he refrained from calling out a floor number; he simply waited, half-turned from the operator. At the sixth floor he remembered: the operator was Wally Planetsky, whom he had last seen on duty at the admission desk of the County Jail, on the top floor of the County Court House. Planetsky had been elderly then, and graying; now he was old, white-haired, and with his thick shoulders heavily stooped. *O tempus!* Grover Doodles grow pots and policemen retire to run hotel elevators. Just the same, Ellery was careful to get out at the tenth floor crab-fashion, back to Wally Planetsky.

A gentleman carrying a salesman's briefcase, who looked like J. Edgar Hoover, got out with him.

The gentleman turned left, so Ellery turned right.

He searched among the wrong room numbers long enough for the gentleman to unlock a door and disappear. Then Ellery went quickly back, past the elevators, noting that his tenth-floor fellow traveler had entered 1031, and hurried on. The Turkey red carpet muffled his footsteps.

He saw 1010 coming up and he looked back briefly without checking his stride. But the corridor behind him was empty and no guilty head popped back into a room. At 1010 he stopped, looking around again.

Nothing.

He tried the door then.

It was not locked.

So it wasn't a bluff.

Ellery pushed the door in suddenly. He waited.

When nothing happened, he went in, immediately shutting the door.

No one was there. No one seemed to have been there for weeks.

It was a single, without bath. In one corner stood a white sink with its plumbing showing; there was a wooden towel bar above the sink. A walk-in closet lay beyond the sink.

The room contained the irreducible minimum prescribed by Boniface's profession. It featured a narrow bed covered by a tan bedspread with purple candlewicking, a night table, an overstuffed chair, a standing lamp, a writing table, and a bureau with a starched cotton runner. Above the bureau hung a mirror, and on the wall opposite, above the bed, there was a dust-peppered print labeled *Sunrise Over the Mt.* The single window was covered with a slick and sleazy curtain in grim écru, whose edge came the traditional two inches above a large, flaking radiator. The floor was carpeted wall to wall in a green Axminster, thoroughly faded. On the night table stood a telephone, and on the writing table was grouped a water pitcher, a thick glass, and a square glass tray with fluted edges. A menu inscribed *Hunting Room, The Hollis Hotel, "Fine Food for Discriminating Diners,"* stood on the bureau, leaning against the mirror.

Ellery looked into the closet.

It was empty except for a new paper laundry bag on the hat shelf and a curious piece of crockery on the floor which it took him a moment to identify. He made the identification with pleasure. It was what an older generation had forthrightly termed a "thunder jar." He returned it to its place gently. This was Wrightsville at its best.

Ellery shut the closet door, looking around.

It was clear that the blackmailer had not engaged the room in the customary way: the towel bar was empty, the window was fastened. Yet Sally's anonymous caller had known as early as yesterday morning that Room 1010 would be available for the rendezvous. It would be essential for him to insure the room's accessibility. He had, then, reserved it, paying cash in advance. But he had not taken open, formal possession. To unlock the door, the blackmailer had therefore used an ordinary hardware store skeleton key; the Hollis's rooms had not yet progressed to the stage of cylinder locks.

It all added up, mused Mr. Queen, seating himself comfortably in the overstuffed chair, to a cautious scoundrel. He would not put in a personal appearance. But there must be contact. Therefore there would be a message.

Ellery wondered how long he would have to wait and how the message would come.

He sat in the chair, relaxed, not smoking.

At the end of ten minutes he rose and began to prowl. He glanced into the closet again. He got down on his knees and looked under the bed. He opened the bureau drawers.

The blackmailer might be waiting to make certain there were no police or hidden confederates about. Or he might have recognized Sally's emissary as a gentleman of some experience in these matters and been frightened away.

I'll give him another ten minutes, thought Ellery.

He picked up the menu.

Roast Pork with Apple Fritters à la Henri . . .

The telephone rang.

Ellery had the receiver off the hook before it could ring the second time.

"Yes?"

The voice said: "Put the money in the right-hand top drawer of the bureau. Close the door. Then go over to Upham House, Room 10. Walk right in. You'll find the letters in the right-hand top drawer of the bureau there."

Ellery said: "Upham House, Room—"

"The letters will be in that room for eight minutes,

just long enough for you to walk over there if you start right now."

"But how do I know you aren't—"

There was a click.

Ellery hung up, raced to the bureau, opened the right-hand top drawer, dropped the envelope of money in it, slammed the drawer, and ran out of the room, shutting the door behind him. The corridor was empty. He swore and punched the elevator button. The first elevator appeared almost at once. There was no one in it. Ellery pressed a dollar bill into the hand of the operator, a red-haired boy with freckles.

"Take me right down to the lobby. No stops!" This was no time for finesse.

It was a rapid trip.

Ellery plunged into the lobby crowd and came up with a bellhop.

"Want to make ten dollars the easy way?"

"Yes, sir."

Ellery gave him the ten-spot. "Go right up to the tenth floor—fast as you can get there—and keep an eye on the door of Room 1010. If anybody comes along, pull a knob-polishing act, anything. Don't do or say anything, just wait there. 1010. I'll be back in fifteen minutes."

He hurried out into the Square.

Upham House was on Washington Street, a hundred feet from the Square. Its two-story wooden pillars were visible from the Hollis entrance. Ellery shoved his way through the crowds circling the Square. He crossed Lincoln, passed the Bon Ton, the pharmacy which had been Myron Garback's, the New York Department Store. He ran across Washington against the signal . . .

The voice was maddening. It kept whispering in his ear. *"Put the money in the right-hand top drawer . . ."* Even a whisper can be revealing. But this whisper . . . Tissue paper! That was it. The speaker had been whispering through tissue paper. It had given the voice a hoarse, vibrant, fluttery quality, completely deforming, desexing, ageless.

Room 10 at Upham House. Ground floor, that would be. There were a few rooms in the west wing. West wing . . . As he hurried along, a tiny hand knocked at a door. For some reason a pleasant black face kept popping up, a young man in the uniform of the United States Army, General Issue. Corporal Abraham L. Jackson! Corporal Jackson and his testimony in the Davy Fox case. How he had delivered the six bottles of grape juice when he had been a delivery boy for Logan's Market. Logan's Market . . . It was still there, beyond Upham House, at the corner of Washington and Slocum, its entrance on Slocum. Jackson had . . . What had Jackson done, and why was it so bothersome now, after all these years? He had carried the carton out to the delivery truck in the alley behind Logan's . . . yes . . . that's what he'd testified . . . the alley which the market shared with the fire exits at the rear of the Bijou Theater and . . . *and the side entrance of Upham House.* Side entrance! West side of the building! That was it. It was a way of getting into the hotel without attracting attention. Ellery glanced at his watch as he strode past the Upham House entrance. Six and a half minutes. There was the alley . . .

He turned into the alley and ran the rest of the way to the side door.

The corridor, carpeted in Revolutionary blue and papered with a flag-red illustration of the Minute Men at Concord Bridge, was deserted. Two doors away stood the door numbered 10.

The door was closed.

Ellery ran over to it and without hesitation turned the knob. The door gave and he darted in and to the bureau and jerked the top right-hand drawer open.

There lay a bundle of letters.

Six minutes and a few seconds later Ellery emerged from the third elevator onto the tenth floor of the Hollis. He had run all the way.

"Boy!"

The bellhop stuck his head out of the doorway marked FIRE EXIT.

"Here I am, sir."

Ellery ran up to him, puffing. "Well?"

"Not a thing."

"Nothing?"

"No, sir."

Ellery looked the boy over carefully. But all he could detect on the face of Mamie Hood's youngest was curiosity.

"No one went into 1010?"

"No, sir."

"Of course no one came out."

"No, sir."

"You didn't take your eyes off the door?"

"Not once."

"You're sure, now."

"Cross my heart." The boy lowered his voice. "You a detective?"

"Well . . . in a way."

"Dame, huh?"

Ellery smiled enigmatically. "Think if a five-spot joined that ten, you could forget all about this?"

"Try me!"

Ellery waited until the boy disappeared in the elevator. Then he ran over to 1010.

The envelope containing the money was gone.

When your wits are your stock-in-trade, to be outwitted is a blow. To be outwitted in Wrightsville is a haymaker.

Ellery walked back to Upper Dade Street slowly.

How had the blackmailer got the money?

He hadn't been hiding in 1010; Ellery had searched the room before and after. The closet was empty. The bureau drawers were empty (logic must take midgets into account). There was no one under the bed. There was no bathroom. There was not even a door to an adjoining room. He could hardly have entered through the window; a human fly would have packed the Square below like Times Square on New Year's Eve.

Yet the fellow had managed to get into 1010 after Ellery's departure and he had managed to get out before Ellery's return. He had managed to get out even earlier than that . . . before the bellboy took up his post on the tenth floor.

Of course.

Ellery shook his head at his own innocence. Unless the hop was lying, the answer lay in a simple time sequence. The room was under observation for all but one short period: between the time Ellery stepped into the down elevator and the time the bellboy stepped out.

In that interval the blackmailer had acted.

He had phoned from inside the Hollis, either from another room on the tenth floor, or in the ninth, or from one of the house phones in the lobby. He had placed a time limit on the letters. Shrewd! Reflection should have shown that either the letters were not in the bureau of Room 10 of Upham House at all, or, if they were, the blackmailer would scarcely risk appearing there at the expiration of a stipulated number of minutes to retrieve them. But he had given Ellery no time for reflection. And he had had still another advantage. Reflection or no, Sally's representative was hardly in a position to disobey instructions. The whole point of the blackmailing operation, from the victims' standpoint, was to regain possession of the letters. To achieve this, even the risk of losing the money and failing to get the letters back had to be run. The blackmailer could count on this. And he had done so.

He had simply entered Room 1010 after Ellery's departure, he had taken the money, he had come out again before the bellhop reached the tenth floor. Probably he had strolled down the fire stairway to one of the lower floors and taken an elevator down from there.

Ellery considered returning to the Hollis and investigating the reservation for 1010, and going back to Upham House for some clue the blackmailer may have left there. But then he shrugged and got into Howard's car. He might wind up, through a suspicious clerk, in the hands of Chief Dakin or a reporter for Diedrich Van Horn's *Record.* The police and the newspapers must be avoided.

He found himself wondering by what insanity he had come to be mixed up in the whole dreary business.

Ellery parked Howard's roadster outside *The Hot Spot* on Route 16 and went in. It was thronged and noisy. He sauntered over to the second booth from the rear, on the left, and said, "Mind if I join you?"

The beer before Sally was untouched but there were three empty whiskey glasses before Howard.

Sally was pale: her lipstick made her look paler. She was dressed in a mousy sweater and skirt, with an old gabardine coat over her shoulders. Howard wore a dark gray suit.

They both stared up at him.

Ellery said: "Shove over, Sally," and he sat down beside her, turning so that his back was to the room. A white-aproned waiter pounded past, saying, "I'll be right with you folks," and Ellery said, without looking around, "No hurry." He slipped something into Sally's lap with his left hand as with his right he picked up her glass of beer.

Sally looked down.

Her cheeks flamed.

Howard muttered: "Sally, for the love of God."

"Oh, Howard."

"Pass them to me."

"Under the table," said Ellery. "Oh, waiter. Two beers and another whiskey."

The waiter grabbed the empty glasses and began to swab the table off with a dirty rag.

"Never mind the damn rag," said Howard hoarsely.

The waiter stared and hurried away.

Ellery felt a hand in his. The hand was small, soft, and hot. Then it was withdrawn, quickly.

Howard said: "All four of them. All four, Sal. Ellery—"

"You're sure they're all there. And the right ones."

"Yes."

And Sally nodded. Her eyes burned at Howard.

"They're the originals, not copies?"

"Yes," said Howard again.

And Sally nodded again.

"Pass them to me under the table."

"To you?"

"Howard, you'd argue with God," Sally laughed.

"Watch it!"

The waiter slapped down two beers and a whiskey, belligerently. Howard fumbled in his back pocket.

"I've got it," said Ellery. "Oh, keep it, waiter."

"Say! Thanks." Mollified, the waiter went away.

"Now, Howard." And a moment later, Ellery said: "Now pass the ash tray over here."

He put his hand on the ash tray, looked around casually, and when he looked back the ash tray was on the booth seat between him and Sally.

"Both of you drink, talk."

Sally sipped her beer, her elbows on the table, smiling, and she said to Howard, "Ellery, I'll thank God every night on my knees for you and for this till the day I die. Every night and every morning, too. I'll never forget this, Ellery. Never."

"Look down here," he said.

Sally looked. There was a pile of small scraps on the big glass ash tray.

"Can you see it, Howard?"

"I can see it!"

Ellery lit a cigaret and then transferred the burning match to his left hand and dropped it into the ash tray.

"Watch your coat, Sally."

He made the burnt offering four times.

When they had gone, separately, Ellery brooded over his third beer. Sally had been first to leave, her shoulders back and her step as light as the flying birds over Quetonokis Lake. There's a quality in pure relief, Ellery mused, which puts a velvet lining on the roughest reality.

As for Howard, he had talked loudly and with exultation.

The letters were retrieved, they were burned, the danger

was over. This was what Sally's step had said, and Howard's tone.

No point in disillusioning them.

He went over the events of the afternoon.

The blackmailer had risked leaving the originals of the letters to be picked up *before* collecting his blackmail. Would any self-respecting blackmailer have done this? Suppose the envelope in the bureau drawer at the Hollis had contained strips of blank paper? The originals would have been repossessed and he would have had exactly nothing for his pains. So of course he had had photostats of the four letters made beforehand. Then returning the originals cost him an insignificant asset. Photostats would serve almost precisely the same purpose, especially in this case. Howard's handwriting was distinctive: a peculiar, very small, engraving-like script identifiable at a glance.

No point in telling them now.

Walk in the sun today, Sally. Tomorrow cloudy.

And when the blackmailer calls again, Howard, then what? If you were forced to steal the first time, how will you satisfy a second demand?

And there was something else.

Ellery frowned into his beer.

There was something else.

What it was, exactly, he didn't know. But whatever it was, it made him uneasy. That old prickly sensation again in the scalp. The tickle of doom.

Something was wrong. Not the adultery, or the blackmail episode, or anything he had yet run into in the Van Horn household. Those things were "wrong," but this wrong was a different wrongness, it covered everything. It was a great wrong, as distinguished from a number of lesser wrongs, component wrongs. That was it—component wrongs! When he tried to isolate the source of his unease, a vaguely satisfying solution arose from the sheer concept of an *all-over* wrong of which these individual wrongs were mere parts. As if they were portions of a pattern.

Pattern?

Ellery drained the beer.

Whatever it was, it was developing. Whatever it was, it could only end badly. Whatever it was, he'd better stick around.

He left *The Hot Spot* on the double and exceeded the speed limit returning to North Hill Drive. It was almost as if something was happening at the Van Horn house and by getting there quickly he might avert it.

But he found nothing out of the ordinary, unless relief is out of the ordinary, and the sudden release of tensions.

Sally at dinner was vivacious. Her eyes sparkled, her teeth flashed. She filled her lord's hall with herself, and Ellery thought how right she looked at the end of the table, opposite Diedrich, and what a pity it would be if not Diedrich sat there, but Howard. Diedrich was in seventh heaven and even Wolfert made a remark about Sally's spirits. Wolfert seemed to take it personally; his remark was edged with malice. But Sally simply laughed at him.

Howard was feeling good, too. He talked volubly about the Museum project, to his father's delight.

"I've started sketching. It feels right. It feels great. I think it's going to be something."

"Which reminds me, Howard," said Ellery. "You know, I haven't even seen your studio. Is it sacred ground, or . . . ?"

"Say! That's right, isn't it? You come on upstairs!"

"Let's all go," said Sally. She glanced at her husband significantly and intimately.

But Wolfert snapped: "You promised to work on the Hutchinson deal tonight, Diedrich. I told him I'd go over the papers with him tomorrow."

"But it's Saturday night, Wolf. And tomorrow's Sunday. Can't that crowd wait until Monday morning?"

"They want to get going Monday morning."

"Hell!" Diedrich scowled. "All right. Darling, I'm sorry. I'm afraid you're going to have to be host as well as hostess tonight."

Ellery had expected something vast and grand, with gargantuan draperies in royal swoops and huge blocks of stone sitting about in various stages of nascence, the whole resembling a sculptor's studio on a Hollywood sound stage. He found nothing of the sort. The studio was large, but it was also simple; there were no great blocks of stone ("You don't have the architectural mind, Ellery," Howard laughed. "This floor would hardly support them!") and the draperies were reasonable. The place was a clutter of small armatures, points, modeling stands, and tools—clamps, gouges, vises, scrapers, chisels, mallets, and so on, which Howard explained had different uses, in wood and ivory carving as well as in stone. Many small models stood about, and rough sketches.

"I use this place for the preliminary work," Howard explained. "There's a big barn of building 'way out in back which I'll show you tomorrow if you like, Ellery. I do the finished work there, I mean on the stone. It has a good solid floor and it'll take a lot of weight. It also simplifies carting the blocks in and the finish out. Imagine trying to hoist a three-ton block of marble up here!"

Howard had done a number of sketches for the Museum figures. "These are all very rough," he said. "Just an all-over visualization. I haven't got down to specifics yet. I'll make more detailed sketches and then get to work with the plasticine. I'll be holed up in the attic here for a long, long time before I'm ready to go ahead in the back studio."

"Dieds told me, Howard," said Sally, "that you wanted some changes made in the studio down there."

"Yes. I think the floor will have to be strengthened and I want another window cut into the west wall. I'll need all the light I can get. And a lot more distance. I'm considering having the west wall knocked out and the studio there enlarged by at least half."

"You mean to hold all your sculptures physically?" asked Ellery.

"No, for perspective. The problem of decorative, monumental sculpture is a lot different from portrait sculpture or even the sort of thing Michelangelo did. You have to get up close to his work really to appreciate it—the textures, details of contour, and so on. At a distance that kind of work tends to blur, get shapeless. My problem is different. These figures must be planned to be seen from a distance, in the open air. The technique will have to be sharp and clear—clear silhouettes, profiles. That's why Greek sculpture appears to such remarkable advantage in the open—why, as a matter of fact, I go for the neoclassic. I'm strictly an outdoor chiseler."

Howard was a different man here. His confusion and introspection were gone, his brow was untroubled, and he spoke with authority and even grace. Ellery began to feel a little ashamed of himself. He had thought of Diedrich's "purchase" of a museum as a rather sickening phenomenon of wealth. Now he saw it as possibly giving a talented young artist an opportunity to create something altogether worth-while. It was a new element in his calculations; one he liked very much.

"All these evidences of creative activity," said Ellery with a grin, "recall me to my own piddling efforts over at the cottage. Would you two consider me very unfriendly if I ducked over there and tormented my typewriter for a while?"

They were properly contrite; and Ellery left them with

their heads together over a sketch, Howard talking animatedly and Sally listening with bright eyes and her lips moist and parted.

So it's all over, is it? Ellery thought grimly. Not all evidence takes the form of letters. He was glad that Diedrich was two floors down, in his study.

Ellery was thinking that it would serve the blackmailer right if Diedrich found out simply by using his eyes and thereby rendered the photostats null, void, and of no value . . . when he saw her again.

He was just rounding the bend in the staircase halfway between the top and second floors. It was the shadow of a shadow, but the shadow's shadow was in the half-bent shape of an angry cat, and he knew it was the old woman.

He leaped noiselessly down the few steps to the second floor and flattened himself against the wall.

She was moving slowly down the hall, an old sickle of a creature with a cowling shawl over her head, and as she moved she mumbled something incredible.

"There the wicked cease from troubling, and there the weary be at rest."

She stopped at the very end of the hall, before a door. To Ellery's astonishment she fumbled in her garments and produced a key. This key she inserted into the lock. When she had unlocked the door she pushed it open and Ellery saw nothing beyond it. It was a rectangle of outer space.

Then the door shut and he heard the snick of the key from the invisible ether.

She lived here.

She lived here, and no one had mentioned her in two and a half days. Not Howard, not Sally, not Diedrich, not Wolfert—not Laura or Eileen.

Why? And who was she?

The old woman had a way of slipping in and out of his consciousness like a witch in a dream.

Guest or no guest, Ellery thought wildly, running down the stairs, here's where I find out what the hell gives.

The Fifth Day

ELLERY HAD JUST reached the foot of the stairway when he heard running and he looked up to see Sally swooping down on him like Superman.

"What is it?" he asked quickly.

"I don't know." She caught at his arm to steady herself and he felt her shaking. "I left Howard just after you did and I went to my room. Diedrich called on the intercom to come right down to the study."

"Diedrich?"

She was frightened.

"Do you suppose . . .?"

Howard came clattering down, white.

"Father just called me on the intercom!"

And there was Wolfert, the skirt of an old-fashioned bathrobe flapping about his skinny legs, his Adam's apple sticking out like an old bone.

"Diedrich woke me up. What's the matter?"

They hurried to the study in a clash of silences.

Diedrich was waiting for them impatiently. The papers on his desk had been brushed to one side. His hair was all exclamation points.

"Howard!" He grabbed Howard, hugged him. "Howard, they said it couldn't be done and, by God, it's *been* done!"

"Dieds, I could strangle you," Sally said with an angry laugh. "You scared us half to death. *What's* been done?"

"Yes! I almost broke my neck getting down those stairs," growled Howard.

Diedrich put his hands on Howard's shoulders, held him off. "Son," he said solemnly, "they've found out who you are."

"Dieds."

"Found out who I am," Howard repeated.

"What are you talking about, Diedrich?" asked Wolfert peevishly.

"Just what I said, Wolf. Oh, we have Mr. Queen at a disadvantage, don't we?"

"Perhaps I'd better be getting on to the cottage, Mr. Van Horn," said Ellery. "I was on my way there when—"

"No, no, I'm sure Howard won't mind. You see, Mr. Queen, Howard's my adopted son. He was left on my doorstep as an infant by . . . well, until now," chuckled Diedrich, "it might just as well have been by the stork. But sit down, sit down, Mr. Queen. Howard, get off those big feet of yours before you fall off 'em. Sally, come sit on my lap. This is something of an occasion! Wolf, smile. That Hutchinson business can wait."

Somehow they were seated and Diedrich went on happily to tell Ellery what he already knew. He managed to convey the proper surprise, while observing Howard out of the corner of his eye. Howard was sitting motionless. His hands were on his knees. The expression on his face was baffling. Was it apprehension that pinched his mouth? Certainly his eyes had a glaze over them; and a little irregular tom-tom was beating in his temple.

"I hired a detective agency in 1917," said Diedrich, his hand on Sally's hair, "when Howard was left with me, in an effort to track down his parents. Wasn't really an 'agency'—or rather, it was a one-man agency. Old Ted Fyfield was the man. He'd retired as police chief and gone into business for himself. Well, I practically supported Fyfield for three years with fees for his work—including all the time I was in the Army—you remember, Wolf. And when he couldn't find a trace after all that time I gave up."

It was hard to tell whether Howard was even listening. Sally saw it, too. She was puzzled, worried.

"It's funny how little things sometimes are the most important," Diedrich went on heartily. "Couple of months ago I was getting a trim in Joe Lupin's chair at the Hollis barber shop—"

"Tonsorial Parlor," murmured Mr. Queen nostalgically. Joe Lupin had come into the Haight case through his wife Tessie, who worked in the Lower Main Beauty Shop. It was The Hollis Tonsorial Parlor, Luigi Marino, Prop., and now that Ellery thought of it, he'd noticed Marino's salt-and-pepper head that very afternoon, bent over a lathered face, as he had sidled through the Hollis lobby.

"—and I got to talking to J. C. Pettigrew, who was under the sun lamp in the next chair. You know, dear. The real estate fellow . . ."

Ellery could still see J. C.'s Number Twelves up on his desk in the real estate office on Lower Main that day he had hit Wrightsville for the first time; the shoes and the ivory toothpick.

"The conversation got around to old-timers who had passed on and somebody—I think it was Luigi—mentioned old Ted Fyfield, who'd been dead for years. J. C. perked up and said, 'Dead or not dead, that Fyfield was a crook and a skunk,' and he went on to tell about the time he'd paid Ted a small fortune in expense money and fees to track down a fellow who'd run out on a realty deal leaving J. C. holding the bag, only to find out that Ted was giving him completely fictitious reports all the time he was collecting J. C.'s money for 'investigating'—that Ted hadn't even left Wrightsville or lifted a finger to earn that money! J. C. said he threatened to have Fyfield's private detective license revoked and the old scoundrel ponied up fast. Well, it gave me a queer feeling, because I'd paid

Fyfield a small fortune myself for three years. Then it turned out that nearly everybody in the barber shop had some discreditable yarn to tell about Ted Fyfield, and by the time they were through I was sick. I hate to be played for a sucker, makes me see red. But more important than that, I'd depended on Fyfield in a matter that . . . well, that was mighty important to all of us."

Sally's frown was deep now. She put her arm around her husband's neck and said lightly: "You should have been a writer, darling. All these *details.* What's the exciting part?"

Wolfert just sat there, in brine.

"Well, sir," Diedrich said grimly, "I played a hunch. I decided to reopen the whole business on the chance that Fyfield had skinned me thirty years ago and not done any real investigating at all. I put the matter in the hands of a reputable agency in Connhaven."

"You never told me." It came out stiff and new, in a strange-sounding voice, not like Howard's at all.

"No, Son, because I figured it was the longest kind of shot—after thirty years—and I didn't want to raise your hopes until I had something definite.

"Well, the long shot came through. Fyfield *had* skinned me, the—" Sally put her hand over his mouth. He grinned. "Just a few minutes ago I got a call from Connhaven. It was the head of this agency. They had the whole story, Son. They couldn't believe their own luck—they'd taken the case on, telling me I was wasting their time and my money. But I played my hunch—and now we know."

Howard asked: "Who are my parents?" in the same stiff way.

"Son . . ." Diedrich hesitated. Then he said gently: "They're dead, Son. I'm sorry."

"Dead," said Howard. You could see him struggling through that intelligence: they were dead, his father and mother were dead, they weren't living, he would never see them, know what they had looked like, and that was bad, or was it good?

Sally said, "Well, I'm not sorry."

She jumped off her husband's lap and perched on his desk, fingering a paper. "I'm not sorry because if they were alive, Howard, it would be the most stupid sort of mess. You'd be a total stranger to them and they to you. It would confuse everybody and do no one concerned the least good. I'm not sorry at all, Howard. And don't you be!"

"No." Howard was staring. Ellery didn't like the way

he was staring. The glaze was thickening over his eyes. "All right, they're dead," he said slowly. "But who were they?"

"Your father, Howard, was a farmer," Diedrich replied. "And your mother was a farmer's wife. Poor, poor people, Son. They lived in a primitive farmhouse about ten miles from here—between Wrightsville and Fidelity. You'll remember, Wolf, how desolate that stretch in there was thirty years ago."

Wolfert said: "Farmer, huh?" The way he said it made Ellery want to stuff his dentures down his throat. Sally slew him with a look, and even Diedrich frowned.

But Howard was impervious to tones of voice. He simply sat staring at his foster father.

"They were too poor to hire hands for the farm, according to the information the agency gathered," continued Diedrich. "Your parents had to do it all themselves. They barely managed to scratch a living from the soil. Then your mother had a baby. You."

"And zing, she tosses me on the nearest doorstep." Howard smiled, and Ellery wished he would go back to staring.

"You were born in the middle of the night during a bad summer thunderstorm," Diedrich smiled back, but no longer was his face happy; he was regretful now, uneasy, and a little sharp, as if he were angry with himself for having misjudged Howard's reaction. And he spoke more rapidly. "The Connhaven agency was able to reconstruct the events of that night from the records they found, and the thunderstorm is important.

"Your mother, Howard, was attended by a Wrightsville man, a Dr. Southbridge, and when you'd been born and taken care of and your mother was comfortable, the doctor started back to town in his buggy, at the height of the storm. Well, on the way back his horse must have been frightened by lightning and got out of control, because the horse, Dr. Southbridge, and the buggy were found at the bottom of a ravine, just off the road. The buggy was smashed, the horse had two broken legs, and the doctor a crushed chest—he was dead when they found him. Of course, he'd had no opportunity to record your birth at Town Hall. The agency thinks that's one of the reasons your parents did what they did. Apparently they felt they were too poor to bring you up right—there were no other children—and realizing when they heard about Dr. Southbridge's accident that he couldn't have had time to record your birth, they saw a chance to put you into the care of someone better off who wouldn't be able to trace you back to them.

"Apparently only they and Southbridge knew about your birth, and the doctor was dead.

"Why they left you on our doorstep, of course, no one will ever know. I doubt if it had anything to do with us personally—it was a pretty prosperous-looking house; at least it must have seemed so to a couple of poor farmers."

"That's all on the assumption," smiled Howard, "that they did it all for little Nameless. But how do you know they didn't do it just because they didn't want little Nameless?"

"Oh, Howard, shut up and stop that breast-beating," snapped Sally. She was terribly concerned; concerned and restless and angry with Diedrich.

Diedrich said hastily: "Anyway, the Connhaven detectives found out all this as a result of locating Dr. Southbridge's appointment book. It was a pocket affair, a notebook, and it had been taken from the doctor's clothes by the undertaker and put among the dead man's effects, winding up in the attic of his old house where the investigators located it. The entry in the doctor's handwriting, apparently made as he was leaving the farmhouse, of the birth of a male child to the farmer's wife corresponds exactly in date to your date of birth, Howard, as given in the note that was pinned to your blanket when I found you; and the agency man tells me—I'd of course kept the note all these years and I'd given it to the agency—that the handwriting on it is absolutely beyond question the handwriting of the farmer—they managed to dig up a sample of an old mortgage. And that, Howard," concluded Diedrich with a sigh of relief, "is the story. So now you can stop wondering about who you were"—his eyes twinkled—"and start being what you are."

"And that's the first *bright* thing I've heard you say tonight, Dieds," cried Sally. "Now how about all of us having some coffee?"

"Wait," said Howard. "Who am I?"

"Who are you?" Diedrich winced. Then he said heartily, "You're my son, Howard Hendrik Van Horn. Who on earth would you be?"

"I mean who was I? What was the name?"

"Didn't I mention it? It was Waye."

"Waye?"

"W-a-y-e."

"Waye." Howard seemed to be tasting it. "Waye . . ."

He shook his head, as if it had no flavor for him at all. "Didn't I have a first name?"

"No, Son. I guess they hadn't given you one—left that job, and it was sensible, too, to the ones who'd bring you up. At least no Christian name for the child appeared in Dr. Southbridge's notation."

"Christian. Were they Christians?"

"Oh, what difference would that make?" said Sally. "Christian, Jewish, Mohammedan—you're what you were brought up. Let's stop this now!"

"They were Christians, Son. What denomination I don't know."

"And you say they're dead, huh?"

"Yes."

"How'd they die?"

"Well . . . Son, I think Sally's right." Diedrich rose suddenly. "We've talked enough about this."

"How'd they die?"

Wolfert's eyes were bright. His glances kept darting from Diedrich to Howard like quick little animals.

"About ten years after they left you with me, a fire broke out on their farm. They were both burned to death." Diedrich rubbed his head in a rather odd gesture of fatigue. "I'm really sorry, Son. This was stupid of me."

The glaze fascinated Ellery. It suddenly occurred to him that he might be witnessing the beginning of an amnesia attack. The thought jarred him.

He said quickly: "Howard, this is all pretty unsettling and exciting, but Sally was right before. It's all for the best—"

Howard did not even glance in his direction. "Didn't they leave anything, Father? An old photo or something?"

"Son . . ."

"Answer me, damn it!"

Howard was on his feet, swaying. Diedrich looked shocked. Sally gripped his arm reassuringly, without taking her eyes off Howard.

"Why . . . why, after the fire, Son, some relative of your mother's saw to the funeral and took away the few things that weren't destroyed in the fire. The farm itself was mortgaged to the hilt—"

"What relative? Who is it? Where can I find him?"

"There's no trace of him, Howard. He moved from here shortly afterward. The agency had no information about his whereabouts."

"I see," said Howard. And then he asked, in a slow thick voice, "And where are they buried?"

"I can tell you that, Son," said Diedrich quickly. "They're in adjoining graves in the Fidelity cemetery. Now how about some of that coffee, Sally?" he boomed. "I know I can use some, and Howard—"

But Howard was on his way out of the study. He was walking wide-eyed, hands raised a little, and he kept stumbling.

They heard his uneven steps going upstairs.

And in a little while they heard the slam of a door from the top of the house.

Sally was so incensed that Ellery thought she was going to be indiscreet.

"Dieds, this was terribly ill-advised! You know how the least emotional upset sends Howard off!"

"But, dearest," said Diedrich miserably, "I thought it would do him good to know. He's always wanted to so badly."

"You might at least have discussed it with me beforehand!"

"I'm sorry, darling."

"Sorry! Did you see his face?"

He looked at his wife in a puzzled way. "Sally, I don't understand you. You've always thought it would be a good thing if Howard learned about . . ."

Sally. This is a clever man you're married to.

"I'm completely out of order," said Ellery cheerfully, "and nobody's asked me to put my two pennies in, but, Sally, I think Mr. Van Horn's done the only possible thing. Of course it's a shock to Howard. It would be to a stable personality. But Howard's ignorance of his origin has been one of the mainstays of his unhappiness. When the shock wears off—"

She caught it. He knew it by the way her lids came down and her hands fluttered down to rest. But she was still angry, woman-wise; perhaps angrier.

All she actually said was, "Well, I can be wrong. Forgive me, dearest."

And then Wolfert Van Horn said a really shocking thing. He had been sitting forward with his skeletal knees drawn up and his torso bent far forward. Now, like Jack-in-the-Box, he sprang to the perpendicular, his bathrobe falling open to reveal his furred and brittle chest.

"Diedrich, how does this affect your will?"

His brother stared at him. "My what?"

"You never did have a head for technicalities." Now

Wolfert's voice was more metallic than acidulous; it had something of the whine of a band saw. "Your will, your will. Wills can be mighty important instruments. In a situation like this they can cause a lot of trouble—"

"Situation? I wasn't aware, Wolf, of any 'situation.' "

"What would you call it—normal?" Wolfert smiled his sucked-in smile. "You've got three heirs—me, Sally, Howard. Howard's an adopted son. Sally is a pretty recent wife—" and Ellery could actually hear the quotation marks around the last word.

Diedrich was sitting very quietly.

"—and as I understand it, we share and share alike?"

"Wolf, I don't get this at all. What's this all about?"

"One of your heirs now turns out to be a man named Waye," grinned Wolfert. "It could make a difference to a lawyer."

"I think," said Sally, "Mr. Queen and I'll take a walk in the garden, Dieds," and Ellery was half out of his chair when Diedrich said gently, "Don't," and then he got up and went over to his brother and stood looking down at his brother and his brother pushed away a little nervously and showed his gray dentures.

"It doesn't, Wolfert, and it won't. Howard is properly identified in my will. His legal name is Howard Hendrik Van Horn. And that's what it stays unless he himself wants to change it." Diedrich loomed unusually large. "What I don't understand, Wolf, is why you'd bring it up it up at all. You know I don't like double talk. What's on your mind? What's behind this?"

And there was that hell again in Wolfert's little avian eyes. The brothers stared at each other, one sitting, the other standing. Ellery could hear them breathing, Diedrich deeply and Wolfert in sniffly spurts. It was one of those interminable moments of pure crisis during which whole histories are written; when the flutter of a fly's wing can start an avalanche. Or that was how it felt. For it was impossible to say that Wolfert *knew*. He was so naturally snide that even his ignorance seemed rotten with meaning; he gave off the unpleasant secrets of corpses.

Then the moment passed, and Wolfert creaked to his feet. "Diedrich, you're a damned fool," he said, and he stalked out of the study like the Scarecrow of Oz.

And Diedrich stood there, in the same position, and Sally went up to him and stood on tiptoes to kiss his cheek; and she said good night to Ellery with her eyes and then she walked out, too.

"Don't go yet, Mr. Queen."

Ellery turned back at the door.

"This hasn't worked out quite as I expected." It sounded plaintive, and Diedrich laughed at his own tone and motioned to a chair. "Life keeps us hopping, doesn't it? Sit down, Mr. Queen."

Ellery found himself wishing Howard and Sally had not gone upstairs.

"I seem to recall defending my brother," Diedrich went on with a grimace, "on the ground that he's unhappy. I forgot to mention that misery likes to have company. By the way, have you got anywhere yet on that twenty-five thousand dollar business?"

Ellery almost jumped.

"Why . . . Mr. Van Horn, it's only been twenty-four hours."

Van Horn nodded. He circled his desk and sat down behind it and began to fuss with some papers. "Laura told me you were out this afternoon. I thought . . ."

Damn Laura! thought Mr. Queen.

"Well, yes, but . . ."

"A thing as simple as this," Diedrich said carefully. "I mean, I thought it would be child's play . . ."

"Sometimes," said Ellery, "the simplest cases are the hardest."

"Mr. Queen," Diedrich said slowly, *"you know who took that money."*

Ellery blinked. He was annoyed with himself, with Van Horn, with Sally, Howard, Wrightsville—but chiefly with himself. He might have known that a man of Diedrich's perspicacity would not be taken in by mumbo-jumbo, even of the superior Queen brand.

Ellery decided quickly.

He said nothing.

"You know, but you won't tell me."

The big figure swiveled behind the desk, turning his face away as if he felt the sudden need for withdrawal. But there were long twists of wrinkle on his shoulder and his very immobility betrayed the forces at work beneath it.

Ellery said nothing.

"You must have a strong reason for not telling me." He sprang to his feet. But then his big body settled and there he was, his hands clasped behind him, looking out into the darkness.

"A very strong reason," he repeated.

But Ellery could only sit there.

Diedrich's powerful shoulders sagged and his hands

contracted in a sort of convulsion; the whole effect was curiously like death. *If an autopsy were to be held at this moment Van Horn would be found to have died of doubt. He knows nothing and he suspects everything—that is, everything but the truth. To a man like Diedrich Van Horn, this could be very like dying.*

Then he turned back and Ellery could see that, whatever it was that had died, Diedrich had already anatomized it and flung it away.

"I didn't get to my age," he said with a grim smile, "without learning how to tell when I'm licked. You know, you won't tell me, and that's that. Mr. Queen, drop the whole thing."

And all Ellery could find to say was, "Thank you."

They talked for a few minutes about Wrightsville, but it was not a successful conversation; at the first opportunity Ellery rose and they said good night.

But at the door Ellery stopped in mid-step.

"Mr. Van Horn!"

Diedrich looked surprised.

"I almost forgot again. Would you mind telling me," Ellery said, "who in heaven's name that very old woman is? The one I've seen in the gardens and upstairs entering a dark bedroom?"

"You mean to say—"

"Now don't tell me," said Ellery firmly, "that you never heard of her. Because I'll run screaming into the night."

"Good grief, hasn't anyone told you *that?*"

"No, and it's driving me mad."

Diedrich laughed and laughed. Finally, wiping his eyes, he fumbled for Ellery's arm and said: "Come on back and have a brandy. That's my mother."

There was no mystery. Christina Van Horn was approaching her hundredth year; rather, her hundredth year was approaching Christina Van Horn, for she had no awareness of time and she was today what she had been for forty-odd years—an arrested creature roaming the barrens of her mind.

"I suppose the reason none of us mentioned her," said Diedrich over the brandy, "is that she doesn't 'live' with us in the usual sense. She lives in another world—the world of my father. Mother began to act queer after Father's death, when Wolfert and I were still boys. Far from her bringing us up, we tended more and more to take care of *her*. She'd come from a very strict Dutch Calvinist home, but when she married Father she really lived with hell's fire, and at Father's death she took up his . . ." Diedrich groped, "his *ferocious* piety as a sort of tribute to his memory. Physically, Mama's a wonderful specimen; the doctors marvel at her stamina. She leads an absolutely independent life. She won't mix with us, she won't even eat with us. Half the time she doesn't even bother to put her lights on. She knows the Bible practically by heart."

Diedrich was surprised to hear that Ellery had seen his mother in the gardens.

"She doesn't leave her room for months at a time. She's perfectly capable of caring for herself and she's almost comically insistent on her privacy. She hates Laura and Eileen," Diedrich chuckled, "and she won't let them into her room. They have to leave her meals on a tray outside her door, and fresh linen, and so on. You ought to see that room of hers, Mr. Queen—she keeps it clean herself. You could eat off the floor."

"I'd like very much to meet her, Mr. Van Horn."

"You would?" Diedrich was pleased. "Well, come on."

"At this hour?"

"Mother's a night owl. Up half the night, does most of her sleeping during the day. She's marvelous. Anyway, as I told you, time doesn't mean a thing to her."

On their way upstairs, Diedrich asked: "Did you see her very clearly?"

"No."

"Well, don't be surprised at what you find. Mama got out of step with the world the day Papa died. She just dropped out of the ranks and there she's stayed, at the turn of the century, while everybody else has gone on."

"Forgive me, but she sounds like a character in a novel."

"She's a character in five novels," chuckled Diedrich. "She's never ridden in an automobile or seen a movie, she won't touch a telephone, she denies the existence of the airplane, and she considers the radio sheer witchcraft. In fact, I often think Mama believes she's living in a literal purgatory—presided over by the Devil in person."

"What will she say about television?"

"I hate to think about it!"

They found the old woman in her room, an unopened Bible in her lap.

Whistler's great-grandmother, was Ellery's first thought. Her face was a mummified, shrunken version of Diedrich's, with a still formidable jaw and proud cheekbones covered loosely with pale leather. Her eyes, like Diedrich's, were the essence of her; they must once, like her elder son's, have been of extraordinary beauty. She was dressed in black bombazine and her head, which Ellery surmised was nearly bald, was concealed under a black shawl. Her hands had a feeble sort of independent life; the thick stiff blue knobby fingers moved ever so slightly, but continuously, over the Bible in her lap.

A tray lay on a table beside her, barely touched.

It was like walking into a different house, in another world, at a distant time. The room bore no relationship to the rest of the mansion. It was poor and old, with battered, very crude handmade furniture, its papered walls yellow with age, and hooked rugs on the floor from which the colors had all but disappeared. There was almost no decoration. The fireplace was of blackened brick, with a handhewn mantelpiece. A Dutch cupboard with chipped and undistinguished delftware stood incongruously beyond the wide and swaybacked bedstead.

There was no beauty in it anywhere.

"It's the room my father died in," explained Diedrich. "I simply took it along with me when I built this house. Mama could never be happy in anything else . . . Mama?"

The ancient woman seemed glad to see them. She peered up at her son and then at Ellery and her withered lips parted in a grin. But then Ellery realized that her pleasure was the pleasure of a disciplinarian about to employ the switch.

"You're late again, Diedrich!" Her voice was remarkably strong and deep, but it had a curious flickering quality, like a radio signal that keeps fading out and in again. "Remember what your father says. *Wash ye, make you clean*. Let me see your hands!"

Diedrich dutifully held out his great paws and the old lady seized them, peered at them, turned them over. During her inspection she seemed to notice the massiveness of the hands she held in her claws, for her expression softened, and she looked up at Diedrich and said: "Soon now, my son. Soon now."

"Soon what, Mama?"

"You'll be a man!" she snapped, and then she cackled at her own wit. Suddenly her glance darted to Ellery. "He doesn't come to see me often, Diedrich. Nor the girl."

"She thinks you're Howard," whispered Van Horn. "Incidentally, she doesn't seem to be able to remember that Sally's my wife. Half the time she calls her Howard's wife— Mama, this isn't Howard. The gentleman is a friend."

"Not Howard?" The news seemed to distress her. "Friend?" She kept peering up at Ellery like an animated little question mark. Suddenly she popped back in her rocker and began rocking violently.

"What is it, Mama?" asked Diedrich.

She refused to answer.

"Friend," said Diedrich again. "His name is—"

"Yea!" said his mother; and Ellery quailed, her glance was so fierce. *"Yea, mine own familiar friend, in whom I trusted, which did eat of my bread, hath lifted up his heel against me!"*

He recognized the Forty-first Psalm with uneasiness. She had mistaken him for Howard; and the word "friend" had sent her untethered mind skittering back to what seemed to Ellery a wonderfully relevant cross reference.

She stopped rocking, snapped, "Judas!" with pure venom, and set herself in motion once more.

"She seems to have taken a dislike to you," said Van Horn sheepishly.

"Yes," muttered Ellery. "I'd better go. No point in upsetting her."

Diedrich stooped over the little centenarian, kissed her gently, and they turned to leave.

But Christina Van Horn had not finished.

Rocking with an energy Ellery found slightly distasteful, she shrieked: *"We have made a covenant with death!"*

The last thing Ellery saw as his host closed the door was the little creature's fierce eyes, still glaring at him.

"Dislike is right," Ellery said with a laugh. "What did she mean by that parting shot, Mr. Van Horn? It sounded rather lethal to me."

"She's old," Diedrich said. "She feels her death is near. She wasn't talking about you, Mr. Queen."

But as Ellery picked his way across the dark gardens to the guest house, he wondered if the old lady might not have meant someone else entirely. That Parthian glare had had a point.

Just as he reached the cottage, a delicate rain began to fall.

The Sixth Day

AND THERE WAS no sleep in him.

Ellery moved restlessly about the cottage. Beyond the picture window Wrightsville frolicked. The bars would be swarming in Low Village; there would be the Saturday night dance at the Country Club in summer formals; Pine Grove would be jumping with bebop; he could actually see the pearly shimmer of *The Hot Spot* and Gus Olesen's *Roadside Tavern* on the silver chain of Route 16; and the decorous blaze above Hill Drive told him that the Granjons, the F. Henry Minikins, the Dr. Emil Poffenbergers, the Livingstons, and the Wrights were "entertaining."

The Wrights . . . All that seemed so long ago, so tenderly pure. And that was laughable, because when it happened it had been neither tender nor pure. Ellery supposed that his memories had undergone the usual metamorphosis through the witchcraft of time.

Or was it that what had been neither tender nor pure appeared so sheerly by contrast with the present reality?

Good sense challenged this theory. The crimes of adultery and blackmail were surely not more heinous than cunning murder.

Then what was it that made him sense a special quality of evil in the Van Horn case? Evil, that was it. *We have made a covenant with death, and with hell are we at agreement . . . for we have made lies our refuge, and under falsehood have we hid ourselves . . . For the bed is shorter than that a man can stretch himself on it; and the covering narrower than that he can wrap himself in it.*

Ellery scowled. It was God with whom Isaiah had threatened Ephraim. Old Christina had misquoted Scripture. *For the Lord shall rise up as in mount Perazim, he shall be wroth as in the valley of Gibeon, that he may do his work, his strange work; and bring to pass his act, his strange act.*

He had the most irritating feeling that he was trying to grab at something as impalpable as it was slick. Nothing made sense.

He was as bad as the mummified crone in her tomb over there.

Ellery put away the Bible he had found on the bookshelf and turned to his reproachful typewriter.

Two hours later he examined what he had milled. It was a stony grist. Two pages and eleven lines of a third, with numerous X-marks and triple word changes, and nothing sang. In one place, where he had intended to write *Sanborn,* he had actually written *Vanhorn.* His heroine, who had been reasonably emancipated for two hundred and six pages, had suddenly turned into an elderly Girl Guide.

He tore up two hours' work, covered the typewriter,

filled his pipe, poured himself a Scotch, and strolled out onto the porch.

It was raining hard now. The pool looked like the moon, and the garden was a black sponge. But the porch was dry, and he sat down in a cane-bottomed bamboo easy chair to watch the attack.

He could see the watery bombardment on the north terrace of the main house and for a long time he gave himself over to simple observation, with no purpose but distraction from his restlessness. The house was as dark as his thoughts; if the old woman was still up, she had turned out her lights. He wondered if she might not be sitting in the dark, as he was, and what she might be thinking . . .

How long Ellery sat there he could not have said. But when it happened he found himself on his feet, the pipe in scattered ashes on the floor beside the empty glass.

He had fallen asleep, and something had aroused him.

It was still raining; the garden was a swamp. He had a faraway recollection of thunder.

But then he heard it again, above the rain.

It was not thunder.

It was a racing automobile engine.

A car was coming around the main house, from the south, from the direction of the Van Horn garage.

There it was.

It was Howard's roadster.

Someone was trying to warm up a cold motor, riding the clutch and pumping the accelerator in short bursts. Whoever it was couldn't know much about cars, Ellery thought.

Whoever it was.

Of course, it must be Howard.

Howard.

As the car got halfway under the porte-cochere, the engine stalled.

Howard.

Ellery could hear the sudden whines of the starter. The engine did not turn over, and after a moment the starter stopped whining. He heard the roadster door open and the sound of someone jumping onto the gravel of the driveway. A dark figure came quickly around and raised the hood. An instant later a slender beam appeared, groping in the motor.

It was Howard, all right. There was no mistaking the long trench coat, the wide-brimmed Stetson Howard affected.

Where was he going? There was a frantic quality in the swift movements of the figure behind the headlights' glare. Where was Howard going in the late night, in a heavy rainstorm, frantically?

And suddenly Ellery remembered Howard's face as it had been in the study a few hours before: the pinchiness about the mouth, the glaze over the staring eyes, the tom-tom in his temple, as his father related the findings of the Connhaven detective agency. His stumbling from the study, his erratic steps mounting to the studio. *Might be witnessing the beginning of an anmesia episode . . .*

Ellery dashed into the cottage, not stopping to switch on the lights. It took him no more than fifteen seconds to find his topcoat and run out again, struggling into his coat as he ran. But already the motor was roaring, the hood was down, the car was in motion.

As he splashed across the gardens Ellery opened his mouth to yell. But he didn't; it was useless; Howard wouldn't hear him above the motor and the storm and the headlights were already swinging away toward the open drive.

Ellery flew.

He could only hope one of the cars in the garage had keys in it.

The first car. . . . Key in the ignition!

He blessed Sally as he sent her convertible hurtling out of the garage.

He was already damp from the run around; within ten seconds at the wheel he was soaked from head to foot. The top was down and he made an attempt to find the switch that controlled it. Not finding it quickly, he gave up; it didn't matter now, he couldn't get any wetter; and the condition of the corkscrew driveway called for concentration.

There was no sign of Howard's roadster anywhere along the drive. Ellery skidded to a stop just outside the entrance to the estate, on North Hill Drive, prepared to turn either way instantly.

Nothing was to be seen to the right, toward Hill Drive.

But to the left, going north, there was a dwindling taillight.

Ellery swung Sally's convertible hard left and stepped on the accelerator.

At first he thought Howard was heading for the Mahoganies, perhaps Quetonokis Lake, which was atonement, or Lake Pharisee, which was original sin. In the grip of amnesia Howard might be moved by some obscure urging to return to the scene of an emotional crisis. All this, of course, if it was Howard's taillight. If it was not, if Howard had turned south on North Hill Drive and headed for town, he was lost for good.

Ellery pressed harder.

At sixty-five he began to gain.

Serve me right, he thought, if I find out it's some upstate drunk's car just as I skid off the road and bring my career as a wet nurse to a messy conclusion.

The rain spouted off his nose. His shoes were so wet that his right foot kept slipping off the accelerator.

But he continued to gain, suddenly with great rapidity, and then he saw the brake light of the car he was following and he jammed on his own brake. Why was the car slowing?

The blinker of an intersection answered him just as the car ahead turned sharply left. But for an instant it was fixed in the convertible's headlights and Ellery saw that the roadster was Howard's. Then it disappeared.

He missed the road sign in the darkness and rain. But left was west, which meant they were flanking Wrightsville. He kept the red light at a constant distance. Howard had decelerated to a mere twenty-five miles an hour, another puzzle; but it enabled Ellery to turn off his brights and become less conspicuous.

So it wasn't either of the lakes.

What was it?

Or didn't Howard himself know?

It occurred to Ellery that for the first time he was justifying his trip to Wrightsville.

All at once he knew why Howard had slowed down.

He was looking for something.

Then the roadster's taillight disappeared for the second time.

So he'd found it.

And Ellery found it a few moments later.

It was a fork in the road. At the fork there was a small local sign, and the sign said:

FIDELITY
2 Miles

The fork had been a dirt road; now it was deep and affectionate glue. It not only clung to the wheels; it twisted and dipped and soared and doubled back like a fox on the run. Within thirty seconds Ellery had lost Howard.

Mr. Queen began to curse, bubbling like a whale as he wrestled with the convertible.

His speedometer sank to 18, then to 14, and finally to 9 miles an hour.

He clung to the wheel doggedly, not caring whether he caught up with Howard or not. He was seated in a small lake and he squished every time he shifted. He could feel cold rivulets coursing down his naked back. He had long since turned his brights on again, but all he could see was the interminable striped wall of the rain and drenched trees to either side. He passed a few miserable houses, cowering by the roadside.

He also passed Howard's roadster before he realized what it was.

There had been no town. It was less than two miles from the fork. Why had Howard stopped here, in the very center of nowhere?

Maybe anmesiacs have their own logic. Ha-ha.

Howard had not merely stopped; he had turned the roadster around, so that now it was facing south.

Accordingly, Ellery straddled the narrow road and persuaded the convertible backward and forward until he, too, could face south. He coaxed the sliding car to a position some twenty-five yards from the roadster, turned off his ignition and headlights, and crawled out of the convertible.

Immediately he sank into mud to the tops of his Oxfords.

The roadster was unoccupied.

Ellery sat down on Howard's running board and wearily rubbed his streaming face with his streaming hand.

Where the hell was Howard?

Not that it mattered. Nothing mattered now except the deliciously unattainable, which was a hot bath and dry clothes afterward. But as a question of simple scientific interest, where had Howard gone?

Ah, for footprints.

But this mud would be as trackless as the sea.

Anyway, he didn't have a flash.

Well, thought Ellery, I'll wait a few minutes. Then if he doesn't show up, the hell with it. Seeing was impossible. No moon . . .

Out of stern habit he got to his feet, although reluctantly, opened the roadster door, and felt around on the dashboard.

Just as he discovered that Howard had taken the keys, he saw the light.

It was a coy light, bobbing and curtseying and for brief moments disappearing altogether. But it kept reappearing. It would fix itself for a moment, then it would bob and curtsey again and disappear again and reappear a few feet away.

The light was performing these antics a good distance off, not up or down the muddy road, but off to the side, beyond the roadster.

Was it a field over there?

Sometimes the light was close to the ground. Sometimes it was waist-high to a man.

Then it steadied for a longer moment and Ellery caught a glimpse of a dark mass surmounted by a broad hat. Howard using a flashlight!

Ellery slogged around the roadster with his hands before him. There was probably a flashlight in the convertible's glove compartment but to go for it might mean missing something. And there was always the possibility that another light might frighten Howard away.

Ellery's hands encountered a wet stone wall beyond the roadster. The wall came up to his waist.

He swung himself up and over, landing neatly in a thorny bush.

At this point Mr. Queen included Heaven itself in his imprecations.

Then, because part of him was pure leech, he wrenched himself from the embrace of the brambles and set a stumbling, groping course toward the light.

It was the most baffling place. He found himself going up little rises and sliding down on the other side. He encountered cold hard wet objects. Once he fell over one and found that it was lying flat on the weedy ground. And occasionally there was a tree, usually encountered first by his nose.

It was the most puzzling terrain he had ever tried to cross in the dark, full of traps for the feet. What made it especially difficult was the necessity for keeping the light continuously in view. If only the damned thing would stay in one place! But it kept moving jerkily, in a sort of dance.

And Ellery made the exasperating discovery that he was not gaining on it.

It danced in the distance like *ignis fatuus,* a snare for the unfortunate traveler, never seeming to come nearer.

The traveler's toe caught on something and he fell for the second time. But this time, as he fell, something happened to his head. It flew right off his shoulders, exploding in a burst of flame, and surely he died, because everything stopped, the rain and the chill and Howard and the dancing light and everything.

Perhaps it was the Providence he had cursed, shaming him with Its beneficence, but when Ellery opened his eyes the light was no more than twenty feet from where he was lying. And, sure enough, there was the trench-coated, Stetson-surmounted mass that was Howard, before the light, which was now steady. It gave enough illumination for Ellery to make out what he was lying on, what he had stumbled over, and what had struck him on the side of the head.

He had stumbled over a weed-choked little mound of earth of rectangular shape, at the head of which stood a column of marble supporting a stone dove.

It was the dove which had struck his temple, and while he lay unconscious Howard had made a rough circle and had found, only a few yards from where Ellery was lying, the graves he had been hunting.

They were in the Fidelity cemetery.

Ellery got to his knees. The marble monument stood between him and Howard. Even if he had knelt exposed, there would have been small danger of Howard's seeing him—his back was to Ellery and he was utterly absorbed in the sight revealed by his flashlight.

Ellery clung to the unknown's monument; he could only stare.

Suddenly Howard lunged. The light made a crazy half circle. Then it focussed again and Ellery saw that Howard had stopped for a handful of mud, mud from one of the graves.

This mud he now hurled with satanic energy full in the face of the broad headstone.

He stooped again, again the light pinwheeled, again it focussed, again he hurled mud.

It seemed to Ellery that this was the strictly logical denouement of the whole nightmare: that a man should drive miles in a pelting downpour in the dead of night to throw mud at a broad headstone. And when the flashlight swooped to the ground and its beam trained itself on the mud-splattered monument and Howard took from one of the pockets of his trench coat a chisel and a mallet and darted forward to strike great blows upon the stone, blows that sent commas, periods, and exclamation points flying through the italic rain into the darkness beyond . . . this too seemed the proper employment for a sculptor groping toward the final shape of the Unknown.

Ellery came to himself in the dark cemetery.

Howard was gone.

All that was left of him was the light going slowly away in the direction of the dirt road.

And even as Ellery got to his feet the light vanished.

A moment later he heard the faint roar of the roadster. Then that too was gone.

He was surprised to discover that the rain had stopped.

Ellery leaned against the dove-topped column in the darkness. Too late to follow Howard.

But even if there had been time, he would not have followed Howard. The ghost of every soul lying beneath his soaked feet could not have dragged him from the burying ground.

There was something to be done, and to do it he would stand here until dawn, if necessary.

Maybe the moon would show up.

Mechanically he unbuttoned his gluey topcoat and fumbled with muddy fingers in his jacket pockets for his cigaret case. It was a silver case and its contents would be dry. He found it and opened it and took out a dry cigaret and stuck it between his lips and returned the case to his pocket and fumbled for his lighter . . .

Lighter!

He had the lighter out and open and a flame cupped between his palms even as he hurdled three mounds to the place where Howard had exorcised his demon.

Ellery stopped, shielding the little flame.

It was necessary to stoop. For this was surely the poorest of the poor, pale soft crumbly stone, a pitiful affair no taller than the crowding weeds but wide as two graves, rounded at the top and cleft between, like the twin tablets of Moses. Weather and its own infirmities had pocked it honorably; but the sculptor's chisel had dealt the final foul blows, and it tottered above the twin graves now, a murdered thing.

Some of the lettering had fallen victim to the furious chisel; what remained was hard to read. He could make out figures, dates of birth and date of death, but these were all but illegible; and there was a motto, which after patient scrutiny Ellery decided had originally read: WHOM GOD HATH JOINED. But there was no question about the names. Across the top of the gravestone, in crabbed clear capitals, ran the legend:

AARON AND MATTIE WAYE

Ellery drove the convertible into the Van Horn garage and parked it beside Howard's roadster with no surprise. Nevertheless, he was relieved. He decided that Howard could wait, and he hurried around the main house to the cottage.

He left his mud-stiffened outer garments on the porch, discarded the rest on the way to the bathroom, and scalded his hide under the shower until the chill seeped out of his bones and his muscles unknotted. He rubbed himself down quickly, got into clean dry clothing, paused in the sitting room only long enough to take a flashlight and a pull from the bottle of Scotch, and then he strode over in the lifting darkness to the other house.

Quietly he went upstairs, past sleeping doors. There were no lights anywhere; he stepped cautiously, feeling his way, not using his flash. On the top floor landing, however, he turned it on. A faint trail of muddy prints on the taupe carpeting led from the stairs to Howard's bedroom. And the bedroom door was half open.

Ellery paused in the doorway.

The mud marks wandered to the bed. On the bed, fully clothed, lay Howard, asleep.

He had not even bothered to take off his trench coat. His soaked hat gaped in a puddle on the pillow.

Ellery shut the door and bolted it.

He drew the Venetian blinds.

Then he switched on the lights.

"Howard."

He prodded the sleeping man.

"Howard."

Howard groaned something unintelligible and turned over, his head thrown back, snoring. He was in a sort of stupor. Ellery stopped prodding him.

I'd better get him out of these clothes first, Ellery thought, or he'll come down with pneumonia.

He unbuttoned the sodden coat. The material was rain-proofed and the lining was dry. He tugged until he got one sleeve off, and then he managed to lift Howard's heavy body sufficiently to pull the coat free and strip it off the other arm. He removed Howard's shoes and socks, and his trousers, which were caked and wet to the knee, and, using the blanket as a towel, he rubbed Howard's legs and feet dry; the bed was a mess, anyway.

Then he went to work on Howard's head.

Under the massage, Howard stirred.

"Howard?"

He thrashed about as if he were fighting something off. He moaned. But he did not awaken. And when Ellery had him all dry, he lapsed into the same semi-comatose sleep.

Ellery straightened with a frown. Then he saw what he was looking for on the bureau and he went for the whiskey bottle.

Howard opened his eyes.

"Ellery."

They were bloodshot and stary.

They took in the bed, himself half undressed, the wet muddy clothing on the floor.

"Ellery?"

He was bewildered.

And then, suddenly, frightened.

He clutched at Ellery.

"What happened?" His tongue was thick; he mouthed it.

"You tell me, Howard."

"It happened, didn't it? Didn't it!"

Ellery shrugged. "Well, something happened, Howard. What's the last thing you remember?"

"Coming upstairs from the study. Pottering around a while."

"Yes, I know. But after that."

Howard squeezed his eyelids shut. Then he shook his head. "I don't remember."

"You came upstairs from the study, you pottered around a while—"

"Where?"

"Where?"

"Oh, you're asking the questions." Howard laughed shakily. "What's the matter with me? I pottered around in the studio there."

"In the studio. And then—nothing?"

"Not a blamed thing. It's a blank, Ellery. Just like . . ." He stopped.

Ellery nodded. "The other times, eh?"

Howard swung his naked legs off the bed. He began to shiver and Ellery pulled the underblanket free and tossed it over his thighs.

"It's still dark." Howard's voice rose. "Or is it another night?"

"No, it's the same night. What's left of it."

"Another attack. What did I do?" Ellery studied him. "I went somewhere. Where did I go? Did you see? Did you follow me? But you're dry!"

"I followed you, Howard. I've changed."

"What did I *do?*"

"Whoa. Wrap that blanket around your feet and I'll tell you—you're sure you don't remember a thing?"

"Nothing! What did I do?"

Ellery told him.

At the end, Howard shook his head as if to clear it. He scratched his scalp, rubbed the back of his neck, pulled his nose, stared at the muddy clothing on the floor.

"And you don't remember any of that?"

"Nope."

Howard looked up at Ellery.

"It's hard to believe." Then he looked away. "Especially that part about where I . . ."

Ellery picked up the trench coat, fished in one of the pockets.

When Howard saw the chisel and mallet he went very pale.

He got off the bed and began to blunder about the bedroom in his bare feet.

"If I could do that, I could do anything," he mumbled excitedly. "God knows what I've done those other times. I've got no right running around loose!"

"Howard." Ellery dropped into the armchair by the bed. "You harmed nobody."

"But why? Why did I desecrate their graves?"

"The shock of learning who you are, after a lifetime of dreading the moment of discovery, sent you off again. In the amnesic state you expressed the deep resentment and fear and hatred you've apparently always felt toward the parents who rejected you . . . I'm speaking psychologically, of course."

"I'm not aware of any hatred!"

"Of course not."

"I'm not aware of ever having felt any!"

"Not consciously."

Howard had paused in the doorway to the adjoining studio. Now he stared into the gloomy room for several seconds. Then he strode through and into the studio and Ellery heard him moving about. The sounds stopped and the lights came on.

"Ellery, come in here."

"Don't you think you ought to get something on your feet?" Ellery struggled out of the armchair.

"The hell with my feet! Come in here!"

Howard was standing beside a modeling stand. A plasticine figure of a little bearded Jupiter occupied the stand.

Ellery said curiously: "What's up?"

"I told you I pottered around in here last night after I came up from the study. This is one of the things I did."

"The Jupiter?"

"No, no. I mean this." Howard pointed to the base of the model. In the plasticine a sharp tool had scratched:

H. H. WAYE

"You remember doing that?"

"Certainly! I even remember why." Howard laughed stridently. "I wanted to see what my real name looked like. I've always signed my work *H. H. Van Horn.* I had to use the *H. H.*—they didn't give me a first or middle name. But *Waye* was mine. And do you know?"

"What, Howard?"

"I liked it."

"You liked it?"

"I liked it. I still do. Downstairs, when father first told me, it didn't mean anything. But later, when I came up . . . it sort of grew on me. Look." Howard ran over to the wall, indicated a series of sketches pinned on a board. "I liked it so much I signed *H. H. Waye* to every sketch I've made for the Museum project so far. I'd damned near made up my mind to make it my professional signature. Ellery, would I have liked it so much if I hated *them?"*

"Consciously? It's quite possible. To conceal your hatred from yourself, Howard."

"I fall in love with my parents' name and then I black out and drive ten miles in a rainstorm to spit on their graves?" Howard dropped into a chair, looking gray. "Then it gets down to this," he said slowly. "When I'm in a normal state, I'm one thing. But when I black out I become another. Consciously I'm a pretty good guy. In amnesia I'm sort of maniac, or devil. Dr. Jekyll and Mr. Hyde!"

"You're dramatizing again."

"Am I? To hack your parents' gravestone to pieces is hardly a 'reasonable' act! It's vile. You know perfectly well that no matter how much cultures may differ, they meet on the common ground of respect for parents. Whether it's called ancestor worship or honoring your father and your mother!"

"Howard, you'd better go to bed."

"If I'd defile my parents' graves, why wouldn't I commit murder? Rape? Arson?"

"Howard, you're running off at the mouth. Go to bed."

But Howard had Ellery's hand in a convulsive grip. "Help me. Watch me. Don't leave me."

His eyes were terrified.

He's transferred his attachment from Diedrich to me. I'm his father now.

Somehow, Ellery got Howard to bed. He remained by the bedside until Howard fell into an exhausted sleep.

Then he trudged downstairs and out of the house and spent a ghastly hour in the garage removing the mud from the convertible and the roadster.

Sunday morning was peering through the cottage windows as Ellery fell into bed.

The Seventh Day

AND HE RESTED on the seventh day from all work he had not made, specifically his novel; and he tried not to think of a certain publisher, and of how same would brandish a contract, displeased. But labor he had in the cause of letters, if not precisely the letters demanded by his bondage; and he basked in the surcease thereof, delinquently.

There was Church.

Of how pertinent this was to become Ellery had no inkling; sufficient unto the day was Reverend Chichering of St. Paul's-in-the-Dingle, whose voice rolled as the prophet's—a modified thunder, to be sure, since this was High Church; but the spirit was Jeremiah's, judging and exhorting and complaining: *"My bowels, my bowels! I am pained at my very heart; my heart maketh a noise in me"*; which was audible to the last pew; *"I cannot hold my peace, O my soul . . . The whole land shall be desolate . . . Woe is me now! for my soul is wearied because of murderers,"* at which Howard all but disappeared and Wolfert grinned and Sally shut her eyes while Diedrich sat quietly grim. At the peroration of his sermon, however, Reverend Chichering without warning abandoned Jeremiah to enter Luke—VI, 38—for a new text: *"Give, and it shall be given unto you; good measure, pressed down, and shaken together, and running over, shall men give into your bosom. For with the same measure, that ye mete withal, it shall be measured to you again,"* for it shortly appeared that a certain vestryman had donated a new sanctuary for the chancel, the rector having used the present sanctuary hardly; and it further appeared that this outgiving servant of the Lord bore a well-known name—"I say well-known," Father Chichering thundered musically, "not in the temporal sense, although it is that also, but in the eyes of Our Father, for this God-fearing Christian soul has performed his good works not by laying up for himself treasures upon earth . . . or rather, he *has* laid up for himself treasures upon earth, but how else could he have done what he has done, which is to lay up for himself treasures in heaven, where neither moth nor rust doth corrupt, in accordance with the Sermon on the Mount? And I think the good Lord will forgive me if I sound a trumpet and tell you that our beneficent brother in Christ is Diedrich Van Horn!"—at which the congregation hummed, craning and beaming at the servant of the Lord as he shrank deeper into the Van Horn pew and glared at his rector with no humility whatsoever. However, this incident served to disperse the gloom cast by the rector's preceding jeremiad; the closing hymn was roared; and the service ended with everyone feeling mightily spiritual.

Even Ellery left St. Paul's-in-the-Dingle exalted.

The rest of the day was given over to good works also, such as roast turkey with chestnut-and-giblet stuffing *à la Laura,* candied yams, lemon sherbet *soufflé,* and so forth; postprandially, Mendelssohn's *Elijah,* which left Sally solemn and Diedrich excited. Howard had bought a new recording of it weeks before and Ellery thought it clever of him to have saved its first performance for today when each, for his secret reason, had need of soul-searching. And then a social evening in the finest Wrightsville tradition—laughing ladies and gracious gentlemen who had mastered the cliché and occasionally even said something interesting, and none of whom Ellery had ever met before, for which he was—obscurely—grateful.

The day even ended agreeably. Sunday evenings are early evenings in Wrightsville. Everyone was gone by eleven-thirty, and Ellery was in bed by midnight.

He lay in the dark thinking how beautifully everyone had behaved all day, even Howard, even Wolfert; how much duplicity there is in humankind, and how necessary for tolerable existence so much of it is; and finally he prayed the Lord his soul not to take until he had finished the damned novel, which he now sternly commanded himself to sail into with unswervable purpose the very first thing in the morning; and then he was diving into Quetonokis Lake in an old bathrobe trying to reach four furry letters gleaming on the loamy bottom at the foot of a pale nude sculpture of Sally, who, reasonably enough, had Diedrich's face.

The typewriter was spitting out hot good words at a furious clip at 10:51 Monday morning when the cottage door burst open and Ellery, jumping a foot, whirled to see Sally and Howard huddled in the doorway.

"He called again."

At once Sunday was as if it had never been and this was Saturday again, at the Hollis Hotel.

Nevertheless, he asked: "Who called again, Sally?"

"The blackmailer."

"The damned porker," said Howard thickly. "The swilling greedy swine."

"The call came just now?"

Sally was shaking. "Yes. I couldn't believe my ears. I thought it was all over."

"The same whispery, sexless voice?"

"Yes."

"Tell me what he said."

"Laura answered the phone. He asked for Mrs. Van Horn. I got on and he said, 'Thanks for the money. Now there's the second installment due.' I didn't understand at first. I said, 'Didn't you get *all* of it?' and he answered, 'I got twenty-five thousand. Now I want more.' I said, 'What are you talking about? I got back what you sold me—' (I didn't want to say 'letters' because Laura or Eileen might have been listening) '—they're gone,' I said. 'Destroyed.' He said, 'I have copies.' "

"Copies," Howard snarled. "What can he do with copies? I'd have told him where to go, Sal!"

"Ever hear of photostatic copies, Howard?" asked Ellery.

Howard looked stunned.

" 'I have copies,' he said," Sally continued in a breathless voice, " 'and they're just as good as the originals. Now I'm putting the copies up for sale.' "

"Yes?"

"I said I had no more money. I said a lot of things. Or tried to. But he wouldn't listen."

"How much does he ask for this time, Sally?" Ellery wished people would avoid having to look frightened afterward simply by taking good advice beforehand.

"Twenty-five thousand dollars. Again!"

"Another twenty-five!" roared Howard. "Where the devil are we going to get another twenty-five? Does he think we're made of money?"

"Shut up, Howard. Sally, let's have the rest of it."

"He said to leave twenty-five thousand dollars in the Wrightsville railroad station waiting room, in one of those self-service parcel lockers they just installed."

"Which locker?"

"Number 10. He said the key would be in the first mail this morning, and it was. I just ran down to the road for it."

"Addressed to you, Sally?"

"Yes."

"Have you handled the key?"

"Why, I took it out of the envelope, looked it over. Howard did, too. Shouldn't we have?"

"I suppose it doesn't matter. This bird's too cagey to leave his fingerprints around. Did you save the envelope?"

"I did!" Howard looked around furtively before he took an envelope from his pocket and handed it to Ellery.

It was a cheap slick envelope, perfectly plain—standard stock of the stationery counters of every five-and-dime in America. The address was typewritten. There was nothing on the flap. Ellery tucked the envelope away without comment.

"And, and here's the key," said Sally.

Ellery looked at her.

She flushed.

"He said it's to be put on top of the tier of lockers, above 10. To push it back out of sight, against the wall." She still offered the key.

Ellery did not take it.

After a moment, timidly, she placed it on the desk before him.

"Did he put any time limit on this second payment?" asked Ellery, as if nothing had happened.

She was looking blindly out at Wrightsville through the picture window. "The money must be in the locker at the station by five o'clock this afternoon or he said he'd send the evidence to Diedrich tonight. To Diedrich's office, he said. Where I couldn't intercept it."

"Five o'clock. That means he intends to pick it up during the rush hour, when the station's jammed," ruminated Ellery. "The Slocum, Bannock, and Connhaven traffic . . . He rather rushes things, doesn't he?"

"You'd think he'd give a person a chance," said Sally.

"What did you expect from a blackmailer—sportsmanship?"

"I know. You warned us." Sally was still not looking at him.

"I'm not rubbing it in, Sally. I simply want to indicate the probabilities for the future."

"Future!" Howard loomed. Ellery tipped back in the chair and looked up at him curiously. "What future? What are you talking about?"

Now Sally *was* looking at him.

"You don't think he's through, do you?"

"But—!"

"Sally, he didn't say anything about *giving* you the photostats, did he?"

"No."

"Even if he had. He could have made ten photostatic sets of the four letters. Or a hundred. Or a thousand."

The woman and the man looked at each other, dumbly.

It was not pretty and Ellery swiveled to the sky. He felt sorry suddenly for both of them. So sorry he forgave them their stupidities and foibles and contemplated a few of his own. As it turned out, he would have been better advised to remain objective, unforgiving, and cynical; but Ellery is a hopeless sentimentalist when his emotions are involved, and they were young and in a mess.

He swiveled back. Sally was curled up in the big chair in a foetal position, her hands hiding her face; Howard was pouring himself a drink with an expression of sheer concentration.

"This is just the beginning," Ellery told them gently. "He'll demand more. And more. And, again, more. He'll take what you have, he'll take what you can steal, and in the end he'll sell the evidence to Diedrich. Don't pay. Go to Diedrich this morning, together. And tell him. Everything.

"Could you do that, both of you? Or one of you?"

Sally burrowed deeper into her hands. Howard stared into the glass of Scotch.

Ellery sighed.

"I know, it's like contemplating a firing squad. But it's much worse than the actuality. One blast—"

"You think I'm afraid." Sally had dropped her hands; she had been crying; but she was angry now, angry as she had been angry Saturday night, although this morning for a different reason. "I tell you it's Dieds I'm thinking of. He'd *die.*" She sprang from the chair. "I don't care about myself any more," she said in a passionate undertone. "All

I want is to forget all this. Start over again. Make it up to him. I can, too. If it became necessary, I'd see that Howard went away. I'd be *ruthless,* Ellery—you don't know how ruthless I could be. But I've got to have that chance." She turned away. "Maybe," she said in a muffled voice, "he'll let a long time go by till the next time. If there is a next time . . ."

"This envelope, Sally," Ellery tapped his pocket, "went through the Wrightsville post office stamping machine at 5:30 P.M. Saturday. *Only a couple of hours after I'd paid him the first twenty-five thousand.* That means he must have mailed it immediately after picking up the envelope in Upham House. Does that look as if he'll let 'a long time go by' before he makes his third demand?"

"Maybe he'll stop altogether," Sally flared. "Maybe when he realizes there isn't any more, he'll *stop.* Maybe he'll . . . maybe he'll *die* in the meantime!"

Ellery said: "And you, Howard?"

"He mustn't find out." Howard tossed off the Scotch.

"Then you'll pay."

"Yes!"

Sally said: "We must."

Ellery laced his fingers across his stomach and asked: "With what?"

Howard threw the whiskey glass into the fireplace with all his strength. It broke against the firebrick in a splash, like a spray of diamonds.

"Like diamonds," muttered Howard. "I wish they were."

"Sally." Ellery sat forward, alarmed. "What is it?"

Sally said, in the queerest way: "I'll be right back."

In the gardens, she began to run. They watched her run around the pool and across the terrace and into the house.

Howard shook his head. "Nothing seems to connect this morning," he said apologetically. "I'm sorry about the glass, Ellery. Boyish, aren't I?" He took another glass and poured another drink. "Here's to crime."

Ellery watched him toss it off.

Howard turned blindly away.

Three minutes later Sally appeared on the terrace. Her hand was rammed into the right pocket of her suit jacket. She crossed the terrace and the gardens sedately. But on the cottage porch she hurried, and when she came in she slammed the door.

Howard gawped at her.

She held out her right hand to him.

Dangling from it was a diamond necklace.

"I took it out of the safe."

"Your *necklace,* Sally?"

"It's mine."

"But you can't give up your necklace!"

"I'm sure twenty-five thousand can be raised on this. It must have cost Dieds a hundred." She turned to Ellery. "Would you like to see it?"

"It's magnificent, Sally." Ellery made no move to take it.

"Yes, so beautiful." Her voice was steady. "Dieds gave it to me on our last anniversary."

"No," said Howard. "No, it's too risky."

"Howard."

"It's bound to be missed, Sal. How would you explain to Father?"

"You took a risk to raise the first twenty-five thousand."

"Why, no, I . . ."

"Wherever you got it, there's some record of it. A note, or something. Of course you took a risk. Now it's my turn. Howard—take it."

Howard flushed.

But he took it.

The sun streaming in through the picture window caught its facets and tossed them about. His hand seemed on fire.

"But . . . it's got to be turned into cash," Howard muttered. "I . . . wouldn't know how to go about it."

Howard the ineffectual. Howard the dependent.

"You know," remarked Ellery from the swivel chair, "this is sheer imbecility."

Howard turned to him hungrily.

"Ellery, I'll never ask you to do anything—"

"You mean you want me to pawn this necklace, Howard."

"You know about these things," stammered Howard. "I don't."

"Yes, and that's why I characterize this entire business as lunacy."

"But we've got to raise that money," said Sally in a hard tone.

Ellery shrugged.

"Ellery." She was begging now, fiercely. "Do it for me. A favor. It's my necklace. I take the responsibility. Howard's right—we won't ever ask you to get mixed up in this again. No matter what happens. But won't you do just this one thing?"

"Let me ask you, Sally," said Ellery clearly. *"Why don't you do it yourself?"*

"I might be seen in town. By Dieds, or Wolfert, or one of their employees. Going into or coming out of the pawnshop. You don't know what a small town's like. It would be all over Wrightsville in no time. Dieds would be bound to hear about it—somebody'd make good and sure he heard about it! Don't you see?"

And Howard jumped in: "Yes, and the same thing goes for me, Ellery." *He hadn't thought of it till Sally brought it up. Now he's grabbing for it.*

"Or the pawnbroker might mention it, or—"

Ellery raised his brows. "Let me get this straight. You want me to pawn this necklace without identifying it as yours, Sally?"

"That's the whole point. That way Dieds couldn't find out—"

"I don't get this. At all." Ellery's face was bleak. "A necklace like this—it must be famous in Wrightsville. Even if the pawnbroker doesn't know it, the minute someone else saw it—"

"But Dieds bought it in New York," said Sally eagerly. "And I've never worn it. Even at home, Ellery, when we've entertained. I've had it only a few months. I've been saving it for an occasion. It's *not* known in town—"

"Or you could pawn it somewhere else," put in Helpful Howard.

"No time to go outside Wrightsville, Howard. You two seem to think a stranger can walk into a pawnshop, plunk down a hundred-thousand-dollar necklace, and walk out with twenty-five thousand of the broker's dollars and no questions asked. There's only one broker in town, old Simpson in the Square, so I can't even shop around. Simpson would want proof of ownership. Or authorization from the owner. He'd have to raise the cash. And at once." Ellery shook his head. "It's not just stupid. It's almost impossible."

But now they were both at him, collaborating their arguments, with a determination he found a little sickening.

"Why, you told me yourself you knew J. P. Simpson," Sally was saying. "From the time you were in Wrightsville visiting the Wrights. The Haight case—"

"I didn't know Simpson, Sally. We met briefly during Jim Haight's trial; he was a witness for the prosecution."

"But he'd remember you," cried Howard. "You're somebody, Ellery. They've never forgotten you in this town!"

"Maybe so, but do you expect Simpson to have twenty-five thousand dollars in his till?"

"He's one of the richest men in town," countered Sally triumphantly. "Has one of the largest accounts at the Wrightsville National. And he does occasionally make big loans. Only last year Sidonie Glannis got herself in an awful mess with some smoothie who swept her off her feet—that was a letter business, too—and he blackmailed her for I don't know how much. Sidonie had a lot of jewels left to her by her mother, and she pawned them at Simpson's to pay this man off before he turned the letters over to Claude—that was Claude Glannis, Sidonie's husband. I don't know how much Simpson gave her, but I've heard it was well over fifteen thousand dollars. They caught the man and the story came out and Claude Glannis blew his brains out, but even before the blackmailer was arrested—he's in prison now—everybody in town knew about it and—"

"Then what makes you think everyone in town won't know about this?"

"Because you're Ellery Queen," she retorted. "All you'd have to do would be to tell Simpson you were in Wrightsville on a very hush-hush case—staying with the Van Horns as a blind—that you couldn't disclose the name of your client but that you had to pawn her necklace, or something like that. You see? I'm even writing your dialogue, Ellery. Oh, do it!"

Every reasonable cell in Ellery's body bade him rise, pack his bag, and flee on the first train out of Wrightsville bound for any destination whatever.

Instead, Ellery said: "Whichever way this turns out, I warn you both now, in advance, that I'll have nothing further to do with this childish, dangerous nonsense. Don't ask me to connive at anything but the truth from now on. I'll refuse. —Now let me have the locker key and the necklace, please."

Ellery returned from town shortly after one o'clock.

They were watching for him, because he had scarcely got his hat off when they appeared in the cottage doorway.

He said, "It's done," and stood there, his silence inviting them to leave.

But Sally came in and dropped into the armchair.

"Tell us about it," she begged. "How did it go?"

"You called the turn, Sally."

"Didn't I tell you? What did Simpson say?"

"He remembered me." Ellery laughed. "It's depressing how gullible people are. Especially the shrewd ones. I keep forgetting it, and every time I do I go wrong . . . Why, Simpson did it all by himself, with hardly a suggestion from me. Assumed I was working on something very big, very secret, and very important. Fell all over himself co-operating." He laughed again.

Sally slowly got out of the chair.

"But the money," Howard demanded. "Did you have any trouble about the money?"

"Not the slightest. Simpson locked his store and went over to the bank in person. Came back with a bagful." Ellery turned to Wrightsville. "He was so very impressed. With the necklace, with me, with his part in what he obviously suspects his international ramifications . . .

"The money's in Locker 10 at the station. The key is on top of the tier of lockers, at the back, against the wall. It's too high to be noticed accidentally; he had it all figured out." And Ellery said, "Do you two have any idea what I feel like?"

He turned around.

"Do you?"

They stood before him, just looking at him and not at each other and after a moment not looking at him, either.

Then Sally's lips parted.

"No thanks are necessary," Ellery said. "Now would you mind very much letting me get on with my work?"

He did not join the household at dinner Monday evening. Laura brought a tray over to him, which he emptied dutifully before her eyes; then she took the tray away.

He worked through half the night.

Ellery was putting his shaving things away Tuesday morning when a voice called from the sitting room: "Queen? You up?"

He could not have been more astounded if the voice had been Professor Moriarty's.

He went to the doorway in his undershirt, razor still in hand.

"Not intruding, I hope." Wolfert Van Horn was all friendliness this morning, eager-beaverish, with a vast dental smile and his hands plunged in his pockets boyishly.

"No, indeed. How are you this morning?"

"Fine, just fine. Saw your door open and wondered if you'd be up. Weren't your lights on most of the night?"

"I worked until almost 3:30."

"That's exactly what I thought." Wolfert beamed at the littered desk; he's the only man I ever saw, Ellery thought, who can look sly with his eyes wide open. "So this is what an author's desk looks like. Wonderful, wonderful. Then you didn't get much sleep, Queen."

So we're going to play games.

"Hardly any," Ellery smiled. "You work yourself into a thing, Mr. Van Horn—everything tight, everything wound up—it sometimes takes a long time to unwind."

"And I've always thought writers live the life of Riley. Just the same, I'm glad you're up."

Here it comes.

"Haven't seen you since Sunday. How'd you like Chichering?"

Not yet.

"Earnest, in an earnest sort of way."

"Yes, ha-ha! Very spiritual man. Reminds me a little of my father," Wolfert laughed deprecatingly, "although Pa was a fundamentalist, of course. He used to scare Diedrich and me so our knees shook. But here, I'm rattling along as if neither of us had a lick to do." Wolfert lowered his voice, cocked his ax of a head, and struck. "You weren't thinking of having breakfast with the family this morning, were you, Mr. Queen? You didn't have dinner with us last night and I thought . . ."

Ellery smiled back. "Something special on the menu this morning, Mr. Van Horn?"

To his horror, Wolfert winked.

"Extra-special!"

"Eggs benedictine?"

Wolfert howled and slapped himself. "Very good! No, it's something a whole lot better'n that."

"Then I'll certainly come over."

"I'd better tip you off first. My brother's a funny coot. Hates formality. To get him to make a speech you practically have to call out the State Militia. Get it?"

"No."

"You hurry up and get dressed, Queen. This is going to be a circus!"

Nevertheless, Mr. Queen was not elated.

Wolfert Van Horn nursed and nuzzled his mystery all through breakfast, chuckling and making obscure remarks to his brother and behaving so remarkably unlike his unwholesome self that even Howard, bogged down in his problems, noticed and said, surprised: "What's happened to *him?*"

"Now, Son," said Diedrich dryly, "let's not look a gift horse in the mouth."

They all laughed, Wolfert the most loudly.

"Don't be mean, Wolf," said Sally with a smile. "Give out."

"Give out what?" said Wolfert innocently. "Ha-ha!"

"Don't rush him, dear," said her husband. "Wolf so seldom allows himself to laugh . . ."

"All right, that did it," said Wolfert, winking at Ellery. "I'll put you out of your misery, Diedrich."

"Me? Oh, I'm the joke."

"Get set, now."

"All set."

So was Sally. So was Howard. Suddenly. *The wicked flee when no man pursueth.*

"Where d'ye think you're going tonight, Diedrich?"

"Going? Not a darned place but home."

"Incorrect. Sally," said Wolfert with a flourish of his cup, "more coffee."

Sally poured with an ever-so-unsteady hand.

"Oh, come on," growled Howard. "What's all the mystery about?"

"Why, Howard. You're in it, too. Ha-ha-ha!"

"All right, Son," said Diedrich quietly. "Well, well, Wolf? And where am I going tonight?"

His brother set bony elbows on the table, took a slup of his coffee, set the cup down, and brandished a forefinger coyly. "I'm not supposed to tell you this, now—"

"Then don't." Diedrich promptly pushed his chair back.

"But it's too good to keep," said Wolfert hastily. "And you'll know, anyway, this morning at the office. They're sending a delegation to invite you."

"Invite me? Where, Wolf? To what? What delegation?"

"All the old girls of the Art Museum Committee—Clarice Martin, Hermy Wright, Mrs. Donald Mackenzie, Emmy DuPré and the rest of that crew."

"But why? Invite me to what?"

"Tonight's shindig."

"What shindig?" demanded Diedrich, with a note of alarm.

"Brother," said Wolfert triumphantly, "you told me you hoped the Committee didn't make a fuss about your donation. Well, sir, tonight you're going to be guest of honor at a grand banquet in the Grand Ballroom of the Hollis—testimonial dinner to that patron of the arts, that benefactor of culture or whatever it is, the Man Who Made the Art Museum Possible—Diedrich Van Horn! Hip-hip! Yayyyyy!"

"Testimonal dinner," said Diedrich feebly.

"Yes, sir. Soup-and-fish, speeches, the works. Tonight the Van Horns become Public Property! The great man in the middle, his beautiful wife at his right, his talented son at his left—everybody all togged out!"—Wolfert laughed again, and it sounded like a snarl "—try getting out of this one, Diedrich. Matter of fact, I'll tell you a secret." There went that wink again. "I was the one put 'em up to it!"

It was fortunate, Ellery thought, that Diedrich reacted in character. His dismay and Wolfert's enjoyment of it enabled Sally to fight the cornered animal in her eyes, and Howard sat slack-jawed, trying to close his mouth.

Ellery felt a little sickish himself.

As Diedrich bellowed and stormed—he'd be damned if he'd do it, they couldn't make him—and Wolfert baited him—banquet's set, dinner's ordered, invitations sent out—Sally and Howard managed to take hold of themselves.

So that when it was all over and Diedrich threw up his hands and said to Sally, "I guess we're stuck, darling. Well, there's one saving grace—it'll give you a chance to doll up. Wear the diamond necklace I gave you, Sally," Sally was able to smile and say, "Naturally, dear," and tilt her face to be kissed—exactly as if wearing the necklace which lay in J. P. Simpson's safe was the most delightful prospect in the world.

Diedrich and Wolfert left. The three conspirators sat. Laura came in and began to clear the breakfast dishes. Sally shook her head and Laura went out, banging the door.

"I think," said Ellery at last, "we'd better go somewhere else."

"The studio." Howard rose, stiffly.

Upstairs Sally collapsed. Her body shook and shook. Neither man said anything. Howard stood wide-legged, only the semblance of a man. Ellery strolled back and forth before little Jupiter.

"I'm sorry." Sally blew her nose. "I seem to have a genius for doing the wrong thing. Howard, what are we going to do?"

"I wish I knew."

"It's like a sort of punishment." Sally held on to the arms of the chair and addressed the rafters tiredly. "No sooner do you get out of one corner than you're trapped in another. It's almost humorous. I'm sure I'd laugh if it were happening to somebody else. We're a couple of frantic bugs trying to get out of a matchbox. *How am I going to explain about that necklace?"*

Ellery did not say that that was a question she should have considered when she decided to pawn the diamonds.

"I thought I had time." She sighed. "I thought, I'll figure out a way when the time comes. And here it is. So soon . . ."

Yes, thought Ellery, that's the remarkable thing about this problem. The pressure. The pressure of events crowding one another. They're piled up now in a space too small to contain them. Something has to give . . . The unusual factor of pressure. Unusual factor . . . The phrase kept repeating itself until his conscious mind took note of its insistence. Unusual . . .

Howard was saying something over and over, too, and not brightly.

"What was that, Howard?"

"It doesn't matter," said Sally. "Howard said maybe I could say the necklace was in my japanned box and was stolen with the other jewels in June."

"And never recovered, Sal! That's the point!"

"Howard, you're not being helpful. I gave Dieds a full list of the contents of the jewel box at the time. The necklace wasn't on the list because the necklace hadn't been in the box. What do you want me to say—that I *forgot* it? Anyway, it's been in his safe downstairs all this time. I told you I went to the study to get it. Dieds *must* have seen it there; he goes to the safe frequently. For all I know, so does Wolfert."

"Wolfert." Howard grabbed at that, black-angry. "If not for that—that corpse, none of this would be necessary!"

"Oh, stop it, How."

"Wait."

"For what?"

"No, wait, wait." Howard's voice was soft, almost unpleasant. "There is a way out of this, Sal. I don't like it, but . . ."

"What way?"

Howard looked at her.

"What way, Howard?" She was really puzzled.

He said very carefully, "Stage a . . . robbery."

"A robbery?" She sat up straight. "A *robbery?*" She was horrified.

"Yes! Last night. Or during the night. Father and Wolfert didn't go into the study this morning, I'm sure of it. We can say . . . We'll open the safe. *Leave* the safe door open. Break a pane in the French door. Then Sal, you can call Father at the office . . ."

"Howard, what are you talking about?"

He's forgotten she doesn't know about the other robbery. Now she's beginning to wonder. Now he sees it. Now he covers up.

"Then you suggest something," he said shortly.

Sally glanced at Ellery but then—quickly—she glanced away.

"Ellery." Howard sounded very reasonable. "What do you think?"

"Lots of things, Howard. None of them pleasant."

"Yes, I know, but I mean—"

"It won't work."

"But what else can we do?"

"You can tell the truth."

"Thanks!"

"You asked me, I'm telling you. This thing is now so involved, so hopeless, that there's no other way." Ellery added with a shrug, "There never was, really."

"No. I can't tell him. I won't. I can't hurt him that much!"

Ellery looked at him.

Howard's glance shifted. "All right, have it your way. I don't want to hurt myself, either."

"But that's not my reason," moaned Sally. "I'm not thinking of myself. I'm not, I'm not."

"We seem," said Ellery in the silence, "to have come to some sort of ending."

Howard said abruptly, "There's nothing you can suggest?"

"Howard, I told you. That pawnshop deal was my last. I'm utterly, immovably against all of this. If I can't stop you from acting the fool, I can at least stop compounding your folly. I'm sorry."

Howard nodded, curtly. "Sally?"

She got out of the chair.

Ellery trailed them to Diedrich's study compelled by a psychology he tried wearily to analyze. The sensible course was to pack up and leave. And yet he persisted in following them in their awkward gyrations as if he were a part of the problem. Maybe it was just curiosity. Or curiosity and a perverted sort of loyalty, or a compulsion of conscience, as if, having agreed to one bargain, he had to stick to the end, even though it had long since been superseded by other bargains to which he was not a party.

They went in and Sally put her back against the study door and Ellery stood in a corner.

None of them said a word.

Howard wadded a handkerchief. It was like watching a pantomime. With it he opened Diedrich's safe. He wrapped the handkerchief around his hand and made violent gestures inside, tumbling things about. His hand came out with a velvet box. He opened it. It was empty.

"This is it, isn't it?"

"Yes."

Howard dropped the box, open, on the floor just below the safe. He left the safe open.

Now what? The scene had a certain academic interest.

Howard strode to the French door. On the way he snatched a cast-iron paperweight from his father's desk.

"Howard," said Ellery.

"What?"

"If you're manufacturing evidence to indicate that the thief was an outsider, don't you think it might be wiser to break the pane from the terrace side?"

Howard looked startled. Then he reddened. And then he opened the French door with his handkerchief-wrapped hand, stepped through, shut the door, struck the pane nearest the handle with the paperweight. Glass showered onto the study floor.

Howard came back in. This time he left the door open. He stood looking around.

"Have I forgotten anything? All right, Sally. That's it."

"What, Howard?" Sally looked at him blindly.

"It's up to you now. Phone him."

Sally swallowed.

She went around her husband's desk, avoiding the glass, sat down in the big chair, pulled the telephone to her, dialed a number.

Neither man said anything.

"Mr. Van Horn, please. No, *Diedrich* Van Horn. Yes, this is Mrs. Van Horn calling."

She waited.

Ellery moved closer to the desk.

"Sally?" He heard the big voice, reduced.

"Dieds, my necklace is gone!"

Howard turned away, fumbling for a cigaret.

"Necklace? Gone? What do you mean, darling?"

Sally burst into tears.

Nor all your Tears wash out a Word of it.

"I just went to take the necklace out of the safe for tonight's affair and . . ."

"It's not in the safe?"

"No!"

Weep, Sally, weep.

"Maybe you took it out and forgot, dear."

"The safe's been opened. The door to the terrace . . ."

"Oh."

And a very queer oh that was, Mrs. Van Horn. You don't know what he knows and what he suspects. Careful now.

"Dieds, what am I going to do?"

Weep, Sally, weep.

"Sally. Dearest. Now stop. Ask Mr. Queen to—Is he there?"

"Yes!"

"Put him on. And stop crying, Sally." *Still odd.* "It's just a necklace."

Sally held the telephone out, mutely.

A mere hundred thousand dollars' worth.

Ellery took it.

"Yes, Mr. Van Horn."

"Have you looked over the—"

"The French door has been broken through. The wall safe is open."

Van Horn did not ask the question about the glass. He waited. But Ellery waited, too.

"You'd better tell my wife not to touch anything. I'll be right home. Meanwhile, Mr. Queen, would you keep an eye on things?"

"Of course."

"Thanks."

Diedrich hung up.

Ellery hung up.

"Well?" Howard's face was all out of shape. Sally just sat there.

"He asked me to keep an eye on things. No one is to touch anything. He's coming right home."

"No one's to touch anything!" Sally got up.

"I think," said Ellery slowly, "he intends to notify the police."

Chief of Police Dakin had grown old. Where he had been lean, he was fragile; his hide was crumbling; his hair was ashes. His big nose seemed even bigger.

But his eyes were still two panes of frosted glass.

Dakin came in between the brothers and it was characteristic that, even though he must have known Ellery would be there, his glances went first to the broken pane, next to the open safe, and only thirdly to Ellery. But then it turned warm; and he came over to pump Ellery's hand.

"We never seem to meet excepting there's trouble," he exclaimed. "Why didn't you let me know you were back among us?"

"I've been more or less in hiding, Chief. And the Van Horns have been covering me up. I'm writing a book."

"Seems to me you could have kept your eye on things better for these folks between paragraphs," said Dakin, grinning.

"I'm humiliated, believe me."

Wrightsville's chief of police stood rubbing his lean jaw.

"Diamond necklace, huh? Oh, hello, Mrs. Van Horn." He nodded to Howard, too.

Sally said, "Oh, Dieds," and Diedrich put his arm around her.

In the doorway, Wolfert said nothing. He kept looking around peckishly. Searching for worms, Ellery thought.

Chief Dakin strolled over to the French door, glanced at the glass on the floor, at the jagged hole in the pane.

"Second robbery since June," he remarked. "Seems like somebody's got it in for you, Mrs. Van Horn."

"I hope I'm as lucky this time, Mr. Dakin."

Dakin drifted over toward the safe.

"Did *you* find anything, Mr. Queen?" Diedrich asked. His jaw was jutting.

"It's a pretty clear case, Mr. Van Horn, as Chief Dakin will tell you. Incidentally, you don't need me with Dakin around. I have a great deal of respect for the chief's talents."

"Say, thanks," said Dakin, picking up the velvet box.

Diedrich nodded rather grimly, as if to say, *So have I.*

Mad clear through, Ellery thought. First the twenty-five thousand, now the diamond necklace. Can hardly be blamed.

Dakin took his time. Dakin always took his time. He had the exasperating deliberateness of a rising tide. You could hardly see it move, and yet you knew it would engulf everything in its own time and that nothing could stop it.

He was fascinating Sally and Howard.

"Mrs. Van Horn."

Sally jumped. "Oh! Everybody's been so quiet. What, Mr. Dakin?"

"When's the last time you saw the necklace?"
"Over a month ago," said Sally quickly.
Too quickly.
"Why, no, dear," said Diedrich, frowning. "It was two weeks ago, don't you remember? You took it out of the safe to show—"
"Millie Burnett. Of course." Sally was crimson. "I'd forgotten, Dieds. Stupid of me."
"Two weeks." Dakin stood digesting the fact. "Anybody see it after that?"
"Did you," said Diedrich, "Howard?"
The ugly face was stone.
"Me?" Howard laughed, nervously. "Me, Father?"
"Yes."
"How could I have seen it? I never have any reason to go to the safe."
Diedrich said in a thick voice, "I just thought you might have seen it, Son."
He suspects. He doesn't know. He suspects, and it's killing him. It's killing him to suspect and not know. Howard? Impossible. Sally? Unthinkable. But . . .
Diedrich turned away.
"It was in the safe Monday morning," said his brother.
"Yesterday?" Diedrich eyed Wolfert sharply. "You're sure?"
"Sure I'm sure." Wolfert smiled his meager smile. "I had to get at those Hutchinson papers and I opened the safe. The necklace was there."
Dakin asked, "In this box, Mr. Van Horn?"
"That's right."
"Box open?"
"No . . . but—"
"Then how'd you know the necklace was in it?" said Dakin mildly. "Have to be careful about these things, Mr. Van Horn. In gettin' the facts, I mean. Or did you happen to, now, open the box, Mr. Van Horn?"
"As a matter of fact, I did." The tips of Wolfert's furry ears were turning fuchsia.
"You did?"
"Just looked at it, that's all." Wolfert was furious. "Or do you think I'm lying?"
Diedrich roared, "What difference does it make? The burglary occurred during the night, that pane of glass was all right late last night. What difference does it make when the necklace was last seen?"
He's sorry already. Sorry he's called Dakin in on this. That was bitterness. This is bitter regret.

The police chief said, "You'll be hearin' from me about this, Mr. Van Horn," and before they grasped that he had said something definite and threatening, Dakin was gone.

Diedrich did not return to town. Wolfert did, but Diedrich remained in his study most of the day behind a closed door. Once, seeking a reference book, Ellery approached the door; but hearing the footsteps of his host blundering about aimlessly, Ellery went back to the cottage. Howard had shut himself up in his studio. Sally was in her room.

Ellery worked.

At five o'clock Diedrich appeared in the cottage doorway.

"Oh, hello."

He had fought his battle and won it. The lines were deeper, but controlled.

"See that deputation of old hens?"

"The Committee? No, I didn't. Working . . ."

"Mountain coming to Mahomet. What could I say? I felt like a fool. Of course, we have to go."

"To each his suff'ring," said Ellery with a laugh.

"What's that in? Job?" Diedrich responded with a slight smile. "Pa used to quote it. Oh, yes. *Man is born unto trouble, as the sparks fly upward.* Some of us look as if we were being attacked by acetylene torches . . . See here, I don't want to disturb you, Mr. Queen, but it occurred to me we hadn't said a word about your coming with us tonight to that blamed testimonial dinner. Of course we want you to—"

"I'm afraid I'll have to beg off," said Ellery quickly, "although it's very kind of you to include me in the family."

"No, no. We'd love having you."

"I have no evening clothes with me—"

"You can wear an extra tuxedo of mine."

"I'd swim in it. Anyway, Mr. Van Horn, this is your show."

"You mean you want to stay here and punish that typewriter."

"It hasn't taken half enough abuse. Frankly, yes."

"I wish we could change places!"

They laughed at that companionably, and after a while Diedrich waved and went away.

A strong man.

Ellery watched the Van Horns leave. Diedrich, magnificent in tails and a silk topper, held the door open for

Sally, who wore a mountainous mink wrap with a gardenia corsage, a white gown sweeping the steps, and a gossamer something over her head; and, behind them, Wolfert, looking like an undertaker's assistant. The Cadillac limousine rolled up with Howard at the wheel, Diedrich and Sally got into the tonneau, Wolfert slipped in beside Howard. The *bon ton* Wrightsville rarely employed chauffeurs.

The big car roared down the drive and around a bend and disappeared.

And it semed to Ellery that none of them had uttered a word through the whole thing.

He returned to his typewriter.

At seven-thirty Laura appeared. "Mrs. Van Horn told me you'd be home for supper, Mr. Queen."

"Oh, Laura. You don't have to bother."

"No *bother,*" said Laura. "Will you be having it in the dining room, Mr. Queen, or would you like me to bring you a tray?"

'Tray, tray. Don't go to any trouble, Laura. Anything'll do."

"Yes, sir," But Laura lingered.

"Yes? What is it, Laura?" That heroine was an increasing pain in the neck.

"Mr. Queen, is . . . somethin' wrong? I mean—"

"Wrong, Laura?"

Laura plucked at her apron, "Mrs. Van Horn in her room cryin' all day, and Mr. Diedrich bein' so . . . And then, him comin' back with the chief of police this morning and all."

"Well, if something's wrong, Laura, it's really none of our affair, is it?"

"Oh. No, Mr. Queen."

When Laura returned with the tray, her mouth was set in a very thin line indeed.

Ellery gathered that she had just discovered the clay in her idol's feet.

He really made progress. The pages flipped off and he heard nothing but the typewriter's chatter.

"Ellery."

He was surprised to find Howard beside him. He hadn't even heard the door open.

"Back already, Howard? Why, what time is it?"

Howard was hatless; his evening topcoat was open and the tails of his white scarf dangled. His eyes made Ellery remember everything.

Ellery pushed back.
"Come over to the house."
"Howard, what's the matter?"
"We just got back from the dinner. We found Dakin waiting for us."
"Dakin. Is *Dakin* here? I've been so absorbed—"
"Dakin sent me over here for you."
"For me?"
"Yes."
"Didn't he say why he . . .?"
"No. He just said to get you."
Ellery buttoned the collar of his shirt, reached for his jacket.
"Ellery."
"What?"
"He's got Simpson with him."
Simpson.
"The pawnbroker?"
"The pawnbroker."
Ellery clamped his mind shut instantly.

J. P. Simpson was a balding, grape-eyed little countryman who always looked as if he was sniffing something. His stained topcoat was buttoned and he clutched his hat tightly. He was seated on the rim of Diedrich's big chair. When Ellery and Howard strode in, he jumped up and scuttled behind it.
Sally was in a shadow near the French door, still in her fur coat. Her white gloves crumpled a menu.
The old baffled look was on Diedrich's face. He had dropped his coat and top hat on the floor; his scarf, like Howard's, was still around his neck; his hair was disorderly. And he was extremely quiet.
Wolfert hovered behind his brother.
Chief Dakin leaned against a bookcase.
"Dakin."
Dakin pushed away from the case, reaching into his pocket.
"I thought we'd better have you in on this, Mr. Queen."
"In on what?"
As if I didn't know.
"Well, here he is," said Diedrich roughly. "Now what's this, Dakin?"
Dakin's hand emerged from his pocket with the diamond necklace.
"This your necklace, Mrs. Van Horn?"

The souvenir menu fell to the floor.

Sally stooped but Dakin was quicker. He had it, and he handed it to her politely, and Ellery thought how beautifully this man worked. The way he had got to her side without making a point of his approach. He was really wasted in Wrightsville.

"Thank you," said Sally.

"Is it, Mrs. Horn?"

Sally let it drip, glittering, over her gloved hands.

"Yes," she said faintly. "Yes. It is."

"Why, Dakin," said Diedrich, "where'd you find it?"

"I'll let Mr. Simpson tell you that, Mr. Van Horn."

The pawnbroker said in an excited voice: "I made a loan on that! Yesterday. Yesterday afternoon."

"Take a look around, Mr. Simpson," drawled the chief of police. "Recognize anybody here as the person who pawned it?"

Simpson shook an indignant finger at Ellery.

Even Wolfert was surprised. But Diedrich was stunned.

"This gentleman here?" he asked incredulously.

"Queen. Ellery Queen. That's him!"

Ellery grimaced. He had told them it wouldn't work. Now they were in for it. He glanced sadly at Sally and Howard. Sally was clutching the necklace and staring at it. Howard was trying to look surprised.

How silly this all is.

"Mr. Queen pawned this necklace?" Diedrich was saying. "Mr. *Queen?*"

"Made me think it was for a client or some such tittle-tottle," cried the little pawnbroker. "Led me by the nose! Took me in! Well, I always said you never can tell about these New Yorkers. Bigger they are, foxier they are. Stolen article all the time—why didn't ye tell me that, Mr. Queen? Why didn't ye tell it was stole from Mrs. Van Horn?" He was dancing behind the armchair.

Diedrich laughed. "Why, I frankly don't know what to say, what to think. Mr. Queen . . .?" He stopped, helplessly.

Your turn, boys and girls . . . Ellery looked at Howard again.

And a strange thing happened.

Howard looked away.

Howard looked away . . .

But he must have caught that glance.

Ellery succeeded in catching Howard's eye again.

Howard looked away again.

Quickly, Ellery glanced at Sally.

But Sally seemed to be counting the diamonds.

Can't be. They can't be this perfidious. Howard! Sally!

This time Ellery compelled her to look up.

Sally looked through him.

And suddenly Ellery felt a tightness around his throat. When he felt it he knew it for what it was. He found himself angry. Angrier than he had ever been in his life. So angry that he did not trust himself to speak.

Diedrich was looking him over now, no longer helplessly; more questioningly now, and with a certain joy that lit up the question and sharpened its outline swiftly.

He'd glad. He's going to hang onto this. He's been floundering; and here's a life preserver flung from nowhere and he's grabbing for it.

Ellery lit a cigaret, deliberately.

"Mr. Queen." Dakin was being respectful. "I don't have to remind you this all looks pretty queer. I'm dead certain you can explain it, but—"

"Yah! Let him explain it!" shouted Simpson.

"Would you please explain it, Mr. Queen?" So respectfully.

Ellery blew out the match. He smoked, he waited.

Dakin's eyes became opaque.

"Well? Mr. Queen!" This was Diedrich. And harsh.

He's grabbed it.

"Writing a book, did he say?" Wolfert Van Horn exploded. He rocked and hawked with the miserable joy of it.

"Mr. Queen." Diedrich again. *Now we're going to be fair. Chance to talk before pronouncing execution. Well, I'll be damned if I . . .* "Mr. Queen, won't you please say something!"

"What can I say?" Ellery smiled. "That I'm humiliated? Insulted? Furious? Astounded?"

Diedrich considered this. Then he said quietly: "This could be very clever."

"Could it, Mr. Van Horn?"

"Because now that I think of it, there are certain facts. Other facts."

"Such as?"

"That other robbery. Friday morning."

Dakin said quickly: "What's this, Mr. Van Horn?"

"My safe was burglarized some time during the early hours of Friday morning, Dakin. Twenty-five thousand dollars in cash were taken."

Jump, Sally. Yes, look at him. Oh, but away. So fast.

"You didn't report that, Mr. Van Horn," said Dakin, blinking.

"Diedrich, you didn't even tell me," said Wolfert. "Why . . . ?"

"You were here then, too, Mr. Queen," said Diedrich.

Ellery nodded thoughtfully.

"That pane in the French door was broken then, too, Dakin. I had a glazier fix it over the week end. But that first time the pane'd been broken from inside the study here. I must admit . . . at the time I thought it was an inside job—I mean . . . one of the help."

Unworthy of you, Diedrich. One of the help? Well, what else can you say?

"But now . . . The job done on that first pane could have been a smart dodge. A trick."

"To make it look like an amateur job?" Dakin nodded slowly. "It could at that, Mr. Van Horn."

"What are you just looking at him for?" shrilled Simpson. "What is he, God or somebody? He buncoed me! He's a crook!"

Diedrich frowned, rubbing his jaw. "Simpson, you *sure* Mr. Queen was the one who pawned that necklace?"

"Am I sure? Van Horn, my business is remembering faces. You bet your sweet life I'm sure. I'm *sure.* I shelled out good American money and lots of it. Ask him. Go ahead!"

"You're quite right, Simpson." Ellery shrugged. "I pawned Mrs. Van Horn's necklace . . . yes."

Sally said, "Excuse me," in a faint voice. She started from the room.

Diedrich said, "Sally," and she stopped in mid-step and turned around a moment later and Ellery saw the oddest expression on her pretty face. Sally stood on the brink of a decision. He wondered grimly whether she would jump or run. "We've got to get to the bottom of this," said Diedrich harshly. "I just can't believe it. Queen, you're no fly-by-night. You're somebody. You'd have to have a tremendous reason to do a thing like this. Won't you tell me what's behind it? Please."

"No," said Ellery.

"No?" Diedrich's jaw settled.

"No, Mr. Van Horn. I'm going to let Howard answer for me."

Not Sally. Sally has to do it by herself. That's important. I'm a fool but that's important.

"Howard?" said Diedrich.

"Howard, I'm waiting," said Ellery.

"Howard?" said Diedrich again.

"Haven't you anything to say, Howard?" Ellery asked gently.

"Say?" Howard licked his lips. "What would I have to say? I mean . . . I don't get this. At all."

Committed, Howard?

"Queen." Diedrich seized Ellery's arm. Ellery almost cried out. "Queen, what's my son got to do with this?"

"Last chance, Howard."

Howard glared at Ellery.

Ellery shrugged. "Mr. Van Horn, Howard handed me that necklace. Howard asked me to raise money on it."

Howard began to shake. "That's a damned lie," he said hoarsely. "I don't know what he's talking about."

Committed. Over.

And Sally?

Sally just stood there.

She's standing there but she's jumped. She would be ruthless, she'd said. And Howard said he'd do anything. To keep Diedrich from learning the truth they'd lie, steal, betray. You weren't kidding, either of you.

There was no reason whatever for keeping Sally out of this. And yet an obscure something checked Ellery's tongue. Pure sentiment, he decided. What's more, she knew it. He could read the little, wicked, triumphant woman's knowledge in her eyes. And yet Sally was neither wicked nor small. Perhaps she was better than any of them, and bigger. He was almost happy to be able to keep her out of it. Unless Howard mucked to the very bottom and dragged her down with him. But Ellery didn't think he would. Not to spare her. To spare himself.

Ellery stopped thinking altogether. But then he pulled himself in. Diedrich was watching him, watching Howard. And then Diedrich did a strange thing. He strode over to Sally and took the necklace from her fingers and ran to the safe and hurled the necklace in and slammed the safe door and twirled the dial.

When he turned to Chief Dakin his face was composed. "Dakin, the matter's closed."

"No charges?"

"No charges."

Dakin's clouded eyes shifted over so slightly. "Mr. Van Horn, it's your property."

"Wait a minute!" screamed J. P. Simpson. "The matter's closed, is it? And what about that money I loaned him on the necklace? Think I'm goin' to be done out of my money?"

"How much was it, Simpson?" asked Diedrich courteously.

"Twenty-five thousand dollars!"

"Twenty-five thousand dollars." Diedrich's lips tightened. "Reminiscent, Mr. Queen, isn't it? By the way, is that right—that figure?"

Diedrich went to his desk and in the intolerable silence wrote out a check.

When Dakin and Simpson had gone, Wolfert seeing them out, Diedrich got up from his desk and put his hand on Sally's arm.

She quivered, but she said, "Yes, Dieds."

He steered her to the doorway. Howard moved, too, but somehow his father's bulk managed to get in the way. The door closed in Howard's face.

Neat.

Howard shouted, "Why'd you come out with it? Damn you, why did you?"

His hands were fists and he was pale and flushed alternately and he seemed about to throw himself at Ellery in a perfect frenzy of outrage.

"Why did I come out with it, Howard?" asked Ellery incredulously.

"Yes! Why didn't you stick by us!"

"You mean why didn't I confess to a crime I didn't commit?"

"You didn't have to say a damned thing! All you had to do was keep your big mouth shut!"

I've got to get hold of myself.

"In the face of Simpson's identification?"

"Father would never have pressed charges!"

He's insane.

"Instead of which you welshed on us! You've made him suspicious! You forced me to lie. And he knows I lied. And if he doesn't get it out of me, one of these days he'll worm it out of Sally!"

Just hold on.

"I rather think, Howard, that Sally will take care of her end very capably. He doesn't suspect she's involved in any way. The only one he suspects is you."

Forced him to lie. Howard believes it.

"Well, that's true." As suddenly as it had begun, the tantrum ended. "I'll give you that much. You kept Sally out of it."

"Yes," said Ellery. "Big-hearted Queen. So now all your father can think is that you're a thief, Howard; he has no reason to learn that you cuckolded him, too. As I said, big-hearted Queen."

Howard went very pale.

He dropped into the armchair and began to bite his nails.

"This whole thing, Howard," said Ellery, "is so completely incredible that frankly, for the first time in my life, I don't know what to say. I ought to knock your head right off your shoulders. If I thought you were normal, I would."

Ellery reached for the telephone.

"What are you going to do?" Howard mumbled.

Ellery sat down on the desk. "If I stay on here, Howard, I can only continue to muddy the existing mess. That's one thing. Another is that I've had a bellyful—I wash my hands of the whole stupid, unbelievable business. You and Sally work it out as you see fit—you never took my advice, anyway. This adultery thing wasn't what brought me up here; had I known about it in advance, I shouldn't have come in the first place. As for your amnesia, my advice—which undoubtedly you won't take—is what it was back in New York: See a really top man or woman in psychiatry and open up.

"The third thing, Howard," said Ellery with a slight smile, "is that I've learned an important lesson, to wit: Never reach a conclusion about a man's character on the basis of a few weeks in Paris, and never, *never* reach a conclusion about a woman on any basis whatsoever."

He dialed Operator.

"You're leaving?"

"Tonight. Immediately. Operator—"

"Wait a minute. You calling for a cab?"

"Just a moment, Operator. Yes, Howard. Why?"

"No more trains out tonight."

"Oh—never mind, Operator." Ellery hung up, slowly. "Then I'll have to stay over in one of the hotels."

"That's silly."

"And dangerous? Because it might get around that Howard Van Horn's house guest spent his last night in Wrightsville at the Hollis?"

Howard reddened.

Ellery laughed. "What do you suggest?"

"Take my car. If you insist on leaving tonight, drive back. You can garage the car in town and I'll pick it up on my next trip in. I've got to run into New York the end of the week anyway to buy some stuff for the Museum project. I'll tell Father you suddenly decided to leave tonight—which is true—and that I lent you my car—which is also true."

"But look at the risk I'm running, Howard."

"Risk? What risk?"

"Of finding Dakin on my trail," said Ellery, "with a warrant charging me with automobile theft."

Howard muttered: "You're very funny."

Ellery shrugged. "All right, Howard. I'll chance it."

Ellery drove steadily. It was very late, there was almost no traffic on the main highway, Howard's roadster hummed the song of escape, there were honest stars to look at, the tank was full, and he felt happy and at peace.

It had been wrong from the start. He'd had no business meddling in Howard's amnesia. But there had been a mystery then, and the human element of liking and curiosity. Later, however, when he learned about the erotic explosion at Lake Pharisee, he should have run rapidly for the nearest exit. Or if he had stayed, he should have refused firmly and finally to act in any capacity whatever in the negotiations with the blackmailer. At any step along the way he might have spared himself the sickening eventuality of Howard's perfidy simply by being sensible. So, really, he had no one to blame but himself.

But it was a comfortable castigation. Peace perched on his suitcase, a therapeutic companion.

It was possible to see Wrightsville now in the perspective of his receding tracks, a sore spot rapidly vanishing. It was possible to see Diedrich Van Horn and his great trouble, and Sally Van Horn and hers. It was even possible to see Howard for what he was—the disturbed and degenerating prisoner of a cruel personal history, an object of sympathy rather than a subject for anger. And Wolfert was simply a little nastiness, to be flicked off. As for Christina Van Horn, she was less than a phantom—the ancient shadow of a phantom, toothlessly mouthing in the darkness of her crypt a few dry morsels of the Bible.

The Bible.

The Bible!

Ellery found himself parked on the side of the road, crouched over the dead wheel, gripping it while his heart labored to right itself and his head filled with the unthinkable.

It took him some time to work it out. There was the wonder to fight clear of, and the deadwood to pick out and throw away. An orderly process had to be set up so that the thing might be seen in its unbelievable image. He had to stand far enough off to be able to encompass its sheer magnitude.

But was it possible? Really possible?

Yes. He couldn't be mistaken. He could not.

Each piece had the terrifying color of the whole, the congruent edges of which, fitted together, revealed the tremendous—the simply tremendous and the tremendously simple—pattern.

Pattern . . . Ellery recalled his uneasy thoughts about a pattern, how he had tried to decipher its hieroglyphs. But this was the Rosetta Stone. There was no possibility of a mistake.

One piece was missing.

Which?

Slowly. One . . . four . . . seven . . .

A pale horse: and his name that sat on him was Death.

Frantically, he started the roadster, shot the car around. His foot kicked the accelerator to the floor, held it struggling there.

That all-night diner a few miles back.

The hollow-eyed night man in the diner stared.

Ellery's hand shook as he dropped the coins into the slots.

"Hello?"

Quickly!

"Hello! Mr. Van Horn?"

"Yes?"

Safe.

"Diedrich Van Horn?"

"Yes! Hello? Who is this?"

"Ellery Queen."

"Queen?"

"Yes. Mr. Van Horn—"

"Howard told me before he went to bed that you—"

"Never mind! You're safe, that's the important thing."

"Safe? Of course I'm safe. Safe from what? What are you talking about?"

"Where are you?"

"Where am I? Queen, what's the matter?"

"Tell me! Which room are you in?"

"My study. I couldn't sleep, decided to come down and do some paper work I've neglected—"

"Everyone in the house?"

"Everyone but Wolfert. He went back to town with Dakin and Simpson, left me a note saying he'd forgotten some contracts on a deal we've been negotiating, that he'd probably work through the night, and—"

"Mr. Van Horn, listen to me."

"Queen, I can't take much more tonight." Diedrich sounded exhausted. "Can't whatever it is wait? I don't *understand,*" he said bitterly. "You pack up and leave—"

Ellery said rapidly: "Listen to me carefully. Are you listening?"

"Yes!"

"Follow these instructions to the letter—"

"What instructions?"

"Lock yourself in the study."

"What?"

"Lock yourself in. Not only the door. The windows. The French door, too. Don't open to anyone, Mr. Van Horn, do you understand? *To anyone but me.* Do you understand?"

Diedrich was silent.

"Mr. Van Horn! Are you still there?"

"Yes, I'm still here," said Diedrich very slowly. "I'm here, Mr. Queen. I'll do as you say. Just where are you?"

"Wait a minute. You, there!"

The counterman said: "Somebody in trouble, bud?"

"How far am I from Wrightsville?"

"Wrightsville? About forty-four miles."

"Mr. Van Horn!"

"Yes, Mr. Queen."

"I'm about forty-four miles from Wrightsville. I'll drive back as fast as I can. Figure forty to forty-five minutes for the trip. I'll come to the French door on the south terrace. When I knock, you'll ask who it is. I'll tell you. Then, and then only, open—and only when you're completely satisfied that it's really me. Is that perfectly clear? There must be no exceptions. You must let no one into the study either from outside the house or from inside. Is that clear?"

"I heard you."

"Even that may not do it. Is that .38 Smith & Wesson still in your desk drawer? If it isn't, don't leave the study to get it!"

"It's still here."

"Take it out. Now. Hold it. All right. I'm going to hang up now and start. As soon as I do, lock up and keep away from the windows afterward. I'll see you in—"

"Mr. Queen."

"Yes? What?"

"What's the point of all this? From the way you're talking anyone would think my life's in danger."

"It is."

The Eighth Day

FORTY-THREE MINUTES LATER Ellery knocked on the French door.

The study was in darkness.

"Who is it?"

It was hard to say just where Diedrich might be beyond the glass.

"Queen."

"Who? Say it again."

"Queen. Ellery Queen."

A key turned. He opened the French door, stepped through, shut the door swiftly, turned the key. He felt around in the dark until he found the pull of the hanging.

Only then did he say, "You may turn the lights on now, Mr. Van Horn."

The desk lamp.

Diedrich was standing on the other side of the desk, the .38 brilliant. The desk top was a confusion of account books, papers. He was in pajamas and robe; bare feet in leather mules. His face was quite pale, a study in planes.

"Good idea turning the lights out," said Ellery. "I should have thought of that myself. Never mind the gun now."

Diedrich laid the weapon on the desk.

"Anything?" Ellery asked.

"No."

Ellery grinned. "That was quite a drive; I'll dream about it. Mind if I take the load off my feet?"

He dropped into Diedrich's swivel chair and stretched his legs.

A muscle at the corner of the big man's mouth was jumping. "I'm pretty much at the end of my patience, Mr. Queen. I want the whole story, and I want it now."

"Yes," said Ellery.

"What's this about my life being in danger? I haven't an enemy in the world. Not that kind of enemy."

"You have, Mr. Van Horn."

"Who?" His laborer's fists took his full weight as he leaned over the desk.

But Ellery slumped until the back of his neck rested on the top of the chair.

"Who!"

"Mr. Van Horn." Ellery rolled his head. "I've just made a discovery so . . . sidereal that it brought me back here when I'd have said an hour and a half ago an Act of Congress couldn't have pulled the trick.

"A great many things have happened since I stepped off that train last Thursday. At first they seemed disconnected. Then the outlines of connections appeared, but only of obvious and ordinary ones. Through it all I was bothered by the feeling that they had, oh, a greater connection, an all-over something . . . a pattern. I had no idea what the pattern was. It was just a feeling—call it an intuition; you develop a special sense when you've poked around the darker holes of what's laughingly called the human soul as long as I have."

Diedrich's eyes remained glacial.

"I put it down to imagination; I didn't pursue it. But just now, driving away from Wrightsville, the flash came.

"The lightning image is a cliché," murmured Ellery, "but there's no substitute for it as an adequate expression of how it happened. It just struck me. 'The bolt from the blue.' By its light I made out the pattern," Ellery said slowly, "the whole, hideous, magnificent pattern. I say 'magnificent' because there's grandeur in it, Mr. Van Horn—the grandeur, say, of Satan who was, after all, Lucifer. There's beauty in the Dark Angel, of a sort; and the Devil can quote Scripture to his purpose. I know. This is gibberish to you. But I'm still not over the," Ellery paused for the word, "the apocalyptic awfulness of it."

"Who?" growled Diedrich. "What did you find out, or figure out, or whatever it is?"

But Ellery said: "The diabolical feature of this pattern is its inevitability. Once it's laid down on the cloth, so to speak, and the scissors taken up, it must cut to the last selvage. It's the perfect thing; it must be perfect, or it's nothing. That's why I knew. That's why I called you. That's why I very nearly broke my neck getting back to you. There's no stopping it. It's got to fulfill itself. Got to."

"Fulfill itself?"

"Go on to the end."

"*What* end!"

"I told you, Mr. Van Horn. Murder."

Diedrich looked at him a moment longer. Then he pushed away from the desk and lumbered over to his armchair. He sat down, put his head back.

With this man only doubt and uncertainty are defeat-

ing. He can face anything if he knows. But he must know.

"All right," said Diedrich in a rumble. "There's going to be a murder. And I take it I'm the murderee. Is that it, Mr. Queen?"

"It's as perfectly sure as—as gravitation. The pattern is incomplete at this point. There's only one thing which can complete it, the crime of murder. And once I identified the pattern and its designer, I knew that you were the only possible victim."

Diedrich nodded.

"Now tell me, Mr. Queen. Who's planning to kill me?"

Their glances locked across the room.

Ellery said: "Howard."

Diedrich rose and came back to the desk. He opened a humidor.

"Cigar?"

"Thanks."

He held the desk lighter over to Ellery's cigar. The flame was untroubled.

"You know," said Diedrich, puffing, "I was prepared for anything but this murder business. Not that I necessarily accept your conclusion, Mr. Queen. I have a lot of respect for you as a craftsman, as I think I made clear when you first came. But I'd be a fool to take your word for anything like this."

"I don't expect you to take my word for it."

Diedrich looked at him through the blue smoke. "You'll prove it?" he exclaimed.

"It proves itself. I told you, it's perfect."

Diedrich was silent.

Then he said. "This Howard thing. Mr. Queen . . . he's my son. It doesn't matter that I didn't actually conceive him. I've read enough detective fiction to get a laugh out of the writers who avoid a blood relationship between a parent and a child when the child, say, is to be the murderer in the story; they do it by making the child a foster child. As if that made any difference! The . . . emotional tie between people is a result of a lifetime of living together and has practically nothing to do with genetics. I've brought Howard up from infancy. What he is I've made him. I'm in his cells. And he's in mine.

"I admit I haven't done a very good job, though God knows I've tried my best. But murder? Howard a murderer, with me his intended victim? It's too . . . too storyish, Mr. Queen. Too unbelievable. We've shared a life for over thirty years. I can't accept it."

"I know how you feel," said Ellery irritably. "I'm sorry. But if my conclusion is wrong, Mr. Van Horn, I'll never make another. I'll . . . I'll quit thinking."
"Big words."
"I mean every one of them."
Diedrich began to walk up and down, the cigar jutting from his mouth at an angry angle.
"But why?" he said harshly. "What's behind it? It can't possibly be for the usual reasons. I've given Howard everything—"
"Everything but one thing. And, unfortunately, that thing is what he wants most. Or thinks he does, which comes to the same thing. Also," murmured Ellery, "Howard loves you. He loves you so self-centeredly, Mr. Van Horn, that, granting certain premises, killing you becomes absolutely logical."
"I don't know what you're talking about," shouted Diedrich. "I'm a plain man and I'm used to plain talk. What's this pattern you claim is going to wind up in my murder? By Howard, of all people!"
"I'd rather explain with Howard here—"
Diedrich started for the door.
"No!" Ellery leaped. "You're not going up there alone!"
"Don't be a fool, man."
"Mr. Van Horn, I don't know how he's going to do it, or when—for all I know, it may be planned for tonight. That's why I . . . What's the matter?"
"Planned for tonight," Van Horn glanced ceilingward, very quickly, but shaking his head almost as he did so.
"What's the matter?"
"No. It's too silly. You've got me as jumpy as . . ." Diedrich laughed shortly. "I'm getting Howard."
Ellery had him by the arm before he could unlock the door.
After a moment Diedrich said: "You're really convinced."
"Yes."
"All right. Sally and I occupy separate bedrooms. But it's so damned far-fetched!"
"It can't be a hundredth as far-fetched as what I've got to tell you, Mr. Van Horn. Go on!"
Diedrich scowled. "After that business tonight, after you left, Sally was terribly nervous. More nervous than I've ever seen her. She told me upstairs there was something important she wanted me to know. Something, she said,

that she'd kept from me and couldn't keep from me any longer."

Too late, Sally.

"Yes?"

Diedrich glared at him. "Don't tell me you know . . . whatever it is . . . too!"

"Then she didn't tell you after all?"

"I'm afraid I was still upset by the necklace business. Frankly, I couldn't take any more just then. I told her it would have to wait."

"But that's not it, Mr. Van Horn! What was it that worried you just now?"

"What's the matter, Queen? Damn it, what's the matter?"

"What worried you?"

Diedrich flung the stub of his cigar into the fireplace with all his strength. "She begged me to listen," he cried, "and I said I had this work to finish tonight and whatever it was could wait. She said, All right—then I'll wait up, I've got to tell you tonight. She said she'd wait up for me in my bedroom. That if I worked very late I might find her asleep in my bed, but that I was to wake her up and—"

"In your bed. *In your bed?"*

Diedrich's bedroom door stood open.

Diedrich jabbed the light button and the room leaped at them and Sally, who was part of the room, leaped more strongly than the bed in which she was lying or any of the other dead things around her.

And this was queer, because Sally was dead, too.

Sally was ugly-dead, distorted-dead, she did not look like Sally at all. The only thing of Sally's that lingered on this wrenched and congested gargoyle of a face was the faint smile which had irritated Ellery so at their first meeting. Now, because it alone remained of all the remembered Sally, it comforted him. He put his fingers in her hair and pulled gently to get her head back so that he might look at what he knew was to be seen, the Van Gogh fingerstrokes on the canvas of her throat painting the story of her death in powerful tones.

She lay twisted in a matrix of violence. Her legs and arms had done this to the bedclothes in her last creative moments.

The flesh of her torn neck was very cold.

Ellery stepped away and jostled Diedrich and Diedrich lost his balance and sat down, hard, on the bed, on one of Sally's legs. He sat there, unconscious, with his eyes open.

Ellery got a hand mirror from Diedrich's bureau and returned to the bed to put the mirror to the dead mouth, knowing it was dead but performing the act through habit. It was hard to breathe for the congestion at the base of his own throat, but he was unaware of the pain. Inside, somewhere, a voice was charging him with responsibility for this great crime; but he was unconscious of that, too. It was only later, when he put the mirror with its print of Sally's lips back on her husband's bureau, that he became aware of what the voice was saying, over and over; but then he went quickly out of Diedrich's bedroom.

Howard was lying on his own bed upstairs, in the bedroom adjoining the big studio.

He was fully clothed and he was in the same stupid trance in which Ellery had found him after that wild night in the Fidelity cemetery.

You were your own best diagnostician, Howard. You hypothecated Mr. Hyde and you foresaw murder most foul.

There was something about his hands.

Ellery raised one of them. Four long soft hairs were caught between two of the powerful sculptor's fingers and under the nails of all the fingers except the thumb were little bloody particles of Sally's throat.

The Ninth Day

CHIEF DAKIN WAS in and out all night and that was a touch of home, for the others were all new. Where was Prosecutor Phil Hendrix of the dove-bill mouth who had replaced young Cart Bradford who was now in the second renewal of his lease on the gubernatorial mansion in the state capital? Where was nervous Coroner Salemson of the asthma and the gooseberry wine? Where old palsied Dunc, of the Duncan Funeral Parlors? Alas. Hendrix was hunting witches in Washington, Salemson slept gratefully in Twin Hills Cemetery, and the elder Mr. Duncan, who had placed two generations of Wrightsvillians into the waiting earth, was one with the air and the wind and the dust, for he had left imploring orders in his will to be cremated.

There was a saturnine young man who persisted in giving Ellery long exploratory looks; his name was Chalanski, and it turned out that he it was who now played

Nemesis to the felons of Wright County; the coroner was a brisk lean surgical fellow named Grupp, with a long nose and scalpel eyes; and the mortician (for Wrightsville was still lacking an official morgue) was the chubby junior Mr. Duncan who, to judge from the shiny-lipped relish with which he discussed the post-mortem problems with the coroner, County Prosecutor Chalanski, and Chief of Police Dakin, had been conceived on a slab, cradled in a casket, weaned on embalming fluid, and had expended the first yearnings of his puberty on some weekend visitor to his father's establishment. Ellery didn't like the way rotund Mr. Duncan looked at Sally; he didn't like it at all.

Some time during Wednesday morning, a stout flat-footed individual with a neck like bark, ploughed in, giving off powerful odors; and this was County Sheriff Mothless, successor to Gilfant. No improvement! Fortunately, Sheriff Mothless lingered only long enough to make sure that the newspaper people outside spelled his name correctly.

And there were others—state troopers, Wrightsville radio patrolmen, civilian-looking people with black bags, and just people—among the latter, Ellery suspected, being some of the more elastic-necked townsfolk who were exercising the traditional American prerogative of tramping around the squire's manse airing a long-smothered curiosity.

Well, he thought, there's no reason why murder in Wrightsville should be sweeter-smelling than murder anywhere else.

Mr. Queen was feeling strangely at peace. In one part of him only, of course; most of him was occupied by fatigues and unpleasantnesses. He had had no sleep; he had unfortunately been compelled to witness the Ayesha-like transformation of Diedrich Van Horn from prime to senescence; he had had to sustain himself through two hours of Wolfert Van Horn, who had trapped him in a corner of the living room and assaulted him wtih reminiscences of Howard's evil tendencies from earliest boyhood: how Howard had hunted garter snakes and chopped them into little pieces, and pulled wings off flies, and once, at the age of nine, had filled his, Wolfert's, bed with thistles and how he, Wolfert, had always warned his brother that no good would come of suckling the brat of the devil knew what parents, and so on. And, of course, there was always Howard himself, his eyes bright red and his hair a tangle and his air of absolute bewilderment, his only activity being frequent visits to the bathroom accompanied by a Wrightsville policeman Dakin called "Jeep," whom Ellery did not know. This officer reported that on these excursions Howard merely scrubbed his hands, so that as hour after hour dragged by Howard's hands became paler and more water-wrinkled, finally looking like something washed up on a beach. Howard was the real trial Wednesday morning, because he could answer no questions; he could only ask them. The chief neurologist of Connhaven State Hospital spent two hours with him on the scene of the crime and emerged looking thoughtful. Ellery talked to this medical gentleman, giving Howard's amnesic history; and the doctor, who was also Psychiatric Consultant to the State Penal Board, nodded frequently, and with that mysterious about-to-pounce-but-never-doing-so air which Ellery found so trying in so many medical men.

Nevertheless, there was that small portion of peace; and this was because something which had been darkness was now light and The End was within reach.

He had informed Dakin and Chalanski that he had something vital to contribute to the case and he asked that before Howard was removed from the premises he, Ellery Queen, be given the opportunity to divulge it in the interests of truth, if not justice, as the case against Howard would be distorted, baffling, and incomplete otherwise; if, indeed, it would make sense at all. And he further requested that the neurologist remain, at which the neurologist looked annoyed, but remained.

At two-thirty o'clock Wednesday afternoon Chief Dakin came into the kitchen, where Ellery was devouring the half-eaten corpse of a roast duck (Laura and Eileen had locked themselves in their rooms and had not been seen all day), and Dakin said: "Well, Mr. Queen, if you're ready, we are."

Ellery gulped one more mouthful of brandied peaches, wiped his lips and rose.

"I note," said Ellery in the living room, "that Christina Van Horn isn't with us. No," he said quickly, as Chief Dakin stirred, "don't bother. The old lady wouldn't have anything to contribute but quotations from the Bible, which might get in the way. She doesn't know much, if anything, about any of this. Let her stay upstairs.

"Diedrich." It was the first time he had addressed Van Horn so, and his Christian name now aroused Diedrich a little, so that he looked up almost with interest. "I'm going to have to say somethings that are going to hurt you, I'm afraid."

Diedrich's hand flapped. "I just want to know what this is all about," he said courteously. Then he added, "There isn't much else left," but that was more to himself.

Howard was all shoulders and knees in his chair, needing a shave, needing sleep, needing solace—an isolated lump already out of touch with reality. Only his eyes kept in touch; and they were hard to look at. In fact, he was rather painfully ignored by everyone but the neurologist and Wolfert, and they looked nowhere else.

"To make this . . ." Ellery hesitated, "this thing intelligible, to make it clear to you at each of its specific and numbered steps, I've got to go back to the beginning. To what happened from the time Howard walked into my apartment in New York over a week ago. I'll recap as briefly as I can."

And Ellery went over all the events of the past eight days: Howard's awakening in the Bowery flophouse, his coming to Ellery, the story of his amnesic attacks, his fears, his appeal to Ellery to come to Wrightsville and keep watching him; Ellery's first night in the Van Horn house, when at dinner Wolfert brought the news that the Art Museum Committee had accepted Diedrich's condition that Howard be the official sculptor of the classical gods who were to decorate the face of the proposed Museum building, and of how Howard had fired to the assignment, making sketches and in the succeeding days even beginning work in plasticine for small models; the second day, when Sally, Howard, and Ellery had driven up to Quetonokis Lake, and how Howard and Sally had told Ellery of their debts to Diedrich—Howard, the foundling who owed Diedrich everything, Sally, who had been Sara Mason of Polly Street, destined to poverty and the life of an ignorant drab, but for Diedrich—and then how they had confessed to him the crime of their passion in the Lake Pharisee lodge and its consummation there (and as Ellery told of this he tried not to look at Diedrich Van Horn out of shame for all the sinned-against, for Diedrich shrank into himself like a paper being consumed into ash); and Ellery told of the four indiscreet, revealing letters Howard had written to Sally afterward, and the story of Sally's japanned box with its false bottom and the blackmailer on the day preceding Ellery's arrival, and of the second call, and of Ellery's part in the negotiations; of his conversation with Diedrich the same night of the excursion to Quetonokis Lake, when Diedrich had told him not only of the June robbery of Sally's jewel box but also of the robbery of the night before, the theft of twenty-five thousand dollars in five-hundred-dollar bills from the wall safe in the study—the very sum in the very bills which Howard had handed to Ellery at the lake in an envelope for payment over to the blackmailer; of the third day, when Ellery had been outwitted by the blackmailer, and of Diedrich's revelation that night that he had finally discovered Howard's origin as the son of two poor farm people named Waye, who were long since dead; of Howard's reaction, and of the Fidelity Cemetery episode in the early hours of Sunday morning, when Howard had attacked the gravestones of his parents with mud and a chisel and mallet during an amnesic seizure, and of how Ellery had brought him back to himself afterward, and of how Howard had shown him the plasticine model of Jupiter on which he had scratched his sculptor's signature, not *H. H. Van Horn* as he had always signed himself, but *H. H. Waye;* and of all the events thereafter, including the third call from the blackmailer, Ellery's pawning of Sally's necklace at Howard's request, and Howard's incredible denial of the truth when Ellery was faced with a charge of grand theft.

And through it all Diedrich wrestled with the arms of his chair and Howard sat sculpturally.

"That's the story to date," continued Ellery. "It may strike you as a series of random incidents, and you may be wondering why I take your time up with a recital of them. The reason is that they're not random at all, but connected—connected so rigidly that no one incident is less important to the whole than another, even though some seem actually trivial.

"Last night," said Ellery, "I was on my way back to New York. I was disgusted with Howard, disappointed in Sally—fed up. A long way from Wrightsville a thought struck me. It was a simple thought, so simple it changed everything. And I saw this case for what it really was. For the first time."

He paused to clear his throat and Prosecutor Chalanski said, "Queen, do you know what you're talking about? Because, frankly, *I* don't."

But Chief Dakin said, "Mr. Chalanski, I've heard this man talk before. Give him a chance."

"It's irregular, anyway. There's no legal ground for this 'hearing'—if that's what it is; I don't know *what* it is—and in any event Van Horn ought to be represented by counsel."

"This is all more a part of the coroner's inquest," said Coroner Grupp. "Maybe it's a trick to lay the ground for some future claim of illegal process or something, Chalanski."

"Let him talk," said Dakin. "He'll say something."

"What?" jeered the prosecutor.

"I don't know. But he always does."

Ellery said, "Thanks, Dakin," and he waited; and when Chalanski and Grupp shrugged, he went on.

"I drew up to the side of the road and went over the case piece by piece. I re-examined everything, but this time I had a frame of reference."

"What frame of reference?" demanded Chalanski.

"The Bible."

"The what?"

"The Bible, Mr. Chalanski."

"I'm beginning to think," said the prosecutor, looking around with a grin, "that you've got a lot more need for Dr. Cornbranch's services, Queen, than this fellow here."

"Let him go on, Chalanski, will you?" said the neurologist; but even then he did not take his eyes from Howard.

"It became clear very quickly," said Ellery, "that Howard had been responsible for six acts, and that these six acts encompassed nine different crimes."

At this Chalanski lost his grin and the coroner unfolded his long insolent legs.

"*Nine* different crimes?" repeated Chalanski. "You know what they are, Grupp?"

"Hell no."

"Let him talk," said Dakin.

"*What* nine crimes, Queen?"

But Ellery said: "The nine crimes were different crimes, and yet in a larger sense they were the same crime. I mean by that that they had continuity, congruity, a pattern—they had an integral relationship; they were parts of a whole.

"Once I understood the nature of that relationship," Ellery continued, "once *you* understand it, gentlemen, you'll see, as I did, that it was possible to predict one crime still to come. It had to be. It was an inescapable conclusion. Nine crimes, and they made the tenth inevitable. Not only that. Once you understand the nature of the pattern, you could predict—as I did to Diedrich Van Horn—precisely what the tenth crime would be, against whom it would be aimed, and by whom it would be committed. I've never run into anything so perfect in all my experience, which has been considerable. Without meaning to be presumptuous, I doubt if any of you ever have, either. I'm tempted to say, I doubt if anyone, anywhere, ever will again."

And now there was nothing to be heard but the breathing of many men and, outside, a state trooper's voice raised in anger.

"The only unpredictable factor was time. I couldn't tell when the tenth crime would take place." Ellery said briskly: "Since it could conceivably have occurred even as I sat in the car almost fifty miles from Wrightsville thinking the thing through, I drove for the nearest phone, ordered Mr. Van Horn to take immediate precautions, and returned here as fast as I could.

"I couldn't have known that Mrs. Van Horn would choose tonight to drop off to sleep in her husband's bed, in her husband's bedroom. Howard's hands felt for his father's throat in the dark and choked the life out of the woman he loved instead. If he hadn't been in the amnesic state his sense of touch would probably have told him of his mistake and he might have stopped in time; as it was, he was simply a killing machine, and the machinery, once set in motion, did its job as machines do."

And Ellery said: "That's the story in general.

"Now let's consider Howard's six acts, the six acts embracing the nine crimes I mentioned, revealing the plan behind them and making the tenth crime predictable.

"One." Ellery paused. And then he took the plunge. *"Howard was engaged in sculpturing figures of the ancient gods."*

And he paused. It was too much to ask of any practical mind that it accept such an extraordinary statement out of context as the utterance of sanity. He could only wait.

"Ancient gods," said the prosecutor, looking dazed. "What kind of—"

"What d'ye mean, Mr. Queen?" asked Chief Dakin, looking anxious. "Is that a crime?"

"Yes, Dakin," said Ellery, "and not one crime. It's really two crimes."

Chalanski sank back, openmouthed.

"Two. Howard had actually reached the point of signing his sculptures—or his sketches and preliminary models—with the curiously significant signature *H. H. Waye.*"

Chalanski shook his head.

"H. H. Waye." It was the coroner who said that, not even resentfully; he merely said it, as if he wanted to hear how it might sound in a familiar voice.

"Is that a crime, too?" demanded the prosecutor with an exasperated grin.

"Yes, Mr. Chalanski," said Ellery, "and a particularly blasphemous one.

"Third. Howard stole twenty-five thousand dollars from Diedrich."

They all relaxed at that, gratefully, as if in the midst of a lecture in Urdu the lecturer had inserted a sentence in English.

"Well, I'll agree *that's* a crime!" Chalanski laughed, looking around. But no one responded.

"You'll agree, Mr. Chalanski, when you grasp the overlying design, that *all* of Howard's acts were crimes, although not all were necessarily penological crimes.

"Four. Howard abused the graves of Aaron and Mattie Waye."

"We're getting on solider ground," said Coroner Grupp. "Now that's a crime, Chalanski—vandalism, or something, isn't it?"

"Not exactly. There's a statute that—"

"The two crimes Howard committed in desecrating his parents' graves, Mr. Chalanski," said Ellery, "will not be found in your statutes. May I go on?

"Five. Howard fell in love with Sally Van Horn. And that constitutes two crimes, also.

"And finally, six. Howard's outrageous lie when he denied that he'd given me Sally's diamond necklace to pawn.

"Six acts, nine crimes," said Ellery. "Nine of the ten worst crimes a man can commit, according to an authority a great deal older than your statutes, Mr. Chalanski."

"What authority would that be?"

"An authority who's usually spelled with a capital *G*."

Chalanski jumped up. "I've had just about—"

"God."

"What?"

"Well, God as we know Him from the Old Testament, Mr. Chalanski—Who, after all, in that form, is still professed by Greek and Roman Catholics and most Protestants, as well as by the ancient Jews who first memorialized Him in the Book. Yes, Mr. Chalanski, God—or *Yahweh*, which is a transliteration of the Hebrew tetragrammaton translated as *Jehovah* in the Christian exegesis; the 'ineffable' or 'incommunicable name' of the Supreme Being, Mr. Chalanski . . . the Lord, Mr. Chalanski, Who in whichever nominal form called Moses into the midst of the cloud on the mount of Sinai and kept him there for forty days and forty nights, *and he gave unto Moses, when he had made an end of communing with him upon mount*

Sinai, two tables of testimony, tables of stone, written with the finger of God.

"IN THOSE SIX ACTS," said Ellery, *"HOWARD BROKE NINE OF THE TEN COMMANDMENTS."*

And now it was the neurologist who stirred; he stirred uneasily, as if he were himself having a significant dream. But all the others sat still, including Howard, who seemed outside the world of real things and in a world uniquely his own. And into this terrifying land no one intruded, not even Ellery.

"By sculpturing the gods of the Roman pantheon," said Ellery, "Howard broke two Commandments: *Thou shalt not make unto thee any graven image and Thou shalt have no other gods before me."*

And Ellery said: "By signing his sculpture *H. H. Waye,* Howard broke the Commandment: *Thou shalt not take the name of the Lord thy God in vain;* and this is an especially fascinating example of how Howard's mind worked in his criminal illness. Here he dabbles in the cabala and emulates the occult theosophists of medieval times who believed, among other things, that each letter, word, number, and accent of Scripture contains a hidden sense. The greatest mystery of the Old Testament is the name of the Lord, which He Himself revealed to Moses; and that name is hidden in the tetragrammaton I mentioned, the four consonants which were variously written —actually in five ways, from *IHVH* to *YHWH,* and from which the supposed original form of God's name has been variously reconstructed; and of these reconstructions the most commonly accepted in the modern world is *Yahweh.* And if you'll take the letters which form the name. *H. H. Waye,* you'll find that they constitute an anagram for *Yahweh."*

Chalanski opened his mouth.

But Ellery said, "Yes. Quite mad, Mr. Chalanski."

And Ellery said: "By appropriating twenty-five thousand dollars from Diedrich Van Horn's safe, Howard broke the Commandment: *Thou shalt not steal."*

And Ellery said: "By desecrating the graves of Aaron and Mattie Waye in Fidelity Cemetery during the early hours of Sunday morning last, Howard broke two other Commandments: *Remember the sabbath day, to keep it holy* and *Honor thy father and thy mother."* He smiled faintly. "I should have asked Father Chichering of St. Paul's-in-the-Dingle to sit in on this, because on one of these points I feel the need for expert advice. I mean about the Sabbath. The 'sabbath day' referred to in the Fourth Commandment—it's the Third to Roman Catholics and Lutherans, I believe, but the Fourth to Jews, Greek Catholics, and most Protestants—is the Sabbath of Israel, which is of course Saturday and which I think the earliest Christians kept observing sabbatically as distinguished from the weekly celebration of the Resurrection, 'the Lord's day,' which was Sunday; I seem to recall now that this double observance was practiced for several centuries after the Resurrection, even though Paul from the start laid down the dictum that the Jewish Sabbath was not binding on Christians. Well, it doesn't matter. To Howard, a Christian, *sabbath* means Sunday; and it was in the early hours of Sunday morning that he dishonored his father and mother."

And Ellery said: "By falling in love with Sally and taking her to bed in the Van Horn lodge at Lake Pharisee, Howard broke the two Commandments: *Thou shalt not covet thy neighbor's wife* and *Thou shalt not commit adultery*."

And, quickly, Ellery passed on to the ninth of his citations, and he said: "By lying when he denied having given me Sally's necklace to pawn, Howard broke the Commandment: *Thou shalt not bear false witness against thy neighbor*."

And now they were under the spell of the gigantic oddity, and they would not have broken it if they could.

And Ellery resumed: "As I sat there on the road last night, in Howard's car, piecing these nine fragments together, I asked myself the natural question: Could all this have been coincidence? Could it have been chance that led Howard to commit just such specific acts as to cause him to break nine of the Ten Commandments? And I had to answer myself: No, that isn't possible; the odds that such a congruency of crimes against the Decalogue might occur by accident are too unreasonably great; those nine Commandments were therefore broken by design; they were broken premeditatedly and systematically, following the Decalogue as a guide.

"But if Howard broke nine of the Ten Commandments," Ellery cried, "he would not, he could not, stop. Ten is the whole, and nine is not ten. The Commandment that was missing, that was still to be broken, was the Commandment above all the others which modern man has held to be the most socially desirable, if not the most morally: *Thou shalt not kill.* Ten is the whole, and nine is not ten, and when the tenth is the moral precept forbidding murder, I knew Howard was holding back murder as the climax of his stupendous rebellion against the world.

"Whom was Howard planning to murder? The answer came out the same whether I considered the outward manifestations of Howard's behavior or its underlying psychological implications. What was it Howard wanted?—or thought he wanted, because it's my admittedly layman's theory, Dr. Cornbranch, that Howard was never really in love with Sally at all, but only thought he was. He wanted, or thought he wanted, Diedrich's wife. Who stood in the way of this? Only Diedrich. By removing Diedrich, then, it would seem to Howard that he achieved Diedrich's wife. The fact that in trying to kill Diedrich he accidentally killed Sally is, logically speaking, of no importance—a tragic irrelevance.

"But you arrive at Diedrich as the intended victim by a psychological route, too. There has never been the least question in my mind—in fact, from the time ten years ago when I got to know Howard in Paris—that the chief propulsive force of Howard's emotional mechanism from early childhood has been Oedipean. His worship of Diedrich Van Horn was naked and unmistakable. The sculptures in Howard's Parisian studio were of Zeus, Adam, Moses—Moses even then—but they were all, in essence, Diedrich; and then, ten years later, I met Diedrich in the flesh, I saw that they had all been Diedrich in feature and physique as well.

"Howard's entire history made his adoration of the father-image almost inevitable: the unknown mother who had rejected him in infancy; the big, powerful, admirable male of males who had taken him in and become his father-protector and served as both father and mother to him. And, as in Oedipus, the seeds of father-murder were there, too. Because love became hatred when the father-image rejected the son and transferred his love, as it seemed to Howard, to a woman, and that woman a stranger. At that moment the seed sprouted: coincidental with the event of Diedrich's marriage to Sally came the first amnesic episode. And then Howard 'fell in love' with the woman who had stolen his father! I stand ready to be corrected, Dr. Cornbranch, but I submit that this was no love at all—it was a double-barreled attempt unconsciously *both to punish the father who had rejected him and to regain the father's love by destroying the father's relationship with the woman who was responsible for the rejection.*

"Now observe this remarkable fact: In plotting the murder of the perfidious father-image, the son employs a technique whereby in the process he murders another father-image!" Dr. Cornbranch looked puzzled. Ellery leaned forward, addressing the neurologist directly. "In this family, where Christina Van Horn, the foster grandmother, in Howard's childhood and thereafter was obsessed with the Word of God—deriving from her marriage to a fundamentalist fanatic who had preached the living Jehovah—how could Howard have escaped being steeped in the concept of the paternalism of God? Whereupon we see how perfect this perfection is: *For in deliberately violating the Ten Commandments of God the Father, Howard breaks the greatest Father-Image of all.*"

Ellery glanced at the unjointed lump that had been Howard with the pity and loathing of all normal men in the presence of the mad, and he said with great gentleness: "And now you know, gentlemen, why I've taken your time with this: The whole concept of Howard's plot is the concept of an unbalanced mind.

"I don't know what name you medical men will give to Howard's madness, Dr. Cornbranch, but it must be apparent even to laymen that to take the Decalogue as the pattern for a series of crimes culminating in the crime of murder, and to follow that pattern with the cunning and the pertinacity which this man, both consciously and unconsciously, has followed in this case, calls for a diagnosis in the consulting room by qualified psychiatrists, not for a trial in a court of law according to the rules of punishment laid down for sane lawbreakers.

"This man has no business being handled or treated as an ordinary murderer. He is, if you please, criminally insane; and I'll tell my story and give my Biblical analysis anywhere you designate, at any time, if by doing so I can help place him where he belongs, which is in a mental institution."

And Ellery looked at Diedrich Van Horn, and then away, because Diedrich was crying.

For some time there was no sound but the sound of Diedrich, and then even that stopped.

Prosecutor Chalanski looked at Dr. Cornbranch.

He cleared his throat.

"Doctor, what's your opinion about . . . about all this?"

The neurologist said: "I'd rather not commit myself on the medico-legal aspects of this case right now, Chalanski. It's going to take some time, and a lot of er—consultation."

"Well!" The prosecutor put his elbows on his knees.

"From a prosecution standpoint—aside from what his attorneys may try to get across—we have a case I'm ready to take into court as soon as the inquest is out of the way."

Chief Dakin stirred. "Connhaven Labs?"

"Yes. I got a preliminary report from them by phone just before this started, Dakin. The four hairs found between his fingers have been scientifically identified as coming from Mrs. Van Horn's head. The fragments of flesh and so on under his fingernails, it's the Lab's opinion, came from Mrs. Van Horn's throat. Practically speaking, there's no doubt about it; but I think we can establish it legally, too. And, frankly, I'm not too concerned right now with whether he killed her knowing it was she or mistaking her in the dark for Mr. Van Horn. We've got a motive either way. He wouldn't be the first adulterer who killed his partner-in-sin. In fact," and something like a smile came over the prosecutor's face, "I'd find it a darned sight easier adducing that as a motive than all this fancy stuff about hating the father-image. Well, I guess that's that—"

Chalanski started to rise.

Howard said: "Are you taking me away now?"

If the plasticine image of Jupiter in Howard's studio had suddenly broken into speech they could not have been more startled.

He was looking, not at Chalanski, not at Ellery, but at Chief of Police Dakin.

"Taking you away? Yes, Howard," said Dakin uncomfortably, "I'm afraid that's about the size of it."

"There's something I want to do before they take me."

"You mean go to the toilet?"

"The oldest dodge in the world," smiled Chalanski. "Not that it would do you any good, Van Horn. Or Waye, is it? The house is pretty well covered, inside and out."

"Nutty, is he?" drawled Coroner Grupp.

"I don't want to run away," said Howard. "Where would I run to?"

Grupp and Chalanski laughed.

"Why don't you listen to him!"

It was Diedrich, on his feet, his face convulsed.

Howard said in the same, reasonable, patient way: "I just want to go upstairs to my studio, that's all."

No one said anything for some time.

"For what, Howard?" asked Chief Dakin finally.

"I'll never see it again."

"I don't see any harm in it, Chalanski," said Dakin. "He can't get away and he knows it."

The prosecutor shrugged. "Custody of the prisoner is your responsibility, Dakin. Me, I wouldn't let him."

"What's your opinion, Dr. Cornbranch?" asked the chief of police, frowning.

The neurologist shook his head. "Not without an armed guard."

Dakin hesitated.

"Howard, just what is it you want to do in your studio?" asked Ellery.

Howard did not answer.

"Howard . . ." And that was Diedrich, too.

Howard just stood there, looking at the floor.

Dr. Cornbranch said, "Why don't you answer the question, Howard? What is it you want to do?"

And Howard said, "I want to smash my sculptures."

"Now that," said the neurologist, "is a reasonable request. Under the circumstances."

He glanced at Dakin and nodded.

Dakin looked grateful. He said to the tall young policeman who was standing behind Howard: "Go with him, Jeep."

Howard turned on his heel and walked steadily out.

The policeman hitched his belt, his right hand feeling for the black butt of his grun. Then he followed Howard from the room, almost stepping on Howard's heels.

"Don't take too long," called Dakin.

Diedrich sat down heavily. Howard had not glanced at him even in leaving.

Or at me, thought Ellery; and he walked over to one of the big man's big windows and looked out over the gardens where three troopers stood in the late afternoon sunshine smoking and laughing.

No more than three minutes had passed by the time the first splintery crash brought all their heads around and up.

It was followed by another, and another, and then by many others in a quickening rhythm of destruction. And the sounds of breakage stopped, and there was the pause of a long breath, and then one final furious iconoclasm.

This time the silence remained.

They were all turned toward the doorway now, through which the foot of the staircase was visible, waiting for the breaker of images to descend into their view followed by the policeman; but nothing happened, no destroyer appeared, no policeman. There was the same empty perspective of hall and staircase.

Dakin went into the hall and put his hand on the bleached oak newel post. "Jeep!" he shouted. "Bring him down now!"

Jeep was silent.

"Jeep!"

This was a roar, with panic in it.

But Jeep did not reply.

"My God," said Dakin. His face, turned momentarily toward them, was clay-pale.

And then he scrambled up the stairs, and they all scrambled after him.

The policeman was sprawled before the closed door to Howard's studio with a purple lump over his left ear, his long legs twitching as he tried to struggle to his feet.

The gun was no longer in his holster.

"Hit me in the belly just as we got to the door," he gasped. "Grabbed my gun. Hit me with it. I went out."

Dakin rattled the door.

"Locked."

Ellery yelled, "Howard!" but Chalanski shouldered him aside and shouted, "Van Horn, you open this door and be damned quick about it!"

The door yielded nothing.

"Got a key, Mr. Van Horn?" panted Dakin.

Diedrich looked at him dumbly. He had not understood the words.

"Have to break it down."

They were gathered a few feet from the door, prepared to lunge in a body, when the shot came.

It was a single shot, followed by the sound of something metallic dropping to a floor.

There was no heavier, duller sound, as of a man's body.

They burst through the door in the first rush.

Howard was hanging from the center beam of his raftered studio. His arms dangled and blood still dripped from his wrists into two pools on the floor; he had slashed himself with a chisel. Then he had climbed onto a chair with a rope taken from a sculptor's block-and-tackle and he had slung the rope over the beam and knotted both ends tightly about his neck and kicked the chair out from under him. Then he had put the muzzle of the policeman's gun into his mouth at an acute angle and pulled the trigger. The .38 slug had torn through the roof of his mouth and emerged, taking a piece of the top of his head with it.

Prosecutor Chalanski, making a face, dug the slug out

of the rafter in which it had lodged and wrapped it in his handkerchief.

Coroner Grupp said, "He sure wanted to die in the worst way."

Plasticine, clay, stone fragments littered the studio floor, and Wolfert Van Horn yelped when he stepped on a large chunk of Jupiter and turned his ankle.

The newspapers did nip-ups.

As Inspector Queen said: "Murder, sex, and God—circulation managers dream about a case like this."

Somehow a full report of Ellery's sermon on the Ten Commandments got to the ears of the first wire service to hook onto the case. Thenceforward it was rugged. *Ellery Queen's Greatest Case, Noted Tec's Ten-Strike, Mosaic Murderer Meets Master, Sleuth Traps Bad Man with Good Book, E. Q. Tops Own Triumphs*—these were merely a few of the original headlines and subheadlines which made the master squirm. Blizzards of clips from newspapers all over the United States and Canada whitened the floor of the Queen apartment as Inspector Queen invested his hard-earned money for the greater glory of his son's scrapbook, which was no idea of his son's but strictly of his son's father. For three weeks wise men and fools beat a widening path to the Queen door, and the telephone rang uninterruptedly. There were reporters for interviews; ghost writers with already typed sagas of the Van Horn case requiring only the master's nod and a modest cut to the apparition; magazine editors at the end of the wire and photographers on the unsafe side of the door; at least two representatives of advertising agencies who thought Noted Sleuth's Endorsement of, in one case, a cream shampoo, in the other, a new perfume to be known as "Murder," would make a dynamic tie-in with the *cause célèbre;* and radio, not to be worsted, came up with an offer to Mr. Queen to appear on Sunday afternoon with a panel of prominent clergymen, representing the Protestant, Roman Catholic, and Jewish faiths, on a program to be entitled "The Holy Bible Versus Howard Van Horn." These in addition to an army of assorted ax grinders who wanted to whittle Noted Sleuth into even more heroic shape, and at uniformly fabulous rates. Ellery threatened wrathfully to perform a little whittling job of his own on the unknown blabbermouth who had given the Ten Commandments story to the press—he swore for months afterward that it had been Dr. Cornbranch, motivated by some abstruse, higher psychology—but Inspector Queen soothed him; and, to withhold nothing, it must be recorded that, after the ninth day of the wonder, when he could do so without fear of being caught at it, Mr. Queen sneaked a few looks into the Inspector's scrapbook, which was now in the final stage of obesity. Whereupon he experienced, willy-nilly, that fine full glow which suffuses the hearts of the most modest at times; and he even read one piece through to the sweet end, the magazine article which called him "the Wonder Boy of West Eighty-seventh Street in his most spectacular performance."

But in all the journalistic literature of that fevered interlude in Ellery's career, none surpassed the neophrastic genius who, in a Sunday feature article for one of the more elevated journals entitled "The Case of the Schizophrenic Bibliomaniac," coined a phrase which was to become part of the dictionary of criminology.

This Einstein of etymology referred to Mr. Queen as "he who must henceforward and for all time be known as The Deca-Logical Detective."

So endeth the book of the dead.
And beginneth the book of the living.

Part II Tenth Day's Wonder

The Tenth Day

HIS PREY was man, and he prowled the bottom lands of iniquity with an enchanted weapon, swelling in fame with each bloody chase. Never had evildoers seemed fiercer, or more cunning, or more willing for the bag. For he was Ellery, son of Richard, mighty hunter before the Law; and none might prevail against him.

The year that followed the Van Horn *tour de force* was easily the busiest and most brilliantly successful of Ellery's career. Cases besieged him, winging in from all directions; some crossed oceans. He made two trips to Europe that year, and one to South America, and one to Shanghai. Los Angeles knew him, and Chicago, and Mexico City. Inspector Queen complained that he might just as well have brought Ellery up to be an advance man for the circus, he saw his son so seldom. And Sergeant Velie actually went ten feet past Ellery on the sidewalk skirting Police Headquarters before a vestigial memory made him turn around.

Nor was there dearth of crime business on the master's native heath. The moors of New York City resounded with his exploits. There was the case of the spastic bryologist, in which Ellery made the definitive deduction—from a dried mass of sphagnum no larger than his thumbnail—and reached into the surgery of one of New York's most respectable hospitals to save a life and blast a reputation; there was the case of Adelina Monquieux, his remarkable solution of which cannot be revealed before 1972 by agreement with that curious lady's executors; and these are cited merely in example—the full list is on the Queen agenda and will in time, no doubt, find publication in one form or another.

It was Ellery himself who called the halt. Never heavily fleshed, he had lost so much weight since September of the preceding year that even he became alarmed.

"It's this blasted running around," said Inspector Queen

over an early breakfast one morning in August. "Ellery, you've got to put the brakes on."

"I've already done so. Saw Barney Kull yesterday and he said if I wanted to die gloriously of coronary thrombosis I was to keep up my pace of the last eleven months."

"I hope that put some sense into your head! What are you going to do, Son?"

"Well . . . I've gathered enough material this year for twenty books and I haven't had time to write, or even plan, one. I'm going to get back to authorship."

"And the Crippler case?"

"I've turned it over to Tony, with my condolences."

"Thank God," said the Inspector piously, for there wasn't room enough on the shelves over his bed for even one more scrapbook. "But why the rush? Why not take a rest first? Go away somewhere."

"I'm sick of going away somewhere."

"No, I don't suppose I can expect you to flop sensibly on your back, where you belong," grumbled the old gentleman, reaching for the coffee pot. "Now, I take it, you'll shut yourself up in that opium den you call a study and I won't see you at all. Say! You've put on that crummy old smoking jacket!"

Ellery grinned. "I told you. I'm starting a book."

"When?"

"Right away. Today. This morning."

"Where you get the energy . . . . Why don't you blow yourself to a new jacket? If you *have* to wear one of those sissy jobs."

"Give up this jacket? It's my writing habit."

"When you start punning," snarled his father, hastily pushing away from the table, "it's every man for himself. See you tonight, Son."

So once again Mr. Queen enters his study, shuts the door, and prepares to give his auctorial all.

Mark that the process involved in preparing to conceive a book is technically different from that involved in preparing to bear it. In the latter stage there are typewriters to examine and clean, ribbons to change, pencils to sharpen, clean paper to be arranged at the precise distance from the arm at which the least exertion is called forth, notes or outlines to be propped at the exactly acute angle to the machine, and so forth. The situation at the outset of the conceptual stage is quite deplorably different. Even assuming that the author's head is fully charged with ideas and giving off impatient sparks, he has utterly no need for paraphernalia or their care or placement. He has only a rug and his miserable self.

So observe Mr. Queen in his study on this fine early morning in August of the year following the Van Horn case.

He is fired with energetic intentions. He paces his rug like a general, marshaling his mental forces. His brow is clear. His eyes are intent but calm. His legs are unhurried and untroubled. His hands are quiet.

Now observe him twenty minutes later.

His legs pump. His eyes are wild. His brows work fiercely. His hands are helpless fists. He leans against a wall, seeking the cool plaster. He darts to a chair, perches on its edge with hands clasped, as if imploringly, between his knees. He jumps up, fills his pipe, sets it down, lights a cigaret, puffs twice, it goes out, it remains between his lips. He nibbles his fingernails. He rubs his head. He explores a dental cavity. He pinches his nose. He plunges his hands into his jacket pockets. He kicks a chair. He glances at the headline of the morning newspaper on his desk but glances away heroically. He goes to the window and soon becomes interested in the scientific aspects of a fly crawling up the screen. He fingers the tobacco grains in his right pocket, rolls a grain in a wad of lint, places the wad in a piece of paper which happens to be in the same pocket. He folds the paper around it, takes the paper out, glances at it.

It says:

Van Horn
North Hill Drive
Wrightsville

1

Ellery sat down in his desk chair. He placed the scrap of paper on the blotter, leaned forward, put his arms flat on the desk, rested his chin on his hands, and stared at the paper two inches from his nose.

Van Horn. North Hill Drive. Wrightsville.

All that's left of the Van Horn case.

He remembered now that scene of almost a year before.

He had been dressed in this same smoking jacket *(by gosh, last time I had it on).*

He had given Howard some money to get home on and walked him downstairs and Howard hailed a taxi and they were shaking hands on the sidewalk when it had struck Ellery that he didn't know where Howard lived. They had laughed over it, and Howard had taken a black notebook out of the suit of Ellery's he was wearing, and he had ripped out a page and scribbled his address.

This page.

And Ellery had gone back upstairs and thought about Wrightsville, and finally he had thrust the scrap of paper into a pocket of the smoking jacket and there it had remained, for he had hung the jacket in his closet the following day, where it had been hanging, uncalled to duty, ever since.

All that's left.

Studying the tiny, etching script, Howard came back to him, and Sally, and Diedrich and Wolfert and the old woman; he thought of them all.

A fly dropped onto the "Van" and stood there, insolently. Ellery pursed his lips and blew. The fly soared away and the paper turned over.

There was writing on the other side!

The same small, engraving-like handwriting. But this side was covered with it.

Ellery sat up and reached for the paper curiously.

Howard's handwriting. Black notebook. But these weren't addresses or telephone numbers. A solid page of minute script. Sentence after sentence.

A diary?

It began in the middle of a sentence:

silly pet names he's invented for S., though he has the grace not to use them except when he thinks they're alone. Why should it annoy me? At his *age,* though. Oh, be honest. You know *why* . . . But the damn silliness of it. Calling her "Lia" before they were married—Lia! ! ! ! ! ! just that way—in his own handwriting in that sappy gush note I f . . .—and then "Salomina" after the wedding. Where did he *get* them? ? ! ! So *cute*—the great D. Van H. So *coy.* Salomina—Sally—Sal—the stupid progression and what the hell was wrong with her real name in the first place? I *like* Sara. I lo—whoa, got to quit this, oughtn't even to write it. It's his right, hers. *Quit it.* Going to bed, *hope* to sleep.

A diary, yes.

One thing Howard had never mentioned.

Lia. Salomina.

Funny how those names stuck.

Lia. Salomina. Where had Diedrich picked those up? A thought shuttled over and dropped suddenly into place and Ellery was back at Quetonokis Lake, sitting beside Sally in the convertible drawn up at the lake's edge. She had turned around and tucked her legs under her, and excellent legs they had been. Howard was off at the mossy boulder kicking at a stone. Ellery had given her a cigaret.

"My name was Sara Mason."

He could hear her voice and the swish of the birds rising from the log in the lake.

"It's Dieds who started calling me Sally, among other things."

Among other things. Lia, and Salomina?

Calling her "Lia" before they were married . . . Before they were married. Not Sara Mason. "Lia Mason." Maybe Diedrich didn't like "Sara." "Sara Mason" conjured up the wrong picture: a tight-lipped school teacher, perhaps; a New England housewife wearing a dustcloth about her stringy hair and going around pulling down parlor blinds. "Lia Mason" was young and soft and even mysterious sounding. It suited Sally better. Also, it told something about Diedrich Van Horn. Something secret, and nice.

Salomina after the wedding. Familiar sounding. No, not really. It's the first two syllables that make it seem familiar. Daughter of Herodias . . . Ellery grinned. Then why not "Salome"? Why "Salomina"? The ending *-ina* was in itself a feminization. No, probably a pure invention of Diedrich's, like "Lia." Certainly musical. Sounded like an invention of Poe's.

He sat back and lit his pipe, puffing enjoyably and holding on to the reins of his reflections; to let go meant having to get back to rug-patrol and desperation.

He picked up a pencil, began doodling on a scrap pad.

Lia Mason?

He wrote the name down. Yes, very nice.

He wrote it again, this time in block capitals:

LIA MASON

O-ho, and what's this? LIA MASON—A SILO MAN!

He wrote down the phrase with the agricultural flavor, and now he had:

LIA MASON

A SILO MAN

He studied the letters of the name for another minute, and then he wrote down:

O ANIMALS

An invocation? He chuckled.

The next variation came quickly:

NAIL AMOS

And then:

SIAM LOAN

MAIL A SON

ALAMO SIN

MONA LISA

SAL

Mona Lisa.

Mona Lisa?

Mona Lisa!

That was it. That was *it*. That *smile*. That wise, sad, enigmatic, haunting, contradictory smile! He'd wondered where he had met Sally before. Why, he'd never met her before at all. Sally had the Mona Lisa smile, as identically as if she, and not La Gioconda, had sat for the da Vinci portrait, and . . .

And Diedrich had seen it?

Undoubtedly Diedrich had seen it. Diedrich had been in love.

Had Diedrich identified it? As such?

Ellery's eyes clouded over.

He studied the scratch pad:

MONA LISA

SAL

Almost automatically he finished the unfinished variant:

SALOMINA

Salomina.

Lia Mason, Mona Lisa, Salomina.

Lia Mason, Mona Lisa, Salomina.

A pulse began to tick in his temple.

A man is in love with a woman. She owns a provocative, familiar smile which he identifies as the smile of Mona Lisa. Her name is Mason. The man is passing his prime and the woman is young and she is his first and only love. His passion would be powerful, the appetite of a starved man. There would be, especially in the premarital state, a total absorption in the object of his hunger. The woman would be an obsession and everything about her would be magnified and sharpened to his eye. And the man is sensitive and discerning to begin with. The Mona Lisa discovery is delicious. He toys with it; it pleases him. He writes it down: *Mona Lisa.*

And suddenly he notices that the five letters constituting his Sara Mason's surname are duplicated in the name "Mona Lisa." He is no longer merely pleased; this delights him. He steals the *M,* one *A,* the *S,* the *O,* the *N* from "Mona Lisa." Three letters are left: *L, I, A.* Why, that's practically a name in itself! It sounds like "Leah" and it looks worlds better. Lia . . . Lia Mason . . . Mona Lisa, Lia Mason.

Secretly, he rebaptizes his love. Henceforth Sara is Lia in the closet of his thoughts.

And then, one day, he opens the door to her. He says it. Aloud. "Lia." Sheepishly. But she is a woman, and this is adoration. She likes it. They now share his secret. When they are alone together, he calls her that: "Lia."

They marry, go honeymooning.

Now is the time of symbiosis, when organisms join and fuse and there is nothing outside the lovers' conjunction: no friends, no business, no distraction or possibility of distraction. Each is absorbed in the other. A life is laid aside. A match is more important than a house, and a name can be the secret of the universe. She asks how he arrived at the name Lia, or, if he has told her previously, he brings it up again. He is gay, daring, inventive. "Lia Mason" will not serve now. She is no longer Mason. Another name must be found. Seize paper and pencil, Diedrich, and demonstrate your infinite resources, what a fine headstrong ingenious romantic young-old dog you are, Hotspur and D'Artagnan, and death to obstacles! Fee-faw-fum! Abracadabra! Presto! "Salomina."

And they had laughed together, and doubtless she had said "Salomina" was the loveliest name since "Eve" but wouldn't it be a little awkward to explain? And he gravely agreed and they compromised, for social purposes, on "Sally," which must have seemed to her at the time small price enough to pay in return for the love of this wonderful titan.

Ellery sighed.

Probably it happened altogether differently.

As if any of this made any difference now.

As if it wasn't all a self-made conspiracy to abort the unborn book.

Well . . .

He got up from the desk and paced to his former position on the rug, preparatory to—

Still, it *was* interesting to learn at this late date that poor Diedrich had had the type of mind which played around with anagrams. He recalled now having spotted a book of Double-Crostics on Diedrich's desk one day in—

Anagrams?

Anagrams! Why, yes, that's what they were. Funny it hadn't struck him before in just that way that "Lia Mason," and "Salomina," being formed of the same letters of the alphabet as "Mona Lisa," constituted an *anagram.*

Because an anagram . . .

Because an anagram . . .

"By signing his sculpture H. H. Waye, *Howard broke the Commandment:* Thou shalt not take the name of the Lord thy God in vain; *and this is an especially fascinating example . . . Here he dabbles in the cabala . . . occult theosophists . . . who believed that each letter, word, number, and accent of Scripture contains a hidden sense . . . And if you'll take the letters which form the name* H. H. Waye, *you'll find that they constitute an anagram for* Yahweh."

H. H. Waye—Yahweh. Anagram. Point whatever-number-it-was, one of the ten nails in Howard's coffin.

Ellery became conscious of the ticking in his head. The same old maid of pulse.

What was all the excitement about? he asked his pulse irritably. So Diedrich played around with anagrams. Diedrich got an intellectual satisfaction out of anagrams. And so did Howard, unfortunately for him.

Unfortunately . . .

Ellery was really angry with himself.

Is it possible for two men living in the same house to have the same bent toward anagrams?

Possible hell. It was just as possible as for two men living in the same house to have the same bent toward bourbon. Anyway, it had happened. Anyway, Howard probably caught it from Diedrich. Anyway, what am I beating my brains out for?

He was furious with himself.

The case is over. The solution was impeccable. You damned fool, stop worrying over a case and a set of people dead and buried for a year and get back to work!

But every idea the Queen brain produced turned out to revolve about an anagram.

Ten minutes later Ellery was seated at his desk again, worrying his nails.

But if Howard probably caught it from Diedrich, if Howard was an anagram man by association—if Howard was an anagram man *at all*—why had he written about the pet names "Lia" and "Salomina" the sentence: "Where did he *get* them??!!"

The names had bothered Howard. He had worried over them. And yet he had remained *ignorant of their derivation.* Ellery was an anagram man, and he had worked out the derivation in five minutes.

Oh, this is stupid!

He tried authorship again.

And he failed again.

It was a few minutes after ten when he put in the long distance call to Connhaven.

It's just a call, he thought. Then I can get back to work.

"Connhaven Detective Agency," said a man's voice. "Burmer speaking."

"Er, hello," said Ellery. "My name is Ellery Queen, and I—"

"Ellery Queen of New York?"

"That's right," said Ellery. "Er, look, Burmer. Something's been bothering me in connection with an old case and I'm doing a little checking just to satisfy myself that I'm an old lady in need of a rocker and a set of knitting needles."

"Well, sure, Ellery. Whatever I can do." Burmer sounded companionable. "Case I was in on?"

"Well, yes, in a way."

"What case was that?"

"The Van Horn case. Wrightsville. A year ago."

"Van Horn case? Say, that was a dilly, wasn't it? I wish I *had* been in on it. Then I'd have got a little of that newspaper space you grabbed off." Burmer laughed, indicating this was man-to-man, inside stuff.

"But you were in on it," said Ellery. "Oh, not in any of the pay dirt, but you did some investigating for Diedrich Van Horn and—"

"I did some investigating for who?"
"For Diedrich Van Horn. Howard Van Horn's father."
"I put the matter in the hands of a reputable agency in Connhaven."
"Killer's old man? Ellery, who told you that?" Burmer sounded surprised.
"He did."
"Who did?"
"Killer's old man. He said, 'I put the matter in the hands of a reputable agency—' "
"Well, it wasn't mine. I never had anything to do with any of the Van Horns, worse luck. Maybe he meant in Boston."
"No, he said in Connhaven."
"One of us is drunk! What was I supposed to be investigating?"
"Tracing back his foster son's real parents. Howard's, I mean."
"Just a few minutes ago I got a call from Connhaven. It was the head of the agency. They had the whole story . . ."
"I don't get it."
"You're the head of your agency, aren't you?"
"Sure thing."
"Who was head of it last year?"
"I was. It's mine. Been in business up here fifteen years."
"Maybe it was an operative of yours—"
"This is strictly a one-man operation, and I'm him."
Ellery was silent.
Then he said: "Oh, of course. I'm not functioning this morning. What's the name of the other detective agency in Connhaven?"
"There is no other detective agency in Connhaven."
"I mean last year."
"*I* mean last year."
"What do you mean?"
"I mean there's never *been* another detective agency in Connhaven."
Ellery was silent again.
"What's this all about, Ellery?" asked Burmer curiously. "Anything I can, uh . . . ?"
"You never spoke to Diedrich Van Horn?"
"Nope."
"Never did any work for him?"
"Nope."
Ellery was silent a third time.

"You still there?" asked Burmer.

"Yes. Burmer, tell me: Ever hear the name Waye? W-a-y-e? Aaron Waye? Mattie Waye? Buried in Fidelity Cemetery?"

"Nope."

"Or a Dr. Southbridge?"

"Southbridge? No."

"Thanks. Thanks a lot."

Ellery broke the connection. He waited a few seconds, and then he let go and dialed the number of La Guardia Airport.

2

It was still early in the afternoon when Ellery alighted from the plane at Wrightsville Airfield and hurried through the administration building to the taxi stand.

His coat collar was up and he kept tugging at the brim of his hat.

He crept into a cab.

"Library. State Street."

Best to avoid the *Wrightsville Record* offices.

Wrightsville was snoozing in the August sun. A few people drifted along under the elms on State Street. Two policemen were wiping their necks on the steps of the County Court House. One of them was Jeep.

Ellery shivered.

"Public library, Mister," said the taxi driver.

"Wait for me."

Ellery ran up the library steps, but in the vestibule he slowed down. He removed his hat and trudged past the stuffed eagle through the open doorway and into Miss Aikin's domain, trying to look like a citizen seeking any port in the doldrums, only providing it was cool. And hoping that Miss Aikin wasn't there. But she was—the same sharp-featured old Gorgon. She was fining a frightened-looking girl of about eleven six cents for a book overdue three days. Miss Aikin glanced up suspiciously as she opened her cash drawer; but the man in the topcoat was wiping his face with a handkerchief, and he kept wiping it until he was past her desk and in the transverse corridor beyond.

Ellery stuffed the handkerchief in his pocket and leaped to the door marked *Periodical Room.*

The periodical librarian's desk was vacant. Only one person was in the Periodical Room, and that was a young lady snoring cheerfully over a file of old *Saturday Evening Posts.*

Ellery tiptoed to the *Wrightsville Record* file. He lugged the heavy volume marked 1917 with exquisite care past the sleeping beauty to a lectern and opened it softly.

"Bad summer thunderstorm . . ."

Nevertheless, he began with the issues of April, in order to cover the spring, too.

The accidental death of a local physician in a runaway en route from a confinement would surely have been front-page news in the leading Wrightsville newspaper in 1917. Still, Ellery glanced through all the pages. Fortunately, the *Record* had been a mere four-pager in those days.

He also ran down the obituary column of each issue *en passant.*

In the middle of December he gave up, restored the file to its place on the shelf, left the cheerful young lady snoring over her magazines, and sneaked out of the Wrightsville Public Library by way of a side door clearly marked NO EXIT.

He felt positively sick.

Ellery shuffled toward Upper Whistling, hands trembling in his pockets.

At the entrance to the Northern State Telephone Building he made an attempt to compose himself; the effort took him several moments.

Then he went in and asked to see the manager.

What story he told that functionary he was unable to remember clearly afterward; but it was not the true story, and it got him what he was after: the Wrightsville telephone directories for the years 1916 and 1917.

It took him exactly twenty-five seconds to ascertain that no one named Southbridge was listed in the telephone book for 1916.

It took him twenty seconds more to discover that no one named Southbridge was listed in the telephone book for 1917.

There was a hunted look in his eye as he called for the directories for 1914, 1915, 1918, 1919, and 1920.

No Southbridge was listed in any of them, physician or otherwise.

He felt positively not well as he reached for his hat.

He avoided the Square. Instead, he walked down Upper Whistling past Jezreel Lane, past Lower Main, to Slocum.

He turned into Slocum and hurried the one long block to Washington.

Logan's Market was alive with flies, and little else. The intersection of Slocum and Washington was deserted. Gratefully, he crossed Washington and darted into the Professional Building. He had glimpsed Andy Birobatyan's one arm and fine Armenian face in the Wrightsville Florist Shop next door and he was altogether disinclined toward flowers and Armenia on this occasion.

He plodded up the wide wooden stairs of the Professional Building, irritated by the noise his own feet made on the aged boards.

At the head of the stairs he turned to the right, and there was the familiar shingle:

MILO WILLOUGHBY, M.D.

He tried out a smile, breathed, and went in.

The door to Dr. Willoughby's examining room was shut.

A farmer with a yellow face and pain-filled eyes was sitting in a chair.

A pregnant young lady was sitting in another, dreamy-eyed.

Ellery sat down and waited, too. Same ugly green overstuffed furniture, same faded Currier & Ives prints on the walls, same old fan clattering overhead.

The examining room door opened and another pregnant lady, not so young as the lady who was waiting, waddled out, beaming. And there was old Dr. Willoughby, again. Really old. Dried out. Shrunken. The sharp eye was blunted and grownover; he glanced at Ellery, a peery sort of glance, and said, "I'll be with you in a few minutes, sir," and nodded to the other lady.

The other lady rose, clutching a small something done up in a brown sack, and she went into the examining room and Dr. Willoughby shut the door.

When she emerged, without the sack, Dr. Willoughby motioned to the farmer.

When the farmer came out, Ellery stepped into the examining room.

"You don't remember me, Dr. Willoughby."

The old physician pushed his glasses up on his nose, peering.

"Why, it's Mr. Queen!"

His hand was soft, and moist, and it shook.

"I'd heard you were in town last year," said Dr. Willoughby, pulling over a chair excitedly, "even before the newspapers broke that dreadful story. Why didn't you look us up? Hermy Wright's furious with you. I was insulted myself!"

"I was in town only nine days, Doctor, and they were sort of busy days," said Ellery with a feeble smile. "How's Judge Eli? And Clarice?"

"Getting old. We're all getting old. But what are you doing here now? Oh, it doesn't matter. Here, let me phone Hermione—"

"Er, please, no," said Ellery. "Thanks, Doctor, but I'm in town only for the day."

"Case?" The old man squinted at him.

"Well, yes. Matter of fact," Ellery laughed, "I'd probably have been ungracious enough not to call on you even today, Doctor, if I didn't need some information."

"And probably lost your last chance to see me alive," chuckled the doctor.

"Why, what do you mean?"

"Nothing. Old joke of mine."

"Have you been ill?"

"Every time somebody asks me that," said Dr. Willoughby, "I think of one of the aphorisms of Hippocrates. 'Old people have fewer diseases than the young, but their diseases never leave them.' It's nothing important. Not enough work, that's it! I've had to stop operating . . ." The sallow skin, stretched and mordant; the squeezed-looking tissues, shrunken, sapless; cancer? "What information, Mr. Queen?"

"About a man who died in an accident in the summer of 1917. Man named Southbridge. Do you remember him?"

"Southbridge," frowned the doctor.

"You've probably known more Wrightsvillians, living and dead, than anyone else in town, Doctor. Southbridge."

"There was a family named Sowbridge used to live in Slocum, ran a livery stable there around 1906—"

"No, this man was named Southbridge, and he was a doctor."

"Medical doctor?" Dr. Willoughby looked surprised.

"Yes."

"In general practice?"

"I believe so."

"Dr. Southbridge . . . He couldn't have practiced in Wrightsville, Mr. Queen. Or anywhere in the county, for that matter, or I'd have heard of him."

"My information is that he practiced in Wrightsville. Confinements and things."

"Somebody's making a mistake." The old man shook his head.

Ellery said slowly, "Somebody's made a mistake, Dr. Willoughby. May I use your telephone?"

"Certainly."

Ellery called Police Headquarters.

"Chief Dakin . . . Dakin? Ellery Queen . . . That's right, back again . . . No, just for the day. How are you?"

"Just dandy," said Chief Dakin's delighted voice. "Come right on over!"

"Dakin, I can't. Simply haven't the time. Tell me, what do you know about a fellow named Burmer up in Connhaven?"

"Burmer? Runs the detective agency?"

"Yes. What's his reputation, Dakin? Is he straight? Reliable?"

"Well, now, I'll tell you . . ."

"Yes?"

"Burmer's the only private detective in the state I'd trust without a second thought. Known him for fourteen years, Mr. Queen. If you're thinking of working on something with him, he's absolutely A-one. His word's his bond."

"Thanks."

Ellery hung up.

"George Burmer's a patient of mine," said Dr. Willoughby. "Comes all the way from Connhaven for treatment. Hemorrhoids."

"Do you consider him trustworthy?"

"I'd trust George with anything I have."

"I think," said Ellery, rising, "I'll be running along, Doctor."

"I'll never forgive you for this short visit."

"I'll never forgive myself. Doctor, take care of yourself."

"I'm being treated by the greatest Healer of all," smiled Dr. Willoughby, shaking hands.

Ellery walked very slowly up Washington Street toward the Square.

Diedrich Van Horn had lied.

Last September Diedrich Van Horn had told a long and involved story, and it had all been a lie.

Incredible. But there it was.

Why? Why invent nonexistent parents for a foster son he had reared in love from infancy?

Wait.

Perhaps Mattie and Aaron Waye were . . . Perhaps there was another explanation.

Ellery climbed quickly into a taxi parked before the Hollis and cried: "Fidelity Cemetery."

3

He had the driver wait.

He scaled the stone wall and made his way among the weed-choked graves swiftly. The sun was low.

He found the adjacent graves after a little search; the low double headstone was almost hidden by the undergrowth.

Ellery knelt, parting the weeds.

AARON AND MATTIE WAYE

There it was, cut into the soft, crumbly stone.

AARON AND MATTIE WAYE

He studied the names.

Somehow, they looked different. But then the whole cemetery looked different. A year ago he had been here during and after a storm, at night. He had examined the headstone by the flame of a cigaret lighter which had flickered, and the legend had wavered and danced.

He leaned forward.

There was something wrong with one of the letters.

That was the difference. It was not an illusion of poor light or a trick of memory at all.

The final letter.

The *E* of *WAYE* was cut differently from the other letters.

It was not so deeply incised. It was less professionally hammered out. On close examination it revealed a clumsiness, an irregularity, not characteristic of the other lettering. The more he studied the final *E,* the more plainly its difference stood out. Even its outlines were sharper. In fact, they were considerably sharper.

Because he was a perfectionist he plucked a long darnel from the grave and, stripping its awns, he used it as a rule to measure the distance from the left edge of the headstone to the *A* of *AARON.* Then, with his thumbnail marking the exact length on the weed, he applied his green rule to the right edge of the headstone.

The distance from the *E* of *WAYE* to the right edge

was less than the distance from the left edge to the *A* of *AARON*.

Still unsatisfied, he set his thumb on the right edge of the headstone to determine where the other end of the darnel fell.

It fell exactly on the *Y* of *WAYE.*

Ellery struggled to avoid the conclusion. But the conclusion was unavoidable.

The monument maker's stonecutter had originally chiseled:

AARON AND MATTIE WAY

Another hand, much later, had added an *E.*

This was the fact.

Ellery dropped the weed and glanced about. He saw a cracked stone bench, with weeds growing up through it, nearby.

He walked over to it and sat down and began chewing weeds.

"Say, Mister."

Ellery came to with a start. The cemetery was gone and he was sitting in a smother of darkness. Before him the darkness showed a yellow rent, conical and puzzling.

He shivered, contracting himself under his coat.

"Who is it?" he said. "I can't see."

"I *thought* you forgot all about me," said the man's voice, "But you're ponying up, Mister, you're payin'. That clock's been workin' all this time. You told me to wait."

It was night, and he was still in Fidelity Cemetery, on the broken stone bench. And this was the taxi driver, with a flashlight.

"Oh. Yes," said Ellery. He got to his feet and stretched. His joints were stiff and they ached, but there was another ache inside him against which stretching was no remedy. "Yes, certainly. I'll pay the clock."

"I thought you forgot me, Mister," said the taxi driver again, with different emphasis and in a mollified tone. "Watch your step! Here, let me use my flash. I'll walk behind you."

Ellery made his way across the dilapidated graves to the stone wall. As he went over the wall it occurred to him, wryly, that he never had found the entrance to the cemetery.

This had been the route of . . .

"Where to now, Mister?" asked the taxi driver.

"What?"

"I said where to."
"Oh." Ellery leaned back in the cab. "Hill Drive."

To get to Hill Drive from Fidelity it was necessary to take North Hill Drive, and Ellery waited.

As the familiar marble monoliths moved by, he leaned forward.

"What's this estate we're passing, driver?"

"Huh? Oh. That's the Van Horn place."

"Van Horn. Oh, yes. I remember now. Is the house open? Occupied?"

"Sure is."

"Van Horn brothers still living there, eh? Both of them?"

"Yeap. And their old lady, too." The driver twisted in his seat. "Place is run down somethin' fierce. Real beat. Ever since Diedrich Van Horn's wife was bumped off. That was last year."

"Is that so?"

"Yep. Old Diedrich took it plenty hard. I hear he's lookin' older than his mother, and his mother's older than God. I guess losin' that son of his didn't help. Name of Howard. He was a sculpture." The man twisted again, lowering his voice. "You know, Howard done it."

"Yes, so I read. In the papers."

The driver turned back to his wheel. "Nobody ever sees Diedrich Van Horn any more and hell, he used to run this town. Now his brother runs everything. Wolfert, his name is. Diedrich just stays home."

"I see."

"Damn nasty business. Well, here's where North Hill Drive becomes Hill Drive. Whereabouts on Hill Drive are you goin', Mister?"

"I think it's the house right there, driver."

"The Wheeler place? Yes, sir."

"Don't bother to drive in. I'll get out at the curb."

"Yes, sir." The taxi stopped and Ellery got out. "Say, this clock looks like the Chinese war debt."

"My own fault. Here you are."

"Say. Thanks!"

"Thank you. For waiting."

The man shifted into gear. "It's all right, Mister. Folks go to cemeteries sort of lose track of time. Say, that's pretty good, ain't it?"

He laughed and the cab ground off down the hill.

Ellery waited until its taillight blinked out around a curve.

Then he began walking up the hill, back toward North Hill Drive.

4

The moon was up as Ellery turned in between the two pylons and began walking up the private driveway.

There used to be lights here, he thought.

There were no lights now.

But the moon was bright, and that was lucky, because the drive was treacherous to feet. The lovely smoothness he remembered had degenerated into ruts, pits, and rubble. As he made his way past the cypresses and yews, beginning the spiral ascent to the hilltop, he noticed that the rare shrubs which had lined both sides of the road, between the spaced trees, had all but vanished under a crazy tangle of uncontrolled vegetation.

Run down is right, he thought.

Ruined. It's a ruin, the whole place.

The front of the main house was dark. So was the side facing north—the north terrace, the formal gardens, the guest house.

Ellery walked around the terrace to the gardens and the pool. The pool was dry; rotting leaves half filled it.

He glanced over at the guest house.

The windows were boarded up; the door was padlocked.

The gardens were unrecognizable—weed-grown, disheveled, untended.

He stood there for a few moments.

Then he went cautiously around to the rear.

Wedges of light drew him. He went over on the tips of his toes and looked into the kitchen.

Christina Van Horn was bent over the sink, washing dishes; that curved and ancient back was unmistakable. But when she turned for a moment with dripping hands he saw that she was not Christina at all, but Laura.

The night was stifling, but Ellery put his hands into his pockets. He felt his pigskin gloves.

He pulled them out and put them on, slowly.

Then he made his way along the rear wall, under the kitchen windows, keeping close to the wall.

He rounded the far corner and paused. A sliver of light stuck out into the darkness on this side, touched the wrought-iron railing of the south terrace.

The light came from the study.

Ellery crept along the wall and up the terrace steps.

He stopped just outside the light's shaft and carefully looked into the room.

The hangings were not quite drawn together.

A segment of the study was visible, long and thin and meaningless. Part of it, at about the height of a seated man, was a fragment of face.

It was a fragment of the face of a very old man, a man with gray loose skin.

Ellery did not recognize the fragment of the face as belonging to any face of his acquaintance.

But then the face moved a little, and an eye fixed itself in the crevice of the darkness. And Ellery recognized it. It was a large, deep, brilliant, beautiful eye; and from this he knew that he was looking at Diedrich Van Horn.

He put his gloved knuckles to the nearest pane of the French door and rapped, sharply.

The eye swiveled out of view. The other eye appeared. It was looking directly at him, or so it seemed.

Ellery rapped again.

He stepped aside as he heard a squeaky sound from inside the room, as of little-used wheels.

"Who is that?"

The voice was as strange as the fragment of face, and in exactly the same way: it was an old gray voice.

Ellery put his mouth close to the French door.

"Queen. Ellery Queen."

He grasped the handle, turning and pushing.

The door was locked.

He shook it. "Mr. Van Horn! Open this door."

He heard a key stumble into the lock and he stepped back.

The door opened.

Diedrich sat beyond it in a wheel chair, a yellow blanket about his shoulders, his hands taut on the wheels; he was staring at Ellery, squinting, straining, as if to see better.

Ellery stepped inside, shut the French door, turned the key, drew the hangings together.

"Why have you come back?"

Yes, as old as his mother. Older. The strength was lost. Even the shell had crumbled. The hair was dirty white, sparse; what there was hung lifelessly.

"Because I had to," said Ellery.

The study was much as he remembered it. The desk, the lamp, the books, the armchair. Only now the room seemed bigger. But that was because Diedrich was smaller.

When he shrinks up and dies, Ellery thought, the room will stretch so in every direction that it will plop out of existence, leaving nothing behind, like an overblown soap bubble.

He heard the squeaks and looked around to see Diedrich retreating in his moving chair, retreating to the center of the study, out of range of the light from the desk lamp. Only his legs were illuminated; the rest was shadow.

"Because you had to?" said Diedrich from the shadow. He sounded puzzled.

Ellery sat down in the swivel chair and slumped on his spine, his coat tumbled about him, his hat still on his head, his gloved hands resting on the chair's arms.

"I had to, Mr. Van Horn," he said, "because this morning I found a page of Howard's diary in a pocket of my smoking jacket and for the first time I read what Howard had written on the other side."

"I want you to go away, Mr. Queen," said the ghost of Diedrich's voice.

But Ellery said: "I discovered, Mr. Van Horn, that you're an anagrammatist. I hadn't known about 'Lia Mason' and 'Salomina.' I hadn't known that your mind worked that way."

The wheel chair was still. But the voice was stronger; it held a note of warmth. "I'd kind of forgotten all that. Poor Sally."

"Yea."

"And that 'discovery' brought you all the way back here, Mr. Queen, to see me? That was kind of you."

"No. That discovery, Mr. Van Horn, made me telephone the Connhaven Detective Agency."

The wheel chair squeaked.

But the voice said: "Oh, yes?"

"And after that call I flew up here. Mr. Van Horn," said Ellery, slumping still lower in the swivel chair, "I've been over to Fidelity Cemetery. I've taken a good look at the headstone of Aaron and Mattie Way."

"Their headstone. Is it still standing? We die, stones live. It doesn't seem fair, now, does it, Mr. Queen?"

"Mr. Van Horn, you never engaged the Connhaven Detective Agency to trace Howard's parents. Undoubtedly you made an attempt through the man Fyfield you mentioned, when Howard was an infant, to trace his parents then; but when he turned up nothing, that was the end. *The rest you manufactured.*

"It was not Burmer of Connhaven who found the graves of Aaron and Mattie Way; it was you, Mr. Van Horn. It was not Burmer who told you the story of Howard's birth; you invented it. God knows who Howard's parents were, but they weren't the Ways. There was never a Dr. Southbridge. You concocted the entire fantasy—after you chiseled an extra *E* on the Ways' headstone, making their name read *W-A-Y-E*. You gave Howard false parents, Mr. Van Horn. You gave Howard a false name."

The man in the wheel chair was silent.

"And why did you give Howard a false name, Mr. Van Horn?

"Because, Mr. Van Horn," said Ellery, "that false name —*Waye* with an *e* it never had—combined with the *H. H.* of Howard's signature, *Howard Hendrik,* made possible a 'new' signature, *H. H. Waye,* with an *e*, which, as I so brilliantly showed in my by now world-famous analysis of last year, Mr. Van Horn, is an anagram of *Yahweh.* And this proved that Howard had broken the Commandment which says: *Thou shalt not take the name of the Lord thy God in vain.*"

Diedrich said: "I'm not the man I was, Mr. Queen. You say things to me that sound threatening and bitter and it's all so confusing. What are you talking about?"

"If your memory is failing," said Ellery, "let me try to restore it. You knew, Mr. Van Horn, that if you provided Howard with a surname but not with a given name, Howard would simply have to retain the Christian name you gave him when you adopted him—Howard Hendrik; and you knew, further, that he always signed his work *H. H. Van Horn.* Then if he were to adopt his supposedly genuine surname of Waye, he would accordingly sign himself *H. H. Waye,* with an *e,* Mr. Van Horn. And since Howard was engaged in a heroic sculpturing project, it was very likely that he'd scratch the 'new' name on his models.

"But if Howard didn't do that, *you* could have done it, Mr. Van Horn. Because you had a tremendous advantage in Howard's amnesic lapses. You could have scratched the name *H. H. Waye*—with an *e*—into his models, and it would be assumed that Howard had done it during one of his blackouts—and who, including Howard, could deny it? You couldn't lose, Mr. Van Horn, either way.

"As it turned out, Howard did sign one of his models *H. H. Waye,* and a number of his working sketches."

"I simply don't know what you're talking about," said Diedrich feebly from the wheel chair. His big hand, all loose flesh and ropy veins, was up to his eyes. "Why in heaven's name would I do a thing like that?"

"You invoke the name of heaven naturally, Mr. Van Horn," said Ellery. "As you did then. Why did you do it?

Because you wanted to impose on Howard an anagram for the name of the Lord."

Diedrich was silent.

But then he said: "I find it hard to believe any of this is really happening. Do you really mean all this—this—I mean, imposing anagrams of the Lord's name on Howard, inventing stories of Howard's birth in order to do it! Most fantastic thing I ever heard."

"Oh, it's fantastic," said Ellery, "but it really did happen. It's the only explanation. There are no alternatives. You lied about Howard's parents, you chiseled an extra *e* on the name in Fidelity Cemetery, and this enabled me to make an anagram out of God's name which in turn enabled me to accuse Howard of having broken one of the Ten Commandments. Fantastic, as you say. Unbelievably farfetched. And yet it happened, Mr. Van Horn, and it happened because you're a man of uncanny insight into human nature and of colossal imagination. You were dealing with a man to whom the fantastic and the farfetched are attractive, Mr. Van Horn. You knew my needs!"

Ellery half rose in an unaccustomed excitement; but then he sank back. And when he resumed, it was in a quiet tone again.

"You had to work toward fantastic ends, Mr. Van Horn, but the means were practical, ordinary, and logical. Your plan called for imposing on Howard an anagram for the Lord's name. In selecting one, you had a choice. Probably you narrowed the choice down to two: Jehovah and Yahweh. But it wasn't easy to work with the name Jehovah. Jehovah, minus the two *H*'s Howard would have to retain, left *j, e, o, v, a,* a discouraging combination of letters to anagrammatize into a credible surname. But Yahweh, minus the two H's, gave you the letters *y, a, w, e,* which could be transposed to form the perfectly acceptable surname of Waye. All that was required then was to find the graves of a couple—or of a woman alone, if you were pressed, but a husband and wife were better—in or around Wrightsville Township, or in Slocum, or Connhaven—anywhere in the county would do, or even in the State—people who had borne the name of Waye and had died after the known birth date of Howard, leaving no family.

"You didn't find *Waye*, but you did find *Way*. The word itself is of Anglo-Saxon origin; the ethnic background of New England is largely English; it would have been remarkable if you hadn't found a *Way*, or a number of *Ways* among whom you could choose. As for Aaron and Mattie Way, it's possible you invented their history, too. Or they may well have been poor farmers, as you said. It didn't really matter; you could shape the facts to your purpose, or your means to the facts; you had a great deal of leeway."

The ache in his abdomen had disappeared; but he still felt cold. He did not look at Van Horn.

The old man in the wheel chair said, "Mr. Queen, what are you attempting to prove with all this—this stuff?"

"That Howard," said Ellery, "did not break all of the Ten Commandments. At this point I was able to say: I now know that at least one of the Commandments whose violation I ascribed to Howard was not Howard's work at all, but was the result of *your* work, Mr. Van Horn.

"So I asked myself as I sat in Fidelity Cemetery in the twilight today, Mr. Van Horn: If Howard didn't break one Commandment, *is it possible he didn't break some of the others?*"

5

Diedrich was seized by a spasm of coughing that made the wheel chair dance. Bent over, his eyes frantic, he made a violent gesture toward the desk.

There was a silver decanter on the desk and Ellery jumped up to pour a glass of water from it and hurry with it to the coughing man. He held the glass to Diedrich's lips.

Finally Diedrich said, "Thank you, Mr. Queen," and Ellery returned the glass to the desk and sat down again.

Diedrich's big chin rested on his breast now; his eyes were closed and he seemed asleep.

But Ellery said: "I asked myself another question. I asked myself which of the ten crimes I'd charged Howard with could I be *sure* he'd committed? Not crimes he was made to appear guilty of, Mr. Van Horn; not crimes he was forced to commit; not crimes imposed on him—but crimes of which he was personally, directly guilty, of his free will. And do you know?" Ellery smiled. "Of the ten crimes I heaped on Howard's head that day a year ago, I could now—a little late, wouldn't you agree?—I could now be *sure* that he'd been unequivocally responsible for only two."

The eyelids flickered.

"I knew beyond possibility of error that Howard had wanted or had thought he wanted Sally; he'd told me that himself. And I knew beyond possibility of error that Howard had slept with Sally; they'd both told me that."

The hands twitched.

"So I *knew* Howard had broken two Commandments: *Thou shalt not covet thy neighbor's wife* and *Thou shalt not commit adultery.*

"But what of the other eight? I'd proved that you were responsible for the Commandment clue involving the name of God, Mr. Van Horn. *Was it possible you were also responsible for the seven remaining unaccounted for?*"

Ellery got up suddenly.

Diedrich's eyes flew open.

"I sat on a broken stone bench in Fidelity Cemetery in the darkness this evening, Mr. Van Horn, and I went through a kind of hell. I'm going to take you with me on that tour of hell, Mr. Van Horn! Do you mind?"

Diedrich's mouth opened. He tried again, and this time a croak came out. "I'm an old man," he said. "I'm confused."

But Ellery said: "Last year I began by 'proving' that Howard broke the Commandments: *Thou shalt have no other gods before me* and *Thou shalt not make unto thee any graven image.* And what did my proof consist of, Mr. Van Horn? This: That Howard was in the process of sculpturing the ancient gods. And this was very good proof—as far as it went, Mr. Van Horn. But, Mr. Van Horn, it didn't go far enough. Because who—when you really examine the facts—made Howard's sculpture of the ancient gods possible?

"You, Mr. Van Horn—you alone. It was you who came to the rescue of the Wrightsville Art Museum Committee when their fund-raising drive failed of its goal by a wide margin. It was you who promised to make up the enormous deficit providing Howard was commissioned to execute the sculptures for the exterior of the proposed Museum building. *It was you who specified as a condition of your financial assistance that the statues Howard was to execute were to be of the classical gods.*"

6

The wheel chair slid back and now Diedrich was altogether in shadow. Ellery experienced a shock of recognition, as if this had happened before. But then he knew it was simply the resemblance between the great lump in the wheel chair and the lump of the old woman as he had first glimpsed her seated in the garden that night so long ago.

"Then I charged Howard with having broken the Commandment: *Thou shalt not steal.* Now there I felt I was on solid ground, Mr. Van Horn. Was there, could there be, any doubt that Howard had stolen the twenty-five thousand dollars which he'd handed me at Quetonokis Lake to pay over to Sally's blackmailer? Not the least bit. The money came from your wall safe here; it was your money; I had your check list of the serial numbers of the fifty stolen five-hundred-dollar bills to compare with the fifty five-hundred-dollar bills Howard had given me—and they checked to the last number. Why am I flogging the point? Howard himself admitted stealing the money from your safe.

"And yet this evening, in the cemetery, Mr. Van Horn, I had to ask myself: But did Howard steal that money because he was naturally a thief, or naturally susceptible to temptation, or did he steal it because something had happened of such an unusual nature, exercising such an unusually strong compulsion, as to *force* Howard to steal it against a nature normally impervious to such temptation? And if events forced Howard to steal your twenty-five thousand dollars, Mr. Van Horn, who created those events?

"And this brings me to the crux of the case."

Diedrich stirred in his cocoon of shadows, almost as if he were preparing to rise.

"Now I knew that Howard had been framed for some of the crimes I'd held him responsible for.

"So I considered the framer.

"I considered the framer, Mr. Van Horn, as a disembodied entity, a factor in a mathematical problem—an unknown. Howard was framed; therefore a framer existed. Immediately I asked myself: What did this ponderable, if unknown, quantity represent? What were his values, this Mr. X?

"Well, out of five Commandments broken, I knew that my X-entity was responsible for three. It began to look bad for Mr. X. It began to look very bad. Because I'd reached an answer last year, and the answer was that Howard had broken the Ten Commandments. Now I knew that had not been true in the important sense. My X had made possible the appearance, the *illusion,* of Howard's violation of the Decalogue, or at least of three of the five parts of it which I'd examined. This, then, seemed to have been X's 'value,' mathematically speaking: *He had manipulated events to make it appear that Howard had set out to break all ten of the Commandments.*

"But if this were so, what did X—Howard's framer—have to know? He had to know this basic fact: That Howard himself, unmanipulated, of his free will, had broken two of the Commandments; or rather that he had committed two crimes against the ethical code which we call the Ten Commandments. I say Framer X had to know this, Mr. Van Horn, because to say otherwise is to say that Framer X arrived at his extraordinary decalogic plan independently of Howard's acts. This is unthinkable. No; it was Howard's breaking of the Commandments against wife-coveting and adultery which gave Framer X the larger, broader, encompassing inspiration of causing Howard to break *all* the Commandments. Or all but one, Mr. Van Horn; but the whole illusion tended to that one and it's the climax of my argument; I'll leave it to its proper place."

Ellery poured a glass of water for himself. He put it to his lips. But after staring at the glass for an instant, he rubbed his gloved finger over the place which his lips had touched and he set the glass down, untasted.

"How could Framer have known that Howard desired Sally and that he subsequently satisfied his desire? In only one way. Two people alone knew in the beginning: Howard and Sally. Neither told anyone but me. And I had told no one. That any of the three of us, but especially Howard and Sally, could have told a fourth was a possibility to be discarded as soon as it was broached. All the trouble they got into was a result of *their refusal to tell.* And I was bound to silence by their wishes.

"How, then, did the Framer know? How could he have known? Did a fact exist which made his knowledge possible?

"Yes! The written record of Howard's feelings and Howard's and Sally's adulterous act; the four letters Howard stupidly wrote after the Lake Pharisee episode.

"Conclusion? *Framer read those letters.*

"But this is remarkable, Mr. Van Horn!" cried Ellery. "Because someone else read those letters . . . the mysterious person whose knowledge of the contents of those letters made it possible for him to blackmail Sally! Did I say someone else? Why should I say someone *else?* Why shouldn't I say . . . Framer X read letters, Blackmailer read letters, *Framer X is therefore Blackmailer?*"

Diedrich was staring at the glass Ellery had set down at the desk. It seemed to fascinate him.

"But now, Mr. Van Horn," said Ellery in a quivering voice, "we can get away from mathematical symbols and back to human quantities. Who was Framer X? I've proved that already: *You, Mr. Van Horn.* But Framer Equals Blackmailer. *Therefore, Mr. Van Horn, you were the one who blackmailed Howard and Sally.*"

Now Diedrich raised his head and Ellery saw his face full. And what Ellery saw in Diedrich's face made him go on more rapidly, as if to falter now was in some baffling way to lose a battle.

"I think this was the low point of my thoughts this evening on that bench, Mr. Van Horn. Because it took me back to last year, to my 'brilliant' analysis, when I was delivering the death blows to Howard with the merciless perfection of my reasoning. And I saw, Mr. Van Horn," said Ellery with a single glance so bitter cold that the great eyes across the room glittered, "that while my reasoning had been merciless, it had been anything but perfect. It had been not only loose, not only superficial, but it concealed a great hole—it had neglected even to bring up the question of the all-important blackmailer's identity! Unconsciously, stupidly, I had absorbed the repeated suggestion that the blackmailer was John Doe, burglar. But there was no John Doe, Mr. Van Horn; there was no burglar. You were John Doe, Mr. Van Horn; you were the blackmailer."

He paused, but Diedrich said nothing; and he went on.

"How did you become the blackmailer? Very simply, I think. In May of last year, or early in June, you discovered the false bottom to Sally's japanned box. You found the four letters. It could have happened quite accidentally: You were putting in or taking out a piece of Sally's jewelry, the box fell out of your hands, the false bottom popped open, you saw the letters, the fact that they were in a hiding place prompted you—out of curiosity or your total absorption in all matters concerning your wife—to read them. Or perhaps you caught a word, or a phrase, without even intending to read them—there was no envelopes; and if it were a certain word, or a certain phrase, then you would be sure to read them. Quite sure."

Diedrich still said nothing.

"You didn't disclose to your son and your wife that you had learned their secret. Oh, no. They misjudged you ludicrously there. How often they assured me you didn't suspect a thing! How frantic they were, how childishly frantic, to keep you from suspecting what you'd known for months! And how consummately you acted the role of unsuspecting innocence.

"But all the time you knew and all the time you were watching for your opportunity. . . . Sally told me that if you found out you'd give her a divorce without a word, settle a fortune on her.

"Poor Sally," said Ellery with a smile.

And he said: "To maintain yourself in the role of pure and unsuspecting cuckold, and to create the atmosphere essential to your greater plan, you took the jewel box and its contents and manufactured the evidence necessary to give the impression that a professional burglar had entered Sally's bedroom and stolen the box for the jewels in it. You cleverly saw to it that the jewelry got to pawnshops in various cities—no doubt that period of your activities last year, if it were checked, would be found to involve several sudden and important 'business trips.' And, of course, you knew the jewelry would be recovered.

"But the letters you kept, Mr. Van Horn, and when the time was right, you used them blackmail-wise; you became the blackmailer. I blush to recall that every time the 'blackmailer' telephoned, and that during the one time that he made a physical if invisible appearance—to take the money from the bureau drawer of that room at the Hollis—*you were away from this house.*"

Ellery took out a cigaret. The action was automatic. But when he saw the cigaret between his fingers, he carefully put it back in his pocket.

"At the time you laid your blackmail plans, back in last May or early June, when you found the four letters, I doubt if the decalogic idea was in your mind; in fact, I'm sure it wasn't. Your purpose then was more likely to prepare the ground for a campaign of assault on Howard's and Sally's nerves. The inspiration was born later, out of independent developments—like the Museum project—and the information in the letters in your possession; and I don't think it reached its full growth until the day Howard phoned you from my apartment in New York to say that I was coming up to Wrightsville as his house guest. But I'll go into that later."

Ellery stirred restlessly.

"Let's move on to the events surrounding the blackmail operation itself. As the blackmailer, you demanded twenty-five thousand dollars in cash from Sally; your first demand. You knew Sally would tell Howard. You knew that neither Sally nor Howard, or the two of them together, had twenty-five thousand dollars. You knew them so well, their gratitude to you, their obsessive dread of hurting you, that you could be certain they would do anything to keep the 'blackmailer' from making good his 'threat' to turn the letters over to you! You knew that both were aware of the large amount of cash you usually kept in the study safe at home here. You knew that, pushed to the wall, Howard would think of that money and that he would take it from the safe; and you saw to it that in the safe there was exactly enough; or perhaps what was in the safe dictated the amount of blackmail you demanded.

"We conclude then, Mr. Van Horn, that when Howard broke the Commandment against stealing, it was because events forced him to; *and it was you who created those events for precisely that purpose.*"

Diedrich rolled his chair forward into the light and he smiled.

He smiled and showed his teeth and he said with energy, almost with good humor: "I've been listening to this remarkable speech of yours, Mr. Queen, with what amounts to awe. So clever, so complicated!" He laughed. "But it's getting to be too much of a good thing, don't you agree? You're making me out some sort of god. God Himself! I created this, I created that—I was 'sure' Howard would do this, I 'knew' Howard would do that . . . Aren't you giving me far too much credit, Mr. Queen, for . . . what would you call it?"

"Omniscience?"

"Yes. How could I or anyone else be sure of anything?"

"You couldn't always be sure," said Ellery quietly. "Nor was it essential always to *be* sure. Your plan was flexible; you had lots of latitude.

"But throughout this infernal business, Mr. Van Horn, you planned and acted from a profound and detailed understanding of what made Howard and Sally tick. You didn't misjudge their characters as they misjudged yours. You were as familiar with the innermost operation of their minds as with your own. Consistently you could, and you did, predict with great accuracy what they would feel, what they would think, and what they would do. You'd had thirty years or so to study Howard, and you knew Sally from the time she was nine, was it? Through all those years of correspondence when, as Sally said, she told you things about herself most girls would hesitate to tell their mothers; and in Sally's case, your knowledge of her was climaxed by the intimate relationship of marriage. In your own way, Mr. Van Horn, you're a master psychologist. It's a pity you didn't apply your talents more constructively."

"Somehow," said Diedrich with a grim smile, "that doesn't sound like a compliment."

"On the other hand, you didn't have to be right each time. If Howard and Sally didn't jump in quite the direction you intended when you jerked the string, because of a lapse in judgment, or an imponderable you couldn't have been aware of, or because of some accident you couldn't have foreseen, you simply had to set into motion another string, actuate another series of events; and sooner or later, Howard would do what you wanted him to do.

"But as it turned out, you were remarkably accurate in your judgments. You provided exactly the right stimuli, exerted exactly the right pressure at the right places, and Howard and Sally moved exactly as you wanted them to move.

"And, I might add," said Ellery in a very low voice, "not merely Howard and Sally."

7

"Go on," said Diedrich Van Horn, after a while.

Ellery looked up, startled, "I beg your pardon.

"So far, then, in my analysis you've imposed three crimes on Howard and forced him to commit a fourth.

"Which event produced my conclusion that Howard had broken the Commandments enjoining: *Remember the sabbath day, to keep it holy* and *Honor thy father and thy mother?* His trip in the dark hours one Sunday morning to Fidelity Cemetery to desecrate the graves of the two people you had told him were his parents.

"I must confess," said Ellery, "that when I reached this point in my reconstruction earlier this evening I was held up. It was quite impossible, with all your shrewd evaluation of Howard, to have been able to count on Howard's desecrating the Ways' graves—and out of the question that you should have been able to count on Howard's doing so on a Sunday. The whole structure of my argument was in danger of collapsing. But then I saw what the answer must be.

"Since you couldn't count on Howard's making that trip, since you couldn't force Howard to make that trip, *you could make it for him.*

"The more I thought about this, the more convinced I became that that was what happened. Not once had I caught a glimpse of Howard's face, or heard his voice. I saw Howard's car, I saw a man about Howard's size wearing Howard's coat and hat, I saw this man use a sculptor's mallet and chisel . . . In view of the fact that your plan called for Howard to make that trip, and you couldn't possibly have made Howard make it, someone else must have been acting the part of Howard that night; and since it was your plan, and you and Howard are of a size, that someone else must have been you.

"A reconstruction was then simple. Suppose that on that Saturday night, quite late, and after the rest of us had got out of the way, you dropped into Howard's studio, or bedroom, for a nightcap. Father and son stuff, Mr. Van Horn. And suppose you handed Howard a drink containing a drug, a drug in a dose sufficient to make him sleep all night, if he was undisturbed. When Howard dropped off, you put on yourself his distinctive and readily identifiable wide-brimmed Stetson and long trench coat, his socks, his shoes, and his trousers. And you left Howard sleeping in his room or studio and went quietly downstairs and outside and to the garage. You put Sally's keys in the ignition lock of her convertible—for my benefit. You got into Howard's roadster. And you drove around to the front, deliberately racing the engine. That was to attract my attention, of course, from the guest house. To make certain, you just as deliberately stalled the car under the porte-cochere . . . to make certain, and to give me time to dress, if I were undressed. Or perhaps you'd scouted me before taking the car out and had seen me dozing on the porch of the guest house; and the engine stall was to give me time to get a coat. And when you saw me begin to run across the garden, you drove off.

"Mr. Van Horn, you played me that night the way a veteran sportsman plays a tarpon. Your timing throughout was superbly delicate. You didn't make the mistake of making it too easy for me. You gave me just enough line to delude me into thinking I was giving you a run for your money. And, if I'd lost you, you'd have seen to it that I picked up your trail again.

"The rain helped, but even if it hadn't rained you were still safe; it was a dark night, and that you could have known in advance. In any event, you knew I wouldn't come too close or try to stop you. You knew I'd be positive you were Howard and that my function was not to interfere but to observe.

"And at the graves of the Ways you attacked the headstone, using a mallet and chisel you'd taken from Howard's studio.

"What happened after that illustrates the impeccability of your judgment of people and situations—a talent, by the way, that undoubtedly accounts for your success in business.

"You left and drove home. You knew I wouldn't follow you at once. You knew I'd examine the headstone after the attack, to check up on it. You knew that when I returned to North Hill Drive the odds were greatly in favor of my changing my wet clothing before going up to see if Howard was back. Yes, you were taking a chance on that; but the calculated risk is part of every careful plan, and the risk was not great. I'd probably not want to leave a trail of mud in the main house which might require explanations the next day—even if I didn't mind risking pneumonia.

"While I was changing in the guest house, you were putting the finishing touches to your master-illusion on the top floor of the house here. You took off Howard's soaked socks and mudcaked shoes and put them on Howard's feet. You took off Howard's wet, muddy trousers and pulled them over Howard's legs. You took off Howard's trench coat and sat Howard up and put his arms through the sleeves and drew the coat around him and buttoned it. Howard's sopping hat you placed on the pillow beside him. And then, calmly, you went to bed."

Ellery said: "You must have calculated that it was even possible I wouldn't come to Howard's room until morning. But whether immediately or after the lapse of several hours, I was sure to come to Howard's room to check up on him. And so I'd find Howard in what would inevitably seem to me to be one of his typical amnesic stupors, fully dressed in the wet and muddy clothing which had made the nasty trip to the cemetery.

"Yes, Mr. Van Horn, it was you who committed the two crimes of breaking the Sabbath and dishonoring How-Howard's 'parents,' doing it in such a way as to fool me into believing the Commandment-breaker had been Howard."

8

And Diedrich said again, "Go on, Mr. Queen."

"Oh, I will," said Ellery. And he said: "And now I come to perhaps the most spectacular example of your psychological shrewdness.

"I blithely proved last year that Howard had broken the Commandment: *Thou shalt not bear false witness against thy neighbor,* when I pointed out that Howard had denied having given me the necklace to pawn. That was true, of course; he *had* given me the necklace to pawn, and he lied when he said he hadn't.

"But here again it was you who, by manipulating events and accurately estimating Howard, placed Howard in the position where, being what he was, he had to lie!

"In your role of blackmailer, Mr. Van Horn, you demanded a second payment of twenty-five thousand dollars—virtually on the heels of the first demand, which had been paid. Obviously, you did this to exert the maximum pressure at the weakest point. For where could Sally and Howard get another twenty-five thousand dollars? There was no more of your cash lying conveniently around to be stolen. You knew they had nowhere to borrow the money, even if they dared leave such a trail. There was only one thing between them which might yield such a large sum: Sally's necklace. It was virtually a certainty, then, that one or the other of them would think of Sally's necklace as the means of satisfying the blackmailer's second demand.

"More than that. You knew I had acted as Sally's go-between in the first negotiations with the blackmailer, so it was a better-than-fair guess that I'd act in the same capacity in their attempt to raise the second payment. And if I didn't you were no doubt ready with another scheme in which I'd have to permit myself to become involved and which would accomplish the same end: Howard's denial of me.

"But I did consent to act, and I acted. And the stage was set for your crowning psychological performance.

"For no sooner had I pawned the necklace and deposited the money in the Wrightsville railroad station, as instructed, than you struck.

"This time your tool was your brother Wolfert, Mr. Van Horn. Just as you knew Sally and Howard, so you knew Wolfert. What did Wolfert say? That you had told him you 'hoped' the Museum Committee wouldn't 'make a fuss' about your donation! To have expressed such a 'hope' to Wolfert, jealous, bitter, and malicious as he is, was to invite him to thwart that hope. Wolfert actually chortled, 'I was the one who put them up to it.' I remember his saying it at the breakfast table that morning. But Wolfert was only partially right. He was only the instrument—your instrument. You played on him, Mr. Van Horn, as you played on your wife and your son. To make you squirm, as he thought, Wolfert prodded the Committee to give you a testimonial dinner, a full-dress affair of the kind he knew you loathed. But this was precisely what you wanted him to do. Because it gave you the natural and innocent excuse for asking *Sally to wear her diamond necklace*—which you knew she no longer had.

"And so Sally would have to reveal that the necklace was gone. Would she tell the truth? Oh, no. To have told the truth Sally would have had to expose the whole mess of the blackmail, and its reason for being. You knew Sally would die rather than disclose that; you knew Howard would kill her before he let her disclose it. Again, it was a reasonable assumption that they'd invent some story to explain the necklace's being gone. Burglary was in the air; Howard had stolen the cash and made an attempt to make it look like an outside thief's work; theft of the necklace in another 'burglary' was indicated.

"And when Sally phoned you at your office to say that the necklace had been 'stolen' from the safe, you knew your calculations had been accurate and you exerted the last pressure: You called in Chief of Police Dakin.

"From that point, nothing could go wrong. Dakin would locate the necklace in Simpson's pawnshop, Sally and Howard would be confronted with the necklace, I would be identified by Simpson as the man who had pawned it, in sheer self-defense I'd have to reveal that Howard had asked me to pawn it—and Howard, to keep the story of his adultery with Sally from coming out, would deny it—would bear false witness," said Ellery, "against a particularly witless neighbor."

And Ellery said: "Nine crimes against the Sinaitic decalogue, only two committed by Howard as a free uninfluenced agent, the other seven imposed by you upon Howard as your dupe or actually perpetrated by you physically in the guise of Howard.

"Nine crimes, and when I recognized the grand pattern and so foresaw the inevitable tenth crime, Mr. Van Horn, you were prepared for me, your stage was fully set for your climax.

"Because it was murder you were leading up to, Mr. Van Horn," said Ellery, "double murder to satisfy your cold fury for revenge . . . the murder of your wife for having been unfaithful to you, the murder of your adopted son for having stolen your wife's affections. I include Howard among your murder victims, Mr. Van Horn, because whether he died by legal execution for a murder he didn't commit or by his own hand because he thought he had committed it, his death was murder just the same—and you were his murderer as surely as if your big hands choked his life out. As, in fact, they had choked the life out of Sally."

9

Diedrich's chin had sunk to his breast again, and again his eyes were closed. And, in the wheel chair, he appeared again to be asleep.

But Ellery continued: "When I telephoned you that night to warn you that your life was in danger, Mr. Van Horn, you knew your great moment had come at last. If you had any doubts, they were dispelled when I said it would take me forty or forty-five minutes to get back here. Nothing could have been better suited to your purpose. Forty or forty-five minutes were ample for what you had to do.

"I think, Mr. Van Horn, that you intended to kill Sally that night whether I discovered the Ten Commandments pattern or not. If I didn't discover it before Sally's murder, I could hardly have avoided discovering it afterward, with the evidence you manufactured. And if the very worst happened, and I stupidly failed to discover and name the pattern, no doubt you were prepared for that, too: Simply by revealing the pattern yourself, or making some subtle suggestion to me which would finally open my eyes. God knows you left little or nothing to chance. You'd kept throwing 'tens' at me all through the case—even going to the exquisite trouble of using Room 1010 for the blackmail rendezvous at the Hollis and Room 10 as the depository of the four letters at Upham House and designating Locker 10 at Wrightsville station for the second twenty-five thousand dollars!

"The time I allowed you, as I said, was ample. Wolfert wasn't home—or was it at your suggestion, Mr. Van Horn, that your brother suddenly found he had urgent and important work at the office so late at night? Your mother would probably not leave her room or, if she did, you could easily have handled her. Laura and Eileen were asleep—Wrightsville domestics retire early. So there was little or no danger of interruption. In the phrase which had served similar purposes since it was first used in 1590, Mr. Van Horn—the coast was clear.

"So while I was risking my silly neck speeding back to Wrightsville in the interests of your 'safety,' you calmly went up to Howard's quarters, again had a nightcap with him, again drugged him. Then you went down to the second floor and you asked Sally to come to your bedroom and you strangled her there and placed her body in your bed. And then you went back upstairs and planted four of Sally's hairs in Howard's hand and with a tweezer inserted minute shreds of bloody tissue from Sally's throat under Howard's fingernails. And then you returned to the study here, locked yourself in as I had instructed, and simply waited for my arrival.

"The thing was done. The final brush stroke on a classic canvas. All that remained were a few more lies, another demonstration of your histrionic ability—no great matter for a man of your extraordinary imagination and gifts. As a matter of fact, you outdid yourself that night. Your lies to me, particularly the one about Sally's insisting on waiting up for you in your bedroom to tell you 'something important'—with the implication that she intended to confess her adultery—were nothing short of inspired. And the *way* you led me around to the discovery that Sally was waiting in your bedroom was sheer genius.

"And I was completely taken in, Mr. Van Horn," said Ellery dully, "taken in on all ten counts. You set up the victim for me and I, Ellery Queen, little tin god of cerebration, furnished the *coup de grâce*. My 'brilliant' deductions, plus the indubitable evidence of Sally's hair and the shreds of her flesh in Howard's hand, left no loophole for Howard . . . or for me.

"Because the truth is," said Ellery slowly, "I implemented your heroic frame-up of Howard, Mr. Van Horn. Without me it couldn't have been the perfect thing it was. So I helped you kill Howard, you see. I was your little-tin-god-accessory before, during, and after the fact."

Now Diedrich's great head came up, and his eyes opened, and his loosely fleshed hand made a gesture of impatience.

"You accuse me of this enormous crime," he said with a certain liveliness, "and I must admit—as you put it, it sounds pretty plausible. But—just in the interests of truth, you know—it strikes me your argument fails to take into account the one thing that destroys it."

"Does it?" said Ellery. "Mr. Van Horn, I'd be overjoyed to hear it. I've never before in my life made an analysis I'm more anxious to tear down."

"Well, then, Mr. Queen, relax," said Diedrich, with almost the old boom in his voice. There was a slight flush in his desiccated cheeks as he trundled the wheel chair closer to the desk. "You say Howard didn't kill my wife—although, of course, the boy did, thinking he was killing me. But if Howard was innocent, Mr. Queen, when you charged him with murder *why didn't he deny it?* That's what an innocent man would have done. And then what does he do? He takes his own life! Don't you see? It doesn't wash. Howard was guilty, all right. The poor boy knew you had him with the goods; he *couldn't* deny it. And when he committed suicide he admitted his guilt."

But Ellery was shaking his head. "No go, Mr. Van Horn. Like so many elements in this case, the two you bring up now are true, but only partially. You've employed the half truth, and the appearance of truth, to tremendous advantage throughout.

"Howard didn't deny guilt, true; but not because he was guilty in fact. He didn't deny being guilty because he *thought* he was guilty!

"Howard didn't know you'd drugged him, Mr. Van Horn; he thought, as I thought, that he'd gone through another amnesic episode. What happened during his blackouts always worried Howard. When he came to me in New York, that was uppermost in his mind. And when he asked me to come to Wrightsville, it was for precisely that reason: to keep watching him, to follow him when he went into another blackout, to find out what he did during episodes—whether he was, as he put it, a Dr. Jekyll and Mr. Hyde—because a feature of his blackouts was that *he remembered nothing afterward.*

"You knew all about Howard's amnesia, Mr. Van Horn; it was the keystone of your arch. Howard's mind was obsessed with fear that during his blackouts he committed criminal acts. You knew that, and you knew that when he recovered from what would seem to him—and to me and to everyone else but you—another blackout and discovered that during his blackout Sally had been strangled and some of her hairs and flesh had been found on his hands . . . you knew Howard would believe himself guilty. The entire psychological history of his amnesia had prepared Howard for the unquestioning acceptance of any evidence of his criminality.

"As for his subsequent act of self-destruction, Howard was always a potential suicide, Mr. Van Horn. The suicide climax is implicit in psychological patterns like Howard's. He told me, for example, that when he snapped out of the blackout he suffered in New York—the one that sent him to me—he seriously contemplated throwing himself out of the flophouse window. As a matter of fact, in my first talk Howard, I suspected suicide as an unconscious pattern, and I asked him point-blank if he'd ever come to—come out of a blackout—in the act of trying to kill himself, and he admitted to three distinct experiences of that sort.

"No, there was nothing remarkable about Howard's act of self-destruction after I demonstrated his 'guilt,' Mr. Van Horn. He was convinced he'd murdered Sally, he knew he was through, and he chose the way out which anyone who knew his make-up well—as well, say, as you knew it, Mr. Van Horn—might quite conceivably have predicted.

"While I'm on the subject," Ellery added suddenly, "it occurs to me that virtually every clue pointing to you as the god of the machine was known to me last year, when I obligingly sent Howard to his death for you. There was even a clue in my possession to your knowledge of psychology—a knowledge without which, as I've already said, you couldn't have begun to plan your crimes. You handed me that clue very coolly the first night I met you, during our dinner-table conversation. You introduced the subject of books, and their relation to practical living. And you included, among the few books you said had had practical value to you, 'certain studies of the human mind.' Which ones, Mr. Van Horn? I'm afraid I didn't look your library over carefully enough."

Diedrich was still smiling a little, but Ellery noticed now that there was a resemblance between his smile and Wolfert's, a resemblance which had not been apparent when Diedrich's face had been fuller.

"I think you know, Mr. Queen, what an admirer of yours I've always been—your work in fiction and in life," Diedrich said. "I should have told you last year, while you were visiting here, that in spite of my admiration I've always considered your method—that justly celebrated 'Queen method'—extremely weak in one respect."

"In more than one, I'm afraid," said Ellery. "But which one do you have in mind?"

"Legal proof," said Diedrich pleasantly. "The kind of proof policemen with no imagination and district attorneys with factual training and judges with rules to judge by demand when a man is accused of a crime. The law, unfortunately, isn't impressed with mere logic, no matter how brilliant. It asks for admissible evidence before it's willing to put a defendant in jeopardy."

"Nice point," nodded Ellery. "I'm disinclined to defend myself beyond saying that I've always left the gathering of evidence to those whose business evidence-gathering is. My function has been to detect criminals, not to punish them. I admit that occasionally someone I've put the logical finger on has given the evidence-gatherers a run for their money.

"However," and Ellery's tone grew grim, "I don't think they're going to find this particular job too much for them."

"No?" said Diedrich, and now his smile was remarkably like Wolfert's.

"No. Your feat has been tremendous in sweep, but here and there you've left a hole. The whole concept of yourself as the blackmailer, while daring and imaginative, was also exactly the sort of thing by which men hang. Last year the various pawnbrokers in whose shops you pawned Sally's jewelry could only attempt to describe a free-floating image; they had no frame of reference. Now it will be possible to show these people a photograph of you, or better still to face you with them. While time is on your side, I think it not unlikely that one or two of the pawnbrokers will identify you as the man who pawned that jewelry.

"Then there was the business of the room at the Hollis and the room at Upham House which the blackmailer engaged for the purpose of collecting the first twenty-five thousand dollars. I didn't follow that up at the time because I was pledged not to endanger the negotiations —something, of course, you counted on. But now a thorough checkback will be made. You must have signed two registers. Experts will identify your handwriting. The clerks may even be able to identify you as the man who engaged those rooms.

"The photostats may have been a bluff, but there's a good chance you had at least one set made in case you had to prove you still held a real threat of producible letters. If that's true, the photostats will be traced back to you. Could you have used the facilities of the *Wrightsville Record* you own, I wonder?

"The money itself: Fifty of your five-hundred dollar bills were taken by Howard from your safe here, turned over to me, and I turned them over to the 'blackmailer'— which is to say, back to *you.*" Ellery leaned forward and said softly: "Did you destroy that twenty-five thousand dollars, Mr. Van Horn? I doubt it. The great weakness of your plan was that you were positive you were never be suspected. To have burned fifty five-hundred-dollar bills —your own money—would hardly have occurred to you, a man who came up the hard way, from poverty, a man of big business. But I doubt that you've yet dared to use them. So you probably have those bills hidden somewhere,

Mr. Van Horn; and, I assure you, you'll get no opportunity to destroy them now. By the way—I still have your memorandum of the serial numbers of those bills. I saved it . . . as a memento of my most spectacular 'success.' "

Diedrich was pursing his lips now, frowning.

"I can't say what you did with the second twenty-five thousand dollars, J. P. Simpson's money, which I left for you in the lockers in the Wrightsville station; but maybe the bank still has its record of those bills, and if you've put them where you keep the other bills, that's another nail in your coffin."

"I'm trying to follow, Mr. Queen," said Diedrich, "With respect, believe me! But am I wrong in pointing out that, even if all this be true, all it would do would be to connect me with the blackmailer?"

"All, Mr. Van Horn?" Ellery laughed. "Proving you were the blackmailer would be the prosecution's important job. Because it would establish that you knew all about the adulterous relations between your wife and Howard. It breaks down the one defense you had, psychologically, throughout the whole affair; the presumption that you were ignorant of what is going on. It gives you motive, Mr. Van Horn; it sets the whole case up against you.

"I should imagine the prosecution's case against you," continued Ellery, "difficult as it would be, would set out to prove two things: That you knew your wife was unfaithful with your son, and that you planned to punish both of them—your wife by outright murder, your son by framing him for her death.

"Proof of your knowledge will be established by proving that you were the blackmailer; proof that you planned to punish them both will be established by showing that you were behind all the events which apparently proved that Howard had deliberately broken all Ten Commandments—that is, that you framed Howard. In this connection, I'm afraid my testimony will be crushing. Your lie about having put the Connhaven Detective Agency to work tracing Howard's parents—I'll nail that one, and so will Burmer (who, incidentally, has an excellent reputation in this State). The nonexistence of 'Dr. Southbridge'—I'll nail that lie, too, squarely to you as the liar. And there's always Wolfert to corroborate my testimony—and that's something I'll watch with a great interest, Mr. Van Horn; I mean the spectacle of Wolfert succumbing to his lifelong hatred of you.

"There are numerous other angles for the police to work on, Mr. Van Horn. Such as the drug you must have used to put Howard to sleep on at least two occasions. It may even be necessary to exhume Howard's body to test for the existence of the drug in his remains; if that can be done, it might not be too difficult to connect you with the purchase of such a drug. And so on."

But Diedrich was smiliing faintly again. "A great many conditional clauses, Mr. Queen. But even granting everything you say, I haven't heard a syllable connecting me with the act itself . . . the murder."

"No," said Ellery, "no, that's true. That may well be impossible. But Mr. Van Horn, very few murderers are convicted on direct evidence. A case will be scraped together, a circumstantial case, admittedly, and you'll be tried for murder . . . Yes," said Ellery, after a moment, "I think that's the important thing, Mr. Van Horn. You'll be indicted, you'll stand trial, the whole story will come out, and the great Diedrich Van Horn, who until now has been the object of public sympathy, the betrayed husband and father, will stand revealed for what he is—the supreme egocentric who committed murder for revenge. Not murder on impulse, in the emotional explosion of betrayal discovered, but coldly deliberate, plotted, premeditated murder.

"You're an old man, Mr. Van Horn, and I don't imagine death as such has many terrors for you—you being what you are. But I do think public exposure has. And that will be a far more painful death for you. A much more terrifying punishment. That's the kind of punishment a man suffers even when he's lying in the bottom of a grave."

And now Diedrich was not smiling, nor did he smile again. He sat very quietly in his wheel chair. Ellery did not disturb him. He merely stood there looking at the old man.

But then Diedrich looked up, and he asked almost bitterly: "And if my purpose was to kill the bitch and frame the dog, why didn't I do just that? Why this high-flown, fancy business of the Ten Commandments?"

When Ellery answered, it was in the same even tone; but there was a deep flush on his face.

"A detective would have one answer," he said, "and a psychologist another. The truth is a combination of both.

"For all your physical structure and the practical affairs of business that occupied you all your life, you're essentially a man of the mind, Mr. Van Horn. Like all tyrants, you think. You've never acted on impulse. Everything must be thought out, planned, like a battle, or a political coup. You molded Howard frrom his infancy to a preconceived shape. You planned Sally as deliberately as Howard planned a statue; she thought you fell in love with her suddenly—she was wrong; she didn't know that you determined to marry her from the day you plucked her out of Low Village and started doing her over into the woman you intended to share your kingdom with years hence.

"Your Ten Commandments idea was in many respects the culminating inspiration of your intellectual life. It had scope, sweep, power. It was gigantic. It was worthy of Diedrich Van Horn.

"It began where all logical processes begin: with a premise. Your premise was twofold: You must punish your betrayers; and in punishing them you must yourself be unsuspected. Or, to put it more crudely, you must get away with murder. The injury you suffered was fundamentally to your ego, the ego of a megalomaniac. So the affronted all-powerful had to avenge the affront to his power; and he had to repair the injury to his ego by avenging with impunity—showing that he was above the laws governing ordinary men, that his power was greater than the power of law.

"But it isn't easy to commit murder and frame an innocent person for the murder and remain safe from suspicion. If you had murdered Sally simply and directly, Howard would have been no more a suspect than you; in fact, you would have been the preferred suspect. And if you had framed Howard simply and directly, Howard may well in sheer panic have blurted out the whole story of his relations with Sally, in which case you'd have been revealed as possessing the strongest motive—almost the exclusive motive.

"So your problem, plan-wise, was to make Howard appear to be the only *possible* suspect. But if Howard had a motive to murder anyone, under the circumstances, that one was you, not Sally. Therefore you had to arrange a crime in which apparently Sally had been murdered by Howard *in mistake for you*. And, what's more, Howard himself had to be convinced he'd done it!

"All this, Mr. Van Horn, as you saw, cut your work out for you. It made a complex plot unavoidable. I imagine you rather enjoyed the prospect. The Napoleonic mentality thrives on difficulties; it even seeks them; and sometimes it creates them.

"You took your time. To cover your discovery of the

letters in Sally's jewel box you took the necessary steps to set up the illusion of an outside thief. But thereafter you rested and schemed. Between June and early September you thought, you analyzed, you crystallized your knowledge of your intended victims. You made tentative plans, but you took no action.

"I think what held you up was your realization that the more complex a crime-plan is, the more dangerous for the planner. Every added complication increases the chances for slips, loopholes, unforeseeable accidents of what Thomas Hardy called 'happenstance.' You were groping toward some solution of this very major difficulty when Howard himself gave you your opportunity."

Ellery suddenly caught Diedrich's eye. Their glances locked, and after that the two men held on in a sort of death grip.

"Howard phoned you from New York that he was bringing me back to Wrightsville, or rather that he was coming right home and I was following within a couple of days.

"Instantly you grasped what that could mean to you. The cover of innocence you required, and which your thinking had not been able to evolve, would be amply provided *by me*. How could anyone doubt your innocence or suspect your guilt *if a well-known detective solved the case your way?* It was the answer to everything.

"Oh," said Ellery, "it had its risks. Greater dangers in some ways than not involving me at all. But the beauty of this conception of Ellery-Queen-the-murderer-accomplice, its breadth, its *kind* of risk, thrilled your imagination. Here was a campaign and a struggle worthy of Napoleon himself.

"I daresay you never hesitated."

He stopped; and Diedrich, his great eyes unwavering, said coldly, "Go on."

"Howard phoned you on a Tuesday morning. I arrived in Wrightsville on Thursday. You had two days. *In those two days, Mr. Van Horn, you conceived the Ten Commandments idea and you prepared every phase of it for my arrival.* You invented the story of the Connhaven Detective Agency and its 'investigation.' You worked out the Yahweh anagram, found the graves of Aaron and Mattie Way in Fidelity, added the *E* to the surname. You set in motion the whole business of the Art Museum project—you told me about that on Thursday evening, saying you'd offered to make up the Museum fund deficit *'yesterday'*—which would make it Wednesday, the day *after* Howard's phone call! You went into action with your long-perfected blackmail plan; need I remind you that the blackmailer's first call to Sally also came on Wednesday, the day after Howard told you I was coming to Wrightsville?

"Everything started to move with the announcement of my visit.

"Yes, Mr. Van Horn, you handed me the part of accomplice and I accepted it as gullibly as you knew I would. And I did everything you planned for me to do—danced to your tune at every step of the way. And that was really your greatest triumph, Mr. Van Horn, because I was really your most obedient puppet."

Ellery paused again. He went on with some difficulty.

"The Ten Commandments business was wholly for my benefit. For me to solve the case your way, you had to prepare the kind of case I have a natural affinity for. You knew me very well. Oh, we'd never met, but you told me yourself how you'd read every book I've ever written, how you'd followed my career in the papers—I think you actually used the phrase, 'I'm a Queen expert.' And so you are, Mr. Van Horn, so you are—in a way I didn't dream of until today.

"You knew me better than I knew myself. You knew my working method. You knew my weakness. You knew you had to give me the kind of case I'd fall for, the kind of solution I'd fight to bring to a triumphant conclusion—that I'd believe in!

"You knew I'd prefer the subtle answer to the obvious, always; the complicated rather than the simple; the pyrotechnical over the commonplace.

"You knew I possess a rather grandiose psychological pattern myself, Mr. Van Horn. That I like to think of myself, whether I ever admitted it or not, as a worker in mental marvels. And that's exactly what you gave me—a sort of marvel to perform. A grandiose concept. A steep, labyrinthine trail. A blinding, stunning climax. And I performed for you, Mr. Van Horn. I worked out this stupendous solution for you, and everyone fell flat on his face being impressed with my cleverness—and you were never once suspected.

"The Ten Commandments," said Ellery. "What did the newspapers say? 'Ellery Queen at his greatest.' "

And Ellery continued in the same even, colorless tone: "But it's interesting to note that, in judging me accurately, and as a result of your analysis giving me the Ten Commandments idea to play with, you betrayed something of fundamental importance about yourself, Mr. Van Horn."

A glitter of curiosity came into the eyes.

"All along I'd diagnosed Howard's emotional troubles as being tied in to his psychoneurotic worship of the father-image. I don't think there can be any doubt of that. But when I extended that diagnosis to include Howard's whole conception of the violation of the Ten Commandments as a deliberate revolt against the greatest Father-Image of all, the Fatherhood of God, I was obviously in error, since the Ten Commandments concept wasn't Howard's at all. *It was yours.*

"Why did your brain conceive and hold to that idea, Mr. Van Horn? How did you come to *think* of it? Why the Ten Commandments? You might have conceived a hundred other ideas possessing the attributes you required to impress me into your service. But no—your chose the Ten Commandments. Why?

"I'll tell you why, Mr. Van Horn—the only thing I'll have told you tonight that I think will come as news to you. *Your very choice of the Ten Commandments idea was a clue to you as the guiding mentality if only I'd had the brains to see it.* Not to Howard, but to you.

"I attempted last year, in expounding my pompous little thesis to Prosecutor Chalanski and Chief Dakin and Dr. Cornbranch, to explain that *Howard's* choice of the Ten Commandments weapon—breaking the Father-Image of God in breaking the father-image of you—must have been rooted in his environment as a child . . . in a home where a foster grandmother was obsessed with religion, and so on. But when you really dig into it, that was a pretty weak point—*as it applied to Howard.* Your mother, Mr. Van Horn, according to your own version, has never been an active influence in your household—at least, in Howard's lifetime. She was hardly ever seen; nobody paid much if any attention to her when she was. And Howard was brought up by nurses and tutors; it was their influence which would dominate, not your mother's. And certainly, aside from your mother, this was not an oppressively religious household.

"But how about *you,* and *your* boyhood environment, Mr. Van Horn?—the environment *you* were raised in during the impressionable childhood years? *Your father was an itinerate evangelist, a fundamentalist fanatic who preached the anthropomorphic, personally vengeful, jealous God of the Old Testament—who, as you told me, used to 'beat the hell out of' you and your brother; you were, you said, scared to death of him.* Howard loved his father, Mr. Van Horn, but you hated yours. And it's out of that hatred that your Ten Commandments idea was born . . . a means by which, unknown to your conscious self, you employed your father's own weapons to kill him fifty years after he dropped dead of apoplexy."

And now Ellery said rapidly: "I think this brings us up to date, Mr. Van Horn. You murdered Sally and framed Howard for it, and so Howard's death is also on your hands; I helped you commit these crimes; and we've both, in our fashion, got to pay the penalty."

"Penalty?" said Diedrich. "Both?"

"In our fashion. Mr. Van Horn," said Ellery, "you've destroyed me. Do you understand that? You've destroyed me."

"I understand that," said Diedrich Van Horn.

"You've destroyed my belief in myself. How can I ever again play little tin god? I can't. I wouldn't dare. It's not in me, Mr. Van Horn, to gamble with the lives of human beings. In the kind of avocation I've chosen to pursue there's often a life at stake, or if not a life then a career, or a man's or woman's happiness.

"You've made it impossible for me to go on. I'm finished. I can never take another case."

And Ellery was silent.

Then Diedrich, nodding, asked with a sort of humor: "And my penalty, Mr. Queen?"

Ellery pushed back the swivel chair and with his gloved hands he opened the top drawer of Van Horn's desk.

10

"Because, you see," said Diedrich, watching Ellery's hand, "there's no good can come fom telling the truth to *them.* The truth won't bring her back, Mr. Queen, or him.

"You just think you're finished, Mr. Queen, but I *am.* I'm an old man. I don't have much time left. I've built something in my lifetime. I don't mean this," his gaunt hand waved vaguely, "or my money, or anything unimportant like that. I mean, a *life.* A name. The sort of thing that makes a man go to the grave with just a little sense of waste.

"You're a man of considerable insight, Mr. Queen. You must know that what I did left me with no sense of triumph or satisfaction. Or if you didn't see it, you can see it now simply by looking at what's happened to me.

What's that line in *Lear? 'Tremble, thou wretch, That hast within thee undivulged crimes, unwhipp'd of justice.'* To a man who's three-quarters dead already, Mr. Queen, isn't that penalty enough?"

And Ellery said: "No."

Diedrich said quickly, "I'm a very rich man, Mr. Queen. Suppose I offered you—"

But Ellery said: "No."

"I'm sorry," said Diedrich, nodding. "I spoke on impulse. That was beneath both of us. We can do a great deal of good, you and I. Name a charity and I'll write out a check for one million dollars."

"Five million."

"Not fifty."

Diedrich was silent.

But then he said, "I know money as such means nothing to you. But think of the power it could give you—"

"No."

Diedrich was silent again.

Ellery, too.

And the study. There was not even a clock.

Finally Diedrich said: "There must be something. Every man has a price. Is there anything I can offer you to keep you from going to Dakin?"

And Ellery said: "Yes."

The wheel chair rolled forward quickly.

"What?" asked Diedrich eagerly. "What is it? Name it, and it's yours."

Ellery's gloved hand came out of the desk drawer.

In it glittered the snub-nosed Smith & Wesson .38 safety hammerless he had seen there on the night Van Horn had shown him the rifled safe.

Diedrich's mouth twitched, but that was all.

Ellery laid the revolver back in the drawer.

He did not close the drawer.

He got to his feet.

"You'll write out a note first. Give any excuse you think will ring true—grief, ill health.

"I'll wait outside the study. I don't think you'll demean yourself further by trying to take a pot shot at me; but if you have any such thought in mind, forget it. By the time you can wheel that chair around to this side of the desk to get the gun, I'll be in the other room; and I'll be in the dark.

"I think, Mr. Van Horn, that's all."

Diedrich looked up.

Ellery looked at him.

Diedrich nodded, slowly.

Ellery glanced at his wristwatch. "I give you three minutes." Then he glanced at the desk, the chair, the floor. "Good-by."

Diedrich did not reply.

Ellery stepped quickly around the desk, passed the silent old man, crossed the study, and walked out into the darkness of the room beyond.

He sidestepped and waited, careful not to lean against the wall. He had his wrist close to his face.

And after a few seconds the illuminated dial of his wristwatch began to take form.

A minute passed.

The study was quiet.

Another twenty-five seconds.

He heard the scratching of a pen.

The pen scratched for seventy-five seconds. Then it stopped, and there was a new sound—the slight squeak of the wheel chair.

The squeak of the wheel chair stopped.

And there was another new sound, a clicking sound.

And, very quickly, a shot.

Ellery backed away from the wall and skirted the edge of the area illuminated by the study until he stood in the darkness beyond.

He glanced into the study.

Then he turned and walked unhurriedly through the dark room to the foyer and the front door.

As he eased the front door open he heard a door open upstairs, then another, and a third. Wolfert? Laura? Old Christina?

He heard Wolfert's thin sawing voice cut through the house. "Diedrich! Was that you down there?"

Ellery closed the front door noiselessly.

Lights were springing up in the house.

But he set his feet on the Van Horn driveway and began the long night walk into Wrightsville.

THE KING IS DEAD

Cast of Characters

I

THE INVASION of the Queen apartment occurred at 8:08 o'clock of an ordinary June morning, with West 87th Street just washed down three stories below by the City sprinkler truck and Arsène Lupin in grand possession of the east ledge, breakfasting on bread crumbs intended for a dozen other pigeons of the neighborhood.

It was an invasion in twentieth-century style—without warning. At the moment it exploded, Inspector Queen was poising a spoon edgewise over his second egg, measuring peacefully for the strike; Mrs. Fabrikant had just elevated her leviathan bottom at the opposite side of the room, preparing to plug in the vacuum cleaner; and Ellery was in the act of stepping into the living room, hands at his neck about to pull down his jacket collar.

"Don't move, please."

There had been no noise at all. The front door had been unlocked, the door wedged back against the wall, and the foyer crossed in silence.

The Inspector's spoon, Mrs. Fabrikant's bottom, Ellery's hands remained where they were.

The two men were standing just inside the archway from the foyer. Folded topcoats covered their right hands. They were dressed alike, in suits and hats of ambiguous tan, except that one wore a dark blue shirt and the other a dark brown shirt. They were big men with nice, rather blank faces.

The pair looked around the Queen living room. Then they stepped apart and Ellery saw that they were not a pair but a trio.

The third man stood outside the apartment, straddling the landing to block the public hall. His motionless back was toward the Queen front doorway and he was looking down the staircase.

Blue Shirt suddenly parted company from his twin. He had to pass Inspector Queen at the dropleaf table, but he paid no attention to the staring old gentleman. He went through the swinging door to the kitchen, very fast.

His mate remained in the archway in an attitude of almost respectful attention. His brown shirt added a warm tone to his personality. His right hand appeared, holding a .38 revolver with a pug nose.

Blue Shirt came out of the Queen kitchen and disappeared in Inspector Queen's bedroom.

The Inspector's spoon, Mrs. Fabrikant's bottom, Ellery's hands all came cautiously down at the same moment. But nothing happened except that Blue Shirt came out of the Inspector's bedroom, crossed to the doorway where Ellery stood, stiffarmed Ellery politely out of the way, and went into the study.

The third man kept watching the stairs in the hall.

Mrs. Fabrikant's mouth was working up to a shriek. Ellery said, "Don't, Fabby," just in time.

Blue Shirt came back and said to his partner, "All clear." Brown Shirt nodded and immediately set out across the room, heading for Mrs. Fabrikant. She scrambled to her feet, creamier than the woodwork. Without looking at her, Brown Shirt said in a pleasant voice, "Take the vacuum into one of the bedrooms, Mother, shut the door, and get it going." He stopped at the window.

Arsène Lupin boomed and flew away, and Mrs. Fabrikant fled.

That was when Inspector Queen found his legs and his voice. Jumping to his full five feet four inches, the Inspector bellowed, "Who in the hell are you?"

The vacuum cleaner began to whine like a bandsaw from Ellery's bedroom beyond the study. Blue Shirt shut the study door, muffling the noise. He wedged his back in the doorway.

"If this is a stickup—!"

Blue Shirt grinned, and Brown Shirt—at the window—permitted himself a smile that only briefly shattered his expression. His glance remained on 87th Street below.

"—it's the politest one in history," said Ellery. "You at the window. Would you get nervous if I looked over your shoulder?"

The man shook his head impatiently. A black town car with a New York license plate was just swinging into West 87th Street from Columbus Avenue. Ellery saw its glittering mate parked across the street. Several men were in the parked car.

Brown Shirt's left hand came up, and two of the men in the parked car jumped out and raced across the street to the sidewalk below the Queen windows. As they reached the curb, the car which had turned into 87th Street slid to a stop before the house. One of the men ran up the brownstone steps; the other swiftly opened the rear door of the car and stepped back, looking not into the car but up and down the street.

A smallish man got out of the town car. He was dressed in a nondescript suit and he wore an out-of-shape gray hat. In a leisurely way he mounted the brownstone steps and passed from view.

"Recognize him, Dad?"

Inspector Queen, at Ellery's shoulder, shook his head. He looked bewildered.

"Neither do I."

Brown Shirt was now at the door of the Inspector's bedroom, so that he and Blue Shirt faced each other from opposite sides of the room. Their foreshortened Police Positives dangled at their thighs. Their companion on the landing stepped up to the newel post, and now his right hand was visible, too, grasping a third .38.

Mrs. Fabrikant's machine kept sawing.

Suddenly, out in the hall, the third man backed away.

The smallish man's shapeless hat and undistinguished suit began to rise from the stairwell.

"GOOD morning," said the smallish man, removing his hat. He had a voice like a steel guitarstring.

Seen close up, he was not so small as he had appeared. He was several inches taller than Inspector Queen, but he had the Inspector's small bones and the narrow face structure of many undersized men. His head broadened at the temples and his forehead was scholarly. His skin was bland and firm, with an undertinge of indoor gray, his hair mouse-brown with a tendency to scamper. His eyes, which were protected by squarish rimless glasses, had a bulgy and heavy-lidded look, but this was an illusion; his blinking stare was unavoidable. A growing pot strained the button of his single-breasted jacket, which could have done with a pressing. He looked as if he ought to be wearing a square derby and a piped vest.

He might have been fifty, or sixty, or even forty-five.

Ellery's first impression was categorical: *The absent-minded professor*. The rather highpitched Yankee voice of authority went with examinations and blackboards. But professors, absent-minded or otherwise, do not go about the city accompanied by armed guards in powerful cars. Ellery revised. A general, perhaps, one of the intellectual brass, a staff man who moved mountains from the Pentagon. Or an oldfashioned banker from Vermont. But . . .

"My name," twanged the visitor, "is Abel Bendigo."

"Bendigo!" The Inspector stared. "You're not the Bendigo—"

"Hardly," said Abel Bendigo with a smile. "I take it you've never seen his photograph. But you see what I'm up against, Inspector Queen. These security people are members of my brother's Public Relations and Personnel Department, which is under the command of a very hard fellow named Spring. Colonel Spring—I doubt if you've ever heard of him. He tyrannizes us all, even my brother or, I should say, especially my brother! And so you're Ellery Queen," their visitor went on without so much as a glissando. "Great pleasure, Mr. Queen. I've never got over feeling a bit silly about these precautions, but what can I do? Colonel Spring likes to remind me that it takes only one bullet to turn farce into tragedy. . . . May I sit down?"

Ellery pulled the old leather chair forward, and the Inspector said, "I wish, Mr. Bendigo, you had let us know in advance—"

"The Colonel again," murmured Abel Bendigo, sinking into the chair. "Thank you, Mr. Queen, my hat will do nicely on the floor here. . . . So this is where all the mysteries are solved."

"Yes," said Ellery, "but I believe what's bothering my father is the fact that he's due in his office at Police Headquarters in about twelve minutes, and it's downtown."

"Sit down, Inspector. I want to talk to both of you."

"I can't, Mr. Bendigo—"

"They won't miss you this once. I guarantee it. By the way, I see we've interrupted your breakfast. Yours, too, Mr. Queen—"

"Just coffee this morning." Ellery went to the table. "Will you join us?"

From the side of the room Brown Shirt said, "Mr. Bendigo."

Bendigo waved his slender hand humorously. "You see? Another of Colonel Spring's rules. Finish. Please."

Ellery refilled his father's cup from the percolator and poured a cupful for himself. There was no point in asking this man questions; in fact, there was every point in not. So he stood by the table and sipped his coffee.

The Inspector gulped his breakfast, throwing side glances at his wristwatch in perplexity.

Abel Bendigo waited in silence, blinking. Blue Shirt and Brown Shirt were very still. The man on the landing did not move. Mrs. Fabrikant's vacuum cleaner kept buzzing in a helpless way.

The moment the Queens set their cups down, the visitor said, "What do you gentlemen know about my brother King?"

They looked at each other.

"Got a file on him, son?" asked the Inspector.

"Yes."

Ellery went into his study, Blue Shirt moving aside. When he came back, he was carrying a large clasp envelope. He shook it over the table and a few newspaper and magazine clippings fell out. He sat down and glanced over them.

Abel Bendigo's prominent eyes behind the glasses blinked at Ellery's face.

Finally Ellery looked up. "There's nothing here that amounts to anything, Mr. Bendigo. Sunday supplement stuff, chiefly."

"You know nothing about my brother," murmured the slender man, "beyond what's in those clippings?"

"Your brother is rumored to be one of the five richest men in the world—worth billions. That, I take it, is the usual exaggeration. However, the assumption may be made that he's a man of great wealth."

"Oh yes?" said Abel Bendigo.

"How great makes an interesting speculation. There is in existence an industrial monster known as The Bodigen Arms Company, munitions manufacturers, with affiliates all over the globe. This company is supposed to be owned lock and stock by your brother King. I say 'supposed to be' because the only 'proof' presented in evidence of his alleged ownership is the rather amusing one that Bodigen is an anagram of Bendigo. If it should happen to be true, I salaam. During World War II a single branch of The Bodigen Arms Company—just one branch out of the dozens in existence—showed profits after taxes of some forty-two millions a year."

"Go on," said Abel Bendigo, blinking.

"Your brother, Mr. Bendigo, is also said to be deeply involved in worldwide oil interests, steel, copper, aluminum—all the important metals—aircraft, shipbuilding, chemicals—"

"Anything, that is," said Inspector Queen, dabbling at his mustache, "relating to materials vital to war. I really must be getting downtown, Mr. Bendigo—"

"Not yet." Bendigo crossed his legs suddenly. "Go on, Mr. Queen."

"Personal data," continued Ellery, "are almost as speculative. Your brother seems extremely shy. Little or nothing is known about his background. A photographer for a Kansas newspaper won a national spot-news photography award two years ago for snapping a picture of King Bendigo and managing to get away with an unbroken plate, although the decoy camera by which he pulled off the trick was smashed to crumbs—by these gentlemen here, for all I know. The photo shows a big man, handsome as the devil—I quote an eye witness—at that time fifty-two years old, which makes him fifty-four today. But he looks little more than forty or so, and he carries himself—I quote again—'with an arrogant self-confidence usually associated with twenty.' 'Dressed to kill,' it says here, and you'll forgive me if I wonder whether the reporter was trifling libelously with the English language when he wrote it."

King Bendigo's brother smiled, but then the corners of his mouth dropped and snuffed the smile out.

"I have in my possession," he said slowly, "two letters. They were addressed to my brother. They're threat-letters.

"Now a man in my brother's position, no matter how careful he is to avoid publicity, can hardly avoid cranks. Colonel Spring's PRPD takes all the necessary precautions against that sort of thing as a matter of routine. These letters, however, are a different run of shad."

Bendigo took two folded sheets of paper from his inside breast pocket. "I want you to examine these, please."

"All right," said Ellery, and he came over.

The Inspector rose, too. "Where are the envelopes?"

"King's secretaries discarded them before their importance was appreciated. My brother's staff opens all his mail for sorting and distribution—all, that is, except letters marked 'confidential' or under special seal. These two letters, I understand, were in the ordinary mail."

Ellery made no move to unfold them. "Was no attempt made to recover the envelopes, Mr. Bendigo? From the wastebasket, or wherever they were tossed?"

"There are no wastebaskets at our offices. Each secretary has beside his desk a chute which leads to a central macerating machine. Discarded paper goes down the chute and is chewed to pulp. The pulp feeds automatically into an incinerator."

"Since smoke," murmured Ellery, "can't be yanked out of a file?"

Abel Bendigo's lips pursed. "We have no u… Queen, for mere accumulations."

"Let's see those letters, Ellery," said the Inspector.

The two sheets of paper were identical. They were creamy single sheets, personal letter size, of a fine vellum-type stationery, unmarked by monogram or imprint. In the center of each sheet there was a single line of typewriting.

"The six-word message was the first," said Bendigo.

The six-word message was:

You are going to be murdered—

The dash was not casual. It was impressed into the paper, as if the key had been struck at that point with force.

The message on the second sheet was almost identical with that on the first. The only difference was the addition of two words:

You are going to be murdered on Thursday—

As in the first message, the dash had been physically emphasized.

The Queens studied the two messages.

Bendigo waited.

Finally, the Inspector looked up. "Where in these notes does it say that *your brother King* is going to be murdered, Mr. Bendigo? I don't see any name on these. Anywhere."

"The envelopes, Inspector Queen."

"Did you see the envelopes?"

"No, but the staff—"

"Did anyone but the secretaries who opened them—and threw them down the chute to be destroyed—see the envelopes?"

"No. But they are reliable people, thoroughly screened. Of course, Inspector, you'll have to take my word for that. The envelopes were addressed to King Bendigo." Bendigo was not irritated; if anything, he seemed pleased. "What do you think, Mr. Queen?"

"I see what's bothering you. Threatening letters are usually hand-printed on cheap paper—the block-lettering, commonly in pencil, is almost always unidentifiable, and the cheap paper untraceable. These letters are remarkable for their frankness. The writer did not try to cover his tracks. He used expensive, distinctive notepaper which should be easy to trace. Instead of printing capitals in pencil, he typed his message on a Winchester—"

"Winchester Noiseless Portable," snapped the Inspector.

"—virtually inviting identification. It's almost," said Ellery thoughtfully, "as if he *wanted* the letters to be traced. Of course, they could be a practical joke."

"No one," said Abel Bendigo, "jokes about the death of my brother King."

"Then they make no sense," said Ellery, "at least to me. Do they make sense to you, Mr. Bendigo?"

"It's your opinion, then, that these are the work of a crank."

"No, indeed," murmured Ellery. "They make no sense because they're obviously *not* the work of a crank. The letters are unfinished: the first ends with an emphasized dash, the second adds a fact and ends with another emphasized dash. There is a progression here. So there will be more letters with more information. Since the first letter promises murder and the second promises murder on a Thursday, logically a third letter will specify on which of the fifty-two possible Thursdays the murder is planned to take place. It adds up to cold calculation, not aberration. Why, then, leave an open trail? That's why I say it makes no sense."

The man in the leather chair seemed to weigh Ellery's words, each one carefully.

"How far apart did the letters arrive?" asked the Inspector.

"The second came Monday. The first a week ago."

Ellery shrugged, turning to the mantel and his pipe. "I don't get it. I mean the purpose of all this, Mr. Bendigo. Your establishment is important and powerful enough to employ a private police force of great efficiency. Determining the authorship of these letters should be a kindergarten exercise to your Colonel Spring. Am I seriously to take it that you're proposing to engage me to do it for him?"

"I haven't made myself clear." Abel Bendigo's blandness remained unmarred. "This matter has nothing to do with Colonel Spring or the security department. I have not permitted it to be put in the Colonel's hands . . . I consider it too special a problem. I'm handling it personally."

"And you haven't got anywhere," grinned the Inspector.

"What worries me—" the prominent eyes chilled—" is that I *have* got somewhere."

"Oh," said Ellery. "Then you know who sent the letters?"

"I believe," said Abel Bendigo, "I do."

The Queens exchanged glances.

"Well," demanded the older man, "and who is it?"

Bendigo did not reply.

Ellery looked at the two guards. They had not relaxed.

It was hard to say that they were even listening. "Shall we send these boys out for a beer, Mr. Bendigo?"

"You misunderstand. I'd rather not disclose what I've found because I don't want to prejudice your investigation. I never jump to conclusions, Mr. Queen. And when I reach a conclusion I invariably double-check it. There's always the possibility—though not the probability—that in this matter I'm wrong. I want you gentlemen to tell me whether I am or not."

"And your brother King? What does he think of all this, Mr. Bendigo?"

"He glanced at the letters and laughed. Threats amuse him. They don't amuse me."

"Then he doesn't know the results of your private investigation? Or even that you've been investigating?"

Bendigo shrugged. "I haven't told him. What he knows or doesn't know is another matter." He said abruptly, "I want you both to come with me."

"This morning?"

"This minute."

Inspector Queen stared as if Abel Bendigo were out of his mind.

Ellery smiled. "My father is a salaried employee of the City of New York, Mr. Bendigo. And while I'm a relatively free soul, the necessity of earning a living has managed to foul me up in responsibilities and commitments. You can't walk in here and expect us to get up and walk out with you—with even you, Mr. Bendigo—on five minutes' notice."

"Your father has been taken care of—"

"Hold it." The Inspector deliberately went back to the dropleaf table and sat down. "And how would you go about 'taking care of' me, Mr. Bendigo?"

But Bendigo said patiently, "As for you, Mr. Queen, you're between novels and you are four issues ahead with the editorial work on *Ellery Queen's Mystery Magazine.* And the only investigation on your calendar at the present time has been taken out of your hands."

"Has it?" said Ellery. "That's news to me."

"If you'll glance through your morning mail, you'll find a note from a man named Harold P. Consideo terminating your connection with his affairs."

Ellery looked at him. He went to the table after a moment and picked up the letters on his breakfast plate. He shuffled through them and came to one that made him stop and look at Abel Bendigo again. Then he tore off the end of the envelope.

A letter fell out. Ellery glanced through it. The Inspector reached over and took the letter and he read it, too.

"Mr. Bendigo," said Ellery, "what makes you think you can interfere in my life this way?" The man in the chair drummed on the leather. "How well do you know Considеo?"

"I don't know him at all. These things are easily arranged. Let's not waste time on Consideo. Are you ready?"

"Me?" said Ellery. "I think not."

"How long will it take you?"

"Too long, Mr. Bendigo, for your busy schedule."

Bendigo opened his pink mouth. But then he shut it and regarded Ellery earnestly. "Why do you take this attitude?"

"A shoehorn has nothing to say about who buys it or the use it's put to. A man wants to feel that he has. Mr. Bendigo," said Ellery, "I like to be asked."

"And I'm his old man," said his father.

"I apologize. We Bendigos live in something of a vacuum. Of course, you're perfectly right." He leaned forward, pudgy hands clasped like a deacon. "Making sure who wrote these letters is of great importance, and not only to me. The assassination of my brother would be followed by the most serious consequences all over the world." He was choosing his words with care. Now he looked up at them with a smile. "Would you gentlemen accept the assignment?"

Ellery smiled back. "Where are your headquarters?"

"On Bendigo Island."

"Bendigo Island . . . I don't believe I know it. Do you, Dad?"

"I've heard tell," said the Inspector dryly, "but I can't tell you where it is."

"It's not well-known," said their visitor. "And you won't find it on any chart."

"Where is it?"

Abel Bendigo looked regretful. "I really mustn't say, Mr. Queen. It's one of our strictest rules. You'll be taken there and returned to this apartment when the job is done."

"How far away is it?"

"I wish I were free to tell you."

"How long does it take to get there from New York?"

"Planes travel fast these days. Not too long."

Ellery shrugged. "I'm afraid, Mr. Bendigo, I'll have to think it over."

"And *I'm* afraid," said Inspector Queen, getting out of his chair, "I'll have to be moseying on down to Centre Street. Interesting experience meeting you, Mr. Bendigo, and I've never meant anything more in my life."

"Call your office first, Inspector."

"What for?"

"You'll find that, as of this morning, you're on leave of absence. On full pay."

"Now I know this is a pipe dream!"

The Inspector, russet about the ears and neck, stamped past Brown Shirt into his bedroom. Abel Bendigo quietly waited. Ellery heard his father's voice, on his direct wire to Police Headquarters, raised in outrage, as if a leave of absence on full pay were cruel and unusual punishment. When the Inspector came out, however, he was looking thoughtful.

"Nobody seems to know how it happened or why!"

Bendigo smiled again. "Mr. Queen, you'll change your mind?"

"I can't very well change it when I haven't yet made it up."

Bendigo rose, glancing at his wristwatch. Something final glittered from his eyeglasses. "I was asked not to use this unless it became necessary, Mr. Queen. You've left me no choice." He handed a long envelope to Ellery. Then he turned to one of the windows, clasping his hands at his back.

The Inspector glared at the envelope. It was addressed by hand to *Mr. Ellery Queen, New York City*. The reverse was heavily sealed with wax.

Ellery broke the seal. The envelope contained a single sheet of very stiff notepaper. The embossing at the top of the sheet made him glance quickly at their visitor.

The letter was entirely handwritten:

MY DEAR MR. QUEEN:

This request has no official status and is made in strictest confidence. Regardless of your decision, I must ask you to destroy this letter immediately upon reading its contents.

Will you put your professional services at the disposal of bearer?

In doing so you would be performing an act of high citizenship, in a matter in which your government has a vital interest but in which it cannot participate by the normal means, for reasons which I may not disclose.

It would be helpful, in the event you undertake the assignment, if your father would make a special point of joining you.

Yours sincerely,

Ellery studied the famous signature for a long moment. "Mr. Bendigo, are you aware of the contents of this letter?"

"I have a fair idea of what it says," was the dry reply.

"But why me?" muttered the Inspector.

"What, Inspector?" Abel Bendigo turned.

"Excuse us, Mr. Bendigo, for just a few minutes," said Ellery.

Bendigo said nothing.

BLUE Shirt stood aside and the Queens went into Ellery's study. Ellery shut the door in the blank face and carefully turned the key.

Mrs. Fabrikant's vacuum cleaner was still keening behind the bedroom door.

"I don't get it," murmured Ellery. "Granted that King Bendigo is large pumpkins, that his activities touch on national interests, and that the Bendigo name drags enough weight to get a letter like this out of Washington —why either of us?"

"If this isn't a forgery, son."

"Somehow I don't see forgery in that fellow's horoscope."

"Call Washington," said his father. "Just for the hell of it."

Ellery put the call through with some excitement and no conviction. Yet six minutes later, against all reason, he heard the voice of the letter writer in his ear. There was no mistaking those dry, easy tones.

"No, it's all right, Mr. Queen, I was hoping you'd check. When B. asked for a letter, I wrote it with care." The speaker chuckled. "In spite of the seal."

"May I talk freely, sir?"

"This is a private line."

"Was it B.'s idea to hire me?"

"Yes."

"You're aware, of course, of the nature of the case?"

"Yes, indeed. Someone is threatening His Majesty's life." The dry tones were drier than usual. "B. thinks he knows who it is, wants confirmation. Since he does, I reminded him that a brace of good heads is preferable to one, and I suggested your father go along, too. I have something—I think I used the word 'special'?—in mind for Inspector Queen. Are you going to accept?"

"Yes, sir."

"Good! The United States government is extremely—

if unofficially—interested in keeping up to date on the state of His Majesty's health. Is your father there?"

"Yes, sir."

"Let me talk to him."

Inspector Queen said, "Yes, sir?" and then he listened for a long time. After which he said, "Yes, *sir,*" and hung up.

"I thought that last paragraph concealed a weenie," muttered Ellery. "What does he want you to do, Dad?"

"Give him a confidential report on Bendigo Island. What's on it, who's on it—plant, personnel, plans, purposes, detail maps if possible—the whole picture, Ellery."

"Do you mean to say our own government doesn't know—!"

"Apparently not. Or what they know is sketchy or not up to date. So I've got to grow a tail in my old age," said the Inspector incredulously, "and make like the Trojan horse."

"What fun."

They grinned at each other suddenly, shook hands, and then Ellery went into his bedroom to calm Mrs. Fabrikant, give her some money and instructions about the apartment, and pack a bag. Before leaving he burned the Washington letter and envelope in the brass ashtray on his night table and used the nozzle of Mrs. Fabrikant's vacuum cleaner to suck up the ashes.

II

THE TWO CARS skirted La Guardia Airport and drew up before a hangar with a gilded roof on which was lettered in black the single giant word, BENDIGO. The hangar was filled with aircraft of varying sizes and types, but all uniformly golden and inscribed with the unqualified name. An immense passenger plane loomed before the hangar, its motors warming up. Attendants in black and gold coveralls swarmed over the plane.

Blue Shirt carried the bags. A Bendigo plane was taking the air from one of the field runways, and Ellery asked him, "Where's that one going? Or is such a question on Colonel Spring's *verboten* list?"

"Buenos Aires, Johannesburg, Teheran—I wouldn't know, sir. Hurry, please."

Brown Shirt was friendlier. "We'll be on the plane with you. . . . Help you up the step, sir?"

The Inspector growled, "Not if you want to stay healthy!"

They found Abel Bendigo waiting for them in the big ship. Its interior made them blink. It was fitted out like a private railroad car, with deep leather chairs, lamps, books, a central bar, and several compartments. The attendants—Ellery counted five, and he suspected others—wore black and gold uniforms. There were no women attendants and no other passengers.

"We're taking off at once, gentlemen," said Abel Bendigo abruptly. "The stewards will see to your wants. I'll have to ask you to excuse me. My work . . ." His voice trailed off as he turned away. Two dark-suited, middle-aged men carrying portfolios were waiting for him at the door of one of the compartments. He brushed by them and they followed him quickly. A moment later the compartment door was shut.

Rather pointedly, Ellery thought.

The ship began to move.

"Would you take seats, please?" said Brown Shirt's pleasantly chill voice.

He strapped them into two of the armchairs.

"You forgot the electrodes," muttered the Inspector.

Ellery said nothing. He was watching Blue Shirt. Blue Shirt was moving from window to window, pulling down metal-vaned black blinds and securing them to the sills.

"ALL this hush-hush," said Ellery. They had felt the lift of the ship and heard the motors settle down to a comfortable thunder, and Ellery had even made a note of the take-off time, but these were mechanical observations in a hopeless cause. "How secret can you keep an island?"

"There probably aren't five men in the United States who know where it is."

"How do you know?"

"I heard an earful from one of the brass who'd been head of liaison at Bendigo Midwestern headquarters, in Illinois, till about two years after the war. He was feeling brotherly after six Martinis—I'd got his son out of a bad jam in New York."

"—I don't get the point of it all," said Ellery, staring at the blinded windows.

"Seems this King Bendigo's always been a secretive gent," said the Inspector reflectively. "Some men never grow up. Play the same games, on a bigger scale. He probably had a dark cellar as a kid, a secret hideout, and buried treasure you got to with a map drawn in blood.

"Take this island of his. There's no earthly reason the General could see why Bendigo would need an island home office. Or why, if he had to have an island, he'd make a mystery of its whereabouts. During the war he operated from the mainland, like anybody else."

"Then Bendigo Island is a postwar development?"

"Yes and no. The way I heard it, the island was owned by one of our allies. England or France, maybe, but I'm guessing. It was one of those islands that never got onto a map, like so many in the Pacific, only this one is supposed to be in the Atlantic."

"I don't believe it. I mean that it's not on the map."

"I'm not asking you to believe it," said his father. "I'm telling you what I heard. The likeliest explanation is that it's on the map, all right, but as an uninhabited island. Maybe surrounded by dangerous reefs and off the regular sea and air lanes.

"Well, during the war," continued the Inspector, "the government that owned the island decided to prepare it for an emergency hideout. It may have been during the Battle of Britain, if it was England. If it was France, it was probably after the fall of Paris but before De Gaulle fell afoul of F.D.R.

"Anyway, the British, or the French Resistance, or what-have-you, began secret construction on the island. It was then known as Location XXX, and only a few of the top brass in Washington knew anything about it. It was done with the consent of the United States government, of course—for all I know, with us supplying most of the materials.

"According to the General's story, they built for keeps—a tremendous administration building, a lot of it underground, shelters, barracks, arsenals, factories, a couple of airfields—the works; they even dredged out an artificial harbor. The idea was that if the government of the country that owned the island had to leave home base in a hurry, this was where they'd evacuate to. The whole shoreline was camouflaged and the waters around the island mined. The development of radar made it possible to anticipate the approach of aircraft, too."

Ellery said darkly, "I've never heard a syllable of this."

"You weren't supposed to. It was one of the best-kept secrets of the war. As it turned out, the island was never used. The installations were finished just about when the European phase of the war ended. And after Hiroshima, atomic developments made the whole project seem kind of silly."

"And Bendigo bought it?"

"Leased it on a ninety-nine-year lease. Complete, just the way they'd built it, right down to the radar. The lease was cleared with Washington, but even if Washington didn't like the idea they couldn't do much about it. Bendigo had been too important during the war. And he's still at it."

The Inspector stopped. One of the uniformed stewards was approaching.

"Would you gentlemen care for your luncheon now?"

Brown Shirt was strolling their way.

"Later, I think," Ellery said. "Unless we land soon?"

"I can't say about that, sir," said the steward.

"Don't you know when we set down? I'm not asking you where. I'm just asking when."

"I can't say about anything, sir, but lunch." The steward retreated, and Brown Shirt turned away.

"Relax," grinned Inspector Queen. "These people are said to go through a screening that makes an F.B.I. atomic project clearance look like a vag booking in the Squedunk Corners pokey." Then he looked grim. "This island of Bendigo's is no joke. Bendigo's supposed to have a private army there. For that matter, his own navy and air force, too."

"Navy?" said Ellery incredulously. "Air force? You mean shooting stuff?"

The Inspector shrugged. "I can only tell you what the General told me. Maybe he was pulling my leg. But he mentioned at least two ex-warships, a light cruiser and a heavy cruiser, and a system of submarine nets and underwater detectors, as well as a couple of submarines. The shoreline's still camouflaged and the radar works twenty-four hours a day. You might say it's a whole new little country. Autonomous. Whom would Bendigo have to account to? I guess that's why Washington is so interested."

"His Christian name begins to impress me. Shooting stuff . . . What's he expect, an invasion?"

"Don't be childish. Nobody invades a man as powerful as King Bendigo. Not because you couldn't wipe him off the map he isn't on, but because he's in too many places at the same time. He's spread all over the globe. Bendigo Island's just the—the concentration of his personality, his court, you might say. It's just that, by the way, from what the General said. Bendigo's added a real palace to the island. . . . No, I imagine the shooting stuff—his 'army,' his 'navy,' his 'air force'—it's all kind of automatic. It goes with power. It's for show, like a throne. No self-respecting royalty without it."

"But it's . . . outmoded, all that," complained Ellery. "He can't be a boy playing with lead soldiers. What are a couple of warships and a few planes in the world of A- and H-bombs? Beanshooters. I don't get it."

The Inspector shrugged again and looked around. The steward anticipated him. There was a bottle at his elbow immediately, and a glass.

Ellery squirmed in the chair. He got up. But then he sat down again.

The Inspector sipped, leaned back, closed his eyes. The motors flowed on like a waterfall. He felt sleepy suddenly.

But his arm was prodded and he opened one eye.

"His family," Ellery mumbled.

"Hm?"

"His family. Does it consist of his brother Abel and himself exclusively? Is King married? Children? Parents? What do you know about him personally, Dad?"

The Inspector struggled awake. "There are three brothers, not two. No sisters, and if their parents are living the General doesn't know about them. Only one of the brothers is married, and that's King himself. No children. Take a snooze, son."

But Ellery said, "Who's the third brother? Where does he fit?"

"Hmm?" The Inspector opened the eye again. "Judah?"

"Who?"

"Judah Bendigo. He's the middle one. King's the eldest of the three. Abel's the baby. Abel is sort of the Prime Minister—he and King are very close. But Judah . . . the General didn't know *what* he did in the outfit. Didn't see Judah do anything but lap up brandy. His impression was Judah's a lush."

"Who is King's wife?"

"The Queen. Who else?" murmured his father with a drowsy grin. "Queen Karla . . . well, almost. The General said Karla's of real royal blood. From Europe. A princess, or grand duchess, or something."

"Now tell me she's a raving beauty, and I'll take on Blue Shirt with one hand behind my back!"

"A knockout, the General said. He had to visit the island several times."

Ellery muttered, "And the Court Jester? Of course, there's a Court Jester."

"Max is his name," nodded the Inspector. "An ex-wrestler, big as a house. Follows King around, works him out, bodyguards him, keeps him laughing. Everything but the cap and bells. Shut up, will you? I'm an old man."

And the Inspector shut the other eye, decisively.

ABEL Bendigo joined them at lunch. He seemed less preoccupied. The two middle-aged secretaries did not appear.

The stewards had set the table for only two, and Ellery remarked that in an organization as perfectly oiled as this it seemed a mighty slip—or was one of them to be starved?

"I never eat lunch," said the Prime Minister with a smile. "Interferes with my afternoon work. A glass of buttermilk sometimes, or yoghurt. But don't let that stop you gentlemen. The chef was detached from my brother's Residence staff especially for the occasion."

The lunch was superb, and the Inspector tackled it with gusto. Ellery ate absently.

"Are your brothers as Spartan as you are, Mr. Bendigo?" asked the Inspector. "My, this is delicious."

"Very nearly. King has simple tastes in food, as I have, and Judah—" Abel Bendigo stopped smiling—"Judah hardly eats at all."

"Judah?" said Ellery, looking up.

"Another brother, Mr. Queen. Will you have some brandy? I'm told this is exceptional, though I don't drink myself."

"Judah," said Ellery. "And Abel. The 'King' doesn't seem to follow, Mr. Bendigo. Or was he a king in Israel from the womb?"

"I think," said Bendigo, "he was." And he looked up. The Queens looked up, too. Blue Shirt and Brown Shirt loomed there.

"What now?" asked the Inspector humorously. "The execution?" Nevertheless he quickly swallowed the last of his brandy.

Bendigo said slowly, "We've come about halfway, gentlemen. From here until we land these two men will remain with you. I'm sure you'll understand, if not appreciate, the necessity to stick to rules. I regret it, but I must ask you to make no attempt to get your bearings. These men are under the strictest orders to prevent it." He got up suddenly. "You'll see me on the island." Before either could open his mouth the Prime Minister had retired to his compartment again.

The twins did not move.

"Halfway," muttered the Inspector. "That means about eight hours out. At, say, three hundred m.p.h., the island's around twenty-four hundred miles from New York. Or is it?"

"Or is it?" said Ellery, looking up at Brown Shirt.

Brown Shirt said nothing.

"Because, of course, we can be flying around in circles. . . . Funny way Bendigo put that parting crack of his, Dad. Why *you'll see me on the island* instead of the more natural *I'll see you on the island?"*

Hours later, in the middle of a nap, Ellery was answered.

He awoke at a touch to find himself in total darkness, and when he heard his father's outraged exclamation he knew that they had both been blindfolded.

III

WHEN the dark cloths were removed, the son and the father found themselves standing with Brown Shirt and Blue Shirt beside the big ship, on a great airfield.

The midafternoon sun rode an intense sky, and they blinked in the backwash of glare.

Abel Bendigo was close by talking to an undersized man. Behind the undersized man stood a squad of tall soldiers, at attention. The undersized man had prim shoulders and large hips and he was dressed in a beautiful black and gold military uniform. The black cap he wore sported a linked-globe-and-crown insignia above the visor and the legend PRPD. This officer, who was smoking a brown cigaret, turned from time to time to stare at the Queens with the friendliness of a fish. Once he shook his head as if it were all too much for him to bear. However, he bore it—whatever it was—with resignation. The Prime Minister talked on.

They faced a camouflaged administration building. Men in black and gold suits moved above in the glassed circle of the control tower. Ground crews swarmed about a dozen large hangarlike structures, also camouflaged. Planes flitted about, field ambulances raced, commissary trucks trundled; all were painted black and gold. A very large cargo ship was just taking the air.

A high wall of vegetation surrounded the field, screening off the rest of the island. The vegetation seemed semitropical and much of it had the underwater look of Caribbean flora. And Ellery had never seen a sky like this in the North Temperate zone. They were in southern waters.

He had the queerest feeling that they were also in a foreign land. Everyone about him looked American and the airfield buildings betrayed a functional vigor inseparable from advanced American design—Frank Lloyd Wrightism at its angriest. It was the air that was alien, a steel atmosphere of discipline, of trained oneness, that was foreign to the American scene.

And then there was the flag, flapping from a mast above the control tower. It was like no flag Ellery had ever seen, a pair of linked globes in map colors surmounted by a crown of gold, and all on a black field. The flag made him uncomfortable and he looked away. His glance touched his father's; it had just come from the flagpole, too.

They said nothing to each other because the Shirts were so attentively at their elbows, and because there was really nothing to communicate but questions and doubts which neither could satisfy.

The Prime Minister finished at last, and the hippy little man in the splendid uniform waved the squad of soldiers away. They wheeled and marched to the administration building and disappeared. Bendigo walked over with his companion. The Shirts, Ellery noted, stiffened and saluted. But it was not Abel Bendigo they saluted; it was the hippy little man.

"Sorry to have kept you waiting," Bendigo said, but he did not explain why. "This is the head of our Public Relations and Personnel Department, Colonel Spring. You'll probably be seeing something of each other."

The Queens said a word or two.

"Anything I can do, gentlemen," said Colonel Spring, offering a limp white hand. His eyes remained fishy. His whole face was marine—greenish white and without plasticity, like the face of a drowned man.

"Isn't the question rather, Colonel," Ellery asked, "anything *we* can do?"

The underwater eyes regarded him.

"I mean, your PRPD seems to lean heavily to the military side. What are our restrictions?"

"Restrictions?" murmured Colonel Spring.

"Well, you see, Colonel," remarked Inspector Queen, "there's never any telling where a thing like this can lead. How free are we to come and go?"

"Anywhere." The white hand fluttered. "Within reason."

"There are certain installations," said Abel Bendigo, "which are out of bounds, gentlemen. If you're stopped anywhere, you'll understand why."

"And you'll be stopped," said the Colonel with a smile. "You're going directly to the Home Office, Mr. Abel?"

"Yes. Excuse us, Colonel."

The little officer rather deliberately ground the butt of his *cigarillo* under his boot heel. Then he smiled again, touched his visor with his delicate fingers, and turned curtly away.

The Shirts instantly followed.

"Valuable man," said the Prime Minister. "Gentlemen?"

The Queens turned. A black limousine had come up on silent treads and a footman in livery was stiffly holding the door open. To the front door was attached a gold medallion, showing two linked globes surmounted by a heavy crown.

Like a coat of arms.

* * *

THE airport was on high ground, and when the car drove through the screen of vegetation the Queens had a panoramic view of half the island.

They realized at once why this island has been selected as the site of a government-in-hiding. It was shaped like a bowl with a mound in the center. The shoreline, which was the edge of the bowl, was composed of steep and heavily wooded cliffs, so that from the sea no evidence of human occupancy or construction in the interior would be visible. The mound in the middle of the bowl, where the airfields lay, was at approximately the same elevation as the wooded cliffs at the shoreline. Between the central airfields and the cliffs on the rim, the ground sloped sharply to a valley. It was in this valley, invisible from the sea, that all the building had been done.

The sight was startling. It was a large island, the valley

was great, and as far as the eye could see the valley was packed with buildings. Most of them seemed industrial plants, vast smokeless factories covering many acres; but there were office buildings, too, and to the lower slopes of the hillsides clung colonies of small homes and barracklike structures which, Abel Bendigo explained, housed the workers. The small homes were occupied by minor executives. There was also, he said, a development of more spacious private dwellings on another part of the island; these were for the use of the top executives and the scientific staffs and their families.

"Families?" exclaimed the Inspector. "You mean you've got housewives and kids here, too?"

"Of course," replied the Prime Minister, smiling. "We provide a normal, natural environment for our employees. We have schools, hospitals, recreation halls, athletic fields—everything you'd find in a model community in the States, although on a rather crowded scale. Space is our most serious problem."

Ellery thought preposterously: *Lebensraum.*

"But food, clothing, comic books," said Inspector Queen feebly. "Don't tell me you produce all that!"

"No, though if we had the room we certainly would. Everything is brought in by our cargo fleets, chiefly airborne."

"You find planes more practicable than ships?" asked Ellery.

"Well, we have a problem with our harbor facilities. We prefer to keep our shoreline as natural-looking as possible—"

"There's the harbor now, Ellery!" said the Inspector.

"I'm sorry," said Bendigo, suddenly austere. He leaned forward to say something to the chauffeur in a low tone. The car, which was speeding along inside the rim of woods, immediately turned off into a side road and plunged down to the valley again. But Ellery had snatched a glimpse, through a break in the vegetation, of a horseshoe-shaped bay very nearly landlocked, across the narrow neck of which rode a warship.

The chauffeur had gone slightly pale. He and the footman sat rigidly.

"We didn't really see anything, Mr. Bendigo," said Ellery. "Just a heavy cruiser. One of your naval vessels?"

"My brother's yacht *Bendigo,*" murmured the Prime Minister.

Inspector Queen was staring down into the valley with glittering eyes. "Yacht my sacroiliac," he snapped. "These food and other supplies, Mr. Bendigo. Do you give the stuff away, or how do you handle it? What do you pay your people off in?"

"Our banks issue scrip, Inspector, accepted by Company stores as well as by individuals all over the island."

"And when a man wants to quit, or is fired, does he take his Bendigo scrip with him?" asked Ellery.

"We have very few resignations, Mr. Queen," said the Prime Minister. "Of course, if an employee should be discharged, his account would be settled in the currency of the country of his origin."

"I don't suppose your people find unions necessary?"

"Why, we have unions, Mr. Queen. All sorts of unions."

"No strikes, however."

"Strikes?" Bendigo was surprised. "Why should our employees strike? They're highly paid, well housed, all their creature comforts provided, their children scientifically cared for—"

"Say." Inspector Queen turned from the window as if the thought had just struck him. "Where do all your working people come from, Mr. Bendigo?"

"We have employment offices everywhere."

"And recruiting offices?" murmured Ellery.

"I beg your pardon?"

"Your soldiers, Mr. Bendigo. They are soldiers, aren't they?"

"Oh, no. The uniforms are for convenience only. Our security people are not—" Abel Bendigo leaned forward, pointing. "There's the Home Office."

He was smiling again, and Ellery knew they would get no more information.

THE Home Office looked like a rimless carriage wheel thrown carelessly into a bush. Trees and shrubbery crowded it, and its roofs were thickly planted. From the air it was probably invisible.

Eight long wings radiated like spokes from a common center. The spokes, Abel Bendigo explained, housed the general offices, the hub the executive offices. The hub, four stories high, stood one story higher than the spokes, so that the domed top story of the central building predominated.

Not far away, Ellery noticed some mottled towers and pylons and the glitter of glass rising from the heart of a wood. The few elements of the structure that could be seen extended over a wide area, and he asked what it was.

"The Residence," replied the Prime Minister. "But I'm

afraid we'll have to hurry, gentlemen. We're far later than I'd intended."

They followed him, alert to everything.

They entered the Home Office at the juncture of two of the spokes, through a surprisingly small door, and found themselves in a circular lobby of black marble. Corridors radiated from the perimeter in every direction. An armed guard stood at the entrance to each corridor. They could see office doors, endless lines of them, each exactly like the next.

In the center of the lobby rose a circular column of extraordinary thickness. A door was set into it at floor level, and Ellery guessed that it was an elevator shaft. Before the door was a metal booth, behind which stood three men in uniform. The collars of their tunics bore the gold initials PRPD.

Abel Bendigo walked directly to the desk of the booth. To the Queen's astonishment, he offered his right hand to the central of the three security men. This functionary quickly took an impression of the Prime Minister's thumb while the man to his right whisked an odd-looking card, like a section of X-ray film set in a cardboard frame, from one of a multiplicity of file drawers before him. This film was placed in a small machine on the desk, and the Prime Minister's thumbprint was inserted in the bottom of the machine. The central man looked through an eyepiece carefully. The machine apparently superimposed on the fresh thumbprint the transparent control print on file, in such a way that any discrepancy was revealed at a glance. This was confirmed a few moments later when the Queens' thumbprints were taken and their names recorded.

"Films of your prints will be ready in a short time," said Bendigo, "and they will go into the control file. No one, not even my brother King, can get into any part of this building without a thumbprint checkup."

"But these men certainly know you and your brother!" protested Inspector Queen.

"Exceptions don't make the rule, Inspector. They break it. Will you step in, gentlemen?"

It was a self-service elevator. It shot upward, and a moment later they preceded their guide into a strange-looking reception room.

It was shaped like a wedge of pie with a bite taken out of its pointed end, the bite being formed by the section of elevator wall giving into the room. They discovered later that the whole pie represented by the floorplan of the dome was composed of three pieces, of which the reception room was the narrowest and smallest. King Bendigo's private office took up half the circle. The third room, for King's staff of private secretaries, and the reception room made up the other half-circle. The elevator had three doors, one to each of the rooms.

The outside wall of the reception room was composed entirely of fluted glass bricks. There were no windows, but the air was cool and sweet.

The room was stark. There were a few functional armchairs of black leather, a low copper table six feet in diameter, a small black desk and chair, and that was all. Not a lamp—the two side walls themselves glowed—not a vase or flower, not a picture. And no rug on the floor, which was made of some springy material in a black and gold design. There was not even the solace of a loud voice, for no receptionist received them in this queer reception room, and it was so thoroughly soundproofed that a voice could not be heard fifteen feet away.

Abel Bendigo said: "My brother is tied up just now." How he knew this Ellery could not imagine, unless the Prime Minister had memorized his sovereign's schedule for days in advance. "It will take—" Bendigo glanced at his wristwatch—"another twenty-three minutes. Make yourselves comfortable, gentlemen. Cigarets and cigars on the table there, and if you'd care for liquid refreshment, there's a cabinet in that wall. And now please excuse me. I was to have sat in at this conference from the beginning. I'll be back for you when King is free."

There were two doors with conventional knobs in the reception room, one in each of the straight walls. Abel Bendigo slipped through the lefthand door and shut it before either man could catch a glimpse of what lay beyond.

They looked at each other.

"Alone," said Ellery, "at last."

"I wonder."

"You wonder what, Dad?"

"Where it's planted."

"Where what's planted?"

"The ear. Of the listening business. If this is where His Nibs keeps visitors waiting, you don't think he'd pass up the chance to find out what's really on their minds? Ellery, how's this setup strike you so far?"

"Incredible."

The Inspector sank uneasily into one of the black armchairs.

Ellery strolled over to the elevator door. Like the one

in the lobby, it had sunk into the floor on their arrival and had risen shut again. The door section fitted so cunningly into the curved shaft wall that it took him a long moment to locate the crack which outlined it.

"You'd need a nuclear can-opener to get this open." Ellery went over to the door in the righthand wall. "I wonder where this goes."

"Probably an outer office."

Ellery tried the door; it was locked. "For his forty-nine secretaries. Do they wear uniforms, too, I wonder?"

"I'm more interested in King King. What are the odds he wears ermine?"

"Nobody trusts anybody around here," Ellery complained. He was over at the door in the lefthand wall now.

"Better not," advised his father. "It might open."

"No such luck." Ellery was right; the door to King Bendigo's office, through which they had seen Abel hurry, was fast. "Sealed in, that's what we are. Like a couple of damned anchovies."

The Inspector did not smile. "We're a long way from Eighty-seventh Street, son."

"Stiff upper." But the quip did not amuse even its author.

Ellery surveyed the small black desk. It was of heavy metal, screwed to the floor. Its empty swivel chair, of the same metal, faced the smooth cylindrical section of the elevator.

"I wonder why the receptionist isn't here."

"Maybe he had to go to the men's room."

"I doubt if the Bendigo code recognizes hand-washing as a legitimate excuse for dereliction of duty. Besides," Ellery tried a few drawers, "the desk is locked. No, here's a drawer that isn't." It was the bottom drawer, a deep one.

His father saw him stare, then drop into the chair. "What is it?"

"Dictaphonic gadget of some sort." Ellery was doubled over. "Of a type new to me. I wonder if . . ." There was a *click!* and a faint whirring sound. Ellery whistled softly. "Do you suppose this can be hooked up to the big boy's office?"

The Inspector jumped out of the armchair. "Careful, son!"

"He'd want records of private talks. Too bad we won't have the chance to lift the record of the one that's going on in there right now—"

"*—overexcited. Sit down, Mr. Minister.*"

The easy male voice boomed in their ears. The Queens whirled. But, except for themselves, the reception room was empty.

"The machine," whispered the Inspector. "Ellery, what did you touch?"

"Does double duty." The voice had not resumed, but the whirring sound continued. "Records the sound, but the pressure of something here amplifies the sound simultaneously— Here it is! You have to keep your finger on this stud."

The man with the easy voice was laughing. It was the laugh of a big man. It filled the room like a wind.

"—no climate for temper, Mr. Minister. Abel, help Señor Minister to a chair."

"Yes, King." Abel's voice.

"Bendigo the First," whispered the Inspector.

"Are you all right?" The easy voice was amused.

"Thank you." This was a bubbly voice with a strong South American accent, struggling to control its fear and anger. *"It is difficult to remain calm, my dear sir, when one has been abducted by brigands from one's home in the middle of the night and spirited out of one's country by an unlawful foreign aircraft!"*

"It was necessary to have a private conversation within walls whose ears we could trust, Mr. Minister. We regret the inconvenience to you."

"Regret! Do not trifle with me. This is kidnapping, and you may be very sure I shall make an international incident of it, with the strongest possible representations to your government!"

"My government? Just where do you think you are?" The voice was still amused, but a power-switch had been flicked on.

"I will not be intimidated!" The foreign voice was shouting now. *"I know very well what you are after, Señor King Bendigo. We have access at last to the secret files of the defunct régime. The new government, which I have the great honor to serve as Minister of War, will not be so complaisant, I promise you! We shall confiscate the Guerrerra works under the powers vested in El Presidente by the National Resources Decree of the fourteenth May, and we will have no dealings with The Bodigen Arms Company or any other of your creature subsidiaries, Señor!"*

Thunder smote the machine in the receptionist's desk.

"Smacked something, His Majesty did," whispered Inspector Queen.

"Let's hope it wasn't Señor Minister of War."

"You miserable anteater—!" It was a bellow.

"Anteater?" screamed the foreign voice. *"You insult, you insult! I demand to be flown back to Ciudad Zuma immediately!"*

"Sit down! How much of this drivel do you think I'm going to stan—" The growl stopped. Then the powerful voice said impatiently, *"Yes, Abel. What is it?"*

There was a long silence.

"The sweet *sotto voce* of reason," murmured Ellery. "Or Abel's passed him a note."

They heard King Bendigo laugh again. This time the voice said smoothly, *"Forgive me for losing my temper, Señor. Believe me, I respect the position of your government even though it is hostile to our interests. But there are no viewpoints—no matter how opposing, Mr. Minister—which can't be reconciled."*

"Impossible!" The angry voice registered several decibels fewer.

"To establish a private cordiality, Mr. Minister? Known, let us say, only to us and to you?"

"There is nothing more to be said!" But now it was merely fuming.

"Well, Abel, it looks as though we're in for a licking."

Abel murmured something; the words did not come through.

"Unless, Mr. Minister, you don't quite see how . . . Let me ask you: Did your predecessor in the War Ministry manage to salvage his yacht in the revolution, Señor?"

"She saved the traitor's life," said the foreign voice stiffly. *"He made his escape in her."*

"Oh, yes. You must have admired her, Señor—your enthusiasm for pleasure craft is well-known. And she's one hundred and twenty feet of sheer poetry, as my brother Judah would say. Did say."

"She was beautiful." The War Minister spoke in the wistful, bitter way of the lover who has lost. *"Had the swine not got to her in time . . . But I presume on your schedule, Señor King—"*

"Her sister is yours."

There was a silence.

"She's identical in every respect, Mr. Minister, except that her designer tells me she's even faster. And speed in a ship is a quality not to be despised, Señor, as your predecessor discovered. Who knows? The politics of your country tend to be somewhat unstable—"

"Señor, you bribe me!" the Minister of War replied

indignantly. But it was not as if he were really surprised. His tone had a flinch in it. *"I thank you for your gift, Señor King Bendigo, but I repudiate it with scorn. Now I wish to leave."*

"Good boy," breathed the Inspector. "He made it."

"After a bit of a tussle," grinned Ellery. "Ah, there's Abel calling time again. Conference in the box. Do they pitch to the Señor or pass him?"

"Here it comes!"

"Gift?" came the dark, rich tone. *"Who said anything about a gift, Mr. Minister? I had something quite legal in mind."*

"Legal . . . ?"

"I'm offering her for sale."

The harassed man laughed. *"At a discount of five per cent, perhaps, because we are such cordial friends, Señor? This is absurdity. I am not a wealthy man—"*

"I'm sure you can afford this, Mr. Minister."

"I am sure I cannot!"

"Don't you have twenty-five dollars?"

There was a very long silence indeed.

"Struck him out," said the Inspector.

"I believe, Señor Bendigo," said the foreign voice, and for the first time it was without heat or distress, *"that would make a bargain I could not afford to ignore. I shall purchase your yacht for twenty-five dollars."*

"Our agent will call on you in Ciudad Zuma next Friday, Mr. Minister, with the bill of sale and the other documents necessary for your signature. Needless to say, the other documents are equally important to the transfer of title."

"Needless to say." The foreign voice stopped for an instant, then it went on amiably: *"Love of the sea is in the blood of my family. I have a son in the Naval Ministry, Señor Bendigo, who is also an ardent yachtsman. There will be no difficulty about the other documents, none whatever, if you will sell me also the eighty-foot* Atlanta IV, *which has only recently, I believe, come off your ways. Possession of such a prize would make my son Cristoforo a happy young man. At the same purchase price, of course."*

"You have a nose for bargains, Mr. Minister," said King Bendigo gently.

"I also keep them, my friend."

"Take care of it, Abel."

After a moment, they heard a door open and close.

"And I mean a nose," came King Bendigo's growl. *"How good an investment is that sucker, Abel?"*

"He's the intellectual strong man of the Zuma régime."

"He'd better stay that way! Who's next?"

"The E-16 matter."

"The mouth-twitcher? I thought that was settled, Abel."

"It isn't."

"The trouble with the world today is that it has too many little crooks running it under the delusion that they're big crooks! All they do is shoot the cost of history higher—they don't change the result a damn. Send him in."

There was a lull, and Ellery mumbled, "In big stuff they send 'em in direct. I wonder if there's another elevator to H.R.H.'s office. Bet there is."

"Shut up," said his father, straining.

King Bendigo was saying heartily, *"Entrez, Monsieur."*

A buttered voice said something in rapid French, but then, with a foreign accent that was not French and was spread with irony, added in English: *"Let us dispense with amenities. What do you want?"*

"The signed contracts, Monsieur."

"I do not have them."

"You promised to have them."

"That was before you raised your prices, Monsieur Bendigo. I hold the folio of Defense in my country, not of clairvoyance."

"Is this your personal decision?" They heard a drumming sound.

"No. Of the entire Cabinet."

"Are you slipping, Monsieur le Ministre?"

"I have been unable to persuade my colleagues."

"You evidently used the wrong arguments."

"You did not provide me with the right ones. Your prices are so high that they would wreck the budget. New taxes are out of the question—"

The voice was frigid. *"This is an annoyance. What of your word?"*

The buttery voice slipped. *"I must repudiate it. I have no choice. It is too risky. A contract with Bodigen Arms at such a price might unseat us. The Actionist Party—"*

"Let's be realistic, Mr. Minister," said King Bendigo's voice suddenly. *"We know the influence you exert in the power group of your country. We admit the risks. What is your price to take them?"*

"I wish to terminate this conversation. Please have me flown back."

"Damn it all—!"

Abel's voice said something.

"What, Abel?"

The brothers played another counterpoint in murmurs, Then the big voice laughed.

"Of course. But before you go, Mr. Minister, may I examine that stickpin you're wearing?"

"This?" The European voice was surprised. *"But certainly, Monsieur Bendigo. How could it interest you?"*

"I'm a collector of stickpins. Yours struck my eye at once . . . Beautiful!"

"It is merely a reproduction in gold and enamel of our national emblem. I am happy that it strikes your fancy."

"Mr. Minister, you know what collectors are—perfect idiots. I must have this pin for my collection."

"I shall send you one this week. They are obtainable at numerous shops in the capital."

"No, no, I want this one—yours, Monsieur."

"I gladly present it to you."

"I make it a rule never to accept gifts. Permit me to buy it from you."

"Really, Monsieur, it is no more than a trifle—"

"Would you accept two hundred and fifty thousand dollars for it?"

"Two hun—" The voice choked.

"Deposited in a New York bank under any name you designate?"

The Queens gaped at each other.

After a very long time, in a voice so low as almost to be inaudible, the Defense Minister said, *"Yes . . . I will sell it."*

"Take care of it, Abel. Thank you for coming, Mr. Minister. I'm sure, on re-examining the situation, you'll find some means of persuading your distinguished compatriots that no sacrifice is too great for a nation to make in this crisis in world history."

"Monsieur has given new strength to my persuasive powers," said the foreign voice in a tone compounded of bitterness, irony, and self-loathing; and the Queens heard it no more.

WHEN the door opened and Abel Bendigo reappeared, Inspector Queen was in the armchair with his head thrown back and Ellery was smoking a cigaret at the glass outer wall, staring as if he could see through it, which he could not.

The Inspector rose immediately.

"Sorry to have kept you waiting, gentlemen. My brother can see you now." Abel stood aside.

The Inspector went in first, Ellery followed, and Abel shut the door.

The hemispherical architecture of King Bendigo's office had been cleverly utilized to impress. The door from the reception room was near the end of the straight wall, so that the visitor on entering the office faced, first of all, the curved glass wall at its narrowest. He naturally made a half-turn toward space, and the long diameter of the room struck him like a blow. And near the other end, behind a desk, sat King Bendigo. The approach to him looked eternal.

There was little furniture in the office. A few heavy pieces designed to fit the curve of the outer wall, several uncompromising chairs and occasional tables, and that was all. As in the reception room, there were no paintings, no sculptures, no ornamentation of any kind. Nothing distracted the eye from that big desk, or the big chair that stood behind it, or the big man who sat in the chair.

The desk was of ebony, and there was nothing on its glittering surface.

The chair was of some golden material.

It was only later that Ellery was able to notice what was set into the straight wall near the desk. It was a room-high safe door. The door, a foot thick, was partly open. On its inner surface, behind glass, was the mechanism of a time-lock.

And just inside the safe leaned a troglodyte. His powerful jaws chewed away at something—chewing gum, or candy. He was so broad that he seemed squat; yet he was taller than Ellery. His face was gorillalike and he stared as a gorilla might stare. His stare never left the visitors' faces. He was dressed in a gaudy black and gold uniform and he wore a beret of black leather with a gilt pompom. He looked ridiculous and deadly.

But that came later. During the endless approach to the eminence of that ebony desk, they could see nothing but the man enthroned behind it.

King Bendigo did not rise. Even seated, he was formidable. He was one of the handsomest men Ellery had ever seen, with pure dark features of an imperious cast, bold black eyes, and thick black hair with a Byronic lock. His ringless hands, resting on the desk, were finely proportioned; they looked capable of breaking a man's back or threading a needle. He wore a business suit of exquisite cut and workmanship which draped itself impeccably at every movement of his torso.

There were deep lines in his face, but he looked no more than forty.

Ellery had the most curious sense of unreality. *Every Inch a King*, starring . . .

There were no introductions.

They were not offered chairs.

They were left standing before the desk, being inspected by those remarkable black eyes, while Abel went around the desk to murmur into his brother's ear.

Abel's attitude was interesting. It was all deference, but without an obsequious slant. Abel, with his lack of stature or grandeur, with his eyeglasses shining earnestly, with his body slightly inclined as he reported to his brother, was a picture of dedication.

Ellery tingled with the annoyance of something not quite grasped.

"Detectives?" They instinctively tightened before the black flash in those eyes. "So that's where you've been! Abel, I've told you those letters are the work of a crank—"

"They're not the work of a crank, King." There was a quiet stubbornness in Abel's voice that aroused Ellery's respect. "On that point Mr. Queen agreed immediately."

"Mister who?" The eyes made another survey.

"Queen. This gentleman is Inspector Richard Queen of the New York police department, and this is his son Ellery."

"Ellery Queen." The eyes became interested. "You have quite a reputation."

Ellery said, "Thank you, Mr. Bendigo."

"And you're his father, eh?" The eyes turned on Inspector Queen and at once turned back to Ellery.

And that takes care of me, thought the Inspector.

"So you think there's something in this, too, Queen."

"I do, Mr. Bendigo, and I'd like to discuss—"

"Not with me, Queen, not with me. *I* think it's a lot of damned foolishness. Play detective all you want to, but don't annoy me with it." King Bendigo turned in his chair. "Who's next, Abel?"

Abel began murmuring in the royal ear, and the royal eyes were immediately abstracted.

Ellery said: "Are you through with us, Mr. Bendigo?"

The handsome man looked up. "Yes?" he said sharply.

"Well, I'm not through with you."

The King leaned back, frowning. Abel straightened up and his prominent eyes began to shuttle between them.

The Inspector rested against a chair, folding his arms expectantly.

"Well?" said King Bendigo.

"Nothing has been said about a fee."

The stare was degrading. "I didn't hire you. My brother did. Talk it over with him."

Abel said, "We'll discuss your fee this evening, Mr. Queen—"

"I'd rather discuss it now."

The King looked up at his Prime Minister. His Prime Minister shrugged ever so slightly. The stare went back to Ellery.

"Really?" drawled the man in the gold chair, and Ellery could have hurdled the desk and throttled him. "And what is this fee of yours, Queen?"

"My services come pretty high, Mr. Bendigo."

"What is the fee?"

It was at this point that Ellery, to conceal the blood in his eye, glanced away, and that was when he first saw the uniformed gorilla standing inside the doorway of the safe, animal eyes fixed on him, jaws grinding away. The King's jester . . . He felt himself tighten all over, and in the next moment all the pressure of hostility and outraged pride that had been building up came to a head.

"I won't talk total fee, since I don't know just what the investigation entails. I want a retainer, Mr. Bendigo, balance left open."

"How much of a retainer?"

Ellery said, "One hundred thousand dollars."

Behind him there was a choked paternal sound.

Abel Bendigo was looking at Ellery thoughtfully.

But King Bendigo neither choked nor took stock. He merely waved and said to his brother, "Take care of it," and then he waved at Ellery and Inspector Queen and said impatiently, "That's all, gentlemen."

Ellery said: "I'm not finished, Mr. Bendigo. I want my retainer in ten certified checks of ten thousand dollars each. You are to have the payees' lines left blank, so that I can fill in the names of ten different charities."

He knew instantly he had taken the wrong tack. Where money was concerned, this man was invulnerable. Money was a power-tool. Anyone who failed to use it as a power-tool was beneath contempt.

King Bendigo said indifferently, "Give it to him, Abel, any way he wants it. Anything, just so they stay out of my hair." In the identical tone, without stopping, he said, "Max'l."

The beast in the beret shot out of the safe, grimacing horribly.

Ellery dodged. The Inspector jumped out of the way like a rabbit.

King Bendigo threw his head back and roared. The wrestler was grinning.

"All right, all right, gentlemen," said the big man, still laughing. "Go to work."

IN the elevator, Inspector Queen broke the rather sick silence.

"I picked this up from the floor on the way out, son. It was at that far wall, all the way across the office from his desk. He must have cracked it between his fingers for exercise and then tossed it away for the help to throw in the trash."

"What is it, Dad?" Ellery's voice shook a little.

His father opened an unsteady hand. On it lay the fragments of the stickpin they had heard King Bendigo buy from his second visitor for two hundred and fifty thousand dollars.

IV

THE SHIRTS were waiting for them in the lobby. Ellery found himself passing the security desk with a stiff back. But the three uniformed men paid no attention to them.

Brown Shirt said, "This way," and Blue Shirt held the outer door open.

Outside, the son and the father breathed again. The sun was low in the west and the western sky was strawberry, copper, and mother-of-pearl. A small, powerful black car gold-initialed PRPD was at the entrance. Blue Shirt took the wheel and Brown Shirt got into the rear seat between them.

Neither Queen felt talkative. Each gazed through his window at the countryside. They might have been traveling along the Mohawk Trail in a quiet fold of the Berkshires, with a city of mills and small homes at their feet, except for the pelagic vegetation and the memory of what they had just heard and seen.

"Who," inquired Ellery, "is at whose orders?"

"We're taking you to the Residence, Mr. Queen," replied Brown Shirt. "Mr. Abel has arranged everything."

"How free are we to move about?"

"You've been given a temporary A-2 rating, sir."

"What's that mean?" asked Inspector Queen, astonished.

"You may go anywhere you want, sir, except those installations marked *Restricted*."

"From what we've seen, that sounds risky. We're not known on the island."

"You're known," Blue Shirt assured him from the front seat.

The Inspector did not look assured.

The car entered a densely wooded area. There were flashes of flying color everywhere, but these were the only evidences of wildlife.

"Beauty for its own sake?" asked Ellery skeptically.

"Karla likes them," said Brown Shirt.

"Mrs. Bendigo?" The Inspector was scrutinizing the woods closely without seeming to do so.

"King's queen," said Ellery.

He had seen it, too, but he and his father continued to look at opposite terrains. There were camouflaged gun emplacements in these woods. Big guns, of the coast artillery type. Probably the whole wooded area bristled with them. And how much of this jungle itself, Ellery wondered, was real?

THEY came upon King Bendigo's home suddenly.

They could see only a little of it because of the trees and shrubs which choked it. The landscaping was positively untidy. Some of the trees were taller than the buildings, and there were heavy branches that actually brushed windows. Even the towers had been so treated that, while they were visible against the sky from the ground, to an airborne eye they must blend into the greenery.

Secrecy again. The original planners had probably been responsible for the camouflage, but then why, when he leased the island, hadn't Bendigo had these trees and the encroaching underbrush cleared away? Was he afraid someone would try to take his precious midocean anchorage away from him?

The Residence stood only four stories high, like the Home Office, but it covered a wider area. The section immediately before them would have been a courtyard had it not been overgrown with shrubbery planted at random. Even the paved driveway ran between two erratic files of trees whose upper branches twined overhead to form a ceiling. Embracing all of this were two projections of the building, running outward from a sort of parent body. From the angle formed by the arms, Ellery suspected others. Brown Shirt, who remained spokesman of the duo, confirmed this and explained the oddity of the architecture. The building was constructed on a plan similar to that of the Home Office, except that where the Home Office had eight arms, the Residence had five.

They were received in a great hall by flunkies in livery. Black and gold. With knee breeches and stocks. The Inspector goggled.

Here, at least, the functional temporized with fussier modes. The furniture was massively modern, but there were medieval French and Swedish tapestries on the walls and a sprinkling of old masters among new, the new chiefly abstractions. Everything in the hall was immense, the hall itself being three stories high; and it was only here and there that one saw a traditional object—such as the classic canvases—as if someone in the household insisted on at least a smattering of an older environment.

A footman conducted them through one of the five portals into a wing, and just inside this corridor Blue Shirt indicated a small elevator. They were whisked up one floor, and they got out to be marched along a soundless hall to a door. The door was open. In the doorway, dwarfed by its dimensions, stood a small bald man in a black suit and a wing collar. He bowed.

"This is your valet," said Brown Shirt. "Whatever you need to supplement what you've brought with you, gentlemen, just inform this man and he'll provide it at once."

"Jeeves?" said Ellery tentatively.

"No, sir," replied the valet Britannically. "Jones."

"Your point, Jones. Does protocol demand evening clothes at dinner?"

"No, sir," said the valet. "Except on given occasions, dining is informal. Dark suit and four-in-hand."

"They'll take my tan gabardine and like it," said the Inspector.

"Yes, yes, Dad," said Ellery soothingly. "Here, Jones, where are you off to?"

"To draw your tubs, sir," said Jones; and he sedately vanished.

The Queens turned to find the Shirts receding shoulder to shoulder.

"Here, wait!" cried the Inspector. "When do we get to see—?"

But they were already far down the corridor.

THEIR sitting room was almost a grand salon, and the two bedrooms were magnificent affairs with lofty ceilings, canopied beds, and historic-looking furnishings. Here, at least, the *décor* was traditional—*ancien régime,* as cluttered with gingerbread as any suite in the Tuileries under the Grand Monarch. Fortunately, as Ellery hastened to discover, tradition did not extend to the sanitary arrangements; but he was amused to find the telephones discreetly hidden in buhl cabinets whose surfaces were intricately inlaid with gold, tortoise shell, and some white metal in the scrollwork, cartouches, and curlicues so dear to the times of Louis Quatorze.

Inspector Queen was not amused at all. He went about from room to room antagonistically examining the grandeur into which they had been thrust; and he reserved his most hostile glare for the valet, who was patiently awaiting an opportunity to undress him. To avoid a homicide, Ellery conveyed Jones to the door.

They bathed, shaved, and dressed in fresh clothes from their suitcases, and then they waited. There was nothing else to do, for they could find no newspapers and the magnificent leatherbound books turned out to be discouraging eighteenth-century works in French and Latin. And from the windows nothing could be seen but foliage. The Inspector occupied himself for some time searching the suite for a secret transmitter, which he was positive was planted somewhere in the sitting room; but after a while he grew tired of even this diversion and began fuming.

"Damn it, what kind of runaround is this? What are we supposed to do, rot here? I'm going downstairs, Ellery!"

"Let's wait, Dad. All this has a purpose."

"To starve us out!"

But Ellery was frowning over a cigaret. "I wonder why we've been brought to the island."

The Inspector stared.

"Abel hires us to investigate a couple of threatening letters received, he says, through the mail. The mail undoubtedly is flown here daily from the mainland by Bendigo's planes. If those letters came through the mail, then, they emanated from the mainland. Why, then, does Abel ask us to investigate *on the island?*"

"Because he thinks the letters came from the island!"

"Exactly. Someone's slipping them into the pouches or into the already sorted Residence or Home Office mail." Ellery ground out his cigaret in a Royal Sèvres dish which was probably worth more than he had in the bank. "Which somebody? A clerk? Secretary? Footman? Guard? Factory hand? Lab worker? For anyone like that, the Prime Minister doesn't have to make a special trip to New York, with a side visit to Washington, to engage the services of a couple of outsiders. That kind of job could be polished off by Colonel Spring's department in about two hours flat.

"So it gets down to . . . what?" Ellery looked up. "To somebody big, Dad."

But the Inspector was shaking his head. "The bigger the game, the less likelihood that Bendigo would call in an outsider."

"That's right."

"That's right? But you just said—"

"That's right, and that's wrong, too. So none of it sets on the stomach. In fact," and Ellery fumbled for another cigaret, "I'm positively bilious."

That was when the telephone tinkled and Ellery leaped to answer it, almost knocking his father down. Abel Bendigo's calm twang said he was terribly sorry but his brother King was being a bit difficult this evening and in Abel's considered judgment it would be a lot smarter not to press matters at the moment. If the Queens didn't mind dining alone . . . ?

"Of course not, Mr. Bendigo, but we're anxious to get going on the investigation."

"Tomorrow will be better," said the Yankee voice in the tones of a physician soothing a fretful patient.

"Are we to wait in these rooms for your call?"

"Oh, no, Mr. Queen. Do anything you like, go anywhere you please. I'll find you when I want you." Perhaps to get by the ironical implications of this statement, the Prime Minister said hurriedly, "Good night," and hung up.

Dinner was served in their suite from warming ovens and other portable paraphernalia by a butler and three servingmen under the cadaver's eye of a perfect official who introduced himself as the Chief Steward of the Residence and thereafter uttered not a single word.

It was like dining in a tomb, and the Queens did not enliven the occasion. They ate in silence, exactly what they could not afterward recall except that it was rich, saucy, and French, in keeping with the *décor.*

Then, in the same nervous silence, and because there was nothing else to do, they went to bed.

* * *

THERE was no note from Abel Bendigo on their plates the next morning, and the telephone failed to ring. So after breakfast Ellery proposed a tour of the Residence.

The Inspector, however, had developed a pugnacious jaw. "I'm going to see how far they'll let me go. Where do you suppose the royal garage is?"

"Garage?"

"I'm borrowing a car."

He went out, his jaw preceding him, and Ellery did not see him until late afternoon.

Ellery prowled about the five-armed building alone. It took him all morning to make its acquaintance. Certainly he made the acquaintance of nothing more animate, for he saw none of the Bendigo family during his tour and the servants in livery and minor officials of the household whom he ran across ignored him with suspicious unanimity.

He was stopped only once, and that was on the top floor of the central building. Here there were armed guards in uniform, and their captain was politely inflexible.

"These are the private apartments of the family, sir. No one is allowed to enter except by special permission."

"Well, of course I shouldn't want to blunder into anyone's bathroom, but I was given to understand by Mr. Abel Bendigo that I could go anywhere."

"I have received no order to admit you to this floor, Mr. Queen."

So Ellery meekly went back to the lowlier regions.

He looked in on the state dining room, the grand ballroom, salons, reception rooms, trophy rooms, galleries, kitchens, wine cellars, servants' quarters, storerooms, even closets. There was an oak-and-leather library of twenty thousand volumes, uniformly bound in black Levant morocco and stamped with the twin-globes-and-crown, which more and more took on the color of a coat-of-arms. The standardization of the books themselves, many of them rare editions raped of their original bindings, made Ellery cringe. None that he sampled showed the least sign of use.

Shortly before noon Ellery found himself in a music salon, dominated by a platform at one end large enough to accommodate a symphony orchestra. In the center of this stage glittered a concert grand piano sheathed in gold. Wondering if this splendid instrument was in tune, Ellery climbed to the platform, opened the piano, and struck middle C. An unmusical clank answered him. He struck a chord in the middle register. This time the horrid jangle that resulted impressed him as far too extreme to be accounted for by mere neglect, and he raised the top of the piano.

Six sealed bottles, identical in every respect, lay in a neat row on the strings.

He took one out with curiosity. It was bell-shaped, with a slender neck, and of very dark green glass, so dark as to be opaque. The antiqued label identified the contents as *Segonzac V.S.O.P. Cognac.* The heavy seal was unbroken, as were the seals of its five brothers, at which Ellery sighed. He had never had the good fortune to savor Segonzac Very Special Old Pale Cognac, for the excellent reason that Segonzac Very Special Old Pale Cognac was priced—where it could be found at all at almost fifty dollars the bottle. He replaced the heavy glass bell on its harmonious bed and lowered the top of the grand piano with reverence.

A man who cached six bottles of cognac in a grand piano was an alcoholic. The middle Bendigo brother, Judah, had been reported by the Inspector's military *tête-à-tête* as an alcoholic. It seemed a reasonable conclusion that this was Judah Bendigo's cache. The incident also told something of the musicality of the Bendigo household, but since this was of a piece with the evidence of the library, Ellery was not surprised.

Apparently Judah Bendigo scorned his brother's vineyards. Unless the Segonzac label was another possession of the all-powerful King . . . It was a point Ellery never did clear up.

The discovery in the music salon led Ellery to poke and pry. An alcoholic who hides bottles in one place will hide them in another. He was not disappointed.

He found bottles of Segonzac V.S.O.P. hidden everywhere he looked. Seven turned up in the gymnasium, four around the hundred-foot indoor swimming pool. Ellery found them in the billiard room and the bowling alley. He found them in the cardroom. And on one of the terraces, where he lunched in solitude, Ellery felt the flagstone under his left foot give and, on investigating, stared down at another of the bell-shaped bottles nestling in a scooped-out hole beneath the flag.

In the afternoon he toured the vicinity of the Residence. Wherever he went he turned up the dark green evidence of Judah Bendigo's ingenuity. The outdoor swimming pool, cleverly constructed to resemble a natural pond, was good for eight bottles, and Ellery could not be sure he had found them all. He did not bother with the stables—there were too many grooms about—but he took an Arab mare out on the bridle path and he made it a point to probe tree hollows and investigate overhead tree crotches, with rewarding results. Another artificial stream, this one stocked with game fish, was a disappointment; but Ellery suspected that if he had worn hipboots he could have waded in any direction through the broken water and found a bottle wedged between the nearest rocks.

"And I didn't begin to find them all," he told his father that evening, in their sitting room. "Judah must carry a map around with him, X marking the spots. There's a man who likes his brandy."

"You might have lifted a couple of bottles," grumbled the Inspector. "I've had a miserable day."

"Well?"

"Oh, I putt-putted around the island. Isn't that what a tourist is supposed to do?" And while he said this, in a tone of lifelessness, the Inspector rather remarkably took a roll of papers from an inner pocket and waved them at his son.

"I will admit," said his son, eying the papers, "this enforced vacation is beginning to bore me, too." He leaned forward and took the papers. "When do you suppose our investigation begins?"

"Never, from the look of things."

"What's the island like, Dad?" Ellery unrolled several of the papers noiselessly. Each showed a hasty sketch of an industrial plant. Others were rough detail maps.

"It's no different from any highly industrialized area in the States. Factories, homes, schools, roads, trucks, planes, people . . ." The Inspector pointed at the papers vigorously.

Ellery nodded. "What kind of factories?"

"Munitions mostly, I guess. Hell, I don't know. A lot of places had *Restricted* signs on 'em with armed guards and electrified fences and the rest of the claptrap. Couldn't get near 'em."

There was one series of sketches of rather queer-looking plants, a scale-frame indicating enormous size.

"Meet anybody interesting?" Ellery pointed to the peculiar sketches and looked inquiring.

"Just Colonel Spring's lads. The working people seem an unfriendly lot. Or they're shy of strangers. Wouldn't give me the time of day." The Inspector's reply to the silent part of their conversation was a shrug and a shake of the head. Ellery studied the sketches with a frown.

"Well, son, I guess I'll take me a bath in that marble lake they gave me to splash around in." The Inspector rose and took his notes back.

"I could use one myself."

His father tucked the papers away in his clothes, and Ellery knew that unless a body search were made, the sketches would not leave their hiding place this side of Washington, D.C.

THAT night they passed through the gold curtain.

The feat was accomplished by means of a piece of paper. At six o'clock a footman with overdeveloped calves delivered a velvety purplish envelope, regally square, and backed out with the kind of bow the Inspector had never seen outside a British period movie. The bow indicated that it was hardly necessary to open the envelope. But they did, and they found inside a sheet of richly engraved and monogrammed stationery of the same color and texture covered with gold ink writing in a firm feminine hand. Inspector Richard Queen and Mr. Ellery Queen were requested to appear in the private apartments of the Bendigo family at 7 P.M. for cocktails and dinner. Dress was informal. The signature was *Karla Bendigo*. There was a postscript: She had heard so much of the Queens from her brother-in-law Abel that she was looking forward with delight to meeting them, and she concluded by apologizing—with what seemed to Ellery significant vagueness—for having been "unable to do so until now."

They had hardly finished reading the invitation before their valet appeared with a dark blue double-breasted man's suit, dully gleaming black shoes, a pair of new black silk socks, and a conservative blue silk necktie. Ellery relieved the man of them and nudged him out before the snarl formed in the Inspector's nose.

"Try them on, Dad. Chances are they won't fit, and you'll have an excuse for not wearing them."

They fitted perfectly, even the shoes.

"All right, wise guy," growled the Inspector. "But the school I was brought up in, if your guests want to show up in their underwear the host strips, too, Who the devil do these people think they are?"

So at five minutes of seven, Ellery in his best oxford

gray and the Inspector uneasily elegant in Jones's finery, the Queens left their suite and went upstairs.

Different guards were on duty in the foyer on the top floor. They were under the command of a younger officer, who scrutinized Karla Bendigo's invitation microscopically. Then he stepped back, saluting, and the Queens were passed through the portals, feeling a little as if they ought to remove their shoes and crawl in on their stomachs.

"That head will roll," murmured Ellery.

"Huh?" said his father nervously.

"If we snitch on him. He didn't fingerprint us."

They were in a towering reception room full of black iron, hamadryads in marble, giant crystal chandeliers, and overwhelming furniture in the Italian baroque style. Across the room two great doors stood open, flanked by footmen in *rigor mortis*. An especially splendid flunky wearing white gloves received them with a bow and preceded them to the double door.

"Inspector Queen and Mr. Ellery Queen."

"Just a little snack with the Bendigos," mumbled the Inspector; then they both stopped short.

Coming to them swiftly across a terrazzo floor was a woman as improbably beautiful as the heroine of a film. But Technicolor could never adequately have reproduced the snowiness of her skin and teeth, the sunset red of her hair, or the tropical green of her eyes. Even allowing for the art, there was a fundamental color magic that startled, and it enlivened a person that was disquieting in form. A great deal of the person was on display, for she was wearing a strapless dinner gown of very frank décolletage. The gown, of pastel green velvet, sheathed her to the knees; from the knees it flared, like a vase. Despite her coloring, she was not of Northern blood, Ellery decided, because she made him think of Venezia, San Marco, the Adriatic, and the women of the doges. Studying her as she approached, he saw earth in her figure, breeding in her face, and no nonsense in her step. A Titian woman. Fit for a king.

"Good evening," she exclaimed, taking their hands. Her voice had the same coloring; it was a vivid contralto, with the merest trace of Southern Europe. She was not so young, Ellery saw, as he had first thought. Early thirties? "I am so happy to receive you both. Can you forgive me for having neglected you?"

"After seeing you, madam," said Inspector Queen with earnestness, "I can forgive you anything."

"And to be repaid with gallantry!" She smiled, the slightest smile. "And you, Mr. Queen?"

"Speechless," said Ellery. Now he saw something else—a sort of grotto deep beneath the sunny seas of her eyes, a place of cold sad shade.

"I have always adored the flattery of American men. It is so uncomplicated." Laughing, she took them across the room.

King Bendigo stood at an Italian marble fireplace taller than himself, listening in silence to the conversation of his brother Abel and three other men. The lord of Bendigo Island looked fresh and keen, although Ellery knew he must have had a long day at his desk. The jester, Max'l, was at a table nearby helping himself to canapés with both murderous hands. Occasionally, while his great jaws ground away, he looked around at his master like a dog.

In an easy chair opposite King sprawled a slight dark man in rumpled clothing. On his sallow face, with its intelligent features, he wore a slight dark mustache; it gave him a gloomy, almost sinister, look. It was an odd face, with a broad high forehead, a nose sharply and crookedly hooked, and a chin that came to a premature point. A bell-shaped dark green bottle stood at his elbow and he was rolling a brandy snifter between his palms as his head lolled on the back of the chair. From the slits of his deeply sunken eyes he was studying Ellery, however, with remarkable alertness.

King greeted them graciously enough, but in a moment he had turned aside with Abel, and it was Karla Bendigo who introduced the other men. The slight dark man in the easy chair was Judah Bendigo, the middle brother; he did not rise or offer his hand. He merely squinted up at them, rolling the snifter between his palms. Either he was already drunk, or rudeness was a hereditary Bendigo trait. Ellery was glad when they had to turn to the group at the fireplace.

One of the three was small, stout, and bald, with the unemotional stare of a man to whom nothing has value but the immediate moment. Their hostess introduced him as Dr. Storm, Surgeon-General of Bendigo Island and her husband's personal physician, who lived on the premises. It did not surprise Ellery to learn that the second man, a tall lean swarthy individual with a catty smile, was also a permanent resident; his name was Immanuel Peabody, and he was King Bendigo's chief legal adviser. The third man of the group looked like a football player convalescing from a serious illness. He was young, blond, broad-shouldered, and pale, and his face was rutted with fatigue.

"Dr. Akst," Karla Bendigo said. "We seldom see this young man; it is a rare pleasure. He buries himself in his laboratory at the other side of the island, fiddling with his dangerous little atoms."

"With his what?" said Inspector Queen.

"Mrs. Bendigo insists on making Dr. Akst out some sort of twentieth-century alchemist," said the lawyer, Peabody, smiling. "A physicist can't very well avoid the little atom, but it's hardly dangerous, Dr. Akst, is it?"

"Say it is dangerous, Doctor," said Karla playfully. But she flashed a glance at the lawyer. It seemed to Ellery the glance was resentful.

"Only in the sense that an experimenter," protested Peabody, "is always monkeying with the unknown."

"Can we talk about something else?" asked Dr. Akst. He spoke with a strong Scandinavian accent, and he sounded younger than he looked.

"Mrs. Bendigo's eyes," suggested Ellery. "Now there's a subject that's really dangerous."

Everyone laughed, and then Ellery and the Inspector had cocktails in their hands and Immanuel Peabody began to tell the story of an old criminal trial in England, in which testimony about the color of a woman's eyes delivered the defendant to Jack Ketch. But all the while Ellery was wondering if his father knew that the tired young man with the humorless Scandinavian voice was one of the world's most famous nuclear physicists. And he thought, too, that in trying to gloss over the nature of Dr. Akst's work on Bendigo Island Immanuel Peabody had only succeeded in calling attention to it. For the rest of the evening Akst made a point of effacing himself and, playing the game, Ellery ignored him.

Karla Bendigo did not refer to him again.

DINNER was sumptuous and interminable. They dined in the adjoining room, a place of suffocating grandeur, and they were served by an army corps of servants. The courses and wines came in a steady parade, many of the delicacies blue-flamed in chafing dishes, so that the whole incredible feast was like a torchlight procession in a medieval festival.

Immanuel Peabody kept pace, with fat and deadly little Dr. Storm not far behind, Peabody telling with the utmost cheerfulness gruesome stories of criminal lore, with Dr. Storm's surgically bawdy. To these last, Max'l was the most appreciative listener; he winked, leered, and guffawed between gulletfuls, missing nothing. Max'l wore his napkin frankly under his chin and he ate with both elbows guarding his plate; he removed one of them only to batter Ellery's ribs at a particularly gusty witticism of Dr. Storm's.

To the Queens' disappointment, neither had been placed beside King or Karla Bendigo. The Inspector was trapped between the loquacious lawyer and the wicked little Surgeon-General, while Ellery sat diagonally across the table between the taciturn physicist, Akst, and Max'l—the father being talked to death, the son given Coventry on one side and a beating on the other. The arrangement was deliberate; nothing here, Ellery knew, happened by chance.

Since most of the lawyer's and the physician's conversation was directed toward the Queens, they found little opportunity to talk to the Bendigos. Karla murmured to Abel at her end of the field-long table, occasionally sending a word or a crooked little smile their way, as if in apology. At the other end sat King, listening. Once, turning suddenly, Ellery found their host's black eyes fixed on him with amusement. He tried after that to cultivate at least an appearance of patience.

It was a queer banquet, full of tense and mysterious undercurrents, and not the least of them swirled about Judah Bendigo. The slender little man slumped to the left of his brother King, ignoring Max'l's feeding antics—Max'l sat between Judah and Ellery—ignoring Storm's sallies and Peabody's forensic yarns, ignoring his food ... giving all his attention to the bottle of Segonzac cognac beside his plate. No servant touched that bottle, Ellery observed; Judah refilled his own glass. He drank steadily but slowly throughout the evening, for the most part looking across the table at a point in space above Immanuel Peabody's head. His only recognition of the menu was to drink two cups of black coffee toward the end, and even then he laced them with brandy. The first cup emptied his bottle, and a servant quickly uncorked a fresh bottle and set it beside him.

The dinner took three hours; and when at exactly 10:45 P.M. King Bendigo made an almost unnoticeable gesture and Peabody brought his story to an end within ten seconds, Ellery could have collapsed in gratitude. Across the table his father sat perspiring and pale, as if he had exhausted himself in a desperate struggle.

The rich voice said to the Queens, "Gentlemen, I must ask you to excuse Abel and me. We have work to do tonight. I regret the necessity, as I'd looked forward to hearing some stories of your adventures." Then why the devil, thought Ellery, did you order Peabody and Storm to monopolize the conversation? "However, Mrs. Bendigo will entertain you."

He did not wait for Karla's murmured, "I will be so happy to, darling," but pushed his chair back and rose. Abel, Dr. Storm, Peabody, and Dr. Akst immediately rose, too. Abel followed his tall brother through one door, and the doctor, the lawyer, and the physicist trooped out through another. The Queens watched them leave, fascinated. It was exactly as if the long dinner had been a scene in a play, with everyone an actor and the curtain coming down to disperse them in their private identities, each registering relief in his own fashion.

As Ellery drew Karla Bendigo's chair back, his eyes met his father's over her satiny red hair.

In three hours, with all the principals present, not one word had been said about the reason for the Queens' presence on Bendigo Island. "Shall we go, gentlemen?"

King's wife took their arms.

* * *

AT the door, Ellery looked back.

Side by side at the littered table sat Max'l and Judah Bendigo. The ex-wrestler was still stuffing himself, and the silent Bendigo brother was pouring another glassful of cognac with an air of concentration and a hand that remained steady.

V

KARLA'S APARTMENT was on another planet, a gentle world of birds and flowers, with casements overlooking the gardens and a small fireplace burning aromatic logs. Watercolors splashed the walls, glass winked in the firelight, and everything was bright and warm and friendly.

A maid, not a flunky in livery, served coffee and brandy. Karla took neither; she sipped an iced liqueur.

"Coffee keeps me awake. Brandy—" she shrugged—"I find I have lost my taste for it."

"Your brother-in-law's influence?" suggested the Inspector delicately.

"We can do nothing with Judah."

"Why," asked Ellery, "does Judah drink?"

"Why does anyone drink? . . . Rest your feet on the footstool, Inspector Queen. Dinner was exhausting, I know. Immanuel Peabody is a fascinating raconteur, but he has never learned that the pinnacle of brilliance in storytelling is knowing when to stop. Dr. Storm is a pig. One of the world's great internists, but a pig nevertheless. Am I being dreadful? It is such a relief to allow myself to be a woman on occasion, and gossip."

The sadness in her eyes interested Ellery. He wondered how much Karla Bendigo knew of the threats against her husband's life, if she knew anything at all.

The Inspector was apparently wondering, too, because he said, "Your husband bowled me over, Mrs. Bendigo. One of the most dynamic men I've ever met."

"That is so characteristic, Inspector!" She was pleased. "I mean, your feeling that. It is the invariable reaction of everyone who meets Kane."

"Who meets whom?" said Ellery.

"Kane."

"Kane?"

"Oh, I forget." She laughed. "Kane is my husband's name. K-a-n-e."

"Then the name King—"

"Is not properly his name at all. We are playthings of the press, *n'est-ce pas?* The newspapers referred to Kane so long and so often as 'the Munitions King' that he began to use the word 'king' as a name. In the beginning it was a family joke, but somehow it has hung on."

"Does his brother Judah address him as King?" asked Ellery. "I don't believe I heard Judah utter a word all evening."

She shrugged. "Judah took it up with as much enthusiasm as he ever shows for anything. Judah's affinity for cognac often leads him into childish irony. He uses 'King' as if it were a—a title. Even Abel has fallen into the habit. I am the only one who still addresses my husband by his given name."

Ellery began to perceive a ground for the sadness in her eyes.

SHE told the story of how she and her husband had met.

It was in an ultrafashionable restaurant in Paris under characteristic Bendigo circumstances. They were at adjacent tables, each in a large dinner party. She had noticed the big, dark, Byronic-locked man with the flashing black eyes when his party entered; it included two members of the French cabinet, a high British diplomat, a famous American general, and Abel Bendigo—there were no women—but it was on the Munitions King that all eyes fastened.

The buzz that filled the restaurant caused Karla to inquire who he was.

She had heard of him, of course, but she had always discounted the stories about him as the inflated gossip of the bankrupt society from which she came. Now, seeing him in the flesh, she was equally sure the stories must be true. In the world in which she lived, men were either cynical petrifactions in high places or useless, usually impecunious, exquisites. Among these people he stood out like a Roman candle. He was all radiant energy, heating and exciting the pale particles among which he moved.

Being a woman, Karla had immediately turned her glance elsewhere.

"I remember feeling thankful that my better profile happened to be turned toward his table," Karla said, smiling. "And wondering if it were possible to make a conquest of such a man. He was said to have very little to do with women. That, of course, is a challenge to any woman, and I was bored to death by my friends and my life.

"I suppose some of this showed in what was visible to him. Which was a great deal, I fear," she added, "for this was immediately after the war and I was wearing a particularly shameless creation of Feike-Emma's. Still, I was surprised when the Baroness Herblay, who was called behind her back 'Madame Roentgen' because nothing escaped her eye, whispered to me behind her lorgnette that *Monsieur le Roi* had been staring at me for some time with the most insulting intensity—'insulting' was the word she used, hopefully."

The Baroness explained at Karla's raised brow that "Monsieur le Roi" was what the leftist French press had taken to calling Mr. King-of-the-Munitions Bendigo.

"I looked around," Karla murmured, "and met Kane's eye. Mine was very cold, intended to freeze him into an awareness that I was not some modiste's mannequin to be looked over with insolence. Instead, I met such a heat in his . . .

"I looked away quickly, feeling myself blush. I was not a convent girl. The war had made us all a thousand years old. Still, at the moment, I was feeling exactly like one. He was so . . . uniquely attractive. . . . And then I howled like a chambermaid, which was the effect Baroness Herblay sought, I am sure, for she was a wicked old woman and she had stabbed my ankle with the stiletto she wore in place of a heel. So I looked up through tears of pain to find him, very darkly imperious and amused, stooping over my chair.

" 'Pardon me if I startled you,' he said in schoolboy French. 'But I had to tell you that you are the most beautiful woman I have ever seen.'

"Of course, in American English it sounds—how do you say?—corny," continued Karla with a twinkle, "but there is something about the French language which gives this sort of sentiment a tone of ever-fresh glamour. And expressed—no matter how awkwardly—in Kane's deep, rich American voice, it sounded as if it had never been said before.

"My cousin, Prince Claudel, was at the head of our table. Before I could find my tongue, Claudel rose and said frigidly, 'And I must tell you, Monsieur, that you are a presuming boor. You will please retire immediately.' "

"There was a brawl," chuckled Inspector Queen.

"A duel," guessed Ellery.

"Nothing of the sort," retorted Karla, resting her shining head on the back of her chair, "although either would have delighted the Baroness. Baron Herblay, who had grown old in the intrigues of Europe, whispered in Claudel's ear, and I saw my cousin go amusingly pale. It was Bendigo money which had supported Claudel in exile while he plotted the destruction of the revolutionary régime in our country and his return there, which would mean eventually his elevation to the overturned throne. Claudel had never laid eyes on Kane Bendigo; it was a minor matter to the Bendigos, handled through agents and bankers in Paris.

"Meanwhile, Kane stood over me paying no attention whatever. It was a coldblooded display, and the restaurant had fallen silent—that horrible public silence which undresses you and leaves you no place to hide.

"Claudel said nervously, 'Monsieur, I spoke hastily, perhaps. But you must realize, Monsieur—you have not been presented—'

"And, without looking up at him, Kane said, 'Present me.'

"Whereupon, even paler, Prince Claudel did so."

"Since this is a romance," grinned Ellery, "I suppose you slapped his face and swept out of the restaurant."

"No," said Karla dreamily, "for this was a realistic romance. I knew the source of our family's support and I had undergone too much privation during the war to jeopardize it over a breach of etiquette. Besides, he was so handsome. And his breach had, after all, been committed over me. . . . But then he made it very difficult for me to remain flattered."

"What did he do?" asked the Inspector.

"He ordered all non-redhaired women out of the restaurant."

"He *what?*"

"He passed a law, Inspector Queen. Only redhaired women, he decreed in a penetrating voice, should be allowed. And he summoned the *maître* and ordered the poor man to escort all brunette, blonde, and grayhaired ladies from the premises. The *maître* wrung his hands and hurried off, while Kane stood by my chair with perfect calmness. The restaurant, of course, was in an uproar.

"I was furnous with him. I was about to rise and leave when the Baroness dug her claws into my arm and hissed at me, whispering something about the Prince. I glanced at my cousin and I could see that he was about to do something suicidally heroic. Poor Claudel! He's had such a hard time of it. So I had to pretend to be amused, and I smiled up at the tall author of the scene and acted as if I were enjoying myself. As, secretly, I was."

Karla laughed again, from deep in her throat. "The *maître* returned with the manager. The manager wrung his hands, too. Monsieur was obviously jesting . . . it was of a truth impossible . . . these distinguished personages. . . . But Monsieur very calmly said that he was not jesting in the least. There was room in the planetary system, he said, for only one sun, which at its most beautiful, he reminded the manager, was of the color red. All non-redhaired women must leave at once.

"The manager threw up his hands and sent for the owner of the restaurant. The owner came and he was adamant. It could not be done, the owner said with respect but firmness. Such an act would be not merely immoral and unprecedented, it would be commercial suicide. He would instantly lose the patronage of the most elevated diners in Paris. He would be sued, wrecked, ruined. . . .

"At this point Kane looked over at Abel, and Abel, who had been quietly listening, rose from their table and came to his brother. They conferred for a moment, then Abel took the owner aside and there was another inaudible conference. While this was going on, Kane said to me soothingly, 'A thousand apologies for this annoyance. It will be over in a moment.' I had to smile up at him again to keep Claudel in hand. . . .

"Then the owner rejoined us, and he was paler than my cousin. If Monsieur Bendigo and his guests would be so gracious as to retire to a private suite, for a few moments only. . . . Monsieur Bendigo smiled and said that would be agreeable to him—if I joined his party."

"And you did?"

"I had to, Mr. Queen, or Prince Claudel would have assaulted him where he stood. I went to Claudel and whispered that I was being most terribly diverted—leaving Claudel speechless—and then I permitted Kane to escort me from the room. The last thing I remember," laughed Karla, "was Baroness Herblay's open mouth.

"Fifteen minutes later the owner of the restaurant presented himself to Kane in the private suite, informed him that all ladies who were not so fortunate as to possess red hair had been 'removed from the premises,' and bowed himself out again. At this Kane nodded gravely, and he said to me, 'I am reasonably sure you were the only redhaired woman present, but if we find that I've made a mistake, I will take appropriate action on some other ground. Will you do me the honor of dining with me and my friends?" And we went back into the restaurant, and not a woman was there—just a few men who had remained out of curiosity. Needless to say, Claudel, the Herblays, and the others had all left."

"But what on earth made the owner change his tune?" asked Ellery. "I assume he was well paid for it, but it seems to me no amount of money, after a stunt like that, would keep his business solvent."

"It was no longer his, Mr. Queen," said Karla. "You see, on the spot, on Kane's instructions, Abel had purchased the restaurant!"

FOUR days later—four of the most exciting in her life, Karla said—they were married. They spent a prolonged honeymoon on the Continent, to the despair of Abel. But Karla was overwhelmingly in love, and it was not until two months later that her husband brought her in state to Bendigo Island.

"Where you've been ever since?" asked the Inspector. "Must get pretty lonely for a woman like you, Mrs. Bendigo."

"Oh, no," protested Karla. "I could never be lonely with Kane."

"But doesn't he work very hard?" murmured Ellery. "Late hours, and all that? From what I've gathered, you don't see much of your husband."

Karla sighed. "I have never felt that a woman should stand between her husband and his work. It is probably my European training. . . . We do have our interludes, however. I often accompany Kane on business trips, which take him all over the world. We spent most of last month, for example, in Buenos Aires, and Kane says we will be going to London and Paris soon." She refilled their brandy glasses, her hand shaking slightly. "You must not feel sorry for me," she said in a light tone. "It is true, I sometimes miss the company of women of my own class, but one must sacrifice something for being married to a phenomenon. . . . Did you know that my husband was a famous athlete in his day?"

It was all rather pathetic, and when Karla insisted on showing them her husband's trophy room they followed her like tourists into what looked like a museum. The room was sternly Greek in spirit, an affair of pure-line marble and slender columns, and it was full of athletic trophies won, Karla Bendigo said, by her extraordinary husband in his youth.

"This is a phase of the great man that never gets into the magazine articles," remarked Ellery, glancing about at the plaques and scrolls and cabinets containing memorial footballs, baseballs, skis, statuettes, cups, lacrosse sticks, foils, boxing gloves, and a hundred other testimonials to athletic prowess. "Did Mr. Bendigo actually win all these?"

"We rather discourage magazine writers, Mr. Queen," said Karla. "Yes, these were all won by Kane at school. I don't think there's a sport he didn't excel in."

Ellery paused to study one silver cup, for water polo, on whose surface the name Kane appeared brighter than the other engraving.

"That one," observed the Inspector over Ellery's shoulder, "looks as if the name Kane's been re-engraved."

Karla looked, too, and nodded. "Yes, it has. I asked Kane about that myself when I first saw it."

"Abel. Judah." Ellery turned suddenly. "I wondered why the Biblical influence didn't extend to the other brother. It did, didn't it, Mrs. Bendigo? Kane—K-a-n-e—isn't his name, either. It was . . ."

"C-a-i-n. That is right, Mr. Queen."

"Can't say I blame him!"

"Yes, for obvious reasons he always loathed it. When he entered private school—some military school, I think—even as a boy he insisted on changing it. He told me he had won this water polo trophy in his Genesis phase, as I always call it, so he had it re-engraved later to read K-a-n-e."

"From his appearance, Mrs. Bendigo," said the Inspector, "your husband must keep up a lot of these sports. When does he get the time?"

"He doesn't. I have never seen him do anything but wrestle and box a little with Max."

"What?" The Inspector looked around the trophy room.

"He takes no exercise to speak of," laughed Karla. "I told you Kane is unique! He keeps his figure and muscles in trim by massage twice a day. For all his stupidity, Max is a skillful masseur and Kane, of course, is Max's religion. Careful food habits—you saw how sparingly he ate tonight—and a constitution of steel do the rest. Kane has so many facets to his personality! In many things he is a little boy, in others a peacock. Did you know that for years now he has been judged one of the world's ten best-dressed men? I will show you!"

King's wife dragged them to another room. It was a large room; it might have been an exclusive men's shop. Closet after closet, rack after rack, of suits, overcoats, sportswear, dinner jackets, shoes—he had everything, in wholesale lots.

"He can't possibly find the time to wear all of these," exclaimed the Inspector. "Ellery, take a gander at that lineup of riding boots! Does he ride much, Mrs. Bendigo?"

"He hasn't been on a horse for years. . . . Isn't it fabulous? Kane comes in here often, just to admire."

They were inspecting this kingly wardrobe with appropriate murmurs when a deep voice said behind them, "Karla, why would our guests be interested in my haberdashery?"

He was in the doorway. His handsome face was fatigued. His voice held a cross, raspy note.

"You would not deprive your wife of the pleasure of boasting about her husband?" Karla went to him quickly, slipped her arm about his waist. "Kane. You are very tired tonight."

She was frightened. There was no trace of it in her expression or attitude, and her voice was merely anxious, but Ellery was sure. It was almost as if she had been caught in an act of treason, discovery of which meant merciless punishment.

"I've had a long day, and some of it was trying. Would you gentlemen join me in a nightcap?" But his tone was icy.

"Thank you, no. I'm afraid we've kept Mrs. Bendigo far too long as it is." Ellery took his father's arm. "Good night."

Karla murmured something. She was smiling, but her face was suddenly bloodless.

Bendigo stood aside to let them pass. The Inspector's arm jerked. A security guard stood at attention just outside the door. They were about to step into the corridor when Bendigo said, "One moment."

They stopped, alert to some new danger. It was puzzling and annoying. Every word this man uttered seemed full of traps.

King Bendigo, however, sounded merely absent. "Something I was to show you. Abel told me not to forget. What the devil was it, now?"

Blocking the corridor at the turn loomed the ape, Max'l. He was holding up a wall as he smoked a long cigar. He eyed them with a grin.

"Yes?" Ellery tried to relax.

"Oh." King's hand went to his breast pocket. "Another of those letters came tonight. By the late plane. It was in the general mail."

He dropped the envelope into Ellery's hand. The envelope had been slit open. Ellery did not remove its contents; he was looking at Bendigo's face.

He could see nothing there but weary indifference.

"You've read this, Mr. Bendigo?" asked Inspector Queen sharply.

"Abel insisted. Same brand of garbage. Good night."

"Kane. What is it?" Karla was clinging to him.

"Nothing to concern you, darling—" The door shut in their faces.

Max'l followed them at a distance of six feet all the way to the door of their suite. Then, to their alarm, he closed the gap in a bound.

"Here!" The Inspector backed up.

Max'l's sapper of a forefinger struck Ellery in the chest, staggering him.

"You ain't so tough. Are you?"

"What?" stammered Ellery.

"Na-a-a." Max'l turned on his heel and rolled contemptuously away.

"Now what in hell," muttered the Inspector, "was *that* for?"

Ellery bolted the door, rubbing his chest.

THE third note was almost identical with its predecessors. The same elegant stationery, the same type—of a Winchester Noiseless Portable—and virtually the same message:

You are going to be murdered on Thursday, June 21—

"June twenty-first," said the Inspector thoughtfully. "Adds the date. Less than a week from now. And again he ends up with a dash, showing there's more to come. What the devil else can he say?"

"At least one other thing of importance." Ellery was scanning, not the enclosure, but the envelope. "The exact hour, maybe the exact hour and minute, on Thursday, June twenty-first. Have you noticed this envelope, Dad?"

"How can I have noticed it when you've hoarded it like a miser?"

"Proves what we suspected all along. King says it was found with the mail brought in by tonight's mail plane. That ought to mean that it went through somebody's post office. Only, it didn't. Look."

"No stamp, no postmark," mumbled his father. "It was slipped into the pouch on arrival."

"An inside job, and no guesswork this time."

"But this is so dumb, Ellery. Doesn't he care? A school kid would know from this envelope that the origin of these notes is on the island. I don't get it at all."

"It's pretty," said Ellery with a faraway look. "Because they don't need us, Dad. Not the least bit. And right now I don't care a toot if they do hear all this in their spy room."

"What are you going to do, son?"

"Go to bed. And first thing in the morning—assert myself!"

VI

THE NEXT MORNING Ellery asserted himself. He deliberately set out to make as much trouble as he could.

Leaving his father at the Residence, Ellery ordered a car. One showed up in the courtyard with Blue Shirt behind the wheel and his alter ego at the door.

"I don't want company this morning, thank you," Ellery snapped. "I'll take the wheel myself."

"Sorry, Mr. Queen," said Brown Shirt. "Get in."

"I was told I could go anywhere!"

"Yes, sir," said Brown Shirt. "We'll take you wherever you want to go."

"My father took a car out without a wet-nurse!"

"Our orders this morning are to stick with you, sir."

"Who gives these orders?"

"Colonel Spring."

"Where does Colonel Spring get them?"

"I wouldn't know, sir. From the Home Office, I suppose."

"The Home Office is where I want to go!"

"We'll take you there, sir."

"Jump in, Mr. Queen," said Blue Shirt amiably.

Ellery got into the car, and Brown Shirt got in beside him.

At the Home Office Ellery strode into the black marble lobby with a disagreeable face. The Shirts sat down on a marble bench.

"Good morning, Mr. Queen," said the central of the three security men behind the desk. "Whom did you wish to see?"

"King Bendigo."

The man consulted a chart. He looked up, puzzled. "Do you have an appointment, sir?"

"Certainly not. Open that elevator door."

The three security men stared at him. Then they conferred in whispers. Then the central man said, "I'm afraid you don't understand, Mr. Queen. You *can't* go up without an appointment."

"Then make one for me. I don't care how you do it, but I'm talking to your lord and master, and I'm doing it right now."

The three men stared at one another.

From behind him, Blue Shirt said, "You don't want to make trouble, Mr. Queen. These men have their orders—"

"Get Bendigo on the phone!"

It was a crisis Ellery thoroughly enjoyed. Brown Shirt must have touched Blue Shirt's arm, because both fell back; and he must have nodded to the central security man, because that baffled official immediately looked scared and sat down to fumble with the controls of his communications system. He spoke in a voice so low that Ellery could not hear what he said.

"The King's receptionist says it's impossible. The King is in a very important conference, sir. You'll have to wait, sir."

"Not down here. I'll wait upstairs."

"Sir—"

"Upstairs."

The man mumbled into the machine again. There was a delay, then he turned nervously back to Ellery.

"All right, sir." One of the trio pressed something and the door in the circular column sank into the floor.

"It's not all right," said Ellery firmly.

"What, Mr. Queen?" The central man was bewildered.

"You've forgotten to check my thumbprint. How do you know I'm not Walter Winchell in disguise? Do you want me to report you to Colonel Spring?"

The last thing Ellery saw as the elevator door shut off his view was the worried, rather silly, look on Brown Shirt's face. It gave him a great deal of satisfaction.

The elevator discharged him in the wedge-of-pie reception room. This time the black desk was occupied. The man behind the desk wore a plain black suit, not a uniform, and he was the most muscular receptionist Ellery had ever seen. But his voice was soft and cultured.

"There's some mistake, sir—"

"No mistake," said Ellery loftily. "I'm getting tired of all this high-and-mightiness. King Kong in his office?"

"Have a seat, please. The King is in an extremely—"

"—important conference. I know. Doesn't he ever hold any unimportant conferences?" Ellery went to the lefthand door and, before the receptionist could leap from behind the desk, pounded coarsely on the panel. It boomed.

He kept pounding. It kept booming.

"Sir!" The receptionist was clawing at his arm. "This is not allowed! It's—it's—"

"Treason? Can't be. I'm not one of your nationals. Open up in there!"

The receptionist got him in a stranglehold. The other hand he clamped over Ellery's mouth and nose.

Things began to turn blue.

Ellery was outraged. Taking his own bad office manners into due consideration, this sort of treatment smacked more of the bouncer in a Berlin East Zone rathskeller than the dutiful clerical worker of a civilized democracy. So Ellery slumped, feigning submission, and when the muscular receptionist's hold relaxed, Ellery executed a lightening judo counterattack which sent his captor flying backward to thump ignominiously on his bottom.

Just as the door to King Bendigo's private office opened and Max'l peered out.

Ellery wasted no strength parleying with the gorilla. Having the advantage of surprise, there was only one way to deal with such as Max'l, and Ellery did so. He stiff-armed the King's jester in the nose and walked in past the outraged carcass. What must follow in a matter of seconds he preferred not to linger over in his thoughts.

The hemispherical room seemed full of distinguished-looking men. They were seated or on their feet about the King's desk, and they were all staring toward the door.

Behind him Ellery could hear the receptionist shouting and a drumming of boots. Max'l was up on one knee, nose bleeding, beret askew over his left eye, and his right measuring Ellery without the least rancor.

Ellery trudged the long mile to Bendigo's desk, side-stepped one of the distinguished-looking men, planted both fists on the ebony perfection, and stared at the man in the golden chair malevolently.

The man on the throne stared back.

"Wait, Maximus." The voice was furry. "Just what do you believe you're doing, Queen?"

Ellery felt Max'l's hot breath on the back of his neck. It promised neither comfort nor cheer.

"I'm looking for the answer to a question, Mr. Bendigo. I'm sick of evasions and double talk, and I won't stand for further delays."

"I'll see you later."

"You'll see me now."

Abel Bendigo was in the group, looking on illegibly. Out of the corner of his eye Ellery also noticed Immanuel Peabody and Dr. Akst, the lawyer's mouth open, the physicist regarding him with an interest not evident the night before. The distinguished strangers looked merely confused.

"Do you have any idea," demanded the master of Bendigo Island, "what you have interrupted?"

"You're wasting time."

The black eyes dulled over. Bendigo sank back.

"Excuse me, gentlemen, just a moment. No, stay where you are. You guards, it's all right. Shut that door." Ellery heard a scuffing far behind him, the click of the distant door. "Now, Queen, suppose you ask me your question."

"Where on your island," said Ellery promptly, "will I find a Winchester Noiseless Portable typewriter?"

Had he asked for the formula of the H-bomb, Ellery could not have met a more absolute silence. Then one of the distinguished visitors permitted himself an undistinguished titter. The giggle shot King Bendigo out of his golden chair.

"In the course of your stupid, inconsequential investigation," thundered the King, "you disrupt what is probably the most important conference being held at this moment anywhere on the face of the earth. Mr. Queen, do you know who these gentlemen are? On my left sits Sir Cardigan Cleets, of the British government. On my right sits the Chevalier Camille Cassebeer, of the Republic of France. Before me sits the Honorable James Walbridge Monahew, of the United States Atomic Control Commission. And you dare to break in on the deliberation of these gentlemen—not to mention mine!—in order to locate a *typewriter?* If this is a joke, I don't appreciate its humor!"

"I assure you, Mr. Bendigo, I'm not feeling the least bit devilish—"

"Then what's the meaning of this? Explain!"

"Gladly," said Ellery. "You've fouled your island up with so many locked doors, armed guards, orders, restrictions, and other impediments to an investigation, Mr. Bendigo, that it would take me five years to do the job properly, and even then I wouldn't be sure I'd covered them all. And I don't have five years, Mr. Bendigo. I want action, and on Bendigo Island it's obvious that to get it you have to go to the top. I repeat: Where on your island will I find a Winchester Noiseless Portable typewriter?"

The black eyes dulled even more. And the fine hands on the desk top trembled a little. But when the big man spoke, it was in a low voice.

"Abel . . ."

Then his control broke. The fine hand became a club, smashing the air. *"Get rid of this lunatic!"*

Abel hurried around the desk to whisper into his brother's crimson ear. . . .

As Abel whispered, the crimson began to fade and the big fist came undone. Finally King nodded shortly, and his black eyes looked Ellery over once more.

Abel straightened up. "We don't have such information at our fingertips, Mr. Queen." There was something secretive and yet amused in his unhurried twang. "I can tell you that all the typewriting machines in the Home Office are electrics, standard in size and weight; we use no portables in this building at all. There may be some, of course, elsewhere on the island, in the personal possession of employees—"

"If you can't give me any more concrete information than that," said Ellery, "I want permission to search the private apartments of the Residence. Specifically, the Bendigo living quarters." He added brutally, looking Abel in the eye, "Nothing like starting in the feedbox, Abel, is there?"

Abel blinked. He blinked very rapidly indeed, and he kept blinking.

That's where I'll find it, thought Ellery.

King Bendigo snapped, "All right, Queen, you have our permission. Now get out, before I let Max'l boot you out."

ELLERY picked his father up in their suite.

"I made myself as obnoxious as possible," he concluded his recital of his adventures in the Home Office, "and I made one discovery, Dad—no, two."

"I know the first," grunted his father. "That you were born with the luck of the leprechaun."

"We'll find the murderous portable somewhere in the Bendigo living quarters," said Ellery. "That's one. The other is that King is an even more dangerous man than I thought. He has not only the power of a tyrant, but a tyrant's whims as well. And he'll become most whimsical when he recognizes power in others. It's a trait I don't trust. Let's see if Abel's carried out his lord's command."

Abel had. They were not stopped by the guards. The officer in charge looked pained, but he saluted and stepped aside without a word.

Each member of the family had a private suite, and the Queens searched them in turn. There was no sign of a machine in Karla Bendigo's suite, and no sign of Karla.

They found a typewriter in the King's study, and one in Abel's, but these were standard machines of a different make. They were approaching Judah's quarters when Ellery noticed for the first time, across the corridor from Judah's door, a large and massive-looking door of a design different from any he had seen in the Residence. He tried it. It was locked. He rapped on it. He whistled.

"Steel," he said to his father. "I wonder what's in here."

"Let's find out," said the Inspector, and he went for the officer in charge.

"This is the Confidential Room, sir," said the officer. "For the use of the King only, and of whoever's helping him. Usually it's Mr. Abel."

"Where the deeper skulduggery is planned, hm?" said Ellery. "Open it, please, Captain."

"Sorry, sir. No one may enter this room except by special permission."

"Well, you've got your orders. I've been granted special permission."

"Nothing was said about the Confidential Room, sir," said the officer.

"Then get something said."

"One moment, sir."

The officer strode away.

The Queens waited.

"Confidential Room," grunted the Inspector. "Fat chance we have to get in there. I suppose that's where he and Abel work nights when they don't want to go back to the Home Office."

The officer came back. "Permission refused, sir."

"What!" exploded Ellery. "After all that—"

"Mr. Abel assures Mr. Queen that there is no Winchester Noiseless Portable typewriter in the Confidential Room."

They watched the officer march away.

"It looks, Dad," said Ellery, "as if Mr. Judah Bendigo is elected."

He was. They found a Winchester Noiseless Portable in Judah's study.

JUDAH Bendigo was still in bed, snoring the spasmodic snores of the very drunk. The Inspector set his back against the bedroom door while Ellery looked around.

There was nothing like Judah's suite anywhere in the Residence. Karla's had been feminine, but it lacked depth and breadth. These were the cluttered, comfortable quarters of a man of intelligence, culture, and artistic passions.

The books were catholic in range, visibly read, and many were rare and beautiful volumes. The paintings and etchings were originals and could not have been gathered by any but a man of acute perception and taste. Many were by artists unknown to Ellery, which pleased him, for it was evident that Judah set no store by mere reputation, seeing greatness still unrecognized elsewhere. At the same time, there were two little Utrillos which Ellery would have given a great deal to own.

One entire wall was given over to music recordings. Perhaps twenty-five hundred albums, a fabulous record collection which must have taken many years to put together. Ellery saw numerous recordings which had long been out of print and were rare collectors' items. Palestrina, Pergolesi, Buxtehude, Bach, Mozart, Haydn, Handel, Scarlatti, Beethoven, Schumann, Brahms, Bruckner, and Mahler were heavily represented; there were whole volumes of Gregorian chants; and one long shelf was devoted to ethnic music. But Bartók was there too, and Hindemith, and Shostakovitch, and Toch. It was a collection which embraced the great music of the Western world since the ninth century.

On a table, in a velvet-lined case which was open, glowed a Stradivarius violin. Ellery touched the strings; the instrument was in perfect tune.

And he opened the Bechstein piano. No bell-shaped bottles here! Here, Judah Bendigo found such subterfuge unnecessary. In the corner of the room behind the piano, piled high, stood six cases of Segonzac cognac.

Ellery glanced at the bedroom door with an unhappy frown.

He shook his head and went to the Florentine leather-topped desk on which the Winchester portable stood.

He did not touch it.

Suddenly he sat down and began to rummage through drawers.

The Inspector watched in his own silence.

"Here's the stationery."

There was a large box of it—creamy single sheets, personal letter size, of a fine vellum-type paper without monogram or imprint.

"You're sure, Ellery?"

"It's of Italian manufacture. The watermarks are identical. I'm sure."

He took one of the sheets from the box and returned the box to its drawer. The sheet he inserted in the carriage of the machine.

"He'll wake up," said the Inspector.

"I hope he does. But he won't. He's stupefied and this is a Noiseless. . . . I don't get it. If this is the same machine—"

Ellery brought out the third threatening note, propped it against a bottle of Segonzac on the desk, and copied its message on the blank sheet.

The machine made a pattering sound. It was soothing.

Ellery removed the copy and set it beside the original. And he sighed, unsoothed. The evidence was conclusive: The latest message threatening King Bendigo's life and setting the date for Thursday, June the twenty-first, had been typed on this machine. Slight discrepancies in alignment, ink flaws in the impression of certain characters, were identical.

"It is, Dad."

They looked at each other across Judah's quiet room.

After a while the Inspector said, "No concealment. None at all. Anybody—Abel, King—could walk in here at any hour of the day or night and in ten seconds find the stationery, the typewriter, make the same test, reach the same conclusion. Or Colonel Spring, or any security guard on the premises. Max'l could do it!"

"Abel did do it."

Brother proposing to take the life of brother, and taking no precautions of any kind against discovery. And another brother discovering this and—most baffling of all—seeking confirmation where no confirmation was even remotely called for. . . .

"Maybe," said the Inspector softly, "maybe Judah's being framed, Ellery, and Abel knows it or suspects it."

"And would that present a problem?" said Ellery, gnawing his knuckles. "On the top floor of the central building of this fortified castle, in the private apartment of one of the royal family? Does that sort of thing require 'experts' flown from New York? When they've got a complete law-enforcement organization here, with undoubtedly the most advanced facilities? All the exploration of that theory would require, Dad, is the simplest sort of trap. A mere fingerprint checkup, for that matter." He shook his head. "It doesn't make sense."

"Neither does this!"

Ellery shrugged. He fished in his pocket and produced a pocket-knife.

"What are you going to do, Ellery?"

"Go through the motions. What else can I do?" Ellery opened the knife to its sharpest blade and carefully nicked both sides of the lower case *o* in Judah Bendigo's typewriter.

"What's the point of that? We know they're being typed on this machine."

"Maybe they were all typed at the same time, long ago. If the *o*'s on the next note are undamaged, they were, and we'll probably be at a dead end. But if they show these nicks, and if we can get a round-the-clock check on who enters this room . . ."

ELLERY said to the captain of the guard, "Get Colonel Spring on the phone for me."

The officer stiffened. "Yes, sir!"

The other guards stiffened, too.

"Colonel? This is Ellery Queen. I'm calling from—"

"I know where you're calling from, Mr. Queen," said Colonel Spring's high voice. "Enjoying your visit?"

"I'd rather answer that question in person, Colonel. If you know where I am, suppose you come here at once."

"Something wrong?" The Colonel sounded alert.

"I'll wait for you."

The drowned face of Colonel Spring appeared in six minutes. He was not smiling or limp now.

"What is it?" he asked abruptly.

"How much are these guards," asked Ellery, "to be trusted?"

The guards, including their officer, were rigidly at attention. Their eyes bulged.

"These men?" Colonel Spring's aqueous glance washed over them. "Completely."

"That goes for all shifts on duty up here?"

"Yes. Why?"

But Ellery said, "They're utterly devoted to the King?"

The little man in the splendid black and gold uniform put one hand on a hip and cocked his fishlike head. "To King Bendigo, you mean? They'd lay down their lives for him. Why?"

"I'll settle for incorruptibility," murmured Ellery. "Why, Colonel? Because, as of this minute, I want a twenty-four-hour-a-day report on the identity of every person who enters the private apartment of Judah Bendigo."

"Mr. Judah? May I ask *why?*"

"You may, but I'm not going to answer, Colonel Spring."

The little man produced a brown cigaret and snapped it to his lips. The captain sprang forward with a lighter.

"Thank you, Captain," said the Colonel. "And is this authorized, Mr. Queen?" He puffed in short, stabbing puffs.

"Check with Abel Bendigo. If he withholds authorization, tell him Inspector Queen and I will expect to be flown back to New York within the hour. But he won't. . . . This report, Colonel, is to be confidential. No one—except Abel Bendigo, and I'd really prefer not to except even him—no one is to know the check is being made. For simplification, maids and other servants are to be barred from Judah Bendigo's rooms on some plausible pretext until further notice. If any leak whatever occurs, or the job isn't done thoroughly, Colonel—"

The green in Colonel Spring's complexion deepened. But he merely said, "I've never had any complaints, Mr. Queen."

In the elevator Inspector Queen said dryly," I wonder how much *he* can be trusted."

Ellery was wondering, too.

VII

THE FOURTH LETTER turned up on the afternoon of the following day.

The day began with a humorous ultimatum from the King's Surgeon-General. Dr. Storm's quarters in the Residence were combined with a hospital wing, reserved for the use of the Bendigo family. Here, against a background of the most advanced equipment, with the assistance of a staff of medical and dental assistants and laboratory technicians, Dr. Storm supervised the daily ritual of examining into the health of the master of the Bendigo empire. The medical examination took place each morning before King Bendigo's breakfast.

On this particular morning the stout little doctor, brandishing a clip of reports, waddled past the guards into the family dining room, as King and his queen were risng from the table, to announce abruptly that there would be no work for his eminent patient that day.

"Something is wrong?" Karla asked quickly.

"Rot," growled King. "I feel fine. A bit pooped, maybe—"

"A bit pooped, maybe," mocked Dr. Storm. "A bit pooped, certainly! I don't like you this morning. I don't like you at all. And it's a heavy, humid day. Bad for you, at your age. You'll do nothing today but relax."

"Go away, Stormy," frowned King Bendigo. "Abel's had to run over to Washington and I have a thousand things on my calendar. It's out of the question."

"I'll go away," said the Surgeon-General, showing his sharp little teeth, "and I won't come back. Do you think I enjoy this exile? Oh, for an excuse, an excuse."

"Why do you stay?" King was smiling.

"Because I detest *genus homo*. Because I've conquered all their little universes and staggered all their little minds and shocked all their little ethical sensibilities, and because you've given me a great hospital to play with—and a wealth of raw material. And because, my lord, I'm in love with you. You're not to go near the Office today, do you hear? Not a step, or find another fool."

"But my appointments, Stormy—"

"What will happen? A dynasty will fall? You'll make ten million dollars less? To hell with your appointments."

"Darling," begged Karla. Her hand was on her husband's arm and her eyes were very bright.

"You, too, Karla?" The great man sighed and turned to inspect himself in a mirror. He stuck out his tongue. "Aaaaa. Does look starchy—"

"It isn't your tongue at all. It's your muscle tone and vascular system. Do you stay, or do I go?"

"All right, all right, Doctor," said the King tolerantly. "What are your orders?"

"I've given them to you. Do anything you like except work. Fly a kite. Get plastered. Make love to your wife. What do I care?"

So that afternoon, oppressed by the heat, nerves jangling, prowling restlessly, the Queens came upon an extraordinary scene. Passing by the Residence's gymnasium, they heard masculine shouts and looked in to find royalty at play. Near the indoor pool there was a regulation prize ring, and in the ring the master of the island was wrestling with Max'l. The two men wore high laced shoes and tights; both were naked from the waist up. Max'l was completely furred; the King's torso was as smooth as a boy's. Beside the other man's bulk, he looked slim.

As the Queens entered, Bendigo broke a vicious armlock by a backward somersault, and the next moment he had spun Max'l about and applied a full nelson. Max'l raised his great arms, hands clenched, and exerted all his strength in a downward pressure. But King's eyes flashed and he held on. And then Max'l sagged and he began to wave his fingers frantically.

"Give up, Maximus?"

"Yah, yah!"

Laughing, King increased the pressure. Max'l's eyes popped in his contorted face. Then, with a sort of contempt, King unlocked his hands and turned away. The great furred body crashed to the mat and lay still. After a moment Max'l rolled over and crawled to a corner of the ring, where he sat dejectedly, like an exhausted animal licking his wounds. He kept rubbing the back of his neck.

King spied them and waved gaily as he vaulted out of the ring.

"Do you wrestle, Queen?"

"After what I just witnessed—no, thank you!"

King laughed. "Karla. Our wandering guests."

Karla looked up. She was in a French bathing suit, lying with goggles on under a sun lamp at the edge of the swimming pool. She sat up quickly.

"There you both are. I sent all over the Residence looking for you to ask you to join us. Where have you been hiding?"

"Here and there, Mrs. Bendigo. It's a jittery day."

King Bendigo was looking down at them, smiling. Ellery wondered what would happen to a man this potentate caught making love to his wife.

Max'l was on his feet now, looking foolish.

And in the pool was Judah Bendigo. There was no sign of Abel.

Judah's white, emaciated body, wearing green bathing trunks, was floating in the pool like a broken lily pad. On the edge of the pool lay a bottle of Segonzac and a glass. As Ellery looked at him, Judah opened his eyes. They were bloodshot and bleared, but they did not blink. To Ellery's stupefaction, one lid moved down and up in an unmistakable wink. And then both eyes closed and Judah paddled a little, moving lazily toward the bottle and the glass.

Karla was saying, "Why don't you two cool off in the pool? There are dressing rooms down here, and we have a central guest-supply room from which we can provide anything."

"I wouldn't bare my scrawniness before a beautiful woman, even at my age," said the Inspector, "if my hide was baking off. Don't mind if I do," he said to an attendant, who had come up with a portable bar. "But my son here, he's kind of proud of his physique—"

"Not any more," said Ellery, glancing at King.

The big man laughed. "You're slighter than I am, but Darius—my receptionist at the Office—tells me you're a powerful boy. Do you box, Queen?"

"Well . . . yes."

"Don't let Kane tempt you into a boxing match, Mr. Queen," said Karla. "There is a photograph in the trophy room—did you notice it the other evening?—showing my husband standing over the prostrate form of a champion."

"Champion?" said the Inspector. "What champion?"

"The heavyweight champion of the world," chuckled King Bendigo. "It was a long time ago—I was in my early twenties. He was barnstorming up around my way, putting on exhibitions and pushing over the yokels, and some of my local admirers persuaded me to climb into the ring with him. I got in a lucky right cross in the first twenty seconds, he went down, and one of my newspaper friends snapped a flash photo of it. He ran like hell, as I recall it, and so did I! That photo is one of my proudest possessions.—Maximo! How you feeling?"

"We wrestle again," grunted Max. "I'll break your arm this time. Come on!"

"No, I feel like showing off. Let's put the gloves on, Max'l. I'm going to knock your block off."

"Oh, this has been the loveliest day," sighed Karla. "Go on, Max'l. Knock his off. I'd love to see your block flying off, darling. . . ."

"You heard the Madame," grinned King Bendigo. "Toss me my gloves."

Two pairs of eight-ounce boxing gloves hung over one of the ring posts. One pair was the regulation color, the other had an iridescent purple cast. It was these gloves that Max'l tossed with a growl down to his master. Ellery noticed a great many pairs of boxing gloves hanging on one of the gymnasium walls; none of them was purple. His stomach crawled.

It was as King was drawing on the left glove that it happened. His big hand stuck midway into the glove, and with a scowl he withdrew his hand. Then he probed with his forefinger.

It came out hooked about a wad of paper.

Cream-colored paper.

Bendigo unfolded it. He exclaimed with annoyance and whirled as if to accuse someone of something. As he whirled, the sole of his gym shoe slipped on the apron of the pool and, with a comical shout, he tumbled backwards into the water, landing with a splash that soaked Ellery and the Inspector to the skin.

Karla, who had not seen him withdraw the note from the boxing glove, cried out in terror; but then, at the sight of her lord and master threshing and floundering about in the pool, she burst into laughter.

"Oh, Kane, I can't help it! That was so funny! Judah, don't just float there like a dead stick. Help him!"

The great man sank, came to the surface, howled, got a mouthful of water, and sank again. Judah sat up in the pool, startled. Then he swam over to his brother with quick strokes and seized the royal chin.

"A miracle! A miracle!" Judah cried. "Ozymandias revealed! Who's got a hook to barb this foot of clay? And watch out for typhoons!"

As Ellery and the Inspector dragged the spluttering man out of the pool, Ellery was thinking that it was the first time he had heard Judah Bendigo's voice.

"Kane, I'm so sorry. Darling, are you all right? But I've never seen you lose your dignity before. Humpty-dumpty!" Karla laughed and laughed, holding his head tenderly.

He shook her off, jumped to his feet, and strode out of the gymnasium. His face was black.

Max'l, who had stood stupidly in the ring through it all, vaulted to the floor and ran after his master.

Karla stopped laughing.

"He is angry," she said slowly. "He laughs a great deal, but never at himself. . . . What was that piece of paper? Another of those threatening notes?"

Then she did know.

"I'm afraid so, Mrs. Bendigo." Ellery had picked up the paper as it fell from Bendigo's hand and had slipped it into his pocket. He produced it now, and Karla and his father read it with him.

Judah was sitting on the edge of the pool, calmly pouring himself a drink.

It was the same kind of paper, and the typing had been done on a Winchester Noiseless Portable.

This time the message said:

You are going to be murdered on Thursday, June 21, at exactly 12:00 o'clock—

"I can't believe it," Karla said. "I have known about the others—I wormed it out of Kane—but it is all silly. So uselessly melodramatic." She drew her robe about her. "Excuse me," she said faintly. "I will dress."

She ran toward the dressing rooms.

And that was when they turned around to find that Judah Bendigo was gone.

With the bottle and the glass.

NEITHER of the Queens bothered to change his wet clothing. They hurried upstairs and dashed for the private elevator.

"The nicks in the *o*," muttered the Inspector. "Six small *o*'s, and every one has the double nick. Now the question is—"

"Your report, Captain," Ellery said to the officer of the guard. "Let me have it, please!"

The officer thrust a time-sheet into Ellery's hand.

They retreated as pell-mell as they had come.

IN their own rooms, with the door locked, they bent over the report.

There was one name on it.

No one had entered or left Judah Bendigo's quarters since Ellery had nicked the *o*'s in Judah Bendigo's typewriter but Judah Bendigo.

Not only had Judah Bendigo's typewriter been used in the composition of the fourth threatening note, but it could only have been Judah Bendigo who used it.

* * *

"ALL right," said the Inspector, pacing. "So now we *know* it. It's Judah Bendigo on the level, and the time is definitely set for Thursday, June twenty-first, twelve o'clock, and that's that."

"That's not that. Twelve o'clock what?"

"What?"

"Noon or midnight? There's going to be a fifth note."

"I don't care about that, Ellery. Right now the important thing is that we know it's Judah. Only now that we know it, what do we do about it?"

"Report to Abel."

"Who's in Washington."

Ellery shrugged. "Then we wait till he gets back."

"Suppose," said his father, "suppose Abel doesn't get back till Friday, June twenty-second?"

Ellery tapped his lip with the edge of the note.

"Or suppose he gets back in time. We report. He says,

'Thank you, gentlemen, that's what I thought, here's your hat—take off!' So we fly into the sunset, or whatever the devil direction New York is from here—and I ask you, *Why?* What were we needed for in the first place?"

"And what," mumbled Ellery, "what do they do with Brother Judah? Skin him alive? Hang him by the neck till he can't even swallow Segonzac? Slap his skinny little wrist?"

"Climb out of those wet clothes, son. No sense getting pneumonia on top of a first-class skull ache."

They undressed in silence.

VIII

WHAT FOLLOWED was intolerable. For what followed was nothnig at all. All the next day Abel did not return to the island. Karla could not see them—she was reported ill, nothing of importance, but Dr. Storm was keeping her in bed. King Bendigo returned to the Home Office and, as if to make up for the day he had lost, remained there until far into the night, working with Peabody. The Queens saw Judah two or three times; he waved amiably but managed to keep out of their way. They had long since discussed the advisability of tackling Judah on their own initiative, without waiting for Abel, but they decided against this.

There was literally nothing to do.

So they wandered over the island.

"Maybe," remarked the Inspector, "I can add to my little bundle of notes and sketches."

Even the Shirts had disappeared. At least, no block was put in their path and no one, so far as they could make out, trailed them.

On the second day after the incident of the boxing glove, they were exploring a part of the island neither had seen before. There were no factories or workers' homes here. It was a barren place, an area of sand dunes and leathery scrub, with the blue glass of the sea rolling in to smash into splinters against the cliff walls. This was one of the spit ends of the island, exposed to the sea on three sides, and it had probably been left in its natural state because of the difficulty of effective camouflage.

"But not entirely," said Ellery. "If you'll look up there—where the thick stuff starts growing—you'll see something that looks like the biggest leaning birch tree you ever saw. Only it's a sixteen-inch gun."

"Who'd want this Godforsaken place, anyway?" snarled his father. "What's that?"

"What's what?"

The Inspector was a little ahead, to one side of a dune, and when Ellery joined him with a stride the stride stopped short.

The cliff wall crumbled at their feet to make a steep but negotiable path down to the beach. Between the shoreline and the base of the cliff there was a concrete building. It was not a large building, and its few iron-barred windows were so small that it looked like a fort in miniature. Palm trees had been planted about the structure, which was streaked and splashed with green and dun-colored paint. From the sea it was probably indistinguishable from its background.

Around the entire area rose a twelve-foot metal fence topped with barbed wire.

Ellery pointed to some camouflaged cables. "Electrified."

There was a little blistery bulb of a lookout on top of the building, with a narrow embrasure through which machine-gun muzzles protruded. Uniformed men, heavily armed, patrolled the enclosure.

"Soldiers of the Kingdom of Bendigo," said Ellery through his teeth. "They must get lonely way out here. Maybe they'll loosen up to a kind word."

Ellery scrambled down the path, the Inspector at his heels. Bits of shale flew from under their feet. The sun was hot.

As they reached the base of the cliff they came upon a small Residence car. There was a key in its ignition lock, but the car was empty. They looked around. There was no beach road. They had had to leave their car up on the cliff some distance away, where the road ended.

"Now how the dickens did this car get down here?"

"A tunnel." Ellery pointed. "Plugged up—see the camouflaged door? It must lead up through the rock and join the main road somewhere back there. Cliff doors, God help us! I tell you, Dad, these people never grew beyond the age of eight."

"They're little hellers, though," said his father dryly.

"Halt!"

The gate was locked. Just inside were two soldiers armed with submachine guns. The guns were trained on the Queens' bellies through the gate. Between the soldiers loomed an officer with a sunblack face and eyes of the color and warmth of oyster shell.

A little to one side, smoking a brown cigaret, stood Colonel Spring.

"Good morning," said Ellery to Colonel Spring.

The Colonel smoked.

"What do you want?" The officer had a harsh, mechanical voice.

"Nothing especially. Just rubbernecking—Major, is it? I'm still not familiar with your insignia system." Maybe Spring didn't like to interfere in the routine duties of his subordinates. He was standing there as if he had never seen them before. "May we come in, Colonel, and look around?"

Colonel Spring smoked.

"Your passes," rapped the officer.

"What is this place, anyway?" muttered the Inspector.

All right, Colonel, if that's your game . . . "Yes, what are you boys playing at way out here, Major?"

"Your passes!" There was no humor in that robot voice.

The Queens stopped smiling.

"We don't have any passes," said Ellery carefully. "Colonel Spring can tell you who we are."

"I know who you are. Your pass."

"We have King and Abel Bendigo's personal permission to go anywhere on the island. Hasn't the word come down?"

"Produce it!"

"Produce what?" Ellery was growing angry. "I've told you. Your King said we could go anywhere we pleased."

"In this place you must produce a written pass signed by Colonel Spring. This is forbidden ground. If you have no pass, leave at once. Do you have a pass?"

"Well, I'll be damned," said the Inspector.

Ellery deliberately looked the Colonel over. The hippy, elegant little man in the uniform might have been watching the antics of a cageful of trained fleas. "All right, Colonel, here we are and there you are. Inspector Queen and I want a pass. Make one out."

The little Colonel smiled. "Certainly, Mr. Queen. But then you'll have to have it countersigned by King Bendigo or Abel Bendigo. Those are the rules. Apply to my office in the usual way. Good morning." He poised the smoldering brown butt of his cigaret delicately, dropped it, and ground it with the heel of his boot into the shaly sand.

"Come on, son," said Inspector Queen.

Four things happened almost simultaneously.

The only visible door of the concrete building opened and the chubby figure of Dr. Storm appeared, carrying a medical bag; behind him towered an enormous guard.

Ellery snatched a pair of binoculars from his pocket, clapped them to his eyes, and trained them on one of the barred windows of the building.

Colonel Spring stiffened and said something to the officer in a sharp voice.

The officer jumped forward, shouting to the lookout in the blister. Apparently the current charging the fence was operated from the tower. The officer seized the gate and unlocked it.

"Arrest these men," said Colonel Spring.

The binoculars were torn from Ellery's grasp by the officer and the next moment the Queens were in the grip of the two armed soldiers.

They were dragged into the enclosure.

"For . . . the love of . . ." The Inspector choked. One of the soldiers had an easy hold on the Inspector's necktie. The old gentleman slowly grew purple.

A cool small voice kept saying to Ellery, *This is ridiculous, it's something you're reading in a book,* as his fist kept cracking against flesh and faces stared into his and blue sky and blue sea and white sand and green palms whirled and pain jolted from every direction and finally exploded in his middle and he found himself prone on the sand with his nose grinding into some shale and a crushing weight on his back.

And then he was lifted clear and smashed to his feet and things came back a little. His father stood nearby, deathly pale, brushing himself off with blind puny strokes. The door of the concrete building was closed again. Dr. Storm, looking like a portly old penguin in his black suit and white shirt, was talking cheerfully to Colonel Spring.

They were ringed with armed soldiers.

Nobody looked menacing.

Nobody even scowled.

Part of the job. All in the day's work. . . . Ellery found himself doubled up, clutching his groin.

Colonel Spring was smoking another brown cigaret, head lowered, listening with a frown to Dr. Storm.

"My rules aren't made to be broken, Doctor."

Dr. Storm kept talking cheerfully.

The men holding him up kept holding. Ellery felt grateful. His father was still brushing himself futilely. A Bendigo plane streaked by deep in the sky.

"All right." Colonel Spring shrugged.

He said something to the officer, turned on his heel and walked over to the building. The door opened instantly. He stepped inside. The door crashed.

"You may leave now, gentlemen."

Ellery looked up. It was Dr. Storm, smiling.

"May . . . !" He heard a strangled voice, sounding nothing like his own.

"I know, I know," said the Surgeon-General of Bendigo Island. "Your manly ego is offended—"

"Offended," gurgled Ellery. He kept digging his fists into his groin. "I want an explanation. I want an apology. I want this man alone in a room with me. I want *something!*"

"You won't get it," said Dr. Storm. "You're lucky I happened to be here. And if you'll take my advice, Mr. Queen, you'll never come here again." And the fat little doctor waved, went through the gate, climbed into the empty car, backed around, and drove into the hole in the cliff.

A moment later there was no hole, just cliff.

"Outside," said the officer's thumb. His oyster eyes had not changed expression.

Ellery felt swollen fists at the ends of his arms.

"Come on, son," said his father urgently. "Do you think you can make it back to our car?"

ELLERY did not start the car. The pain was going away from his groin, but his nose burned where the shale had cut it and his body ached in a dozen places.

The Inspector sat limply, hands in his lap, staring at the peaceful sea.

They sat there, without a word, for a long time.

Then his father said, "Who was it you spotted in that building?"

"Dr. Akst." His tongue tasted bitter.

"Akst? The big blond young physicist?"

"Yes."

"Can that be Akst's hush-hush lab? Where he fiddles around with his atoms? That would explain the electrified fence, the guards—"

"It's too small a building for physical research. Anyway, Akst had his hands up to the bars. They were manacled."

"Manacled!"

"He's a prisoner." Ellery stared at his overstuffed hands. "I wondered why we hadn't seen him around. He's been tapped for out."

"Oh, come on," said the Inspector vehemently. "That's a bit thick even for this hellhole. After all—"

"After all what? That enclosure is Bendigo Island's version of Dachau. Who's to tell His Mightiness the King what he can or can't do? He's squatting on this island in the ocean, absolute monarch of it and everyone on it."

"But Akst—a man like Akst—"

"Disappears. Or false reports are cleverly broadcast. That wouldn't be a problem, Dad."

"But *why?*"

"Lèse majesté. Treason to the Crown. Or he's found that what he's been working on sticks in even his scientific craw. Who knows why? Probably Akst's loyalty came under suspicion. He was investigated, or he's in the process of being investigated. Or he's refused to go on, and this is a little persuasive treatment. Meanwhile, he's in chains in the King's private concentration camp. . . . Are there courts on Bendigo Island, I wonder?"

* * *

THE Inspector patched up Ellery's wounds, gave him a hot bath, and made him lie down. Ellery did not sleep. It was impossible to sleep.

Inspector Queen paced and paced. They had a nameless need to remain together. Had his father gone into the next room, Ellery would have followed.

At last he jumped out of bed and dressed in fresh clothes.

"How about lunch, son?"

"No."

"Where you going?"

But Ellery was already limping up the corridor. The Inspector hurried after him.

When they got to the Home Office, Ellery marched up to the desk with the air of a man who is prepared to slash and broadax a path to his objective.

"Open that elevator door. I want to see this King of yours!"

The central of the three security men said, "Yes, sir."

Thirty seconds later, the muscular receptionist was holding the door of the big office open.

"Interrupting me seems your only strong point, Queen," said the powerful voice at the other end of the room. "Well, come in."

The receptionist closed the door behind them softly.

King Bendigo was seated behind his desk. In a chair by his side sat Immanuel Peabody, immersed in some papers. A man they had never seen—a large stout man with flabby cheeks—stood facing them. The large stout man was standing between two armed soldiers.

Bendigo seemed calm and relaxed, one hand on the desk. As Ellery and his father approached, the handsome man lazily moved a finger and the soldiers stepped to one side, yanking the stout man with them.

"Mr. Bendigo—" began Ellery.

"Is this what you came for?" said the King, smiling.

His other hand appeared. In it was Ellery's pair of binoculars.

Ellery stared at him across the ebony desk. The black eyes were sparkling. Bendigo clearly had been expecting him. He wanted some entertainment, and what would entertain him best, Ellery saw suddenly, was the outraged fury of a helpless man.

The only defense was a feeble one. Having no choice, Ellery used it. He reached across the desk, took his binoculars from the arrogant fingers, and turned on his heel with a matching arrogance.

"Just a moment, Queen."

He felt calm. He would never lose his temper with this man again.

"When you were given carte blanche we thought you, as a man of intelligence, would understand that it was only relative. This is the original tight little isle; we like to keep our secrets. You're a guest here. We don't expect our guests to go snooping in our closets."

"Especially," said Ellery, "those with the skeletons in them?"

"Put it that way if you like. By the way, do you have a camera—any photographic equipment?"

"No."

"Do you, Inspector Queen?"

"No."

"Well, just in case. Cameras are not permitted on Bendigo Island. They are confiscated and smashed, and the film burned, whenever and wherever found. There are also certain . . . forfeits involved. That's all, gentlemen."

He turned toward Peabody.
"Mr. Bendigo."
Bendigo looked back sharply. "Yes?"
"As long as we're going down the Mosaic tables," said Ellery, "I think I ought to tell you that my father and I have guns with us. Are guns on your contraband list, too?"
Bendigo laughed. "No, Queen. We're very fond of guns here. You may have all the guns you can carry." His lips thinned until they almost disappeared. "But no cameras," he said.
Again their glances crossed.
And this time Ellery was able to smile.
"We understand, Your Highness," he said gravely.
"Wait!" King Bendigo sat taller on his throne. At the note in his voice Immanuel Peabody, for the first time, looked up from his papers. "I don't believe you do understand, Queen," Bendigo said slowly. "No, I don't believe you do.... Sit down and watch what you interrupted. Over there!"
His thumb stabbed toward two chairs at the curved wall.
Ellery felt a twitch of alarm. The drawl had been unpleasantly without inflection. It reminded him of the voice of the robot officer behind the electrified fence. He was vaguely sorry now that he had come. To conceal his apprehension, he went abruptly to one of the chairs. The Inspector was already at the other, looking gray.
They sat down, tense without knowing quite why.
"You may go ahead now," said Bendigo curtly to Peabody.
Peabody rose. His master leaned back and closed his eyes for a moment. It was theatrical, but it failed to give the reassurance of playacting. For in another moment Bendigo had opened his eyes and turned them on the large stout man between the two soldiers. And what glittered in the black arctic depths of those eyes made the Queens look at the large stout man really for the first time.
His knees sagged, as if his body were too heavy for his legs. His flabby cheeks were pale and wet, although air conditoning made the office very pleasant. He kept screwing up his eyes, as if he were having trouble focusing; occasionally, he would blink. His whole appearance was that of an exhausted man who feels he must pay the closest attention to the proceedings. Ellery had seen men look like that who were defendants in murder cases.
And it occurred to him suddenly that the rhetorical

question he had asked in the car after their experience at the concentration camp was being answered here and now.

Yes, there were courts on Bendigo Island. This was one of them, the highest.

The large stout man with the rubbery knees was about to be tried.

And when Immanuel Peabody began to speak, there was no doubt left. He spoke in the crisp, confident tone of the experienced prosecutor. King Bendigo listened with the aloof gravity of the supreme judge.

Peabody was outlining the charge. It had something to do with the stout man's failure to carry out certain instructions. Ellery could not follow it closely, for his thoughts were a bottleneck of jammed impressions—the handsome immobility of Bendigo, the slightly nervous fuss the lawyer's fingers made as he talked, the desperate concentration of the stout man, the glow of the glass brick walls, the powerful mastication of Max'l's jaws as he rapidly fed himself hulled nuts in the doorway of the open safe, apparently his favorite lounging place. Had Max'l been there all the time? . . .

Peabody became more specific. He enumerated dates, names, facts. None of them meant anything to Ellery, who was growing more and more confused. All he could gather was that something or some things the accused had done or had not done had resulted in the severance of an important secret contact somewhere in Asia, which in turn had brought about the loss of an armaments contract. At least it seemed to concern an armaments contract, although Ellery was not sure even of that; it might have involved oil, or raw materials, or ships. Whatever it was, the stout man stood accused of a major crime against the Bendigo empire: bungling.

Ellery held down an impulse to laugh.

And at last King's counsel came to the end of his argument, and he sat down and patted his papers together into a tight, neat pile. Then he leaned back, crossed his dapper legs, and stared with some interest at the stout man.

"Anything to say?" This was evidently the King's juridical voice, cold, solemn, and above-it-all.

The stout man licked his lips and blinked rapidly, struggling with a great wish to produce sound. But then his lips sagged along the lines of his cheeks, and he lapsed into helplessness.

"Speak up, Norton." The voice was sharper, more personal. "Do you have anything to say?"

Again the stout man struggled, the sag lifting. He was no more successful this time, but his failure ended with a shrug—the weariest, most hopeless shrug Ellery had ever witnessed.

Ellery felt his father's fingers on his arm. He sank back.

King made a flicking gesture with his shapely right hand.

The stout man might have been a fly.

The guards took him out, each wrestling an arm. The knees kept buckling, and a step before the door they collapsed altogether.

The trio disappeared.

The splendid office sunned itself. There was a siesta mood over everything. No one said a word.

King Bendigo sprawled on his throne, chin thoughtful, black eyes dreamy.

King's advocate Peabody kept his legs comfortably crossed, one hand on his neat, tight pile of papers. However, his head was cocked.

The rapid-fire motion of Max'l's feeding hand had stopped. The hand was suspended before the mouth.

They were waiting. That was it.

But for what?

A laugh that would shatter this dream—wake everyone up and restore the sanity of the world?

A shot?

Nonsense, absurd. . . .

Anyway, the walls were soundproof—

Ellery jumped.

King Bendigo had risen. Lawyer Peabody uncrossed his legs. Max'l's hand popped to his mouth, dipped for a fresh supply of hulled nuts.

It was over.

Whatever had happened, it was over.

The King was speaking graciously to the lawyer. There was a matter of a tax suit for sixty million dollars pending in the high court of some European country. Bendigo was discussing the incomes of the judges and inquiring for more information of the same personal nature.

Peabody replied busily.

At the door, waiting for his father, Ellery glanced back. The King and his Lord Advocate were seated again, their heads together. They were deep in conversation. The curved wall glowed and the long office was serene. Max was tossing nuts into the air now and balancing under them with his mouth open, like a seal.

Ellery stumbled out.

IX

WEDNESDAY night came, and there was still no word of Abel Bendigo. Peabody, whom Ellery chased for half a day, merely looked blank when asked about Abel's mission to Washington. Karla knew nothing about it.

His talk with Karla left Ellery unhappy.

"It is a long time since I shook at every threat," she said with a toss of her red hair. "I had to make up my mind early that I had married a unique personality, one who would always be the target of something." She smiled her crooked little smile. "Kane is better guarded than the President of the United States. By men at least as devoted and incorruptible."

"Suppose," Ellery said carefully, "suppose, Mrs. Bendigo, we found that your husband's life is being threatened by some one very close to him—"

"Close to him!" Karla threw her head back and laughed. "Impossible. No one is really close to Kane. Not even Abel is. Not even I am."

Ellery went away dissatisfied by this transparent sophistry. If Karla suspected anything, she was keeping it to herself.

As the night wore on and Thursday approached, Ellery's skin began to itch and he found it difficult to remain in one spot for more than a few minutes. The more nervous he became, the angrier he grew with all of them—with King, for treating the subject of his own death first with amusement, then with contempt, and finally with irritation, as at a minor but persistent infraction of some Company rule; with Abel, for dragging them into the case and then, unaccountably, staying away from them; with Karla, for being candid when candor was meaningless, and inscrutable when candor would have been helpful; with Judah, for being a man who drank brandy from morning to night and smiled vaguely when his bloodshot eye was caught . . . surely one of the most unsatisfying assassins in history.

The Inspector was no help. He spent most of Wednesday grumpily in his bathroom, locked away from the world of Bendigo. He was copying his sketches of the island's restricted installations, filling in details as best he could, and transcribing his notes in a minute shorthand.

THE call came just as the Queens were about to go to bed Wednesday night.

"I understand you've been asking for me, Mr. Queen."

"Asking for you!" It was Abel Bendigo. "The latest note—"

"I've been told about it."

"Has there been another one? There's going to be another one—"

"I'd rather not discuss it over the phone, Mr. Queen."

"But has there?"

"I don't believe so—"

"You don't *believe* so? Don't you realize that tomorrow is the twenty-first? And you've been away—"

"It couldn't be helped. I'll see you in the morning."

"Wait! Can't we talk now? Why don't you come down here for a few minutes, Mr. Bendigo—"

"Sorry. King and I will be up half the night on the matter that took me to Washington. In the morning, Mr. Queen."

"But I've found out—!"

"Oh." There was silence on the wire. Then Abel said, "And what did you find out?"

"I thought you didn't want to discuss it over the phone."

"Who is it?" The twang vibrated the receiver.

"Your brother Judah," said Ellery brutally. "Does that agree with your conclusion?"

There was another silence. Finally, Abel's voice said, "Yes."

"Well, what do my father and I do now, Mr. Bendigo? Go home?"

"No, no," said Abel. "I want you to tell my brother King."

"Tonight?"

"Tomorrow morning, at breakfast. I'll arrange it with Karla. You're to tell him exactly what you've found out, and how. We'll proceed from there, depending on my brother's reaction."

"But—"

But Ellery was left holding the receiver.

ALL night he tossed over the problem of Abel Bendigo's apparent diffidence, and he came with his father to the breakfast table in the private dining room without having solved it. But as he took his seat he suddenly had the answer. Abel, a planner, could plan nothing where his brother King was concerned. King was an imponderable, a factor who would always remain unknown. In a crisis as personal as this, he might fly off in any one of a dozen directions. Or he might fold his royal wings and refuse to fly at all. *We'll proceed from there, depending on my brother's reaction.* . . . This was probably why Abel, who had detected Judah's guilt at once, called for outside confirmation before revealing his knowledge. He could only pile up his ammunition and wait for developments to tell him which way and how much to shoot.

The King was in a sulky mood this morning. He stamped into the dining room and glared at the Queens, not greeting them. His black eyes were underscored by his nightwork; he looked almost seedy, and Ellery suspected that this had something to do with his mood—King Bendigo was not a man to relish strangers seeing him at less than his best.

Abel was there. Max'l. And Judah.

It was Abel unquestionably who had engineered Judah's presence at breakfast—a considerable engineering feat, to judge by Judah's almost normal appearance. In spite of the early hour, the dark little assassin could sit in his chair reasonably straight-backed. His hand shook only a little. He was gulping his second cup of coffee.

And Abel was nervous. Ellery rather enjoyed that. Abel's gray schoolmaster's face was far grayer than usual. He kept touching the nosepiece of his eyeglasses, as if he felt them skidding. All his gestures were jerky and full of caution.

"Something special about today?" King glanced darkly about, his hand arrested in the act of picking up his napkin. "Our troublemakers from New York—and you, Judah! How did you manage to get up so early in the morning?"

Judah's sunken eyes were on the fine hand of his brother.

The hand completed the act of picking up the napkin.

An envelope tumbled to the table.

Max'l shouted something so suddenly that Karla gripped

the arms of her chair, going very white. Max'l was on his feet, glaring murderously at the envelope.

"Who done that?" he roared, tearing the napkin from his collar. "Who, who?"

"Sit down, Maxie," King said. He was looking at the envelope thoughtfully. All his sulkiness had disappeared. Suddenly his mouth curved in a brief malicious smile. He picked the envelope up. His name was typed on it: *King Bendigo*. Nothing else. The envelope was sealed.

"Today is Thursday, the twenty-first of June, Mr. Bendigo—that's what's special about it." Ellery was on his feet, too. "May I see that, please?"

King tossed the envelope onto his brother Judah's plate. "Pass it to the expert, Judah. This is what he's getting paid for."

Judah obeyed in silence.

Ellery took the envelope with care. His father hurried around the table with a knife. Ellery slit the envelope.

"And what does this one say, Mr. Queen?" Karla's tone was too light. She was still pale.

It was the same stationery. The *o*'s were nicked. Another product of Judah Bendigo's Winchester portable.

"What does it say!" Abel's voice cracked.

"Now, Abel," mocked King. "Control yourself."

"It's a duplicate of the last message," said Ellery, "with two differences. A single word has been added, and this time it ends not with a dash but with a period. *You are going to be murdered on Thursday, June 21, at exactly 12:00 o'clock midnight.*"

"Midnight, period," muttered Inspector Queen. "That's it. There won't be any more. There's nothing more for him to say."

"For who to say?" bellowed Max'l, inflating his ape's chest. "I kill him! For who?"

King reached across Judah, seized Max'l's dried-apricot ear, and yanked. Max'l fell back into his chair with a howl. The big man laughed. He seemed to be enjoying himself.

"Kane, let us go away today." Karla's hand was smoothing the damask cloth. "Just the two of us. I know these letters are nothing, but—"

"I can't go away, Karla. Too much to do. But I'll take a raincheck on that. Oh, come! You all look like professional pallbearers. Don't you see how funny it is?"

"King." Abel spoke slowly. "I wish you'd take this seriously. It isn't funny at all. . . . Mr. Queen has something to tell you."

The black eyes turned on Ellery, glittering. "I'm listening."

"I have something to ask you first, Mr. Bendigo." Ellery did not look in Judah's direction. "Where would you normally be at midnight tonight?"

"Finishing the confidential work on the day's agenda."

"But where?"

"Where I always work at that hour. In the Confidential Room."

"That's the room with the heavy steel door, across the hall from your brother Judah's quarters?"

"Yes."

Abel said quickly: "We usually spend an hour or two in there, Mr. Queen, starting at eleven or so. Work we can't leave to the secretaries."

"If Abel is away, I take his place," said Karla.

Her husband grinned at the Queens. "All in the family. Where the big plots are hatched. I'm sure you suspect that."

"Kane, stop making jokes. You're not to work there tonight."

"Oh, nonsense."

"You are not to!"

He looked across at his wife curiously. "You're really concerned, darling."

"If you insist on working there tonight, I insist on working with you."

"On that point I yield," he chuckled, "seeing that Abel's going to be occupied elsewhere, anyway. Now let's have breakfast, shall we, and forget this childishness?"

The servants, who had been standing by frozen, sprang to life.

"I would like to suggest, Mr. Bendigo—" began Ellery.

"Overruled. Now see here, Queen. I appreciate your devotion to the job, but the confidential work stops for nothing, the idea of murder is ridiculous, and in that room impossible. Sit down and enjoy your breakfast. You, too, Inspector Queen."

But the Queens remained where they were.

"Why impossible, Mr. Bendigo?" asked the Inspector.

"Because the Confidential Room was built for just that purpose. The walls, floor, and ceiling are two feet thick—solid, reinforced concrete. There isn't a window in the place—it's air-conditioned and there's artificial daylight lighting in the walls. There's only one entrance—the door. Only one door, and it's made of safe-door steel. As a matter of fact, the whole room is a safe. So how would anyone get in to kill me?"

King attacked his soft-boiled eggs.

Max'l looked uncertain. Then he sat down and pounded the table. Two servants jumped forward, getting busy.

But Karla said uncomfortably, "The air-conditioning, Kane. Suppose someone got to that. Sending some sort of gas—"

Her husband roared with laughter. "There's the European mind for you! All right, Karla, we'll station guards at the air-conditioning machinery. Anything to wipe that look off your face."

"Mr. Bendigo," said Ellery. "Don't you realize that the person who wrote those letters is not to be laughed away? He knows exactly where you'll be at midnight tonight—in what amounts to the classic sealed room, guarded moreover by trusted armed men. Since he warns us, he must know that that room tonight will be absolutely impregnable. In other words, he chooses the time and place apparently worst for his plan, and he insures by his warning that even farfetched loopholes will be plugged. Doesn't that strike you as queer, to say the least?"

"Certainly," replied the King briskly. "Queer is the word, Queen. He's queer as Napoleon. It just can't be done."

"But it can," said Ellery.

The big man stared. "How?"

"If it were my problem, Mr. Bendigo, I'd simply get you to let me in yourself."

He sat back, smiling. "No one ever gets into that room except a member of my family—" He stopped, the smile disappearing.

The room was very quiet. Even Max'l stopped chewing. Karla was looking intently at Ellery, a crease between her eyes.

"What do you mean?" The voice was harsh.

Ellery glanced at Judah now, across the table from him. Judah was tapping a bottle of Segonzac cognac softly with a forefinger, looking at no one.

"Your brother Abel did some investigating on his own before calling us in," said Ellery. "We've compared conclusions, Mr. Bendigo. They're the same."

"I don't understand. Abel, what's all this?"

Abel's gray face seemed to go grayer.

"Tell him, Mr. Queen."

Ellery said: "I located the typewriter on which all the notes have been typed. I also found the notepaper; it comes from the same place as the typewriter. I nicked the lower-case *o* on the machine, and all *o*'s typed in the two notes since have shown the nicks. This checks the typewriter identification.

"As a further check, I arranged to have the room where the machine is located watched by your guards. The result was conclusive, Mr. Bendigo: During the period in which the fourth note must have been typed, only one person entered and left those rooms—the person who belonged there. Your brother Judah."

King Bendigo turned slowly toward his small, dark brother. Their arms, on the table, almost touched. A flush began to creep over the big man's cheeks.

Max'l was gaping from his master to Judah.

Karla said in a breathless way, "Oh, nonsense, nonsense. This is one of your cognac jokes, Judah, isn't it? Isn't it?"

Judah's hand as he reached for the bottle was remarkably well controlled. He began to uncork the bottle.

"No joke, my dear," he said hollowly. "No joke."

"You mean," began King Bendigo incredulously. Then he began again. "Judah, you mean you wrote those notes? You're threatening to kill me? *You?*"

Judah said: "Yes, O King."

He did it well, Ellery thought, for a man who was so taut you could almost hear the tension in him. Judah raised the bottle of Segonzac high. Then he brought it quickly down to his mouth.

King watched his brother drink. His eyes shimmered with amazement. They went over Judah, the crooked nose, the droop of the bedraggled mustache, the stringy neck, the rise and fall of the Adam's apple. But then Judah lowered the bottle and met his brother's glance, and something passed between them that made King seem to swell.

"At midnight, eh?" he said. "Got it all figured out."

"At midnight," said Judah in a high voice. "At exactly midnight."

"Judah, you're crazy."

"No, no, King. You are."

The big man sat quietly enough. "So you've had it in for me all these years. . . . I admit, Judah, I'd never have thought of you. Has anyone ever given a damn about you but me? Who else would put up with your alcoholic uselessness? The very fact that you've had all the booze you can soak up you owe to me. So you decide to kill me. Are you out of your mind completely? Is there any sense to it, Judah—or should I say Judas?" Judah's pallor deepened. "I'm your brother, damn it! Don't you feel anything? Gratitude? Loyalty?"

"Hatred," said Judah.

"You *hate* me? Why?"

"Because you're no good."

"Because I'm strong," said King Bendigo.

"Because you're weak," said Judah steadily, "weak where it counts." Now, although his face was like a death mask, the eyes behind it kindled and flamed. "There is strength that is weak. The weakness of your strength, brother, is that your strength has no humanity in it."

The big man looked at the little man with eyes dulled over now, clouded and secretive, in a sort of retreat. But his face was ruddy.

"No humanity, O King," said Judah. "What are human beings to you? You deal in corporate commodities—metals, oil, chemicals, munitions, ships. People are so many work-hours to you, such-and-such a rate of depreciation. You house them for the same reason you house your tools. You build hospitals for them for the same reason you build repair shops for your machines. You send their children to school for the same reason you keep your research laboratories going. Every soul on this island is card-indexed. Every soul on this island is watched—while he works, while he sleeps, while he makes love! Do you think I don't know that no one caught in your grinder ever escapes from it? Do you think I don't know what that devil Storm is up to in the laboratory he had you build for him? Or why Akst has disappeared? Or Fingalls, Prescott, Scaniglia, Jarcot, Blum before Akst? Or what's going on in Installation K-14? Or," Judah said in a very clear, high voice, "why?"

Now the flush was leaving the handsome man's face, and the face was settling into grim, contemptuous lines.

"The dignity of the individual, the right to make choices, to exist as a free man—that's been done away with in your empire as a matter of business policy. All the old laws protecting the individual have been scrapped. There's no law you recognize, King, except your own. And in carrying out your laws, you're judge, jury, and firing squad. And what kind of laws are they that you create, administer, and execute? Laws to perpetuate your own power."

"It's such a small island," said King Bendigo in a murmur.

"It covers the planet," retorted his scrawny brother.

"You needn't act the amused potentate for the benefit of the Queens. That kind of remark is an insult to their intelligence as well as mine. Your power extends in every direction, King. Just as you're cynical about the sovereignty of individuals, you're cynical about the sovereignty of nations. You corrupt prime ministers, overthrow governments, finance political pirates, all in the day's work. All to feed orders to your munitions plants—"

"Ah, I wondered when we'd get to that," said his brother. "The unholy munitions magnate, the international spider—Antichrist with a bomb in each hand. Isn't that the next indictment, Judah?"

Judah made thin fists on the cloth. "You're a plausible rascal, King. You always have been. The twist of truth, the intricate lie, the wool-pulling trick—you're a past master of that difficult technique. But it doesn't befog the issue. Your sin isn't that you manufacture munitions. In the world we live in, munitions are unfortunately necessary, and someone has to manufacture them. But to you the implements of war are not a necessary evil, made for the protection of a decent society trying to survive in a wolves' world. They're a means of getting astronomical profits and the power that goes with them."

"The next indictment," said his brother with a show of gravity, "is usually that I create wars."

"No, you don't create wars, King," said Judah Bendigo. "Wars are created by forces far beyond your power, or the power of a thousand men like you. What you do, King, is take advantage of the conditions that create wars. You stoke them, blow on them, help them go up in flame. If a country's torn by dissension, you see to it that the dissension breaks out into open revolt; if two powers, or two groups of powers, are at odds, your agents sabotage the negotiations and work for a shooting war. It doesn't matter to you which side is *right;* right and wrong have no meaning in your dictionary except as they represent conflicts, which mean war, which mean profits. That's where your responsibility lies, King. It's as far as one man's responsibility can go. It's too far!"

Judah's fists danced as he leaned toward his brother. "You're a murderer, King. I don't mean merely the murders you've committed on this island, or the murders your thugs have committed here and there throughout the world in the execution of some policy or deal of the moment. I mean the murders, brother, of which historians keep a statistical record. I mean the war murders, brother. The murders arising out of the misunderstandings and tensions and social and economic stresses which you encourage into wars. You know what you are, King? You're the greatest mass-murderer in history. Oh, yes, I know how melodramatic it sounds, and how you're enjoying my helplessness to keep it from sounding so! But the truth is that millions of human beings have died on battlefields which would never have been except for you. The truth is that millions upon millions of other human beings have been made slaves, stripped of the last rag of their pride and dignity, thrown naked into your furnaces and on your bone piles!"

"Not mine, Judah, not mine," said his brother.

"Yours! And you're not through, King. You've hardly begun. Do you think I'm blind merely because I'm drunk? Do you think I'm deaf just because I shut my ears to your factory whistles? Do you think I don't know what you're planning in those night sessions in your Confidential Room? Too far, King, you go too far."

Judah stopped, his lips quivering. King deliberately edged the bottle of Segonzac closer to him. Judah wet his lips.

"Dangerous talk, Judah," said King gently. "When did you join the Party?"

Judah mumbled: "The smear. How could I be a member of the Party when I believe in the dignity of man?"

"You're against them, Judah?"

"Against them, and against you. You're both cut from the same bolt. The same rotten bolt. Any means to the end. And what end? Nobody knows. But a man can guess!"

"That's typically muddled thinking, Judah. You can't be against them and against me, too. I'm their worst enemy. I'm preparing the West to fight them—"

"That's what you said the last time. And it was true, too. And it's true now. But a twisted truth that turns out to be no truth at all. You're preparing the West to fight them, not for the reason that they're a menace to the free world, but because they happen to be the current antagonist. Ten years from now you'll be preparing the West—or the East, or the North, or the South, or all of them put together!—to fight something or someone else. Maybe the little men from Mars, King! Unless you're stopped in time."

"And who's going to stop me?" murmured King Bendigo. "Not you, Judah."

"Me! Tonight at midnight I'm going to kill you, King. You'll never see tomorrow, and tomorrow the world will be a better place to live in."

King Bendigo burst into laughter. He threw back his handsome head and laughed until the spasm caused him to double up. He put his fists on the table's edge and heaved to his feet. There were actually tears in his eyes.

Judah's chair went over. He scrambled around the corner of the table and sprang at his brother's throat. His hands slipped. He beat with his thin fists on that massive chest. And as his little blows drummed away, he screamed with hate and outrage. For a moment King was surprised; his laughter stopped, his eyes widened. But then he only laughed harder. He made no attempt to defend himself. Judah's fists kept bouncing off him like rubber balls from a brick wall.

Then Max'l was there. With one hand he plucked the shrieking, flailing little man from his master and thrust Judah high in the air, holding him up like a toy. Judah dangled, gagging. The gagging sounds made Max'l grin. He shook Judah as if the little man were made of rags, shook him until his face turned blue and his eyes popped and his tongue stuck out of his mouth.

Karla whimpered and put her hands to her face.

"It's all right, darling," wheezed her husband. "Really it is. Judah doesn't mind punishment. He loves it. Always did. Gets a real kick out of a beating—don't you, Judah?"

Max'l flung the little man halfway across the dining room. Judah struck a wall, thudded to the floor, and lay still.

"Don't you worry," Max'l said, grinning at his master. "I take care of him. After I eat."

And he sat down and seized his fork.

"Don't be more idiotic than nature made you, Max. When the times comes—midnight, did he say? he'll be blind drunk and about as deadly as an angleworm." King glanced at the heap in the corner. "That's the trouble with democracy, Queen. You're one of the intellectual, liberal, democratic world, aren't you? You never get anywhere. You stick your chin out and happily ask for another crack on the jaw. You poison yourselves into a coma with fancy talk, the way Judah poisons himself with alcohol. All you do is jabber, jabber, jabber while history shoots past you into the future."

"I think we had a little something to do with the orbit of history, Mr. Bendigo," Ellery found himself saying, "not so very long ago."

"You mean I did," chuckled the King, lowering himself into his chair again.

The servants leaped forward as he picked up his napkin. But he waved them away.

"And you, Maxie. You leave Judah alone," he said severely. "He's had a strenuous morning. *Max.*"

The gorilla had leaped from his chair. Judah was stirring. There was blood on Judah's face.

"Sit down."

The gorilla sat down.

"Here, Judah, let me help you—" began Inspector Queen.

Judah raised a hand. Something in the way he did it stopped the Inspector in his tracks.

Judah's brothers looked on, Abel gray as evening, King with no flicker of pity.

Judah crept out of the dining room. They watched him go. His right leg took a long time getting out of the room. But finally it, too, disappeared.

"Karla, my dear," said King briskly. "Karla?"

"Yes. Yes, Kane."

"I'll be at the Home Office all day and most of the evening—I'll have dinner there. You meet me at eleven at the Confidential Room."

"You mean to work tonight, Kane? In spite of—?" Karla stopped.

"Certainly, darling."

"But Judah—his threats—"

"He won't lift a pinkie when the time comes. Believe me, Karla. I know Judah.... Yes, Queen? You were going to say something?"

Ellery cleared his throat. "I think, Mr. Bendigo, you tend to underestimate the intellectual, liberal democrat when aroused. I don't know why I say this—it's certainly nothing to me whether you live or die—"

"Or maybe it is," said King Bendigo, smiling.

Ellery stared at him. "All right, maybe it is. Maybe after what I've seen here I'd greet the news of your death with cheers. But not this way, Mr. Bendigo. I'm an anti-murder man from way back—was indoctrinated from childhood by the Bible and I happen to believe in democracy. They both teach the ethics of the means, Mr. Bendigo. And murder is the wrong means—"

"You'd like to see me die, but you'll lay your life down to protect mine from violence." King laughed. "That's what's wrong with you people! Could anything be more hopelessly asinine?"

"You really believe that?"

"Certainly."

"Then it would be a waste of your valuable time to discuss it." And Ellery went on in the same painful way, "What I have been trying to say is that your brother Judah not only wants to kill you, Mr. Bendigo, he's made plans about it. So he must have some weapon in mind. Prepared. Does he own a gun?"

"Oh, yes. Pretty good shot, too, even when scuppered. Judah practices sometimes for hours at a time. On a range target, of course," the big man said dryly. "Nothing alive, you understand. Makes him sick. Judah couldn't kill a mouse—he's often said so. Don't be concerned about me, Queen—"

"I'm not. I'm concerned about Judah."

The black eyes narrowed. "I don't get that."

Ellery said slowly, "If he gets blood on his hands, he's lost."

"Why, you're nothing but a psalm-singer," King said impatiently. "You're through here. I'll have you flown out this morning."

"No!" Abel jumped up. He was still shaken. "No, King. I want the Queens here. You're not to send them away—"

"Abel, I'm getting tired of this!"

"I know you," shouted Abel. "You'll put a gun in his hand and dare him to shoot! King, I know Judah, too. You're underestimating him. Let the Queens stay. At least till tomorrow morning."

"Let Spring handle it."

"Not Spring, no. King, you've got to let me handle this my way!"

His brother scowled. But then he shrugged and said, "All right, I suppose I can put up with these long-faced democrats another day. Anything to stop this gabble! Now get out, the lot of you, and let me finish my breakfast."

X

BY WRITTEN ORDER of Abel Bendigo, the Queens were permitted that afternoon to inspect the Confidential Room. Colonel Spring himself, looking a wee bit flustered, unlocked the big steel door. The Colonel, the officer in charge of the household guards, and two armed guards went in with them and watched them as closely as if it were the bullion vault of Fort Knox.

It was a great empty-looking room painted hospital gray. There was only one door, the door through which they had entered. There were no windows at all, the walls themselves glowing with a constant, shadowless light. A frieze of solid-looking material ran around the walls near the high ceiling; this was a porous metal fabric invented by Bendigo engineers to take the place of conventional heating and air-conditoning vents and grilles. "It's a metallic substance that actually breathes," explained Colonel Spring, "and does away with openings." The air in the room was mild, sweet, and fresh.

No pictures, hangings, or decorations of any kind broke the blankness of the walls. The floor was of some springy material, solidly inlaid, that deadened sound. The ceiling was soundproofed.

In the exact center of the Confidential Room stood a very large metal desk, with a leather swivel chair behind it. There was nothing on the desk but a telephone. A typewriter-desk, its electric typewriter exposed, faced the large desk; this one was equipped with an uncushioned metal chair. Solid banks of steel filing cases lined the walls to a height of five feet.

Above the door, and so in direct view of the occupant of the large desk, there was a functional clock. It consisted of two uncompromising gold hands and twelve unnumbered gold darts, and was imbedded in the wall.

And there was nothing else in the room.

"Who besides the Bendigo family, Colonel, uses this room?" asked Inspector Queen.

"No one."

Ellery said: "Does Judah Bendigo come in here often?"

Colonel Spring cocked a brow at the officer of the guard. The officer said: "Not often, sir. He may wander in for a few minutes sometimes, but he's never here very long."

"When was the last time Mr. Judah visited this room?"

"I'd have to consult the records, sir."

"Consult them."

The officer glanced at Colonel Spring. The Colonel nodded, and the officer went away. He returned shortly with a ledger.

"About six weeks ago was the last time, sir. And a week before that, and three weeks before that."

"Would these records show if at those times he was in this room alone?"

"Yes, sir."

"Was he?"

"No, sir. He never comes in here when the room is unoccupied. He can't get in. No one can but Mr. King and Mr. Abel. They have the only two keys, aside from an emergency key kept in the guardroom in a wall safe. We have to open the room daily for the maids."

"The maids, I take it, clean up under the eye of the guards?"

"*And* the officer on duty, sir."

The Queens wandered about the Confidential Room for a few minutes. Ellery tried a number of filing cases, but most of them were locked. The few that were not locked were empty. In one of the unlocked drawers he found a bottle of Segonzac cognac, and he sighed.

Ellery examined the steel door. It was impregnable.

When they left the room, Colonel Spring tried the door with his own hands and gave the key to the captain of the guard. The officer saluted and took the key to the guardroom.

"Is there anything else I can do, gentlemen?" asked the Colonel, rather plaintively, Ellery thought. "My orders are to put myself completely at your disposal."

"Just the matter of the air-conditioning unit, Colonel," the Inspector said.

"Oh, yes. . . ."

Ellery left them and crossed the hall. He knocked on Judah Bendigo's door. There was no answer. He knocked again. There was still no answer. So he went in.

Max'l was straddling a chair the wrong way, his chin on his hairy hands. Only his eyes moved, following like a watchdog's the movements of Judah Bendigo's hands. An empty bottle of Segonzac lolled on Judah's desk. Judah was opening a fresh bottle. He had torn away the tax stamp and was just running the blade of a pocketknife around the hard wax seal. He paid no attention to the troglodyte, and he did not look up when Ellery came in.

ELLERY spent the rest of the day trying to save Judah Bendigo's soul. But Judah was doomed. He did not resist salvation; he shrugged it down. He was looking more like a corpse than ever—a corpse who had died of violence, for his cheekbone was bruised, swollen, and purple from its encounter with the dining room wall, and a split lip gave his mouth a sneering grin such as Ellery frequently saw at the morgue.

"I'm not enjoying this, Ellery, really I'm not. I don't care for the idea of killing my brother any more than you do. But someone has to do the dirty job, and I'm tired of waiting for the Almighty."

"Once you shed his blood, how do you differ from King, Judah?"

"I'm an executioner. Executioners are among the most respectable of public servants."

"Executioners do their work by sanction of law. Self-appointed executioners are simply murderers."

"Law? On Bendigo Island?" Judah permitted his ragged mustache to lift. "Oh, I admit the circumstances are unusual. But that's just the point. There are no sanctions I can evoke here except the decent opinions of mankind, as expressed in a handful of historic documents. The conscience of civilization has appointed me."

At another time—toward dusk—Judah interrupted Ellery to say, simply, "You're wasting your breath. My mind is made up."

It was at this point that it occurred to Ellery that Judah Bendigo was talking like a man who expects to consummate his crime.

"Let me understand you, Judah. Granted the firmness of your resolve, hasn't it sunk home that you've been detected *in advance?* You don't think we're sitting by and letting you execute your plan, whatever it is? Max'l alone in this room with you would be enough to thwart whatever you have in mind. There's going to be no murder, Judah." By this time Ellery was talking as if Judah were a child. "We simply can't allow it, you know."

Judah sipped some cognac and smiled. "There's nothing you can do to stop me."

"Oh, come. I'll admit that a man bent on violence may sooner or later find an opening, no matter what precautions are taken. But we know the exact time and place—"

Judah waved a thin white hand. "It doesn't matter."

"What doesn't matter?"

"That you know the time and place. If I cared whether you knew or not, I'd never have written the note."

"You'll do it in spite of the fact that we're forewarned?"

"Oh, yes."

"At that time? In that place?" exclaimed Ellery.

"Midnight tonight. The Confidential Room."

Ellery looked at him. "So that's it. You have another

plan entirely. This was all a red herring to foul up the trail."

Judah seemed offended. "Nothing of the sort! I give you my word. That would spoil it. Don't you see that?"

"No."

Judah shrugged and tipped his bottle again.

"Of course, none of this is really necessary," Ellery said, "since you have my personal assurance you won't leave this room tonight and your brother King won't enter it. So I can afford to play games, Judah. Tell me this: You announced the time of the murder, we know the exact place—if you stick to your word about the time—so do you mind telling me by what means you intend to kill your brother?"

"Don't mind at all," said Judah. "I'm going to shoot him."

"With what?"

"With one of my favorite guns."

"Nonsense," said Ellery irritably. "My father and I have searched these rooms twice today, and neither of us is exactly a novice at this sort of thing. Including, if you'll recall, a very thorough body-search. There is no gun on these premises, and no ammunition of any kind."

"Sorry. There's a fully loaded gun right under your nose."

"Here? Now?"

"It's not six feet from where you're standing."

Ellery looked around rather wildly. But then he caught himself and grinned. "I must watch that trick of yours. It's unsettling."

"No trick. I mean it."

Ellery stopped grinning. "I consider this downright nasty of you, Judah. Now, on the off chance that you may be telling the truth, I've got to search the place all over again."

"I'll save you the trouble. I don't mind telling you where the gun is. It won't make any difference."

It won't make any difference. . . . "Where is it, Judah?" Ellery asked in a kindly voice.

"In Max'l's pocket, where I slipped it when you started searching."

Max'l jerked erect. He began to paw at his coat pocket. Ellery ran over, flung his hand aside, and explored the pocket himself. It was crowded with pieces of candy, nuts, and other objects Ellery's fingers could not identify; but among the sticky odds and ends there was a hard cold something. He drew it out.

Max'l glared at it.

It was a rather silly-looking automatic pistol. It was so snubnosed it could be concealed in a man's hand, for the barrel was only about one inch long—the entire length of the weapon was scarcely four inches. It was a German Walther of .25 caliber. For all its womanish size, Ellery knew it for a deadly little weapon, and this one had a used look. The ivory inlays on the stock were rubbed and yellow with handling, and the right side of the grip was chipped—a triangular bit of the ivory was missing from the lower right corner.

Judah was gazing at it fondly. "Beauty, isn't it?"

The automatic was fully loaded. Ellery emptied the magazine and chamber, dropped the little Walther into his pocket, and went to the door. By the time he had unlocked and opened it, Inspector Queen blocked the doorway.

"What's the matter, Ellery?"

"I've extracted Judah's teeth." Ellery put the cartridges in his father's hand. "Hold on to these for me."

"Where the devil— Maybe he's got more!"

"If he has, they're not in there. But I'll look again."

Ellery relocked the door and regarded Judah thoughtfully. Why had he disclosed where the gun was? Was it a trick designed to head off still another search which would turn up a second gun—the gun Judah had intended to use from the beginning?

Ellery said to Max'l, "Watch him," which was quite unnecessary, and searched Judah's two rooms and bath again. Judah kept drinking with every appearance of indifference. He made no protest when Ellery insisted on another body-search. Afterwards, he redressed and reached for the bottle again.

There was no other gun, not a single cartridge.

Ellery sat down facing the thin little figure and looked it over searchingly. The man was either insane or so fogged with alcohol that he could no longer distinguish between fancy and reality. For practical purposes it really did not matter which. If the German automatic was the weapon he had meant to use, its teeth were drawn; Judah would not and could not leave the room; and it had been arranged between the Queens, with Abel Bendigo's unqualified consent, that King Bendigo would be prevented by force, if necessary, from crossing the threshold of Judah's quarters.

There was simply no way for the dedicated assassin to kill the tyrant. And if Judah's antics masked a plan whereby some bribed or hired killer was to attempt the murder, that was taken care of, too.

At exactly eleven o'clock that night King and Karla Bendigo appeared in the corridor. Six guards surrounded them. Karla was pale, but her husband was smiling.

"Well, well," he said to the Inspector. "And are you gentlemen enjoying yourselves?"

"Don't joke about it, Kane," begged Karla. "Nothing is going to happen, but . . . don't joke about it."

He squeezed her shoulder affectionately and produced a key from a tiny gold case attached to his trousers by a gold chain. Inspector Queen glanced about: two guards were at Judah Bendigo's door across the corridor, one of them with his hand on the doorknob, gripping it tightly. On the other side of that door, the Inspector knew, Judah was being guarded by Max'l and Ellery. Even so, he was taking no chances.

"One minute, Mr. Bendigo." King had unlocked the massive door and Karla was about to precede him into the Confidential Room. "I have to ask you to let me search this room before you step inside."

The Inspector was already in the doorway, barring the way.

King stared. "I was told you searched it this afternoon."

"That was this afternoon, Mr. Bendigo." The Inspector did not move.

"All right!" King stepped back peevishly. Three guards managed to slip between him and the doorway. They stood there shoulder to shoulder. Something about the maneuver restored the magnate's good humor. "What's he had you men doing today, rehearsing? You did that like a line of chorus girls!"

The room was exactly as the Inspector had left it during the afternoon. Nevertheless he prowled about, glancing everywhere—at the filing cases, the desks, the chairs, the floor, the walls, the ceiling.

"Mr. Bendigo, I want your permission to look in these desks and filing cases."

"Denied," came the brusque answer.

"I've got to insist, Mr. Bendigo."

"Insist?"

"Mr. Bendigo." The Inspector came to the doorway. "I've been given a serious responsibility by your brother Abel. If you refuse to let me handle this as I think it ought to be handled, I have your brother's permission to keep you from entering this room—by force, if necessary. Mr. Abel wanted your consent to my searching those drawers and cases, but he recognizes the necessity for it. Do you want to see his personal authorization?"

The black eyes engulfed him. "Abel knows that no one outside my family—no one!—is allowed to see the contents of those drawers."

"I promise not to read a single paper, Mr. Bendigo. What I'm looking for is a possible booby trap or time bomb. A glance in a drawer will tell me that."

King Bendigo did not reply for several moments.

"Kane. Do whatever they say. Please." Karla's voice sounded as if her tongue were stiff.

He shrugged and unhooked the little gold case from the end of his chain. "This key unlocks the file drawers. This one the drawers of my desk. The drawers of the small desk are not locked."

The Inspector took the two keys. "Would you permit me to shut this door while I search?"

"Certainly not!"

"Then I must ask you and Mrs. Bendigo to step aside, out of range of the doorway. These three guards," the Inspector added with a certain bitterness, "can keep watching *me*."

He searched thoroughly.

When he came out into the corridor he said, "One thing more, Mr. Bendigo. Is there a concealed compartment of any kind in that room, or a concealed door, or a panel, or a passageway, or anything of that sort? Anything of that sort whatsoever?"

"No." The big man was fuming at the delay.

The Inspector handed him the two keys. "Then it's all right for you to go in."

When the master of the Bendigo empire had entered the Confidential Room followed by his wife, and the great door had swung shut, Inspector Queen tried the door. But it had locked automatically; he could not budge it.

He set his back against the door and said to one of the guards. "Do you have a cigaret?" Ellery's father resorted to cigarets only in times of great stress. For the first time it had occurred to the Inspector that he had just risked being blown into his component parts to save the life of a man whose death under other circumstances would have caused him no more, perhaps, than a mild humanitarian regret.

JUDAH was well into his current bottle of Segonzac, and by 11:20 P.M., it was almost empty and he had settled down to serious drinking. He had politely inquired if he might play some music, and when Ellery, before consenting, re-examined the record-player, Judah shook his head dolefully as if in sorrow at the suspicious nature of man.

"Don't go near those albums," said Ellery. "I'll get what you want."

"Do you suspect my music?" exclaimed Judah.

"You can't have a weapon concealed in those albums." retorted Ellery, "but there might be a cartridge tucked away in one of them that I somehow missed. You sit just where you are, impaled by Max'l's glittering eye. I'll handle your music. What would you like to hear?"

"You would suspect Mozart. Mozart!"

"In a situation like this, Judah, I'd suspect Orpheus. Mozart?"

"The Finale of the C-Major symphony—there, the Forty-first. There's nothing as grand in human expression except parts of Shakespeare and the most inspired flights of Bach."

"Window dressing," muttered Ellery, perhaps unjustly; and for a few minutes he listened with grudging pleasure to *l'Orchestre de la Suisse Romande* under the baton of Ansermet. Judah grudged nothing. He sprawled in the chair behind his desk, a snifter between his palms, eyes wide and shining.

Mozart was in full swing when Ellery glanced at his watch and saw that it was 11:32. He nodded at Max'l, who was as impervious to the counterpoint as a Gila monster, went quietly to the door, and unlocked it. Before pulling it open, he glanced back at Judah. Judah was smiling.

At the sound of the door the Inspector came quickly across the corridor. He blocked the opening with his back, still watching the door of the Confidential Room.

"Everything all right, Dad?"

"Yes."

"King and Karla still in there?"

"The door hasn't been open since they went in."

Ellery nodded. He was not surprised to see Abel Bendigo across the hall, standing among the guards before the locked room. Abel glanced at Ellery anxiously and came over to join them.

"I couldn't work. It's ridiculous, but I couldn't. How has Judah been, Mr. Queen?"

"He's hard to figure out. Tell me, Mr. Bendigo—does

your brother Judah have any history of mental disturbance?"

Abel said: "Because he's threatened to kill King?"

"No. Because even though he knows we're aware of his intentions, he still talks as if he's going to do it."

"He can't, can he?" Abel said it quickly.

"Impossible. But it's a word he apparently doesn't recognize."

"Judah has always been a little peculiar. Of course, his drinking . . ."

"How far back does his alcoholism go?"

"A good many years. Do you think I ought to talk to him, Mr. Queen?"

"No."

Abel nodded. He went back across the hall.

"He didn't answer the question," remarked the Inspector.

Ellery shrugged and shut the door. He turned the key and put it back in his pocket.

WHEN the symphony was over, Ellery put the records away. He turned from the album shelves to find Judah regarding his empty glass. The would-be fratricide picked up the cognac bottle and tilted it. Nothing came out. He grasped both arms of his chair, raising himself.

"Where are you going?" asked Ellery.

"Get another bottle."

"Stay there. I'll get it for you."

Ellery went behind the Bechstein and took a new bottle of Segonzac from the case on top of the pile. Judah was fumbling in his pockets. Finally he produced his pocketknife.

"I'll open it for you."

Ellery took the knife from him, slit the tax stamp, and scraped the hardened seal off the bottle's mouth. The knife had a corkscrew attachment; with it Ellery drew the cork. He placed the bottle on the desk beside the empty glass.

"I think," he murmured, "I'll borrow this, Judah."

Judah followed his knife in its course to Ellery's trouser pocket.

Then he picked up the bottle.

Ellery glanced at his watch.

11:46.

AT 11:53 Ellery said to Max'l: "Get in front of him. I'll be right back."

Max'l got up and went to the desk, facing Judah seated behind it. The great back blocked Judah out.

Ellery unlocked the door, slipped outside, relocked the door from the corridor.

His father, Abel Bendigo, and the guards had not changed position.

"Still in there?"

"Still in there, son."

"The door hasn't been opened at all?"

"No."

"Let's check."

Ellery rapped.

"But Judah . . ." Abel glanced across the corridor.

"Max is standing over him, the door's locked, and the key's in my pocket.— Mr. Bendigo!" Ellery rapped again.

After a moment the lock turned over. The guards stiffened. The door opened and King Bendigo towered there. He was in his shirt sleeves. At the secretarial desk, Karla twisted about, looking toward the door a little blankly.

"Well?" snapped the big man.

"Just making sure everything's all right, Mr. Bendigo."

"I'm still here." He noticed Abel. "Abel? Finish with those people so early?"

"I'll wind it up in the norning." Abel was tight-lipped. "Go in, King. Go back in."

"Oh—!" The disgusted exclamation was lost in the slam of the door. The Inspector tried it. Locked.

Ellery looked at his watch again.

11:56:30.

"He's not to open that door again until well after midnight," he said. He ran across the hall.

When Ellery relocked Judah's door from inside, Max'l backed away from the desk and padded to the door to set his shoulders against it.

"What did he do, Max?"

Max'l grinned.

"I drank cognac," said Judah dreamily. He raised the snifter.

Ellery went around the desk and stood over him.

11:57:20.

"Time's a-ticking, Judah," he murmured. He wondered how Judah was going to handle the moment of supreme reality, when he was face to face at last with the stroke of midnight.

He kept looking down at the slight figure in the chair. In spite of himself, Ellery felt his muscles tighten.

Two minutes to midnight.

Judah glanced at the watch on his thin wrist and set the empty glass down.

And turned in his chair, looking up at Ellery.

"Will you please be good enough," he said, "to give me my Walther?"

"This?" Ellery took the little automatic out of his pocket. "I'm afraid there isn't much you can do with it, Judah."

Judah presented his upturned palm.

There was nothing to be read in his eyes. The light Ellery saw in them might be mockery, but he was more inclined to ascribe it to cognac. Unless . . .

Because he was what he was, Ellery examined the Walther, which had not left his pocket since he had removed its ammunition.

The automatic, of course, was empty. Nevertheless, Ellery examined it even more closely than before. It might be a trick gun. It might, somehow, conceal a bullet, and a pressure somewhere might discharge it. Ellery had never heard of a gun like that, but it was possible.

Not in this case, however. This was an orthodox German Walther. Ellery had handled dozens of them. It was an orthodox German Walther and it was not loaded.

He dropped the little automatic into Judah's hand.

He could not help feeling an embarrassed pity as Judah transferred the empty gun to his right hand and took a firm grip on the stock, his forefinger curled at the trigger. Judah was intent now, making small economical movements, as if what he was about to do was of the greatest importance and required the utmost in concentration.

He pushed downward with his left hand on the desk top and got to his feet.

Ellery's glance never left those hands.

Now Judah raised his left forearm. He stared down at the second hand of his wristwatch.

Thirty seconds.

His right hand, with the empty gun, was in plain view. There was nothing he could do with it, no sleight-of-hand, not a trick, not a bluff, not an anything. And if he could? If, by an unreasonable miracle, he could materialize a cartridge and load the gun with it with Ellery at his elbow, what could he do with it? Shoot Ellery? Hypnotize Max'l? And if he got out into the corridor, what then? A locked door of safe steel. A hallful of armed, alert men. And even then, no key.

Fifteen seconds.

What was he waiting for?

Judah raised the Walther.

Max'l moved convulsively, and Ellery almost sprang. He had to check his own reflex. Max'l uttered a growly chuckle, rather horrible to hear, and relaxed against the door again.

It was too stupid. There was nothing Judah could do with that empty little gun, nothing. Too, an obscure curiosity stayed Ellery. There was nothing Judah could do, and yet he was preparing to do something. What?

Seven seconds.

Judah's right arm came up until it was straight out before him. He was apparently taking aim at something, getting his sight set for a shot he couldn't possibly fire. A shot he couldn't possibly fire at a wall he couldn't possibly penetrate.

Five seconds.

A theoretical extension of Judah's right arm with the Walther at the end of it would make a line through the wall of his study, across the corridor, through the wall of the Confidential Room, into the approximate center of that room and—perhaps—the torso of a seated man.

Three seconds.

Judah was "aiming" at his brother King.

He was mad.

Two seconds.

Judah watched his upheld wrist.

One second.

And now, Judah?

At the tick of midnight Judah's finger squeezed the trigger.

HAD the little Walther flamed and bucked at that instant Ellery could not have been so astounded. A gun that went off in spite of the impossibility of a gun's going off would at the least have made reasonable the unreasonable play that went before. It would have been a physical miracle, but it would have given Judah's actions the dignity of logic.

The little Walther, however, neither flamed nor bucked. It merely went *click!* and was quiet again. No roar reverberated through the room, no hole appeared in the wall, no voice cried out.

Ellery squinted at the man.

He was incredible, this Judah. He was not acting like a man who had just pulled the trigger of a gun that could not and did not go off. He was acting like a man who had seen the flame and felt the buck and heard the roar and the cry. He was acting like a man who had successfully fired a shot.

Judah lowered the Walther slowly and with great care put it down on his desk.

Then he sank into the chair and reached for the bottle of Segonzac. He uncorked it slowly, slowly poured several ounces of cognac, slowly and steadily drank, the bottle still gripped in his left hand. Then he flung bottle and glass aside and, as they crashed to the floor, he put his face down on the desk and wept.

Ellery found himself going over the facts indignantly. No bullet in the gun. A wall, a corridor, then another wall two feet thick made of reinforced concrete. And a man safely beyond it. Safely. Unless . . . unless . . .

Impossible. *Impossible.*

Ellery heard a harsh voice, hardly recognizable as his own. "You act as if you shot your brother."

"*I did.*"

The words were sobby. Thick with grief.

"As if you really killed him, I mean."

"*I did.*"

He didn't understand. He couldn't have said—

So he had said it. Ellery passed his hand over his mouth. The man *was* insane.

"You did what, Judah?"

"*King is dead.*"

"Did you hear what he said?" Ellery glanced bitterly across at Max'l.

Max'l tapped his temple, grinning.

Ellery took hold of Judah's shoulder in a burst of annoyance and pulled him upright, holding him against the back of the chair.

Crying, all right.

He let go. Judah stopped crying to bite his lower lip with his uneven, stained teeth. He fumbled for something in his back pocket. His hand reappeared with a handkerchief. He blew his nose into it and relaxed, sighing.

"They can do what they want with me," he said in a high monotone. "But I had to do it. You don't know what he was. What he was planning. I had to stop him. I had to."

Ellery picked up the Walther. Glared at it.

He tossed it back on the desk and strode across the room. He said stridently to Max'l, "Get out of my way."

He unlocked the door.

The corridor was at peace. The Inspector and Abel Bendigo were leaning against the door of the Confidential Room, talking in lively voices. The guards lounged in visible relief.

"Oh, Ellery." The Inspector looked around. "Well, that's that.—What's the matter? You're pale as a ghost."

"Is Judah all right?" asked Abel quickly.

"Yes." Ellery gripped his father's arm. "Did . . . anything happen?"

"Happen? Not a thing, son."

"You didn't hear . . . anything?"

"What?"

"Well . . . a shot."

"Of course not."

"Nobody's gone in or out of the Room?"

"No."

"The door's remained shut—locked?"

"Certainly." His father stared at him.

Abel, the guards . . .

Ellery felt like a fool. He was furious with Judah Bendigo. Not merely a lunatic—a malicious lunatic. Still . . .

He stepped up to the big steel door, looked at it.

The men around him watched him, puzzled.

Ellery knocked.

After a moment he knocked again, harder.

Nothing happened.

"There's no use standing there waiting," said a tired voice.

Ellery whirled. Judah had come out into the corridor. Max'l had both of Judah's arms locked behind his back. Max'l was grinning.

"What does he mean?" asked the Inspector, nettled.

Ellery began to pound on the steel door with both fists. "Mr. Bendigo! Are you all right?"

There was no answer. Ellery tried to turn the knob. It remained immovable.

"Mr. Bendigo!" shouted Ellery. "Unlock this door!"

Abel Bendigo was cracking his knuckles and muttering. "He would go into his high-and-mighty act. But why doesn't Karla . . . ?"

"Get me a key, somebody!"

"Key?" Abel started. "Here. Here, Mr. Queen. Oh, why doesn't he—? He'll roar, but . . . Here!"

Ellery snatched the gold case from Abel. It was a

duplicate of King's. He jabbed the key in the lock, twisted, jerked, heaved. . . .

Karla was lying on the floor beside her husband's desk. Her eyes were shut.

King Bendigo was seated in the leather swivel chair behind his desk, and his eyes were open.

But the way he sat and the way he looked made Ellery's blood stop running.

Bendigo was slumped in the chair off the perpendicular, one shirt-sleeved arm between his knees and the other dangling overside.

His head lolled back on his shoulder and his mouth was open, too.

The white silk of his shirt, on the left breast, showed a stain roughly circular in shape, and in color bright red.

In the center of the red circle there was a small, black bullet hole.

XI

THE FIRST THING Ellery did had nothing to do with miracles at all. He turned to Abel Bendigo and said, "Do you want Colonel Spring in on this?"

He was barring the doorway, arms and legs spread. Unbelieving eyes stared over his shoulders into the room.

"Mr. Bendigo." He tapped Abel's arm and repeated the question.

"No. My God, no." Abel came to life. "Don't let the guards in! Just—"

Ellery pulled Abel in. He pulled Judah in; Max'l came along as if he were on the end of a line. He pulled his father in.

He shut the door in the faces of the guards.

He tried the door. Locked. Automatically.

Ellery went over to the man in the chair. Inspector Queen dropped on his knees beside Karla. The brothers remained near the door, almost touching. Judah looked exhausted; he leaned against a filing case. Abel kept mumbling something to himself. Max'l was stunned; there was no ferocity left in him. His breathing deposited flecks of spittle on his lips. He kept staring at the quiet figure in the chair with awe.

The Inspector looked up. "She didn't get it."

"What is it?"

"A faint, I guess. I can't find any wound or contusion."

Ellery reached for the telephone on King Bendigo's desk. When the operator answered, he said, "Dr. Storm. Emergency."

The Inspector glanced from Ellery to the body in the chair. Then he lifted Karla very carefully and carried her over to the secretarial chair behind the typewriter-desk and laid her over the chair face down. He took off his coat and wrapped it about her. He raised her legs, keeping her head low.

"Dr. Storm?" said Ellery. "This is Queen. King Bendigo has been shot. Serious chest wound, near the heart. He's not dead. Bring everything you'll need—you may not be able to move him for a while." He hung up.

"Not dead!" Abel took a forward step.

"Please don't touch him, Mr Bendigo. We can't do a thing until Dr. Storm gets here."

Abel's face was pocked with perspiration. He kept swallowing and glancing at his brother Judah.

Where before Judah had seemed spent, as at a task executed at great physical cost, now—with the news that he had not killed successfully after all—he was dazed. His eyes mirrored some shock Ellery could not quite make out. Ellery was in no mental condition to draw a bead on subtleties, but he had the feeling that Judah had shot his bolt.

"Max." Ellery touched the massive arm. "Watch Judah."

Max'l wiped his lips on his sleeve. He turned to Judah. His head sank into his shoulders and he took a step toward the dark man.

"No, Max, no," Ellery said patiently. "You're not to touch him. Just make sure he doesn't go near King."

Karla moaned, rolling her head. The Inspector began to slap her cheeks. After a moment he sat her up.

She did not cry. The blood, which had rushed to her head, receded swiftly, leaving her face whiter than before. She stared across the desks at the slumped figure.

"He's not dead, Mrs. Bendigo," said the Inspector. "We're waiting for Dr. Storm. Relax, now. Take deep breaths."

What he said apparently had no meaning for her. The man in the chair looked dead.

The door was pounded. Ellery, on his hands and knees peering under the big metal desk, sprang to his feet and raced to the door.

"I'll open it!" he said to Abel Bendigo. "Keep away, please."

He opened the door. Dr. Storm rushed by him. The corridor was crowded with guards and people of the Residence staff. A hospital emergency table was pushed through the doorway by a white-coated man, and a portable sterilizer was wheeled up by another. But Ellery refused to allow the attendants to cross the threshold. Other things were handed in; the inspector took them while Ellery stood guard. Elbowing his way through the jam came Colonel Spring. He shouted, "Wait, don't shut that door!" Ellery said to Abel Bendigo over his shoulder, "You'd better tell him yourself." From behind Ellery, Abel shook his head at the charging Colonel. "No one else, Colonel, no one else." Ellery shut the door in Spring's set green face.

He knew the door locked automatically, but he tried it anyway.

"You men. Help me get him onto the table." There was nothing in Dr. Storm's voice but preoccupation. The sterilizer was going. The contents of his kit were spread out on the desk.

Under the doctor's direction they transferred the wounded man from the chair to the hospital table. His heavy body seemed without life.

"What's the prognosis, Doctor?"

Storm waved them away. He was preparing a hypodermic.

Ellery took the small metal chair from the secretarial desk to a corner of the room, and the Inspector led Karla to it. She went submissively. She sat down, her eyes on the still figure of her husband and Dr. Storm's fingers. Max'l stood over Judah in the other corner of the room, on the same side. Neither man moved.

"Mrs. Bendigo," the Inspector said. He touched her. "Mrs. Bendigo?"

She started.

"Who shot him?"

"I do not know." Suddenly she began to cry, without lowering her face or putting her hands to it. They did nothing. After a while she stopped.

"Well, who came into the room, Mrs. Bendigo?" asked Ellery.

"No one."

Abel was going about the room gathering up papers—from the secretarial desk, from the floor where they had been thrown by Dr. Storm in clearing the top of King's desk. There was something pitiful about the action, a mechanical gathering up of the secrets of a man who might never put them to use . . . the good and faithful servant going through the motions of preserving order in a house from which all reason for order had passed away. Abel stacked the documents in precise piles, transferring them to filing cases which he opened with a key and re-locked afterwards. He seemed grateful for having something to do.

"No one passed through that door, Mrs. Bendigo?" Ellery kept looking around the room, his glance baffled and tormented.

"No one, Mr. Queen."

"Neither in nor out?"

"No one."

"Was there a phone call?"

"No."

"Did either you or your husband make a call?"

"No."

"No interruptions of any kind, then."

"Just one."

"When was that?" Ellery's eyes came around quickly.

"At a few minutes to midnight, Mr. Queen, when you rapped on the door."

"Oh, yes." Ellery was disappointed. "And that was the only interruption? You're sure?"

"Yes."

"Ellery," said his father patiently, "we've gone all through that. Abel and I were outside the door—"

Ellery's glance took up the search again. "And then what happened, Mrs. Bendigo?"

"It recalled the whole dreadful thing to me, but only for a moment." Karla glanced at the hospital table again, quickly shut her eyes. "When Kane closed the door and returned to his desk, he immediately resumed work on his papers. I was at the other desk, going over some reports for him. My back was to the door, where the clock is, so I had no idea what time it was ... that the time was so close ..."

Her voice trailed. They waited.

"I had to concentrate on what I was doing. I forgot ... again. The next thing I knew the clock was chiming—"

"Chiming?" Ellery's glance went to the golden hands set into the wall above the door. "The clock?"

"Yes. It chimes the hours. I looked up and around. The chimes had just begun. The clock was striking twelve. And I remembered again."

"What happened?" And now Ellery gave her his whole attention.

"I turned from the clock to look at Kane, wondering if the chiming of midnight would recall it to him, too." Karla opened her eyes; she looked once more across to the man on the table, with the pudgy figure in white working over him. And she went on rapidly: "But he was immersed in what he was doing. He had dismissed the whole affair as beneath his notice. Oh, if only he had felt a little fear—just a little! Instead, he sat there behind his desk in his shirt sleeves making notes on the margin of a confidential report. Then—it happened."

"What?"

"He was killed. Wounded."

"How?" exclaimed the Inspector.

"One moment, Dad. The clock was still chiming, Mrs. Bendigo?"

"Yes.— How? I do not know. One instant he was sitting there writing, the next his body ... jerked with great violence and he fell back in his chair. I saw a . . . I saw a hole, a black hole, in his breast and a red stain spreading . . ." Her mouth worked uselessly. "No, I am all right ... if only I can be of help ... I do not pretend to understand it ... I rushed around my desk to the side of his, with no thought but to take him in my arms .. it had happened so suddenly I had no feeling of death—merely that he needed my help ... I put out my hand to touch him, and that is all I remember until Inspector Queen revived me. I must have fainted as my hand went out."

"Listen to me carefully, Mrs. Bendigo." Ellery leaned over her chair, his face close to hers. "I want you to think before you answer, and I want you to answer with absolute fidelity to *fact*. Are you listening?"

"Yes?" Her face was tilted anxiously.

"Did you hear a shot?"

"No."

"You didn't think first," Ellery said gently. "You're ill and upset, a great deal has happened in a few minutes.— Think. Think back to that moment. You are sitting, facing your husband, who is at his desk. One instant he's writing away. The next his body jerks and falls back and a black hole and stain appear on his shirt. Obviously he was shot. Someone fired a gun at him. Wasn't the jerk of his body accompanied by a *sound?* Of *some* sort? Maybe it wasn't a loud report. Maybe it was a sharp crack. Even a pop. Even a metallic click. Wasn't there a click?"

"I remember no sound at all."

"Did you smell anything at that moment, Mrs. Bendigo? Like something burning?"

She shook her head. "If something burned at that moment, I did not smell it."

"Smoke," said the Inspector. "Did you see any smoke, Mrs. Bendigo?"

"Nothing."

"But that can't be!"

Ellery put his hand on his father's arm. "You see, of course, that someone must have been in this room with you and your husband, Mrs. Bendigo. *Must* have been. Couldn't someone have been hiding here without your knowledge?"

"But that can't be," said the Inspector again, testily. Ellery touched his arm again.

"I don't see how," said Karla vacantly. "I had just looked around at the clock, as I have told you. I would have to have seen him had he been somewhere behind me. There is no place in this room to hide, as you can see. Besides, how would someone have got in?" She shook her head. "I do not understand it. I can only tell you what happened."

Ellery straightened. He took his father's left hand and held his own by its side.

Their wristwatches agreed.

Both men automaticaly glanced up at the clock above the door.

The clock, their watches, synchronized perfectly.

So they turned back to each other in a total embarrassment of the imagination. Ellery had already told his father the fantastic story of Judah's actions in his study.

Karla's testimony only compounded the fantasy.

At precisely the moment Judah had aimed his empty pistol in the direction of his brother King—with two thick walls and a corridor full of men between them—and squeezed his powerless trigger . . . at that precise moment, in spite of men and walls and locked doors and no ammunition, King Bendigo had slumped back with a bullet in his breast!

JUDAH was saying, "I need a drink. Tell him to take his hands off me. I want a drink."

Abel said, "I'll take care of him, Max."

Max gave up his hold. Judah moved out of his corner, rubbing his arm with a grimace. Max moved after him.

"You'll have to wait for your drink." Ellery came over quickly. "You can't leave this room."

Judah went by him. He paused before the filing cases, licking his lips, squinting, forehead tightened in thought. Then he sprang at one of the cases, and he pulled. The steel drawer gave and, with a little cry of triumph, he groped inside. His hand came out with a bottle of Segonzac. He began to fumble in his pockets.

"I'd forgotten about that," said Ellery dryly, "but apparently where your hidden treasures are concerned, Judah, you have the memory of a map."

"My knife! You took it!" Judah's hands twitched.

"I'll open it for you." Ellery produced Judah's pocketknife. He cut the tax stamp and seal off the top of the bottle, and removed the cork with the corkscrew.

Judah seized the bottle. His Adam's apple rose and fell. A little color began to stain his sallow cheeks.

"That's enough now, Judah—enough!" muttered his brother Abel.

Judah lowered the bottle from his lips. His eyes were still glassy, but the glass had a sparkle. He held the bottle out. "Anyone for a nip?" he asked gaily.

When no one answered, he moved back to his corner and let himself slide to the floor. He took another drink on the way down and set the bottle of cognac on the floor beside him.

"There, all tidy," said Judah. "Don't let me keep you gentlemen. Go about your business."

"Judah." Ellery sounded comradely. "Who did shoot King?"

"I did," said Judah. "You saw me do it." He brought his knees up suddenly to wrap his thin arms about them. Hugging himself.

"Judah!" Abel sounded ill.

"I said I'd kill him at midnight, and I did it." Judah rocked a little.

"He's not dead," said the Inspector, looking down.

Judah kept rocking. "A detail," he said obscurely, waving his hand. "Principle's the same." His hand fell on the bottle. He raised the bottle to his mouth again.

They turned away from him. All except Max'l, whose hands were opening and closing within inches of Judah's throat.

Judah paid no attention.

DR. STORM said, "Our great man is going to live. What are bullets to the gods? Here, who wants this?"

He spoke without stopping his work, offering his hand sidewise. Inspector Queen took a wad of bloodstained cotton from the hand. On the cotton lay a bullet.

Ellery joined him quickly as Abel and Karla came timidly over to the desk and stared across at the man on the hospital table. Karla turned away at once.

"Back, stand back," said Dr. Storm. He was unrolling some bandage. "You're not sterile—none of you is. Neither am I, for that matter. The great Storm—country sawbones! Poor Lister is rotating rapidly in his grave."

"He's still unconscious," said Abel softly.

"Of course, Abel. I didn't say he could jump off the table and do a handstand. He's had a narrow squeak, this emperor of ours, and he's still a mighty sick emperor. But he'll make it, he'll make it. Constitution of Wotan. In a little while I'll have him moved down to the hospital. Get out of my way, Abel! You, too, Mr. Queen. What are *you* sniffing at?"

"I want," said Ellery, "to see his wound."

"Well, there it is. Haven't you ever seen a bullet wound before, or do you solve your cases in a vacuum?" The stout little doctor worked swiftly.

"It's a real wound," said Ellery, "isn't it?" He stooped and picked up the shirt. Storm had cut it from the King's body. "And no powder marks."

"Oh, move back!"

"PERFECT," said Inspector Queen. They were staring down at the bullet on the stained cotton in his palm. "Not a bit deformed. Did you spot a shell anywhere, Ellery?"

"No," said Ellery.

"If this came from an automatic, the shell should be here."

"Yes," said Ellery, "but it isn't."

The Inspector enveloped the bullet in cotton. He went over to the typewriter-desk and opened drawers until he found an unused envelope. He tucked the cotton wad into the envelope and sealed the envelope and put it into his inside breast pocket.

"Let's get over there," he said mildly, "out of the way."

They went to an unoccupied corner. Ellery wedged himself into the corner and his father turned his back on the room.

"But it isn't," said the Inspector. "All right, mastermind, let's look at this thing like a couple of Missouri mule traders instead of two yokels billygoogling at a shell game."

"Go ahead," said Ellery. "How does the mule shape up?"

"It's a mule," murmured his father, "not a damned mirage. Get that into your skull and keep it there. Judah says he shot King. Judah is lying through his alcoholic teeth. I don't know what his point is, or even if he had a point, but the thing's impossible. The bullet Storm extracted from King's chest didn't get there by osmosis or the mumbling of three sacred words. It was *in* King's chest and Storm took it out of King's chest—I saw him do it, and he wasn't pulling a Houdini when he did it, either. He really dug it out. That means the bullet was part of a cartridge that was fired from a gun. Whose gun? Which gun? Fired where?"

Ellery said nothing. The Inspector ran the edge of his forefinger over his mustache, savagely.

"Not Judah's, my son. Or at least it certainly wasn't the gun in Judah's mitt at the dot of midnight across the hall in that apartment of his. That gun, according to your own story, was empty—you'd unloaded it yourself and you gave me the cartridges. Judah didn't have another cartridge—you searched his quarters a couple of times—and even if he had, you examined his Walther a few seconds before midnight and it was still empty. You didn't take your eyes off it, you say, from that second on. He pulled the trigger and there was a click. The gun didn't go off, it shot nothing. It couldn't. That takes care of Mr. Judah Bendigo. He ought to be in an asylum."

"Go on," said Ellery.

"So it was another gun that went off. Fired from where? From outside the Confidential Room? Let's see. The walls of this room are reinforced concrete two feet thick. Hole bored through beforehand? Where is it on these bare walls? I haven't spotted it and, while we'll do a thorough check, you know and I know we won't find such a hole. How could it have been bored without the guards, on duty twenty-four hours a day a few yards away, hearing it? The door? Closed and locked, and it's solid steel. No opening of any kind except the keyhole, which is far too small and narrow to fire a bullet through; besides, the interior lock mechanism would stop it. No window. No transom. No peephole. No secret passageways or secret compartments or secret anything, according to King himself. The air-conditioning and heating business running around the walls up there at the ceiling? Some sort of specially designed metal fabric, Colonel Spring said, that 'breathes.' Look at it—solid mesh. And not a hole visible in it anywhere. Besides, a shot from up there would make an impossible angle."

'Your conclusion is—?"

"The only conclusion that makes sense. The shot was fired from inside this room. And who was in this room? King Bendigo and his wife—and you didn't see any powder marks on his shirt, did you?"

Ellery stared at Karla Bendigo over his father's shoulder.

"But of course," murmured the Inspector, "you've known that all along."

"Yes," said Ellery. "But tell me: Where is the gun?"

"In this room."

"Where in this room?"

"I don't know where. But it's here."

"I've been over the room, Dad."

"Not the way it ought to be gone over," said his father tartly. "Not the way it's *going* to be gone over. . . . No, it's not *on* her. Where would she hide a gun in that gown she's wearing? Besides, when I carried her over to the chair and went to work on her in that phony faint she pulled, I made sure. I don't like to take liberties with another man's wife, but what can you do? It's here, Ellery. It's got to be. Nobody's left the room. All we have to do is find it. Let's get started."

"All right," said Ellery, pushing away from his corner. "Let's."

He said it without the least conviction.

THEY searched the room three times. The third time they divided it into sections and went at it by the inch. They got the key to the filing cases from Abel and they examined every drawer. They cleared each one, case by case, of suspicion of concealing a secret compartment. They went through every cubic inch of the interior of both desks, and they went over the desk legs and frames for hollow spaces. They climbed to the tops of the filing cases and fingered every inch of the walls. Ellery set the metal chair on the cases and went over the metallic frieze at the ceiling, following it all around the room. He examined the clock with special care. They determined the immovability of the cases, which were permanently attached to the walls. They took the two desk chairs apart. They dismantled the telephone. They probed the typewriter. They even examined the hospital table with the unconscious man on it, the sterilizer, Dr. Storm's medical bag, and the other equipment that had been brought in after midnight.

There was no gun. There was no shell.

"It's on one of them," said the Inspector through his denture. He raised his voice. "We're going to do a body search. On everybody. I'm sorry, Mrs. Bendigo, but that includes you, too. And the first thing I'm going to ask you to do is take your hair down. . . . You can console yourself with the thought that I'm an old man who thinks life's greatest thrill is that first cup of coffee in the morning. Unless you people would like to call us off—here and now?"

Abel Bendigo said quietly, "I want to know about this. Start with me, Inspector."

The Inspector searched Abel, Karla, and Max. Ellery searched Judah, Dr. Storm, and the man on the table. Ellery spent a great deal of time over the man on the table. He even contemplated the possibility of the bandages on that big torso as a place of concealment. But that possibility was an impossibility; a glance told him that. Dr. Storm hovered over him like an angry bantam.

"Careful! Oh, you idiot! If he dies, my fine fellow you're a murderer. What do I care about somebody's gun!"

The gun was on none of them. Neither was the shell. Any shell.

The Inspector was bewildered. Ellery was grim. Neither said anything.

Abel began to pace.

Karla stood by the hospital table, her makeup smeared, her hair tangled, just touching her husband's marble hand. Once she stroked his hair. Judah squatted in his corner sipping cognac peacefully; his glassy eyes were dull again. Max'l's great shoulders had developed a droop.

Dr. Storm prepared another hypodermic.

The Queens stood by, watching.

Abel was working up to something. He kept glaring at Judah as he paced, apparently struggling with unfamiliar emotions and losing the struggle. Finally he lost control.

He sprang forward and seized Judah by the collar. The attack was unexpected, and Judah came up like a cork, clutching his bottle frantically. His teeth were gleaming, and for a horrible moment Ellery thought he was laughing.

"You drunken maniac," Abel whispered. "How did you do it? I know that brain of yours—that diseased, dissatisfied brain! We were always too ordinary for you. You always hated us. Why didn't you try to kill me, too? How did you do it!"

Judah put the bottle to his lips, eyes popping from the pressure on his neck. Abel snatched the bottle from him. "You're not drinking any more tonight—ever, if I can help it! Did you really think you were going to be allowed to get away with this? What do you suppose King will do when he gets on his feet again?"

Judah glugged. His brother hurled him back against the cases. Judah slid to the floor and looked up.

He *was* laughing.

THEY searched everyone again before each left the room. Dr. Storm. King Bendigo, still unconscious on the table. Judah, lurching and grinning to himself. Max'l. Karla. Abel . . .

The Inspector did the searching and Ellery passed them out. One by one, so that there was no possibility of a trick. The Inspector also made a final search of the equipment that went out.

There was no gun. No shell.

"I don't understand it," said Abel, the last to leave. "And I've got to find out. My brother will want to know. . . . I give you gentlemen full power. I'm telling Colonel Spring that in anything connected with this business he and the entire security force are under your orders." He glanced at the bottle in his hand, and his lips thinned. "Don't worry about Judah. I'll see that he gets no further opportunity to do anyone any harm."

He strode out, and Ellery made sure the door was locked.

Then he turned around. "Inspector Queen, I presume . . ."

"Very funny," said his father bitterly. "Now what?"

"Now we *really* search," said Ellery.

FORTY-FIVE minutes later they faced each other across King Bendigo's desk.

"It's not here," said Ellery.

"Impossible," said his father. "Impossible!"

"How was King shot? From outside this room?"

"Impossible!"

"From inside this room?"

"Impossible!"

"Impossible," nodded Ellery. "Impossible from outside and impossible from inside—there's positively no gun in this room."

The Inspector was silent.

After a moment, Ellery said: "Ourselves."
"What?"
"Search yourself, Dad!"
They searched themselves.
They searched each other.
No gun. No shell.
Ellery raised his right foot and deliberately kicked King Bendigo's desk. "Let's get out of here!"

THEY slammed the door of the Confidential Room and Ellery tried it for the last time.
It was locked.
There was no sign of Colonel Spring. Colonel Spring evidently preferred to transfer his authority *in absentia*.
"Captain!"
The captain of the guards hurried up. "Yes, sir."
"I want some sealing wax and a candle."
"Yes, sir."
When they were brought, Ellery lit the candle, melted some of the wax, and smeared it thickly over the keyhole of the steel door. He waited a moment. Then he pressed his signet ring into the wax directly over the keyhole.
"Put a guard before this door day and night on three-hour tricks. That seal isn't to be touched. If I find the seal broken—"
"Yes, sir!"
"I believe there's a reserve key to the Confidential Room kept at the guard station up here? I want it."
They walked down the corridor and waited for the key to be brought. A guard was already stationed at the door of the Confidential Room.
"You have the other two keys, Dad, haven't you?"
The Inspector nodded. Ellery handed him the third key. The Inspector tucked it carefully away in one of his trouser pockets.
"We'd better get some sleep."
The Inspector started for the elevator. But then he stopped, looking back. "Aren't you coming?"
Ellery was standing where his father had left him. There was a queer expression on his face.
"Now what?" snarled the Inspector, stamping back.
"That bullet Storm extracted from King's chest," Ellery said slowly. "What caliber would you say it is?"
"Small. Probably .25."
"Yes," said Ellery. "And Judah's gun is a .25."
"Oh, come on to bed." The Inspector turned away.

But Ellery seized him by the arm. "I know it's insane," he cried.

"Ellery—" began his father.

"I'm going to check."

"*Damn it!*" The Inspector stamped after him.

THERE was a guard at Judah's door, too. He saluted as the Queens came up.

"Who put you here?" grunted the Inspector.

"Mr. Abel Bendigo, sir. Personal orders."

"Judah Bendigo's in his rooms?"

"Yes, sir."

Ellery went in. The Inspector went past him to the door of Judah's bedroom. The room vibrated with snores. The Inspector switched on the lights. Judah was lying on his back, mouth open. The room reeked; he had been sick.

The Inspector turned the lights off and shut the door. "Got it?"

Ellery had his hand over the little Walther. It was on the desk, where he had tossed it after Judah's exhibition of murder-by-magic at midnight.

"Now what? What are you staring at?"

Ellery pointed with his other hand.

On the rug, behind Judah's desk, lay a cartridge shell.

The Inspector pounced on it. Out of his pocket he brought one of the unexploded cartridges Ellery had taken from Judah's Walther before midnight and handed over for safekeeping.

"It's a shell from the same make and caliber of cartridge. The same!"

"He didn't fire it," Ellery said. "It never went off. No shell came out when he went through that hocus-pocus. The gun was empty, I tell you. It's a trick, part of the same trick."

"Let's see the gun!"

Ellery handed it to his father. The Inspector examined the German automatic with its ivory-inlaid stock and the triangular nick in the corner of the base. He shook his head.

"It's sheer lunacy," said Ellery, "but do you know what you and I are going to do before we go to bed?"

The Inspector nodded numbly.

They left the room without words, the Inspector carrying the gun, Ellery carrying the shell. Once the Inspector tapped his breast pocket, where the bulge was of the envelope containing the cotton-wrapped bullet from King Bendigo's body.

At the guard station Ellery said to the officer in charge, "I want a fast car with a driver. Get your ballistics man, whoever and wherever he is, out of bed and have him meet Inspector Queen and me at the ballistics lab, wherever that is, in ten minutes!"

THEY never did learn the name of the ballistics man. And they could never afterward recall what he looked like. The very laboratory in which they passed through the final episode of the nightmare remained a watery blur to them. Once during the next hour and a half the Inspector remarked that it was the finest ballistics laboratory he had ever seen. Later, he denied having said it, on the ground that he hadn't really seen anything. Ellery could not argue the point, as the machinery of his memory seemed to have stopped operating, as well as all his other long-functioning equipment.

The shock was too great. They hovered over the ballistics man, watching him work over the shell and the bullet and the little Walther—firing comparison shots, washing, ammoniating, magnifying—watching him angrily, jealously, hopefully, guarding against a trick, anticipating more magic, smoking like expectant fathers, even laughing at the absurdity of their own antics.

The shock was too great.

They saw the results themselves. It was not necessary for the ballistics man to point out what he pointed out, nevertheless, in the most technical detail—firing-pin marks, extractor and ejector traces, marks from the breech block. This was all about the shell they had picked up from the floor of Judah's study. And they studied the near-fatal bullet and the test bullet in the comparison microscope, eying the fused images of the two bullets unbelievingly. They insisted on photographic corroboration and the ballistics man produced it in "rolled photographs" showing the whole circumference of the bullet on a single plate. They peered and compared and discussed and argued, and when it was all over they faced the paralyzing conclusion:

The bullet Dr. Storm had dug out of King Bendigo's chest had been fired from the gun Judah Bendigo had aimed emptily at his brother with two impenetrable walls and a lot of air space crowded with hard-muscled men in the way.

It was impossible.

Yet it was a fact.

XII

JULY CAME—the first, the Fourth.

There was a ceremony of sorts before the Home Office, with the American flag raised beside the black Bendigo standard and a short speech by Abel Bendigo. But this was for the benefit of the Honorable James Walbridge Monahew, unofficial representative of the United States to The Bodigen Company—a courtesy such as the sovereign power extends to a friendly government. Present were Cleets of Great Britain and Cassebeer of France. There was a cocktail party afterwards in the Board Room, which neither Ellery nor his father was invited to attend. They learned later that several toasts were drunk—to the health of the absent King Bendigo, the President of the United States, the King of England, and the President of the Republic of France, in that order.

Bendigo was still confined to the hospital wing at the Residence, under twenty-four-hour guard. Ambiguous bulletins posted by Dr. Storm gave the impression of a rapid recovery. By July fifth the patient was reported sitting up. Still, no visitors were permitted except his wife and his brother Abel. Max'l was not classified as a visitor; he never left the sickroom, feeding there three times a day and bedding down on a cot within arm's reach of his divinity.

Karla spent most of her days in the hospital. The Queens saw little of her except at dinner, when she would chat in a strained, preoccupied way about everything but the subject uppermost in their minds. Abel they saw rarely; with the King helpless in bed, the Prime Minister was a busy man.

Judah was the surprise. For the first week after the attempted assassination he was confined to his quarters under guard, and the six cases of Segonzac cognac behind his Bechstein grand were removed at Abel Bendigo's order. But Judah kept mellow. His apartment was searched repeatedly, and a bottle or two was found occasionally in a rather obvious hiding-place; the guards suspected him of trying to keep them happy. The chief source of his supply they never located. For a few days it was a game which Judah showed every evidence of enjoying in his sardonic fashion. After his confinement was lifted and he was given freedom of the Residence, with the exception of the hospital wing, all attempts to keep him sober were abandoned. It would have taken a general of logistics commanding an army corps of Carry Nations to track down half his secret caches.

The Queens wondered grimly about Judah's release, and they spent several days seeking an explanation. Finally they succeeded in ambushing Abel. It was late one night, as he entered the Residence bound for bed.

Honestly, gentlemen, I haven't been avoiding you. With King down, there's been no time to breathe." Abel looked grayer than usual and his narrow shoulders sagged with fatigue. "What's on your mind?"

"Lots of things," said Ellery, "but a good place to start would be: Why did you order Judah's release?"

Abel sighed. "I should have explained that. Do you mind if we sit down? . . . One of the critical things that's been occupying me—perhaps the most critical—is keeping the real story of what happened on the night of June twenty-first from getting out. You'll have noticed that Mr. Monahew and Sir Cardigan and Monsieur Cassebeer are under the impression that King is indisposed because of influenza. If it became known that he was the victim of an assassination attempt that nearly succeeded, the news would cause the most serious repercussions. Throughout the world. Our affairs are normally very delicate, gentlemen, and they're so spread out that—as a great European statesman remarked only the other day—let King Bendigo stand in a draft and the whole world sneezes."

Abel smiled faintly, but the Queens remained grim.

"What's that got to do with your brother Judah?" asked the Inspector.

"The gentlemen from the United States, Great Britain, and France are very astute. If Judah were kept out of sight for any length of time, they would start speculating. They might put two and two together—King's sudden 'illness,' Judah's sudden disappearance." Abel shook his head. "It's safer this way. Judah can't possibly get to King. And he's being watched closely without seeming to be."

The Queens said nothing for a while.

Then the Inspector said: "Another thing, Mr. Bendigo. We've been trying to see Dr. Storm's patient without being permitted within a hundred yards of his bed. There are some questions we'd like to ask him. How about arranging a visit to his bedside?"

"Dr. Storm won't allow it. My brother's still a very sick man, he says."

"We understand *you* see him daily."

"For just a few minutes. To relieve his mind about pending matters; he frets a good deal. That's all, really."

Ellery said quietly: "Have you asked him anything about the shooting?"

"Of course. He's been no help at all. And I can't press him. Storm says he must not be excited."

"But he must have said something. He was shot in the breast. How can you be shot in the breast at close range without seeing who's shooting you?"

Abel said earnestly: "Exactly what I asked King, knowing it's the one thing you'd want answered. But he says he can't remember anything happening except that he woke up in the hospital." Abel rose. "Is there anything else, gentlemen?"

"Yes," said Ellery. "The most important question of all."

"Well, well?" said Abel, a trifle impatiently.

"What are we doing here?"

Abel stared his illegible, unavoidable stare. They could see his features smooth out as if under a hot iron. When he spoke, he was the Prime Minister. "I hired you to confirm my own findings about the authorship of the letters. You did so. I then asked you to stay on to help in a delicate family situation. Which isn't settled yet."

"You want us to keep going, Mr. Bendigo?" There was nothing to be read in Ellery's face, either.

"Most certainly I do. Especially during the next few weeks. When King is allowed out of bed we'll have the whole problem of Judah on our backs again. I can't keep him under lock and key—"

"Why not?" demanded the Inspector. "With King back on his feet, anything you do with Judah won't be noticed."

The Prime Minister vanished. Abel sat down again, shaking his head, his glasses twinkling a little. "I don't blame you. It must all seem very strange to you. The truth is, what we have most to contend with is not so much Judah as King himself. Contrary to my expectations, King won't allow Judah to be locked up. He has his weaknesses, you know. Courage to the point of foolhardiness is one of them. Tremendous pride is another. To lock Judah up, according to King's code, would be a personal defeat. I realize that now. And then the family relationship . . . I'm sure I don't have to go on. . . . Of course, there's still the matter of the way Judah did it. That bothers me, Mr. Queen, bothers me enormously. And King. We can't make head or tail of it. Have you made any progress at all?"

Ellery shifted to the other foot. "You can hardly progress, Mr. Bendigo, when you're caught between the irresistible force and the immovable object. The facts say the attack on your brother was a physical impossibility—and yet, here he is with a bullet hole near his heart. Did you find time to read our report on the ballistics tests?"

"Incredible," murmured Abel.

"Exactly. Not to be believed. And yet there's no room for doubt. That the bullet dug out of your brother's chest was fired from Judah's gun when Judah's gun couldn't possibly, under the ironclad circumstances, have fired it, is a scientific fact. It's something new under the sun, as far as my father and I are concerned."

"And that bothers *you*. Of course. A man of your training, you exceptional talents, Mr. Queen . . . No offense, Inspector." Abel smiled. "You and I are in the same class—good, solid plug-horses. But the pace of the thoroughbred—" He shook his head as he rose again. "You keep on it, Mr. Queen. I know if anyone can make sense out of it, you're the man."

It was only when the private Bendigo elevator had closed on Abel's smallish figure, the narrow bland face, the broad disturbing brow, that the Queens found themselves totting up the items of their conversation with him. And reaching the sum total of zero.

As usual, Abel had really not answered anything.

THEY were at breakfast in their suite the next morning when Abel phoned.

"I got to thinking last night, as I was getting ready for bed," Abel's twang said, "about our talk, Mr. Queen. It seems to me Dr. Storm is being overcautious. King is really getting along very well. And I see no reason why you should have to rely on secondhand answers to your questions when you can get them directly from King. I've arranged with Dr. Storm for you and Inspector Queen to visit my brother at eleven o'clock this morning. Storm gives you only a few minutes—"

"That's all we want," Ellery said quickly. "Thank you!" But when he hung up he did not speak quickly at all. "Abel's arranged for us to see King this morning, Dad. It's his way of telling us he knows we were skeptical or dissatisfied with his report of what King said about the shooting. I wonder what it means."

"I wonder what anything means!"

They were admitted to the hospital wing without a question, and a guard escorted them to the door of King Bendigo's room. As they walked up the beautiful corridor they met Immanuel Peabody. The lawyer had just emerged from the royal sickroom with a briefcase under his arm, and he hurried past them with a frown and a wave of the hand. "The White Rabbit," muttered Ellery. " 'Oh, my ears and whiskers, how late it's getting!' "

"I wonder where *he* was when Judah pulled his miracle," grunted his father. "And what the devil he carries in that briefcase!"

Then they were admitted to the presence.

The King looked very well, as his brother had remarked. He was thinner and his complexion had paled, but his black eyes were as lively as ever and there was scarcely a trace of weakness in his gestures.

And Max'l was eating nuts again, in a chair beside his master's bed.

Dr. Storm stood Napoleonically before one of the windows, his back to them. Without turning he snapped, "Five minutes."

"Fire away," said the King. He wore white silk pajamas. The crown surmounting the two linked globes was embroidered in metallic gold thread on the breast through which his brother's bullet had gone.

"First," said Inspector Queen. "Do you remember the clock's chiming midnight, Mr. Bendigo?"

"Vaguely. I was absorbed in what I was doing, but it seems to me I remember the chimes."

"All twelve of them?" asked the Inspector.

"No idea."

"At that moment—when you heard the midnight chimes—you were sitting at your desk?"

"Yes."

"In what position, Mr. Bendigo? I mean, taking the front edge of the desk as a line of reference, were you sitting squarely to it? Facing left? Facing right? How?"

"Squarely. I was leaning over, writing."

"Looking down, of course?"

"Naturally."

"When you heard the shot—"

"I didn't hear the shot, Inspector Queen."

"Oh, I see. There was no shot?"

The man in the bed said dryly, "So that's the way you fellows do it. Yes, of course there was a shot."

"Why do you say that, Mr. Bendigo?"

"There must have been. There's nothing imaginary about the bullet hole in my chest."

"You didn't hear the shot. Did you *see* anything? A flash? A sudden movement? Even something you can't identify?"

"I saw nothing, Inspector."

"Did you smell anything unusual?"

"No."

"One moment you were writing, the next you were unconscious. Is that it, Mr. Bendigo?"

"Yes.— Queen. You haven't opened your mouth. Don't you have a question to ask?"

"Yes," said Ellery. "How do *you* think it was done, Mr. Bendigo?"

"I don't know," said the King grimly. "Isn't that your department?"

"I'm not running it too well. The facts and the results are totally contradictory. We were hoping you'd recall something that would give us a clue to what happened. Ordinarily, the fact that you didn't hear, see, or smell anything at the moment you were shot might simply mean that you blacked out instantaneously from a near-fatal wound. But Mrs. Bendigo didn't hear, see, or smell the shot, either, and she wasn't wounded—in fact, she was conscious long enough to see you slump back in your chair with the point of the bullet's entry visible and the blood oozing out to stain your shirt around the bullet hole. So your testimony, Mr. Bendigo, only tends to confirm your wife's and confuse matters further.— All right, Doctor, we're leaving."

FOUR weeks to the night after the attempt on King Bendigo's life, Ellery made the decision which changed the course of their investigation and turned it at last into a channel with a discernible port.

He and his father were parked in one of the Residence cars. They had driven off into the soft summer night after dinner that evening in an attempt to escape from the headsplitting maze in which they were trapped. Ellery drove absently, and it was with some surprise that he found himself emerging from the camouflage belt of woods surrounding the island. He pulled over to the raw edge of the cliffs and turned off his motor. At their feet lay the harbor of Bendigo Island, twinkling with a thousand lights and even at this hour the scene of an insect-like activity. In the bay formed by the embrace of the harbor's arms lay a great number of vessels, and they could see, lying athwart the narrow entrance to the bay, the riding lights and big guns of the heavy cruiser *Bendigo,* King Bendigo's yacht."

"Seems like ten years since that first day, when Abel made the airport car turn sharp inland the minute we caught a glimpse of the harbor," remarked the Inspector after a few moments. "I wonder why they've stopped tailing us and shooing us away from the hush-hush installations. It's weeks since I've seen the Bobbsey Twins."

"The who?" Ellery automatically fingered the Walther in his pocket. He had been carrying Judah's little gun about with him ever since the night of June twenty-first.

"The colored-shirt boys."

"Oh, they're in the States somewhere on an assignment."

"That's where I'd like to be, gol ding it. I can't take much more of this, son, Washington or no Washington."

"King's being discharged from the hospital this Saturday, according to the grapevine."

"Maybe Judah'll put the hex on him and he'll turn into gold or something," the Inspector said hopefully. "Anything for a little action!"

They were silent for a long time.

"Dad."

"What, son?"

"I'm leaving here."

"So am I, if I live that long," said his father gloomily. Then he turned to stare. "You're *what?*"

"Leaving."

"When?"

"Tomorrow morning."

"Suits me," said the Inspector with celerity. "By golly, let's go back right now and start packing."

"Not you, Dad. Just me. You'll have to stay."

"Of all the dirty, lowdown tricks," exclaimed his father. "What's the idea?"

"Well . . ."

"What do you have to cover up, your reputation? With me holding the potsy? Why do *I* have to stay? I mean, *why* do I have to stay? I've got as much in my spy notes as I can hope to get, and the oilskin pouch has given my belly a permanent itch. It's *your* end that's not finished—remember?"

"One of us has to keep a line open here, Dad. And an eye on Judah. There's something I've got to look into."

The Inspector eyed him. "You've got something?"

"No," mumbled Ellery. "No, I've got nothing. But a hunch, that is. When there's nothing else to latch onto, a hunch can look mighty comforting."

After a moment his father sank back and looked glumly down at the lights of the harbor. "Well, give my regards to Broadway."

"I'm not going to Broadway."

"You're not? Where you going?"

"To Wrightsville."

"*Wrightsville!*"

"I made up my mind this afternoon, while you were dunking in the pool. I meandered into the gardens and ran across Judah doing a Ferdinand. He was lying under a royal poinciana waving a peacock flower under his crooked nose and sipping guess-what. We had a long chat, Judah and I. He was unusually voluble.

"What's all this got to do with Wrightsville?"

"Judah says that's where he, King, and Abel were born."

"You're kidding!"

"That's what he told me. And enough more about their boyhood there to make me damned curious."

"The big boy was *born* there?"

Ellery shifted in his seat. "It gave me a queer lift, Dad. You know how Wrightsville's mixed in my life in recent years. I've become a little superstitious on the subject. I suppose it's inane—after all, the Bendigos are Americans by birth . . . they had to be born somewhere in the United States . . . and Abel's twang never came out of anything but a New England nose. Still, learning it was my old Wrightsville jabbed me in the seat of the pants. The moment Judah uttered the magic word—he *is* a magician!—I knew I'd have to run up there for a session with the town. Because the secret's probably buried there, just waiting to be dug up. The way Wrightsville secrets have a way of doing."

Ellery looked out to the dark sea.

"What secret?" demanded his father petulantly.

"*The* secret." Ellery shrugged. "The secret of what makes these people tick. Of how this case came to happen, Dad. I'm no longer obsessed with the answer to how Judah pulled that marvelous flimflam. We'll get to that in due course. . . . Up there in Wrightsville something's waiting to be discovered about Kane, Abel, and Judah Bendigo that's going to restore my self-respect. I feel it in my bones and, by God, I'm flying there tomorrow morning!"

XIII

THE LAST THING Ellery saw was his father on the roof of the observation building waving his hat under a flapping Bendigo flag. The steward pulled and fastened the last black blind, and Bendigo Island disappeared. This time Ellery did not mind. He was thinking of people, not places.

The big trimotor took off.

There were three other passengers—Immanuel Peabody, with the inevitable briefcase; an eagle-nosed man in a wing collar and blue polka-dot foulard tie; and an old woman with a Magyar face and badly stained fingers who was wearing a silly-looking Paris hat. Peabody hurried into a compartment, already unbuckling the straps of his briefcase, and he remained invisible until the plane—its windows free again—circled Gravelly Point for a landing at the National Airport in Washington. The old woman in the hat chain-smoked Turkish cigarets in a long gold holder and read a magazine throughout the trip. When she set it down to eat her lunch Ellery saw that it was not a copy of *Vogue* but a highly technical scientific journal in the German language, published, he knew, in Lausanne. Immediately the old woman in the silly hat ceased to be an old woman in a silly hat and became—he now recalled those Magyar features—one of the world's most famous research chemists. The man in the wing collar he never did identify. Neither attempted to speak to him, but all through the trip Ellery was afraid one or both of them would. He was relieved when they got off the plane with Peabody at Washington.

The people Ellery was turning over in his mind were the Bendigos, particularly Abel. He had rather neglected Abel, he thought, but he could not quite settle on why this should seem a serious oversight. Abel's attitude throughout the affair had been in the tradition of high politics, a puzzling mixture of the right words and the wrong actions. Like the camouflaged shore batteries of Bendigo Island, Abel effaced himself against his background; like them, he concealed a powerful potential. But a powerful potential for what?

And always Ellery came back to the question he had asked himself from the beginning: Why had Abel brought him into the case at all? It was a question as remarkably lacking in answerability as the riddle of the little gun that could not possibly have fired the shot, and yet had.

Ellery's jaw shifted. There was an answer; all he had to do was find it. And as the plane flew farther north, he had the curious feeling that he was approaching the answer at the exact m.p.h. shown on the pilot's instruments.

It was midafternoon when the big black and gold Bendigo ship set Ellery down at Wrightsville Airport. He waved to the pilot and copilot and hurried up the steps of the administration building lugging his bag.

Outside, the taxi man was someone he didn't know, a smartly capped youngster with red-apple cheeks. The cab was a new one, bright yellow, with black-and-white-striped trim and a meter.

Gone are the Wrightsville owner-driven cabs of yesteryear, the dusty Chevvy and Ford black sedans with the zone maps showing the quarter, half-dollar, and seventy-five-cent trip areas, and drivers like Ed Hotchkiss, who called John F. Wright by his Christian name, and Whitey Pedersen, who had started hacking back in the horse-and-buggy days, when the stone base of the Jezreel Wright monument in the Square (which was round) actually watered the buggy and surrey horses of the farmers-come-to-town instead of being planted to geraniums, as now, by the ladies of the Keep-Wrightsville-Beautiful Committee of the Civic Betterment Club.

"Where to?" asked the youngster with a smile.

Wrightsville Airport lies in the valley running north by west between the Twin Hills-Bald Mountain section and the foothills of the great Mahoganies. North Hill Drive is almost due south; it's quite a climb, the road running southeast up the hump past the eastern terminus of "The Hill" (Hill Drive) and the western terminus of Twin-Hill-in-the-Beeches. Hill Drive is not to be confused with North Hill Drive, where the "new" millionaires have their estates. "The Hill" is the residential section of the real thing, the bluestocking families who go all the way back to the 1700s—the Wrights, the Bluefields, the Livingstons, the Granjons, the F. Henry Minikins. Twin-Hill-in-the-Beeches is the town's newest "good" development (not the smartest; Skytop Road facing Bald Mountain farther north is the smartest). It's full of fine, bright, sort of modern homes, though, built by well-to-do business people like the MacLeans ("Dunc MacLean—Fine Liquors," on the Square next door to the Hollis Hotel; Dunc gets all the hotel trade), people who couldn't crash any of the Hill Drive properties for all the cash in Hallam Luck's vaults at the Public Trust Company. And don't think the MacLeans and their crowd don't know it; they don't even try!

"The Hollis," said Ellery, leaning back. The mere sound of the name made him feel as if he had come home.

* * *

ELLERY checked in at the Hollis Hotel, and when he checked out sixteen days later he paid a bill for $122.25, $80.00 of which was for rental of his room. Laundry and pressing took up most of the balance. He ate one meal in the main dining room, but he found it so full of the thunder of organizational ladies and business-group lunchers that he never went back.

High Village hadn't changed much. About the only difference in the Square was that the old Bluefield Store on the north arc, where Upper Dade comes down from North Hill Drive, was gone, replaced by a fluorescent beauty of a shop with a brand-new purple neon sign outside saying *It's Topp's for T-V*. There were a few other changes, more minor than that, but those were chiefly on Wright Street, which had always been a "dead spot" for business.

Death had been there in the past year or so—Andy Birobatyan of the florist shop in the Professional Building on Washington Street was among the departed, Ellery sorrowed to learn. The flower business Andy had built up with his one arm (he had left the other in the Argonne Forest in 1918) was being run by his two-armed son Avdo, and not half so well, according to report. Ellery was inclined to salt this rumor, as Avdo was the one who had eloped with Virgie Poffenberger, Dr. Emil Poffenberger's daughter, and made a go of it, too, though it ruined his father-in-law's social standing, caused Dr. Poffenberger's "resignation" from the Country Club, and subsequently the sale of his dental practice and his removal to Boston. And Ma Upham of Upham House had died of a stroke and her Revolutionary-type hostel had been sold to a Providence syndicate, causing a D.A.R. boycott and a series of fiery editorials in the *Record.*

Ellery spent his first evening and all of the next day lining up his sights: looking up old friends, greeting acquaintances, strolling along familiar streets, catching up on the gossip, and generally enjoying himself. It was not until he had been in Wrightsville for thirty-six hours that he realized why his enjoyment was so thorough. It was not merely the re-experience of old times in a place he loved; it was that he had just left a place he detested, called Bendigo Island, with its electrified fences and swarming guards and secret police with blank faces and robotized employees and its soft, curiously rotten, air. This, on the other hand, was Wrightsville, U.S.A., where people lived, worked, and died in an atmosphere of independence and decency and a man never had reason to look back over his shoulder. This air, even mill-laden, could be breathed.

It made Ellery all the more inquisitive about the Bendigos.

On the second morning after his arrival he went to work in earnest. His object was to get a biographical picture of King Bendigo and his brothers Abel and Judah from conception, if possible, with the emphasis on King.

He consulted town records, he hunted up Wrightsvillians strange to him, he spent long hours in the morgue of the Wrightsville *Record* and the reference room of the Carnegie Library on State Street. He hired a Driv-Ur-Self car at Homer Findlay's garage down at Plum Street in Low Village and he made numerous trips—Slocum Township, Fyfield, Connhaven, even to little Fidelity, in whose dilapidated cemetery he had an old grave marker to hunt up. Once he flew to Maine.

Especially helpful was Francis "Spec" O'Bannon, who was still in Wrightsville running Malvina Prentiss's *Record* (Malvina, the eternal Rosalind Russell, returned from newspaper publishing when she married O'Bannon but retained her maiden name!); O'Bannon kept the *Record* morgue copiously supplied with bourbon while Ellery was dug in there. And, of course, there was Chief of Police Dakin, who was beginning to look more like Abe Lincoln's mummy than Abe Lincoln; and Hermione Wright, who had never looked more radiant; and Emmeline DuPré, the Town Crier, who practically bayed for an entire afternoon; and many others.

Ellery had two whole weeks of it, digging up the pieces, jigsawing them; crosschecking the testimony, establishing the facts, integrating them with world events, and finally arranging them in roughly chronological order. At the end he had a picture of "the oldest Bendigo boy" and his brothers which, kaleidoscopic as it was, delineated them with photographic brutality.

Excerpts from E. Q.'s Notes

DR. PIERCE MINIKIN:

(Dr. Pierce Minikin is 86, retired from practice. Semi-invalid, cared for by Miz Baker, old Phinny's widow, since Phinny died and the *Record* lost the best pressman it ever will have. Dr. Pierce is great-uncle to F. Henry Minikin, but two branches not on speaking terms for over a generation. Dr. Minikin has very small income from some Low Village property. Still lives in Colonial Minikin house on Minikin Rd. between Lincoln and Slocum Sts. In bad shape, needs painting, etc. Dated 1743, squeezed between Volunteer Fire Dept. and Slocum Garage, backyard overlooks Van Horn Lumber Yard. Old fellow a tartar with frosty twinkle and sharp tongue. Physically feeble, mentally very alert. We had several wonderful visits.)

"King" Bendigo? My dear young fellow, I knew that great man when he was mud in his father's eye. Brought all three Bendigo boys into the world. From what I've heard, I owe the world an apology. . . .

His father? Well, I don't suppose anybody remembers Bill Bendigo in Wrightsville except a few old hasbeens like me. I liked Bill fine. Of course he wasn't respectable—didn't come from a high-toned family, didn't go to church, was a regular heller—but that didn't cut any ice with me, I liked my men hard and my women patients to bear down, haha! Bill was hard. Hard drinker, hard feeder, hard boss—he was a building contractor, built that block of flats over on Congress Street near the Marshes they're just getting round to tearing down—and a hard lover? Boys at the Hollis bar used to call him Wild Bill. There's many a story I could tell you about . . .

Well, no, can't say I do. No, not Italian, that's on their mother's side. Don't know how they got the name Bendigo, except that Wild Bill's people were Anglo-Saxon. Came over from England around 1850. . . .

Big man, six foot three, a yard wide, and a pair of hands on him could bend a crowbar. Champion wrestler of the Green. The Green? That's before it was named Memorial Park. Boys used to grapple there Saturday afternoons. Nobody ever pinned Bill Bendigo. They used to come from all over the County to try. Handsome devil, too, Bill was—blue-eyed, with dark curly hair and lots of it on his chest. If you didn't know about the English, you'd have said Black Irish. . . .

The lover part. Well, now, I didn't know *all* Bill's secrets! But when he fell in real love it was all the way. Worshiped the ground Dusolina walked on. Little Low Village girl from an Italian family. Can't remember her maiden name to save my life. Yes, I do. Cantini, that's what it was. Her father'd been a track walker for the railroad, killed by an express train in '91. No, '92. Left a big brood, and his wife was a religious fanatic. Dusolina—Bill called her Lena—fell just as hard in love as Bill, and they had to elope because Mrs. Cantini threatened to kill her if she married a Protestant. Dusolina did, anyway; they were married by Orrin Lloyd, he was Town Clerk before Amos Bluefield. Orrin Lloyd was the brother of Israel Lloyd, who owned the lumber yard then—grandfather of Frank Lloyd who owned the *Record* up to a few years ago . . . Where was I?

Yes. Well, I was the Bendigo family doctor and when Dusolina got pregnant I took care of her. She had a hard time, died a few days later. Child was a great big boy, weighed almost thirteen pounds, I recollect that clearly. That was Bill's first son—your great man. Bill took little Dusolina's death hard, the way he took everything. Didn't blame me, thank the Lord—if he had, he'd have crippled me. He blamed the baby. Unbelievable, isn't it? Said the baby was a natural-born killer! And Bill said there was only one name for a natural-born killer, and that was Cain, like in the Bible. And Cain was what he had me register the baby in the Town Hall records. Only child I ever delivered by that name. That was in 1897, young man, fifty-four years ago, and I remember it as if it were yesterday . . .

SARA HINCHLEY:

> (Of the Junction Hinchleys. Trained nurse. Miss Sara is arthritic, getting anile, lives in the Connhaven Home for the Aged, private institution, where I saw her. Supported by her nephew, Lyman Hinchley, the insurance broker of Wrightsville. Was Jessica Fox's day nurse during J.F.'s fatal illness in 1932.)

That's right, sir, Nellie Hinchley was my mother. She died in . . . in . . . I don't remember. Except for my brother Will—that was my nephew Lyman's father—and myself, none of my mother's children lived. They all died in infancy, and she had seven. We were very poor, so my mother did wet-nursing, as they called it in those days. She always had a lot of milk and after she lost one she would . . .

Dr. Minikin told you that? Well, of course she wet-nursed so many, and I was just a girl. . . . Oh, that one! Let's see, now . . . Mr. Bendigo's wife died delivering his first child . . . yes . . . and Mama wet-nursed the baby for a year. He had a queer name . . . I don't remember. . . . But she did use to say he was the hardest she ever nursed. He'd just about suck the life out of her. What *was* his name? . . . Cain? Cain . . . Well, maybe it was. I don't remember things as good as I used to. . . . I think Mama stopped when Mr. Bendigo got married again. Or was that with the Newbold child? . . .

ADELAIDE PEAGUE:

(One of Cain's earliest living grade-school teachers. Now 71, retired on pension, keeps house for Millard Peague, her first cousin, of the locksmith shop at Crosstown and Foaming. Brisk and very bright, with a jaw like a plowshare.)

I most certainly do, Mr. Queen! I'm not one to bow and scrape and forget the way it *used* to be just because a pupil of mine becomes *famous*, although frankly I don't know what he's famous for except that if he's anything like the way he *was* . . .

No, not the Piney Road school that Elizabeth Schoonmaker taught. The one I taught in is still standing, though of course it's not a schoolhouse any more, it's the D.A.R. headquarters. . . .

He was an impossible child. In those days we taught the first four grades in the same room. The boys were hellions, and if a teacher didn't go about armed with a brass-edged ruler she didn't last a term. . . . Cain Bendigo was the worst, the *worst*. He was the ringleader in every bit of mischief, and some of the things he did I simply cannot repeat. I'll bet he remembers *me*, though. Or his knuckles do. . . .

Yes, I suppose his name had something to do with it, although I'm not one of these advanced people who test everything by psychology. He *did* hate to have me call on him, and now that I think of it, it was probably because of course I had to use his hame. Did you ever hear the like? He did take a lot of joshing because his name was Cain, and any time one of the other boys ragged him about it there was a fist fight. He was big and strong for his age and he would fight at the drop of a hat. In the four years I taught him he licked every blessed boy in school, just about, and some of the girls, too! There was no nonsense about chivalry in *that* child. . . .

Oh, he stopped them making fun of it, yes. Toward the end of the fourth grade—when Opal Marbery inherited him, thank goodness!—no, she's been dead for many years—toward the end, as I say, while he was still having plenty of fights, they weren't about his name. But he and I had a feud over it to the bitter end. I always felt that it was a very unfair thing for a child to do. After all, *I* couldn't help his name being Cain, could I? I had to call the little devil *something*. . . .

URIAH SCOTT ("U.S.") WHEELER:

> (68, principal of Fyfield Gunnery School. Kin to the Wheelers of Hill Drive. Kept referring to his family's hero, Murdock Wheeler, Wrightsville's last surviving vet of the G.A.R., who died in 1939, as if the old fellow had been General Grant himself. Was Cain's teacher at the Gunnery School in 1911, when Cain was 14.)

My dear Mr. Queen, on the contrary I consider it an honor. I have always allowed myself to brag that I had a little something to do with shaping the character, and therefore the destiny, of Mr. Bendigo. Although I've lived in Fyfield ever since coming to teach at Gunnery in 1908 as a very young man, I have always retained a soft spot in my heart for the town of my birth, and Mr. Bendigo is without doubt Wrightsville's greatest living citizen. It's high time indeed that someone like yourself collated the facts of his early life among us humble folk for posterity. . . .

Yes, of course, about his name. Excellent point of character! His father enrolled him at Gunnery as Cain Bendigo—C-a-i-n—as nasty a trick to play on a future great man as I've ever heard of, haha! We used to joke about it in the Faculty Room. But he soon changed all that. A mere boy, sir, in a school in which discipline has always been preached and practiced as a cardinal virtue. My kinsman, Murdock Wheeler, who did distinguished service for our country in the Civil War, used to say . . .

He changed it! Just like that. One day he marched into the Administration Office and *demanded* that the spelling of his hame be changed on the school's roster from C-a-i-n to K-a-n-e. He had already begun heading his papers in his various classes with his first name in the revised spelling. He was confined to quarters for three days for his disrespectful tone and attitude. When he returned to classes, he immediately marched into the Administration Office and made the identical demand—in, I might add, haha, the identical tone! He was again punished, more severely this time. Nevertheless as soon as he was released, there he was again. His father was summoned to Fyfield. Mr. Bendigo Senior, on hearing what had occurred, forbade the school authorities to alter the spelling of his son's name. The boy listened in silence. When he came to my class that very day, his first action was to head a paper "K-a-n-e Bendigo." It made a very pretty problem for us!—and I must confess it was a problem we never solved. He never wrote his name "C-a-i-n" again, to the best of my knowledge. And when he was graduated and saw that the name on his diploma was spelled "C-a-i-n"—the school had no choice, you see—he marched into Principal Estey's office, tore the diploma in quarters before Dr. Estey's nose, flung the pieces on the desk, and marched out again! . . .

CAIAPHAS TRUSLOW:

(Town Clerk. 'Aphas succeeded Amos Bluefield as Clerk after old Bluefield's death on Columbus Day eve in 1940. 'Aphas helpful throughout.)

Yep, here it is, Mr. Queen. *William M. Bendigo and Ellen Foster Wentworth, June 2, 1898.* My father knew Mr. Bendigo well. And Ellen Wentworth was the sister of old Arthur Wentworth, who was attorney for John F. Wright's father. The Wentworths were one of the real old families. All dead now. . . .

Well, yes, except for the two younger Bendigo brothers, and they don't count, now, do they?" . . .

About this marriage, that was Mr. Bendigo's *second.* His first was . . .

They were married in the First Congregational Church on West Livesey Street. Reason I know is I was a choir boy at the ceremony. Way I heard it, Ellen Wentworth insisted on a church wedding just because her folks were against the match. She had a lot of spunk for a girl in those days. Wasn't a soul there—not a soul in the pews, not even her family! No, there was one—Nellie Hinchley, who was holding Mr. Bendigo's first child by his first wife on her lap. . . .

Old Mr. Blanchard was pastor then—no, no, he's been dead and gone for forty-two years—and he was so fussed he messed up the service. Mr. Bendigo got so riled at poor old Mr. Blanchard he puffed up to twice his size just holding himself in—and he looked like a mighty big man to us kids! . . .

DR. PIERCE MINIKIN:

. . . delivered the second boy, too. Different mother this time, one of the Wentworths. Ellen, her name was. Not as pretty as Dusolina. Dusolina was little and dark and had a face shaped like a valentine and big black eyes. Ellen was blonde and blue-eyed and on the skimpy side—looked a little bloodless. But she had breeding, that girl. And money, of course. Leave it to Bill Bendigo to pick up a bargain. There were lots of men from good families in Wrightsville tried to shine up to Ellen. But she wanted love. And I reckon she got it, haha! . . .

Oh, Bill was wild the second time, too. Not because the mother of the child died, though Ellen never was very strong and soon after developed the heart condition that in a few years made her a semi-invalid. It was because for his second child he'd made up his mind to have a girl. And damned if the baby didn't outsmart him this time, too! Turned out to be a boy again. Bill never did get over that. If he hated young Cain for being a mother-killer, he had nothing but contempt for the second boy for not turning out a girl. Wouldn't spit on him. These days a doctor would send a man like Bill to a psychiatrist, I guess. Those days all you could do was take a buggy whip to him, only Bill was too big. So when he said to me, "Doc Pierce, my wife has birthed a sneaky little demon who spent nine months in the womb figuring out how to cross me up, and there's only one name for a baby like that. You go down to Town Clerk Orrin Lloyd and you register this child's name as Judas Bendigo," I tell you, young fellow, I was horrified. Said I wouldn't do any such thing and he could damned well put that curse on his own child himself. And he did. Bill Bendigo had a cruel sense of humor, and he was cruelest when he was mad. . . .

Don't know how he squared it with Ellen. She found out pretty early in married life that there was only one boss in Bill Bendigo's house. Of course, having a heart condition . . . Often wondered what became of Bill's second boy. Imagine naming a boy Judas! . . .

MILLICENT BROOKS CHALANSKI:

(69, aunt of Manager Brooks of the Hollis Hotel. Married Harry Chalanski of Low Village. Chalanski was Polish immigrant boy whom M.B. tutored in English, fell in love with, helped through State U. Their son is young Judson Chalanski who succeeded Phil Hendrix as Prosecutor of Wright County, when Hendrix went to Congress. One of the happiest *mésalliances* in Wrightsville!)

No, I will *not* call him Judas. I taught that poor child on and off for four years when Adelaide Peague and I alternated with the lower grades in the old ridge Road school, and I could never see him without a tug at my heart. He was a frail little boy with very beautiful eyes that looked straight through you. One of the quietest children I've ever taught, the soul of patience. His eyes were always sad, and I don't wonder. He wanted to play with the other children, wanted it desperately, but there's always one child the others pick on, and Judah was that one. I was convinced it was because of his name. The other children never let him forget it. You know how mean young children can be. I could see him cringe every time the hated name was flung at him in the play yard, cringe and turn away. He never fought like the other boys. He would just go very pale when he was taunted about being a "traitor" and a "coward," go pale and then walk away. His brother Cain, who was older, fought a lot of his battles, and it was Cain who protected him from the parochial school boys when they walked home from school.

. . . told his father what I thought of a man who'd give a child a name like that, while his mother sat by wrapped in lap rugs, not saying a word. Mr. Bendigo just laughed. "Judas is his name," he said to me, "and Judas it's going to stay." But I'd seen the look in Mrs. Bendigo's face, and that was all I needed. The next day I took the boy aside during recess and I said to him, "Would you like to have a new name?" His pinched little face lit up like a Christmas tree. "Oh, yes!" he cried. But then his face fell. "But my father wouldn't let me." "Your father doesn't have to know anything about it," I said. "Anyway, we don't have to change it much, just one letter, so that if he does see the new name on a report or something, he'll think it's simply a mistake. From now on, dear, we'll just drop the *s* and put an *h* in its place, and you'll be *Judah* Bendigo. Do you know what 'Judah' means? It means someone who is praised. It's a fine name, and a famous one, too, from the Bible." The child was so overcome he was unable to speak. He looked at me with his big, sad eyes, then his lips began to tremble and before I knew it he was in my arms, sobbing. . . .

It didn't take the other children long. Just about one term. I called on him by his new name as frequently as I dared. By the next year they were all calling him Judah, even his brother Cain. I don't know how Mr. Bendigo took it, and I didn't care. He was going through a lot of business troubles at that time, his wife was sick—I suppose he was too busy to make an issue of it. . . .

DR. PIERCE MINIKIN:

Let's see, remarried in '98—the second boy was born in '99, which makes him two years younger than Cain Bendigo. The third boy was born five years after the second, which would be 1904. My Lord, Abel's forty-seven! . . .

Don't know, can't say, but I'll guess. My guess is the third one was an accident. I know I'd warned Bill about his wife's health, and taking it easy, but Bill being what he was . . .

No, I don't know why he named the third one Abel. Figured he'd keep his Biblical string running, I guess. I do remember he had no more interest in Abel than in the other two. Just had nothing to do with them. And Ellen was getting sicker, and after a while she developed a chronic whine, which was exactly what those three boys could have done without. The truth is the Bendigo boys grew up without any real love or affection, and whatever's happened to them is no surprise to me whatsoever, young fellow, *what*soever. . . .

MARTHA E. COOLYE:

(67, Principal of Wrightsville High School.)

I'm not really *that* ancient, Mr. Queen. I was very, very young when I taught Cain Bendigo in the upper grades. . . .

Student is hardly the word. I don't believe he stuck his nose into a book ever in his life. Certainly not while *I* taught him. I don't know how that boy got by. . . .

Cain's forte was violence. If there was a fight at recess, you could be sure Cain Bendigo was at the bottom of the heap. If a window was broken, you checked up on Cain first. If one of the girls came to you in tears exhibiting a braid which had been dipped in an inkwell, you knew in advance who had done the dipping. If you turned to the blackboard in class and jumped at a B-B shot on your backside, you looked for the peashooter in Cain's desk. . . .

He led the boys in everything. Except, of course, scholarship. He was ringleader of the worst boys in school. I was always having to haul him down to Mrs. Brindsley's office to be disciplined. . . .

Athletics? Well, of course, we didn't have organized athletics in the lower grade schools in those days the way we have them today. But there was one game Cain Bendigo excelled at while *I* was his teacher, and that was the game of hookey. . . . No, I didn't say hockey, Mr. Queen. He was the champion hookey player of the school! . . .

CHARLES G. EVINS:

(Director, Wrightsville Y.M.C.A.)

My father, George Evins, was truant officer for the town between 1900 and 1917. He never forgot Cain Bendigo. Used to call him "my best customer." He called the Bendigo boys "The Three Musketeers," which was funny, because Abel, the youngest, was only seven when Cain graduated from grade school. I remember myself how Cain would go off with Judah and Abel after school to fool around in the Marshes, and that was unusual for a boy in the eighth grade—he and I graduated together. Usually we big boys kicked the little kids aside. Cain was the first to do the kicking, except where his little brother Abel was concerned. He fought a lot of bloody battles over Judah and Abel. Way I've figured it out, it was Cain's way of getting back at his father. He hated his father with a burning hatred, and anything his father was against, he was for. Of course, he led the younger boys around by the nose, but they never minded. To Judah and Abel Cain was God, and whatever he said went. . .

I've often wondered how Cain Bendigo turned out. I know he's supposed to be a multimillionaire and all that, but I mean as a man. Even as a boy he was a contradiction. . . .

WRIGHTSVILLE *Record,* July 20, 1911:

(In 1911 the Wrightsville *Record* was published only once a week, on Thursdays.)

Wrightsville buzzed this week over a deed of heroism done by a 14-year-old boy.

Cain Bendigo, eldest son of William M. Bendigo, well-known High Village building contractor, risked his life last Saturday to save his brother Abel, 7, from drowning while the two boys and their other brother, Judah, 12, were on a tramp through the woods in Twin Hills.

According to the young hero's account, they had gone to the rocky pool at the foot of Granjon Falls, which is a favorite "swimming hole" of Wrightsville's younger element. The 7-year-old boy, who does not know how to swim, was sitting at the edge of the pool watching his brothers when he somehow fell into the water, struck a jagged rock, and was borne unconscious by the fast current toward the rapids at the foot of the Falls. Cain, who was on shore, saw little Abel being swept away to certain destruction. Showing rare presence of mind for a lad of 14, Cain did not try to swim after Abel. Instead he raced alongshore and plunged in to meet his brother's body rushing towards him. In rough water and fighting the strong current, Cain managed to struggle ashore with the little boy and, exhausted as he himself was, he worked over Abel until Abel regained consciousness.

Cain and Judah then carried Abel down Indian Trail to Shingle Street, where the three boys were picked up by Ivor Crosby, farmer, who was driving his team to Hill Valley. Mr. Crosby raced the boys back to town. Medical treatment was administered by Dr. Pierce Minikin of Minikin Rd., the Bendigo family physician. Dr. Minikin said Cain did a fine job of resuscitation. Abel was taken home shortly thereafter, little the worse for his experience.

Cain Bendigo was graduated from Ridge Rd. Grade School this June. . . .

SAMUEL R. LIVINGSTON:

(84, Wrightsville's elder statesman. Dean of the "Hill" Livingstons and all his life a power in local politics. In 1911 he was in his 6th year as First Selectman.)

The medal was ordered from a Boston house and it was a month getting here. We had the ceremony on the steps of the Town Hall. Everybody came out for it—it was like Fourth of July. They packed the Green solid and overflowed into the Square. Course, I'd picked a Saturday for it, when everybody was in town anyway, but the boy deserved it, he surely did. . . .

That Cain Bendigo, he stood up straight as a soldier when I pinned the medal on him. The crowd called for a speech, which I thought was pretty rough on a boy of fourteen, but it didn't faze him one bit. He said he thanked everybody in Wrightsville for the medal, but he didn't feel he really deserved it—anybody would have done the same. That made a real hit with the townspeople, I'm here to tell you, and I said to myself then and there, "Sam Livingston, that boy is going places." And he surely did! . . .

WRIGHTSVILLE *Record*, August 17, 1911:

. . . as follows: 24-jewel Waltham open-face watch with black silk fob, presented with the compliments of Curtis Manadnock, High Village Jeweler. A Kollege Klothes brand suit with new style accessories presented with the compliments of Gowdy & Son Clothing Store, The Square. Wright & Ditson tennis racquet, with press, New York Department Store. Ten-volume set of *The Photographic History of the Civil War*, Semicentennial Memorial Edition, just published by The Review of Reviews Co., New York, presented with the compliments of Marcus Aikin Book Shop, Jezreel Lane. Good-natured hilarity greeted the announcement that Upham's Ice Cream Parlor on Washington St., High Village, would present the young hero with a full month's supply of Upham's Banana Splits Supreme at the rate of one per day. An Iver Johnson bicycle, presented with the compliments of . . .

(From the 1911 Files of Fyfield Gunnery School.)

C O P Y

FYFIELD GUNNERY SCHOOL

August 15, 1911

Mr. Cain Bendigo
Wrightsville

DEAR MR. BENDIGO:

It gives me the greatest pleasure to inform you that, for manifesting the high qualities of manly character which are prerequisite to matriculation in Fyfield Gunnery School, the Scholarship Board at a special meeting has voted to present you with a full four-year tuition scholarship, to take effect at the opening of the Fall Term next month.

If you will present yourself with your parent or guardian during Registration Week, September 8-15, with proof that you duly completed your grade school requirements as prescribed by the laws of the State, arrangements for your immediate enrollment at Gunnery will be concluded.

With warmest good wishes, I remain,

Yours very truly,

(Signed) MELROSE F. ESTEY
Principal

MFE/DV

BEN DANZIG:

(54, prop. High Village Rental Library and Sundries.)

Cain Bendigo was certainly the big squeeze in Wrightsville the rest of that summer before he went off to Gunnery. I remember the rush he got from the girls, and it made the rest of us boys, who'd graduated from the Ridge school with him and were going on to just Wrightsville High, kind of jealous. But there was one kid in town who'd have got down on his hands and knees and licked Cain's shoes if Cain had let him and that was his little brother Abel. I never saw such worship. Why, that kid just followed Cain around all over like a puppy. . . .

Judah? Well . . .

EMMELINE DUPRÉ:

(52, better known as the Town Crier. Teaches dancing and dramatics to the youth of the Hill gentry.)

Where was Judah during the accident? Why didn't *he* help save Abel's life? Those were the burning questions of the day, Mr. Queen. There was one boy in our class—I was in Judah's class, so I'm in a position to discuss this *intelligently*—this boy, his name was Eddie Weevil, rather a nasty boy as I recall, it wasn't long before he was being seen down in Polly Street and that sort of thing, but he did say he'd seen it, and after all even a chronic liar can tell the truth some time, don't you agree, Mr. Queen? Well, Eddie was going around telling the boys in the seventh grade—that was just after Cain went off to Gunnery—that he'd been up around Granjon Falls that day and just happened to witness the whole incident. Eddie Weevil said Judah didn't do *anything*. Didn't even *try*. The pure craven. Eddie said Judah was *closer* to Abel than Cain and could have fished him out easily if he'd had half the spunk of a ground hog, but that he ran away and cried like a baby and let Cain do the whole thing all by himself. . . .

Well, yes, he *was* asked that, but Eddie said the reason he didn't come forward with his story at the time was he didn't want to get Judah Bendigo in trouble. Of course, I don't know, the Weevil boy may have made the whole thing up just to call attention to himself, but it *was* funny, don't you think, that Judah didn't have a word to say about his part in the rescue, and Cain didn't either? . . .

REVEREND ALAN BRINDSLEY:

(52, Rector, First Congregational Church on West Livesey St.)

I occupied the seat next to Judah Bendigo in the seventh grade. I think I was probably the only boy in the class Judah trusted. He never said much about himself, though, even to me. I do know that he suffered horribly during the first few months after the rescue incident. Somehow the rumor spread that he had funked the chance to save his little brother and had run away instead of helping, or something of the sort. Even if it had been true, it was unfair to condemn a twelve-year-old boy as a coward, as if physical bravery were the highest good. Not all of us have what it takes to be a hero, Mr. Queen, and I'm not sure it would be a good thing if we had. Judah was a highly intelligent, sensitive boy who'd been branded from birth with surely the wickedest name ever given a child, I mean his given name, which was Judas. . . .

It got to the point where it was too much for me to bear. Some of the boys began to call him "coward" to his face, rough him up in front of the girls, dare him to fight, challenge him to "swimming" races—you can imagine. Judah merely hung his head. He never replied. He never struck back. I used to beg him to come away, but he would stand there until they were through, and only then would he turn his back. I realize now what courage—what truly great courage—this must have taken. . . .

DR. PIERCE MINIKIN:

Judah as a boy was what the fancy fellows these days would call a masochist. He enjoyed punishment. . . .

REVEREND ALAN BRINDSLEY:

It subsided eventually. It took about six months, I'd say. Then the whole thing was forgotten. By everyone, I'm sure, but Judah. I'm sure he remembers that Golgotha to this day. You say you've seen him recently. Does he brood? Is he lonely still? What happened to him? I always detected something Christlike in Judah. I was sure he would leave the world a little better than he had found it. . . .

WRIGHTSVILLE *Record*, November 28, 1912:

BENDIGO'S 4 TOUCHDOWNS CRUSH HIGH 27-0

WRIGHTSVILLE *Record*, June 12, 1913:

BENDIGO'S HOMER IN 9TH BEATS SLOCUM 6-5

WRIGHTSVILLE *Record*, April 30, 1914:

GUNNERY TAKES TRACK-FIELD MEET WITH 53 POINTS

Big Ben Breaks 3 Marks, Scores 29 Points

WRIGHTSVILLE *Record*, February 11, 1915:

KANE BENDIGO KO'S JETHROE IN 4TH

Gunnery Star Takes State Junior Light-Heavy Title

"DOC" DOWD:

(76, Director of Athletics at Fyfield Gunnery School 1905-1938; retired, now living in Bannock.)

Kane Bendigo was the finest all-round athlete produced by Gunnery in the thirty-three years I directed the school's athletics. . . .

PRINCIPAL WHEELER (OF FYFIELD GUNNERY):

I'm sure my memory can't be that much off, Mr. Queen. . . .

I'm astonished. Graduated forty-ninth in a class of sixty-three! I could have sworn the records would show he stood far, far higher than that. Of course, Gunnery's scholastic standards have always been extremely stringent. . . .

—

WRIGHTSVILLE *Record,* July 1, 1915:

SEN. HUNTER CONSIDERING WRIGHTSVILLE APPOINTEE TO U. S. MILITARY ACADEMY

If Kane Bendigo Named, Will be First Wrightsville West Pointer Since Clarence T. Wright in '78

DR. PIERCE MINIKIN:

There was a lot of pressure put on Bob Hunter to name the boy, I remember. He wanted to, too—it would have been good politics, because Bob was always weak in Wright County. But in the end he had to say no. The boy's marks just wouldn't stand up. And, as Bob told me himself, he couldn't let Bendigo take the entrance examinations because if he failed that would be a nice big Senatorial black eye. So he gave it that year to a boy from up Latham way. . . .

Kane was furious, deathly mad. I was in the Bendigo house on a professional call to his stepmother when the news came. His face got black, I tell you. The only way he showed his disappointment in *action* was pretty mild, I thought, considering that look on his face. He kicked the cat through one of the stained-glass side windows of the vestibule. That cat never was the same again, haha! . . .

WRIGHTSVILLE *Record,* July 29, 1915:

KANE BENDIGO TO ATTEND MERRIMAC U. THIS FALL

CHET ("IRON MAN") FOGG:

(By long-distance phone to his home in Leesburg, Va. Fogg was football coach at Merrimac University from 1913 to 1942, when he retired.)

I never made any bones about it, and I don't today. Kane Bendigo put Merrimac U. on the college athletic map. He was real big-time, the kind of athlete a coach dreams about. He was as good as Jim Thorpe any day. There wasn't anything Kane couldn't do, and do better than anybody else. He ran wild in the backfield the two seasons he played Varsity. He played baseball like Frank Merriwell—or was it Dick?—anyway, whichever one was Superman, that's the one he played like. He made track records that still stand. He was a natural-born boxer, and he slugged his way to the state college heavyweight championship—and if he'd ever gone into his senior year, my money would have been on him to take the national. No college wrestler ever took a fall over him, though that's one he used to say he owed to his old man—the only thing, he'd say, he did owe "the old bastard." And if you'll look it up, you'll find that in 1918 he was named by *Collier's* magazine the most promising all-round college athlete in the U.S., even though by that time he was in the Army. . . .

That's right. He left to enlist in the middle of his junior year—around Christmas of 1917, I think it was. . . .

WRIGHTSVILLE *Record,* October 10, 1918:

KANE BENDIGO WINS NATION'S HIGHEST MILITARY AWARD

Wrightsville Hero of Saint-Mihiel Gets Congressional Medal of Honor

WRIGHTSVILLE *Record*, September 4, 1919:

WAR HERO FETED; ANNOUNCES PLANS

Kane Bendigo, Wrightsville's Congressional Medal of Honor hero of the late conflict, was given a roaring welcome today when he returned to the city of his birth after being mustered out of the U.S. Army. . . .

After the reception, Mr. Bendigo granted an exclusive interview to the *Record*. Queried as to his postwar plans, Mr. Bendigo said: "I have had all sorts of offers to go back to college, and a dozen pro offers in various fields of athletics, but I am through with that stuff. I am going into business, where I can make some real money. I saw too many young fellows die in France to waste any part of my life on rah-rah stuff or working for somebody else. When my father was killed last year in that construction accident, he left a sizable estate. Most of it is in my stepmother's name, but she and my brothers have agreed to let me handle the money and I know just what to do with it. I am going into business for myself. I have something all lined up. . . ."

Excerpts from E. Q.'s Digest

Between January 1920 and November 1923 K. B. had four business failures. He went into the manufacture of sports equipment in Wrightsville and at the same time tried to run his father's contracting business. Result: Both went into bankruptcy. His next venture was to take over a factory that manufactured metal containers. He ran this into the ground in a little over a year, filing a petition in bankruptcy in January of 1922. He then negotiated a deal whereby he took over the Wrightsville Machine Shop in Low Village for the manufacture of light machinery. By November of 1923 this had flopped, too. His main trouble, as I was able to piece it together, seems to have been that he always bit off more than he could chew. He constantly made grandiose plans, overextended himself, and fell flat on his face. What he did have, as evidenced by the record, was the ability to charm hardboiled New England monied people into loosening up. . . .

Note historic parallel: About the time Kane Bendigo was broke and discredited, apparently a total failure, a man in Germany named Hitler was lying wounded in prison as the result of the collapse of his ambitious Beer Putsch march on Munich. Both were at the nadir of their careers. . . .

Abel had had a brilliant scholastic record, and at 17 (Sept. 1921) entered Harvard on a scholarship. He quit college at the end of his junior year (June 1924). Note that between November of 1923 and June of 1924, Kane was licking his commercial wounds. But he wasn't entirely idle, he was back at his old charm routine. He must have been, because coincidentally with Abel's leaving Harvard to join him in Wrightsville, we find Kane starting a new enterprise with the financial backing of such a goulash as John F. Wright, Richard Glannis, Sr., the then-young Diedrich Van Horn, and old Mrs. Granjon. Kane took over an abandoned factory on the outskirts of town and went into the manufacture of shell-casings for the U.S. Navy. Abel went in with him. . . .

At this time Judah was in Paris studying music at the Conservatoire. . . .

Mrs. Bendigo, mother of Judah and Abel and stepmother of Kane, died in 1925. . . .

. . . prospered from the start. The small plant mushroomed into a large plant, the large plant became two large plants. The expansion was incredibly quick. Apparently Abel's native business brilliance exactly complemented Kane's charm, drive, and unbounded ambition. They went more and more deeply into the field of munitions. The further they expanded, the smaller dwindled the group which had financed them. One after another Kane bought out his original backers. At this time the company was known as The Bendigo Arms Company (it was in the early 30s that the company name was quietly changed to Bodigen), and Kane was apparently determined to give himself exclusivity in fact as well as in title. There is reason to believe that Kane did not gain total control without a struggle, as the profits and dividends were beginning to be considerable. Talked with old Judge Martin, Samuel R. Livingston, one of the Granjon sons, and with Wolfert Van Horn. The Judge recalls John F. Wright's battle only vaguely, and Livingston was mysterious. Van Horn cagey but transparent. Convinced me that Kane brought lots of pressure to bear and used methods the victims never talked about as a matter of pride. Considering Wolfert Van Horn's own business reputation, this shows genius of the lowest order....

By 1928 all the inside outsiders were outside looking in, and the Bendigos owned all the shares in the parent company, which now had six immense plants in operation....

October 29, 1929, was the turning point. On the ruins of the stock market Kane Bendigo built his fabulous fortune. He had sold out all his holdings early in October, at the peak highs, after buying everything in sight on dangerous margin at the lows. The crash made him a multimillionaire. Just how much he made cannot be determined; there is reason to believe his profits ran to the hundreds of millions of dollars. This was the effective beginning of the Bendigo empire. Kane was 32. Abel was 25!!!!! ...

They began expanding immediately. Bought out a very large munitions company. In rapid succession several smaller ones. These plus what they already had became the nucleus of the gigantic overall organization, of which The Bodigen Arms Company today is only a part....

In the summer of 1930 the Bendigos left Wrightsville. It had become like a whale trying to maneuver in a pond. They had to get to where they could move around. They built a whole city in southern Illinois, an industrial city of 100,000 population. Their main offices were in New York. They began to open branches in foreign countries....

Some of the original Bendigo plants are still operating in Wrightsville, although the ownership is so tangled up it would take an army of experts to work its way through....

There is no evidence that either Kane or Abel Bendigo has set foot in Wrightsville since that day. Dr. Minikin, who recalls the old days with far greater clarity than the recent past, "thinks" Judah was back during the mid-30s for a few days, alone, but I have found no one who remembers having seen him, and a search of the register records of the Hollis, Upham House, and the Kelton for that period has not turned up his name. . . . William M. Bendigo's grave in the little Fidelity cemetery is untended, overgrown, and almost obliterated. Ellen Wentworth Bendigo is buried in the Wentworth family plot in the Wrightsville cemetery....

June 22, 1930: Government of Bolivia overthrown.
Aug. 22-27, 1930: Peruvian government ditto.
Sept. 6, 1930: Argentine government ditto.
Oct. 24, 1930: Brazilian government ditto.

ITEM: Between January and June of 1930 all plants of The Bodigen Arms Co. (year name-change effected) worked on double shift. Sales almost exclusively South American.

NOTE: It is clear, in the light of this and certain other evidence, that Bendigo provided the explosive force which blew up four South American governments within five months. . . .

NOTE: Bendigo did not *cause* the revolutions. He merely made them possible. . . .

NOTE: Obviously, these were King Bendigo's practice sessions, trying out his muscles. Small stuff—in one of the insurrections there were a mere 3000 casualties. . . .

Jan. 2, 1931: Panama Republic overthrown.
Mar. 1, 1931: A second overthrow of the Peru government.
July 24, 1931: By-by existing régime of Chile.
Oct. 26, 1931: Ditto Paraguay.
Dec. 3, 1931: Ditto Salvador.

NOTE: Five more tests of power. What might be called the buildup of the body beautiful, with biceps and chest expanding rapidly. But this is mere gym work, with setups; he's about ready to step out into the big time. . . .

IN 1932 we find peaceful consolidation, improvement, and further expansion. The organization is unwieldy. There is weeding out of personnel all along the line. Companies are merged, finances consolidated and redistributed, soft spots strengthened, production streamlined, new industries absorbed. The speed of K. B.'s empire building is stupendous; there is only one precedent in modern times, and it stumbles by comparison. This is the kind of industrial story that could never be invented in fiction. No one would believe it. . . .

June 4, 1932: Another revolution in Chile.

This was apparently the result of an error in calculation, or overzealousness on the part of some Company supersalesman. It was immediately remedied by . . .

Jan. 30, 1933: Adolf Hitler named Chancellor of Germany.

The global phase, to which the other was the merest preliminary, begins here.

FINDING Capt. Mike Bellodgia has been a stroke of greatest good luck. The famous round-the-world flyer was put under contract by K. B. toward the end of 1932. He had one job—to fly King Bendigo. He was King's personal chief pilot for almost 13 years—until, in fact, a bit after the end of World War II, when Bendigo was persuaded that Bellodgia was getting too old to be trusted with his precious passenger.

Bellodgia is still bitter about it, probably the real reason why he allowed me to take a look at his diaries, although we both pretended he believed my story that I was there in the interests of posterity. I flew up to Maine, where he now lives, and spent several days with him. He lives very handsomely, I must say—Bendigo was generous with him to the point of prodigality, and Bellodgia is financially secure for the remainder of his days. Bellodgia remarks dryly that he earned it; he says that never once in 13 years of flying Bendigo all over the world did he have to make a forced landing or develop serious engine trouble.

Capt. Bellodgia's diaries are really not diaries at all but personal logs. He doesn't seem to realize what he has, and I have not enlightened him.

By juxtaposing Bellodgia's record of King Bendigo's flights, destinations, dates, and lengths of stay with historical events, it has been possible to place Bendigo pretty accurately in his true perspective between Hitler's ascension to power in Germany and the end of World War II. . . .

* * *

IN 1933 the Reichstag voted absolute power to Hitler. The following day a German newspaper which had been the most powerful pro-Nazi propaganda organ was sold to a German. It had been owned by Kane Bendigo for two years. The conclusion is evident: With Hitler's position secure, Bendigo no longer needed the newspaper. . . .

On Oct. 14, 1933, Germany quit the League of Nations and withdrew from the Disarmament Conference. On Oct. 12, 13, and 14 of that year Bendigo was in Berlin, spending most of his time at the Chancellery. He flew back to his New York headquarters on the night of Oct. 14. . . .

On Apr. 27, 1934, an antiwar pact—previously agreed on at the Pan-American Conference in Montevideo—was signed in Buenos Aires by the U.S. and certain Central and South American countries; Mexico and others had signed on Oct. 10, 1933. The record of Bendigo's air trips at this time is illuminating; they tripled in number. The Bendigo munitions works, now spread to South America and Europe, were working around the clock. The Bodigen Arms Company, then, in the midst of peace talks and pacts was playing the world short. . . .

On June 15, 1934, the U.S. Senate ratified the Geneva Convention for the supervision of international trade in arms, ammunition, and implements of war. Bendigo was not in Washington, D.C. at any time during June 1934. . . .

On Aug. 1, 1934, he flew back to Berlin. He remained there for nearly 3 weeks, until Aug. 20. During those 3 weeks President von Hindenburg died and the offices of President and Chancellor were consolidated in the single office of Leader-Chancellor. One of Der Fuehrer's first acts in his new official capacity was to decorate Herr Kane Bendigo in a strictly private ceremony. The next day Bendigo left Berlin. . . .

On Jan. 10, 1935, Italy resumed fighting in Ethiopia. Between 1934 and the middle of 1936 the Company made huge shipments to Italy. . . .

On Mar. 16, 1935, Hitler broke the Versailles Treaty, ordered conscription in Germany, and began expansion of the German Army. Only one month before, the Company had acquired four more giant plants in widely scattered locations. In Mar. 1935 these were running at full capacity. . . .

On June 5, 1936, Léon Blum, leader of the Socialist Party in France, formed the first Popular Front ministry. Within 6 weeks a far-reaching program of social reform was introduced, including (July 17) nationalization of the munitions industry. Bendigo was in and out of France frequently between the end of July 1936 and June 1937, when the Blum cabinet was forced to resign. Contiguity of additional Bendigo visits to France with significant dates—November, when the Cagoulards were frustrated in their revolutionary plot against the Republic; Mar. 1938, when the Chautemps government fell; Mar.-Apr. 1938, when Blum's second ministry failed, to give way to the cabinet of Édouard Daladier—indicates that Bendigo from the very beginning worked to defeat the Popular Front and its social and nationalization program. . . .

In 1937 the Japanese renewed fighting in China, Hitler repudiated German war guilt, Italy withdrew from the League, civil war raged even more violently in Spain. The

Bodigen Arms Company in 1937 enjoyed its greatest year to that time. . . .

On Mar. 11, 1938, Hitler's troops crossed the Austrian frontier. Sept. 29-30, 1938—Munich. Mr. Kane Bendigo, the ordinarily tireless, was "forced" to desert the arduous cares of business for a "rest." He took a one-month vacation. The month: Sept. 1938. The place: A small hotel in Pfaffenhofen. Pfaffenhofen is some 50 kilometers from Munich. . . .

In Mar. 1939 the Spanish war ended. In a private ceremony in Madrid, El Caudillo decorated Señor Kane Bendigo for unnamed reasons. . . .

Czech Bohemia and Moravia . . . Memel . . . Lithuania . . . Albania . . .

Aug. 1939: Bendigo's connection with the events leading up to the diplomatic revolution which shook the world, the Nazi-Soviet nonaggression pact, remains obscure. Certain entries in Bellodgia's diaries are strongly suggestive. That it was to Bendigo's advantage to see the Soviet power temporarily neutralized so that Hitler might feel free to invade Poland and risk British and French declarations of war is childishly evident. K. B. had several sessions with Hitler and von Ribbentrop in early August, and there is reason to believe that he had a meeting with, or was present at a conference which was attended by, Molotov. . . .

Sept. 1, 1939: Poland. On Sept. 3 Prime Minister Chamberlain announced in Parliament that a state of war existed between Great Britain and Germany: "Hitler can be stopped only by force."

King Bendigo could have told Mr. Chamberlain that some time before. . . .

THE picture is monotonous and unmistakable. It clearly shows this man riding the rollers of history. It must be emphasized again that Bendigo does not cause events; he insinuates himself into their midst and diverts them to his purposes.

It is of no interest to him whether a Hitler comes to power, or a Stalin; he has done business with both. His dealings with the Soviet have been far more obscure than those with the Nazis, but only because there is virtually no data on them available. That they have been considerable and far-reaching is not to be doubted.

Bendigo is completely above loyalties or duties, isms or ologies. Patriotism to him is a device, not an ideal. His politics are fluid; they flow in every direction at once. . . .

A Few Further Excerpts from the Notes

In the bombing of Rennes in 1940, 4500 persons were killed. Bancroft Wells, the philanthropist, heading a committee of distinguished people, formally asked Mr. Kane Bendigo to act as honorary chairman of an international committee dedicated to the future restoration of the historic cathedral. Mr. Kane Bendigo accepted with an indignant speech denouncing "the barbaric practices of the enemies of civilization. . . ."

On May 10, 1941, London suffered its worst air raid of the war—1436 lives lost. King Bendigo left London in his private plane on May 9. *Inevitable speculation: Did he have advance information? . . .*

Dec. 7, 1941: Capt. Bellodgia records a rare item. For the one and only time in his long association with King Bendigo, Bellodgia was privileged to see the great man howling drunk. "He kept beating his chest like Tarzan in the movies—it was positively embarrassing. Also kind of out of place, I thought, seeing that Pres. Roosevelt had only just announced the Jap attack on Pearl Harbor. . . ."

I WAS curious to see—purely as a point of character—exactly when and under what circumstances he met, wooed, and married Karla. The four-day period of their courtship in Paris provided the clue, and Karla had intimated that it was just after the war . . . I worked it out. They met in Paris on July 25, 1946, and they were married on July 29. On July 29, 1946, the first peace conference of World War II began—in Paris.

Between busy seasons, as it were.

XIV

THE INSPECTOR embraced him without shame.

"I thought you were never coming back, son."

"Dad—"

"Wait till wet get in the car. I purposely drove down to the field so we could have a few minutes alone." When they were in the little Residence car, he said, "Well?"

"First," said Ellery, "how is King?"

"Up and about, and as far as I can see he's good as new. Storm won't let him do more than a couple of hours' work a day, so he's taking mild exercise and spending a lot of time with Karla. What have you got?"

"The whole story."

His father scowled. "Isn't that ducky."

"You don't seem pleased!"

"Why should I be? Because you've got the whole story of what they did as kids in Wrightsville? How does that help us get off this damned reef?"

"The whole story," said Ellery, "of the attempted murder. What's behind it . . . and what, I think, is ahead of it."

And Ellery started the car.

"Wait!" cried his father.

"Do you know where King is now?"

"When I left, he and Karla and that Max were lying around the outdoor pool. But Ellery—"

"Then I'd better hurry."

"What are you going to *do?*"

"Look for something first. Something," muttered Ellery, "I don't expect to find."

ELLERY lingered outside the Residence long enough to ascertain that the royal couple was still basking on the bank of the outdoor pool. He did not go near the pool; he investigated from behind a bird-of-paradise bush in the gardens, and the Bendigos remained unaware of his presence. He could see Max'l's furred body and bullet head rolling around in the water. Karla was stretched out on a beach pad; her skin, usually so fair, was red-gold, as if she had been spending her days in the sun. King dozed in a deck chair. He was in light slacks, but he had removed his shirt and Ellery saw the puckered scar of the wound against his dark skin. The wound looked entirely healed.

They took the private elevator to the Bendigo apartments.

The captain of the guard saluted and then shook hands. "We heard you were expected back, sir. There's no one in just now but Mr. Judah."

"I'll want to see him in a few minutes. . . . I notice the seal on the Confidential Room, Captain, is broken."

"Yes, sir," said the officer uneasily.

"King himself broke the seal, Ellery. He was angry, and it was all we could do to convince him that these men weren't at fault but were just following orders. I had to give the boss man back his key."

Ellery shrugged and went directly to King's suite, his father following eagerly.

"This is it, I think."

They stepped into King Bendigo's wardrobe room.

"Shut the door, Dad." Ellery looked around.

The Inspector shut the door and leaned against it. "Now what?"

"Now we take inventory," said Ellery. "You watch and make sure I don't overlook any closet, drawer, or shelf. This has to be thorough." He approached the first closet to the left of the entrance and slid back its door. "Suits . . . suits . . . and more suits. Morning, afternoon, evening, formal, informal, semiformal . . ."

"Am I supposed to take notes?" asked his father.

"Mental notes . . . And so forth. But all suits. Next." Ellery opened another closet, ran his hand along the racks. "Coats. Topcoats, overcoats, greatcoats, fur coats, storm coats, raincoats— What's up here? Hat department. Fedoras, Homburgs, derbies, silk toppers, golf caps, hunting caps, yachting caps, et cetera et cetera. . . ."

"What a man."

"Isn't he."

"I meant you," said his father.

"Ah, the shoe department. From patent leathers to hunting boots. Ever see anything like this outside a store? Dressing gowns . . . bathrobes . . . smoking jackets . . . *And* the sports division! Sports jackets, shooting jackets, slacks, ski outfits, yachting suits, riding clothes, gym clothes, wrestling tights, tennis whites—"

"Is there anything he's missed?" said the Inspector. "He couldn't wear half these things out if he lived to be as old as I feel right now."

"Shirts, hundreds of shirts, for every occasion. . . . Underwear . . . pajamas—whew! . . . socks . . . collars . . and look at these ties! . . . Handkerchiefs . . . sweaters . . . mufflers . . . gloves . . . everything in wholesale lots—"

"And I'm not getting any younger," muttered the Inspector.

"Belts, suspenders, garters, spats, cufflinks, collar buttons, studs, tiepins, tie clasps, key chains . . . and wallets. Dad, will you look in this drawer? I wonder what this is made of. If this isn't elephant hide—"

"You missed that one," said his father.

"Which? Oh . . . Walking sticks. About a hundred, wouldn't you say, Dad? And if this isn't a sword-cane, I'll . . . There you are. Sword-cane, too."

"Umbrella rack."

"And the drawer under it . . . Rubbers. Overshoes. Hip boots—have I left anything out?" Ellery went over to the wall beside his father and pressed a button. "We'll make sure."

"I suppose," sighed his father, "you know what you're doing. Because I don't."

There was a precise knock behind his back. The Inspector opened the door. A thin man in black stood there.

"Yes, sir?" The voice sounded unused.

"Are you the King's valet?" asked Ellery.

"Yes, sir. I must ask you, sir—"

"Do the contents of this room represent Mr. Bendigo's entire wardrobe?"

"On Bendigo Island—yes, sir. Sir, this room is—"

"There's no other place in or out of the Residence where his personal garments are kept?"

"Not on the island, sir. A similar wardrobe room exists in each residence maintained by Mr. Bendigo. There is one in New York City, one in Bodigen, Illinois, one in Paris—"

"Thank you," said Ellery; and when the valet lingered, he said, "That's all." The valet backed away reluctantly.

"That was all I wanted to know," Ellery said as they made their way to Judah Bendigo's quarters.

"That King has the biggest personal wardrobe this side of the Milky Way and that it's all in that room?"

"That he has the biggest personal wardrobe this side of the Milky Way," said Ellery, "with one very odd exception."

The Inspector stopped short. "You mean there's somebody has a *bigger* one?"

"I mean there's something missing."

"Missing! From *there?*"

"What I was looking for, Dad, is not in that room. Not one of them. But we'll make sure."

Judah was at his Bechstein playing a Bach prelude. There was an open bottle of Segonzac on the piano, and an empty glass.

Blue Shirt rose quietly from a chair and Brown Shirt turned from the window as the Queens came in. Judah paid no attention. Rather remarkably, he did not slouch at the piano. He sat well back on the bench, his back straight, his shallow chest out, head thrown back, hand playing from the wrists in beautiful, dancelike rhythms. His eyes were open and staring out across the strings at some vista visible only to himself. There was a frown on his forehead.

He came to the end of the prelude. With the last chord his hands dropped, his back and chest collapsed, his head came forward, and he reached for the bottle of cognac.

"You should play Bach more often," said Ellery.

Judah turned, startled. Then he jumped up and hurried forward with every appearance of pleasure. "You're back," he exclaimed. "I've missed you. Maybe there's something you can do about these two barbarians—I've talked to your father about it, but he merely looked wise. Do you know what this one wants me to play? Offenbach!" Judah had the bottle and glass in his hands and he began to pour himself a drink. "Where have you been, Ellery? No one would tell me."

"Wrightsville."

Judah dropped the glass. The bottle remained in his hand, but only by a sort of instinct. He looked down at the rug, foolishly.

Blue Shirt began to pick up the pieces.

"Wrightsville." Judah laughed; it sounded more like the croak of a blackbird. "And how is dear old Wrightsville?"

"Judah, I want you to come with us."

"Wrightsville?"

"The outdoor pool."

Brown Shirt said from his window, "Mr. Judah is confined to his apartment, Mr. Queen."

"I'm unconfining him. I'll take the responsibility."

"We'll have to come with him, sir."

"No."

"Then I'm sorry, sir. We have our orders from the King himself. No one else can countermand them."

"He kind of surprised Abel, I think," murmured Inspector Queen. "He doesn't seem to want any more holes in his hide than he has already, in spite of what Abel told us."

Ellery went to Judah's desk. He said into the telephone, "This is Ellery Queen. Connect me with Abel Bendigo. Wherever he is, whatever he's doing."

The connection was made quickly. Ellery said, "No, from Judah's apartment, Mr. Bendigo. Where are you now?"

"At the Home Office." Abel sounded curious. "I was beginning to think you'd walked out on us."

"If I did, I'm back in again with both feet."

"Oh?"

"Mr. Bendigo, I want to take Judah from his quarters, without a guard. It's a private matter. I understand your brother King himself ordered Judah confined. Will you take these men off the hook?"

Abel was silent. Then he said, "Let me talk to one of them."

Ellery held out the phone to Brown Shirt. Brown Shirt said, "Yes, Mr. Abel?" After a moment, he said, "But Mr. Abel, the King himself—" and stopped. Then he said again, "But Mr. Abel—" and stopped again and said nothing at all for sixty seconds. At last he said, "Yes, sir," in a worried voice, and he handed the receiver back to Ellery. He nodded to Blue Shirt, who was frowning. The two plainclothesmen went quietly out.

"Thus spake Zarathustra," murmured Judah. "And now do we move toward Armageddon?" He put the mouth of the bottle to his lips and threw his head far back.

"One other thing, Mr. Bendigo," Ellery was saying into the phone, his eyes on Judah. "Please meet us at the outdoor pool immediately."

Again Abel was silent. Then his Yankee voice said, "I'll be right over."

KARLA was looking frightened again, and King black at the sight of his brother Judah. Max'l swooped through the water and was out of the pool like a seal.

Ellery stepped before Judah. "It's all right, Max," he said, smiling.

"Max." At his master's tone the almost naked beast came to heel. He kept glowering over Ellery's shoulder at the thin little man with the green bottle. "So you're back," King Bendigo said grimly. "You're an annoying customer, Queen. How did you persuade the guards to turn my brother over to you?"

"Abel gave the order at my request."

The big man sat very still in the deck chair. "Where is Abel?"

"He'll be here in a minute. . . . Here he comes now."

The slightly tubby figure of the Prime Minister appeared, hurrying through the gardens toward them. The group at the pool waited in silence. Karla had sat up. Now she reached for a robe and threw it about her, as if she were suddenly cold. Her red hair kept glittering in the sun nervously. Judah took another pull from his bottle.

"I got here fast as I could—" panted Abel.

"Abel, I don't understand." His brother's voice was arctic. "You knew my order. What has this fellow done, hypnotized you?"

Abel stooped over his brother's chair, saying something in an earnest whisper. But King's cold face did not soften. He kept looking at Ellery as he listened.

"I still don't understand, Abel."

Abel straightened. And a curious thing occurred. As he straightened he seemed to grow tall, and as he grew tall his bland bankerish face seemed to thin, until it looked almost gaunt. It was now as rigid as the face of his brother.

The brothers stared at each other for some time.

Suddenly King Bendigo sprang from his chair. He was trembling. "I'll clear this up later," he exclaimed. "Right now I want to know what *you're* up to, Queen. You went away, now you're back. What did you find out?"

"Everything."

"Everything about what?"

"About what matters, Mr. Bendigo."

"I'm not impressed. What about the bullet I stopped? That's what I'm interested in, Queen, and I want it without frills—in business English. If you can't tell me how the trick was done, pack your bag, take your father, and get the hell off my island. I'm sick of seeing your faces around here."

"I'll be happy to tell you about the murder attempt, Mr. Bendigo." Ellery walked over to the edge of the pool. He stood there, his right hand in his jacket pocket, looking down at the water. Karla was staring up at him; once she glanced at her husband. Abel was no longer looking at his brother; he watched Ellery closely.

Judah clutched his bottle and surveyed them all with unusual warmth.

The Inspector edged back. He felt a certain joy. He stopped very near Max.

Ellery turned to King, bringing his hand from his pocket as he did so. The little Walther nestled in his palm.

"This is the weapon, Mr. Bendigo," Ellery said, "which your brother Judah aimed at you through two walls. The problem is curious. I testify myself that when Judah raised the gun it contained no cartridges. When he squeezed the trigger, there was no shot. Still, the ballistics tests proved that the bullet Dr. Storm dug out of your chest had been fired from this gun and no other. Would you mind examining it, please?"

The big man had been listening stonily, but with attention. Now he strode to the edge of the pool and put out his hand for the automatic.

Ellery's right hand moved to meet it. King Bendigo stepped closer, and with a sweep of the left arm Ellery struck him a heavy blow at the side of the neck and toppled him over the edge into the pool. The King landed with a cry that was smothered in a great splash.

Ellery immediately wheeled. The Walther in his hand was now gripped at the stock and his finger was curled about the trigger.

"You're not to help him," he said. "I loaded this gun fifteen minutes ago."

Behind Max, the Inspector said, "One move and I blow a hole clear through to your gut."

Max stood still. His brutal face was convulsed.

Abel was making stiff little gestures toward the pool. Judah kept looking at Ellery. And Karla swayed on her knees, reaching.

"Mrs. Bendigo, I must ask you," said Ellery, looking at the men, "to get away from the edge."

"Son." The Inspector sounded urgent.

"Cover them, Dad."

His father stepped back; there was a Police Positive in his hand.

Ellery turned to the pool again. Bendigo was flailing the water with his arms, bellowing and strangling. He went under, immediately reappeared, and immediately began to sink again.

Ellery flung himself on the pool's edge and reached far out. He caught the sinking man's hair, but somehow his quarry got away. He grabbed at a clutching hand. This time he held on, and a moment later he had pulled the big man out of the pool onto the shore.

King lay on his stomach, gagging.

Ellery stood over him. The Walther dangled. He made no attempt to touch Bendigo again.

After a while the big man pushed himself to an all-fours position. He was breathing awkwardly. He struggled to his feet, turned around.

He was unrecognizable. The hair that had given way in Ellery's hand was floating in the pool; all that was left on the magnate's head was a dank black fringe. And something had happened to his face. The vigorous cheeks had become hollow, and the strong mouth had changed its shape and outline. Little wrinkles radiated from their corners. The flesh of his neck was suddenly pouchy.

But the change was more than a matter of a lost toupee and dentures. Something far more vital had gone out of him. The black fires in his eyes had been quenched; the proud confidence that had kept his belly in and his shoulders square had been soaked and rotted out of him. Now he was a sagging and drooping as well as a bald and lined old man.

A beaten and a broken old man.

He did not look at them. His wife made an involuntary movement toward him, full of pity, but then she checked herself.

He stumbled off the camouflaged apron of the pool and made his way through them in a ploddy shuffle, difficult to watch. His long arms bobbed and swayed with his shambling progress, mere appendages. He left a thin trail of water which under the hot sun began at once to dry.

They watched him move through the gardens to the rear entrance of the Residence. He did not once look up or back.

Finally he disappeared.

Max'l cried out and plunged away and through the garden, trampling flowers and making frantic gestures to the Residence.

Karla got to her feet. She seemed strangely calm. And she went to Abel Bendigo and stood close by him.

And Judah Bendigo went to both of them.

After a moment, as if one of them had spoken, the three turned and went side by side at a good pace around the garden and one of the five arms of the Residence and so out of the Queens' sight.

"WILL you tell me," said Inspector Queen, "will you tell me what *any* of this means?"

Ellery was eying the toupee, floating like a black crab in the pool. "You know, Dad, I had no idea he wore a toupee. Or false teeth. He looked a thousand years old."

The Inspector hefted his Police Positive. "If you don't open up," he said, "so help me Hannah—"

Ellery laughed. "Not here," he said. "Suppose I take you for a ride."

XV

THEY WALKED through the great hall of the Residence to the courtyard. There was a disturbing clatter and buzz all about. It seemed to come from everywhere. Servants and minor flunkies bustled about, doors banged, guards ran here and there. Outside, where they had left the Residence car, there was a traffic jam. An armed PRPD man was trying to untangle it; he was shouting for help. Finally the tangle was unsnarled and vehicles began to move through the gates. There were a great many trucks. On the road outside other trucks and cars struggled toward the Reisdence, bumper to bumper.

The Inspector stuck his head out of the car window. "Look at the sky!"

It was alive with aircraft. They were all big ones—transports, trimotored passenger planes. Curiously, as many seemed to be coming in as taking off. The island shook under their thunder.

"What's happening!"

"Maybe the King has declared himself a war," said Ellery, inching the car forward. "This has all the earmarks of a mobilization which has been thoroughly worked out in advance, with everything ready to roll at the touch of a button."

"The way he's feeling right now, he couldn't declare a dividend. Turn off this road if you want to get somewhere. This is worse than the Merritt Parkway on Labor Day."

Just past the belt of woods surrounding the Residence, Ellery found a side lane, scarcely wider than a bridle path, which was free of traffic. He swung into it. A truck driver shouted enviously after him.

"I think this comes out near the cliffs somewhere," said the Inspector. "Near the harbor."

"Sounds like just the place for a quiet talk."

A few minutes later they were parked on the edge of the cliffs. The harbor lay below them.

The sight confounded them. The bay was clogged with ships of all lengths and tonnages. The cruiser *Bendigo* had withdrawn from the neck of the bay; it was anchored some distance at sea, near a light cruiser which the Queens had not seen before. Launches darted and skipped about loaded with passengers. The turrets of several big submarines were surfacing. The docks were piled high with crated goods; they were being loaded at a furious tempo into the holds. The roads leading down from the interior of the island looked like ant trails. And from the entire harbor area rose a confused roar that increased in volume with each moment.

"Whatever they're doing," said the Inspector wonderingly, "they sure had everything ready. What's come over this place? Did you have anything to do with this?"

"No," said Ellery slowly. "No, I don't see how I could have." He shook his head. "Well, do you want to see what I brought back from Wrightsville?"

"Brought back?"

Ellery reached over to the back seat of the car. He opened the suitcase he had carried off the plane that morning. A bulky Manila envelope lay on his haberdashery. He took this and sat back.

"This is what I was doing in Wrightsville," he said, unclasping the envelope. "You'd better read it. To the end."

It was a thick manuscript, and the Inspector took it with a glance at the harbor. But he read slowly, without looking up.

While his father read, Ellery watched the harbor. A fleet of seaplanes had landed in the bay to add to the mess. They were taking on passengers. Before the Inspector had finished they took off, making their runs along a narrow channel cleared by a squad of fast launches, evidently of the harbor traffic police.

When the Inspector had put down the last page, he stared incredulously at the frantic activity below them. "I hadn't realized the extent of his power. . . . I suppose," he said suddenly, "this is all on the level?"

"Every word of it, Dad."

"It's hard for a schmo like me to believe. It's too . . . colossal. But, son." The Inspector eyed the manuscript Ellery was stuffing back into the envelope. "You said—"

"I know what I said," Ellery interrupted fiercely. He tossed the envelope behind him. "And I say it again. What's been happening on this island in purgatory is all in that envelope. Not the details, not the little techniques of circumstance and plot! But the backgrounds, the reasons."

Ellery took Judah's little Walther out of his pocket. He pointed it absently through the windshield at the heavy cruiser. And pulled the trigger. The Inspector ducked. But nothing happened. The gun was empty after all.

"Take the problem of Judah's miracle," Ellery said. "It was really no problem at all. What made it a problem was not its impossibility, but the positions of the people involved in it. *Those* were the impossibilities—until you knew the story that began in 1897, the story that exposed the people for what they were and are . . . the story that's in the envelope. Then the people were no longer impossibilities and the human problem—the big problem—was solved."

The Inspector said nothing. He did not understand, but he knew that soon he would. It had happened a hundred times before, in just this way. Still, for the hundredth time, he wondered.

"The physical aspects of Judah's miracle first," Ellery said, toying with the Walther. "It was such a very simple miracle. A man points an empty gun at a solid wall, and two rooms away, across a corridor filled with men, with another and even thicker wall intervening, another man slumps back with a bullet in his breast.

"An empty gun can't shoot a bullet. But even if it could, no bullet could have entered the other room from outside. So Judah didn't shoot King. No one shot King—" the Inspector started—"from *outside* the Confidential Room. It was materially impossible. But King *was* shot while in that room. I'd seen him, with my own eyes, unwounded, only three and a half minutes before the shot. So had you. We'd seen him close that door, automatically causing it to lock, and you yourself swore that the door was not opened again until we went in together after midnight. And that was the only way in or out of the room. Conclusion: King was shot from inside the room. He must have been. There's no other possibility."

"Except," remarked his father, "that that was impossible, too."

"There's no other possibility," repeated Ellery. "Therefore the appearance of impossibility is an illusion. He was shot from *inside* the room. That being the fact, only one person could have shot him. There were only two persons in that room, and there is no possibility from the circumstances that there could have been more than two, less than two, or two different ones. The two persons who entered that room, who remained in that room, and whom we found in that room were King and Karla. King could not possibly have shot himself; there were no powder marks on his shirt. Therefore Karla shot him."

The Inspector said, "But Karla had no gun."

"Another illusion. Why did we assume that Karla had no gun? Because we couldn't find one. But Karla did shoot him. Therefore our search was at fault. Karla *must* have had a gun, and since it couldn't possibly have left the room by the time we entered it to find King unconscious from his wound, then it was still in the room when we entered."

"And the door was immediately shut," retorted his father, "and no one was allowed to leave while we searched, and we searched everything and everyone there, and before anyone was passed out through the door we made another body-search, and before anything was passed out through the door we searched it, too, and still we didn't find the gun. Now that's really an impossibility, Ellery. That's what hung me up. If the gun had to be in that room, why didn't we find it?"

"Because we didn't look in the place where it was hidden."

"We looked in *every*thing!"

"We couldn't have. We must have neglected one thing."

The Inspector mumbled, "Whatever it was . . . Too bad King broke the seal you put on the door. By this time it's been removed from the room."

"It was removed from the room before I sealed the door."

"Now that," cried his father, "*is* impossible! Not a thing was taken out before you sealed the lock—that we didn't search!"

"I'd have sworn, too, that we searched everything that passed out before we locked and sealed the room. But later I remembered that there was one thing we let go through that we clearly, definitely did not search."

"We searched every human being that passed through that doorway," said the Inspector angrily, "including the wounded man himself. We searched the hospital table he went out on. We searched Dr. Storm's medical kit and every last article of equipment he'd brought in. Do you admit that?"

"Yes."

"Then what are you talking about?" The Inspector waved his arms. "Nothing else went out!"

"One other thing went out. And that thing we didn't search. Therefore it was in that thing that the gun left the room."

"*What* thing!"

"The bottle of Segonzac cognac Judah took out of the filing case while we were all in the room after the shooting."

INSPECTOR QUEEN was dazed. "The gun went out hidden *in a bottle of cognac?* A *gun?* In a *bottle?* Are you out of your ever-loving mind? I suppose he just eased it down through the neck of the bottle—trigger guard, stock, and all! What's the matter with you? Besides, that was a brand-new bottle. You yourself sliced off the government tax label and the wax seal and removed the cork with a corkscrew!"

"So I did," said Ellery. "And that's what bamboozled me, as it was planned to do. But you can wriggle from yesterday to doomsday, and the fact stands: There must have been a gun in that room, the gun must have left the room, the only thing that left the room without being searched was Judah's bottle of cognac, therefore it was in Judah's bottle of cognac that the gun left. If we accept that fact, as we must—"

"Accept it!" muttered his father. "How can I accept an impossibility? You weaseled out of two impossibilities only to get yourself . . . bottled up, God help us, in a third!"

"If you accept the fact, then the bottle as a carrier can't be impossible, it must be possible. How can a bottle conceal a gun? Well, let's have a look at a Segonzac bottle." Ellery reached over again to his suitcase and brought out one of the familiar bottles. "I took this sample along on the trip to keep reminding me of my fatheadedness. Since the Segonzac bottles are uniform in shape and size, this one will serve as a model for the one Judah had stashed away in the Confidential Room.

"True, it has a conventional neck—in fact, the neck is on the slender side. So the gun couldn't have been inserted through the mouth and neck, as you so reasonably pointed out. *But it has a broad base—the Segonzac bottles are bell-shaped.* And this Walther .25 that fired the shot—according to the ballistics tests—is how big? It isn't big at all. On the contrary, it's absurdly small. The barrel is only an inch long. *The total length of the gun is scarcely four inches.* Add to the bottle's broad bottom and the tiny size of the weapon the felicitious fact that the Segonzac bottles are also a very dark green in color—*so dark as to be opaque*—and the impossibility melts away, leaving a simple answer."

Ellery tossed the bottle aside. "The bottle Judah took out of the filing case in the Confidential Room that night was specially made, Dad. It had a false bottom. The false bottom must have been lined with cotton, or felt, or some other sound-deadening material. The false bottom in a bottle of opaque glass would easily conceal the Walther from our eyes, and the lining of the compartment would prevent any clink, as the bottle was held or moved, from betraying its contents to our ears. All this in a bottle with a faked government tax stamp, professionally corked and sealed, and the illusion was set."

The Inspector said, "She shot him—he got the bottle out of the drawer. ... Karla and Judah were in this together!"

Ellery nodded, his eyes on the frenzied harbor scene below. "Each had a part to play, worked out in advance. Judah wrote and sent the threatening letters and with considerable histrionic talent staged and played the scene in which he solemnly aimed and fired an empty gun . . . a gun whose existence and whereabouts he was careful to point out to me beforehand. And in the Confidential Room, where the shooting was to take place, Karla pulled the trigger of the actual murder gun—and in her nervousness bungled the job—hid the gun in the false bottom of the prepared bottle, put the bottle back in the filing case, and then 'fainted.' They were accomplices, all right—"

"Just a minute," said his father. "King was shot with Judah's gun—the gun you took off Judah's desk after the shooting—the gun you're holding right now. That's a fact proved by ballistics tests. But this gun was in Judah's study! How could Karla have shot King with a gun that wasn't in the Confidential Room at any time?"

"Go back to the actual shooting of King," replied Ellery. "Karla has fired the shot at her preoccupied husband, who is wounded and unconscious before he can see who shot him. Karla then hides the murder gun in the false bottom of the bottle. After we all enter the room, Judah removes the bottle from the drawer, allows me to open it for him—daring touch, that—drinks from it—and subsequently the bottle is taken *out* of the room under our eyes.

"Remember, you and I stayed behind, after the others left, to make a last search for the gun which was no longer there. This gave the person who'd taken it out of the room in the bottle the opportunity to cross the corridor, enter Judah's study, shut the door, take the murder gun out of the false bottom of the bottle, remove any remaining cartridge from the gun . . . and then place *that* gun, the one which had shot King in the other room, on Judah's desk for us to find later! The gun which I had seen Judah pretend to fire at midnight—the always-empty gun—was then taken away. By the time you and I searched the Confidential Room for the last time, locked and sealed the door, and went to Judah's study, the switch had long since been made. The gun I picked up from Judah's desk was no longer the one I had seen Judah pretend to fire in that hocus pocus at midnight—*it was now the gun Karla had fired at King in the other room.*"

"Identical guns . . ."

"In outer appearance only. It was easy enough to get hold of a pair of guns of the same make, type, and caliber, and deliberately to chip similar slivers of ivory out of the inlays of both stocks. But they couldn't fool ballistics so far as the interior mechanisms of the two guns were concerned, and they knew we'd make the lab tests. That's why there had to be two guns that looked alike: so that a switch could be made after the shooting, putting the murder gun where the dummy gun had been and thereby completing the illusion of a single gun and consequently an impossible crime."

"But why?" cried the Inspector. "Why did they want it to look like an impossible crime?"

"Because an impossible crime, a crime that 'couldn't' have happened, even though a man was shot in the impossible process," said Ellery dryly, "would protect the criminals from detection, or at least from prosecution. If the gun we found outside the room was demonstrably the gun that had been fired at King *inside* the room—when the gun that had been fired inside the room couldn't possibly have got out!—then neither Judah outside nor Karla inside could be tagged for the job. You could suspect and theorize, but unless you could demonstrate how it was done, they were safe."

Ellery was tapping the wheel with the little gun, frowning at the activity below them. "I wonder," he began, "if King *is* mobilizing—"

But his father was not listening. "Karla put the gun in the bottle, Judah took the bottle out of the drawer. . . . I don't seem to recall *Judah's* taking that bottle out of the room. Or Karla, either. It was—"

He glanced at Ellery in bewilderment.

"It was Abel," said Ellery absently. "Abel, who went out of character to lose his temper, grab Judah by the collar, make a hammy, emotional speech . . . snatch the bottle of Segonzac out of Judah's hand, *and leave the room with it.* So it was Abel who crossed the corridor and switched the guns in Judah's study. Yes, Abel was in the plot, too, Dad. And now you see why Abel brought us here and has kept us here on what seemed a trivial assignment. Our function was purely and simply to witness the 'impossible' crime—as representatives of the world outside—so that we could testify later to the facts which seem to clear Judah and Karla."

XVI

INSPECTOR QUEEN was silent.

"They were all in it," said Ellery, still frowning at the harbor. "Judah, Karla, Abel. The wife and both brothers. Conspiring to kill the great King—an assassination in the approved historical tradition. Abel, the leader, the other two acting under his orders."

"Yes," said the Inspector, "it would have to be Abel who led them. Judah's a feeler, and Karla wouldn't be able to conceive such a plan. But Abel's a thinker."

Ellery nodded. "And a brilliant one. A man who's always been run by his head. Who's run his brother King."

"What?" said his father.

"We had proof of that the first hour we were on the island, Dad, if we'd only had the sense to see it. Abel parked us in the reception room while he went into King's office. We overheard what went on in there . . . Mr. Minister of War of the South American accent got King roaring mad; he almost wrecked a delicate deal. And then King stopped roaring to say, 'Yes, Abel. What is it?' and Abel either whispered to him or passed him a note. Immediately King Bendigo became a very smooth article. He handled Mr. Minister of War exactly right, and Mr. Minister of War walked out with two yachts in his pocket and the Guerrerra works belonging to Bodigen Arms was safe.

"And a few minutes later King ran into trouble again, with the very smooth Monsieur the Minister of Defense. Monsieur the Minister of Defense is a stone; he demands to be flown back. 'What, Abel?' says King, and after a whispered confabulation with Abel, King again pulls off a successful deal and another arms contract is saved for the Company. When Abel is silent, King blusters and blunders. When Abel whispers, King becomes the negotiator supreme."

Ellery stared at the seething bay. "Think back to my notes, Dad. Between 1919 and 1924 Kane Bendigo—flying solo, as it were—cracks up three times. And that's not counting his father's old, established business, which Kane's run into the ground in record time. Then, backed by a Wrightsville group hypnotized by his personality, he starts his first munitions plant and suddenly he's off to the races. Did he start that business alone? Oh, no. Abel has left college to join him—Abel, at the age of twenty! And King's ridden high, wide, and handsome ever since, and Abel's never left his side.

"King knows what he wants. He's always known that. But while he can set the goals, he can't plan and execute the moves needed to reach them. It's Abel who's done the practical work, who's performed industrial miracles behind the plausible, glittering façade of King. Without Abel, King would have been a man with grandiose ideas who couldn't have run a successful newsstand. With Abel, he's become the most powerful man in the world."

The Inspector was shaking his head. "And still it doesn't make sense to me, Ellery. I can see how Karla and Judah would turn on King. Karla's a decent sort, for all her background. She found out the truth about the man she married, what a power-mad lunatic he is—maybe found out a lot about his plans we don't know. Judah's a disappointed artist, a man with a deep feeling about people, and he considers his brother the biggest mass-murderer in history—isn't that what he said? And both Judah and Karla stuck on this nightmare of an island, stewing in the fumes from those damned munitions and atomic plants . . .

"I see those two fine. But Abel's been an active partner in this thing for twenty-seven years, Ellery! You say yourself he's the one who's made it possible. You might say he plotted King's death because of personal ambition. But I don't see that. A man like Abel always prefers the background. He gets a kick out of pulling the wires and hiding in the shadow of his front man.

"And those notes of yours. . . . You can't doubt, from reading them, that Abel's worshiped his brother Kane ever since they were boys in Wrightsville. Ever since Kane saved his life in that swimming hole when Abel was seven years old." The Inspector shook his head again. "It doesn't go down, Ellery. It doesn't wash."

"It goes down, and it washes," said Ellery. "Just because of that life-saving incident."

"How do you mean?" His father stared.

"Remember the day in the gym, when King found Judah's fourth letter in one of his boxing gloves and got so irritated he slipped on the tiles at the edge of the indoor pool and fell in?"

"Yes?"

"Didn't that strike you as awfully queer, Dad? His sinking, floundering, spluttering? His having to be pulled out of the water? The incident stuck in my mind. It bothered me.

"Then in Wrightsville," said Ellery, "I learned the details of his athletic prowess as a youth. He was an all-round athlete, participated in almost every sport. Football. Baseball. Boxing. Wrestling. Track. Field. But never once did I run across his name in connection with swimming."

"But—" his father began in perplexity.

"Today I took inventory of his wardrobe. There are dozens, scores of every conceivable article of male apparel. Except one, which should have been there—judging from the quantities of everything else—by the dozen or the score, too. *Yet there was not a single pair of swimming trunks, not a single bathing suit or swimming accessory.*"

"That's why you knocked him into the pool!"

"As a last check," Ellery nodded. "And he almost drowned. He would have drowned if I hadn't pulled him out. That's what's behind Abel's motive, Dad: *King can't swim.*"

"But . . . that silver cup awarded to 'Kane Bendigo' for water polo! Did you ever try playing water polo without knowing how to swim? He *must* be able to swim!"

"The 'Kane Bendigo' was re-engraved. Karla even explained that his original name was C-a-i-n and that he had changed it to K-a-n-e, and since he'd won the water polo trophy under his orginal name, he'd had the cup changed to read K-a-n-e later. She specifically told us that *he* had told her that. . . . Dad, we've seen the proof twice since we got to Bendigo Island that the man doesn't know how to swim. So he lied to his wife about the reason for the re-engraving on that trophy. It couldn't have been his. It had been awarded to someone else, and he'd had the name re-engraved not from Cain to Kane, but from someone else's name to Kane!

"This man with the false hair and the false teeth and the false front has been living another lie. For forty years. Because if King can't swim now, he couldn't swim in 1911. *Once he's learned, no one ever forgets how to swim.*

"Then it wasn't King who jumped into that mountain stream and saved seven-year-old Abel from drowning that day in the hills above Wrightsville. Who could it have been? Only the three brothers were involved, and Abel was the victim. So it could only have been Judah who rescued Abel. We know Judah can swim—we saw him do it in the indoor pool the day King accidentally fell in."

"Judah saved Abel's life," said the Inspector softly, "*and King took the credit.*"

Ellery nodded over the flame of a match. He puffed and tossed the match out his window. "There's the explanation in a phrase. The record shows that, even as a boy of fourteen, Kane had a domineering unscrupulous character. Because Judah was a timid, sensitive boy, younger and physically weaker, and could be bullied into keeping his mouth shut, Kane deliberately stole the credit for Abel's rescue from Judah. Accepted a medal for it—even made an amazing little speech about it, you'll recall, saying modestly that he didn't really 'deserve' the medal, 'anybody' would have done the same? And Kane—as King—has taken the credit, stolen the spotlight, been the big shot ever since. In everything. That single incident, way back in 1911 in what was then one-horse Wrightsville, illuminates each of the three Bendigo brothers.

"Take King. Deep inside, he's afraid. He must have been, he must still be, deathly afraid of the water—a boy who excelled in so many different sports and yet didn't participate in one of the commonest sports of all, swimming, must have had a powerful psychological reason for not learning. . . . He knows the truth about himself. He knows he's no hero, that in reality he's an inferior human being. But once that incident occurred, once he publicly proclaimed himself a hero as a swimmer—and probably his fear of water was what prompted him to do it—then he shaped his whole future development. He had to repress that sickening truth, in himself as well as to the world, and in order to do so he developed an enormously aggressive personality. Eventually his aggressiveness turned into grandiose channels, and with Abel's implementation of his megalomaniac goals he's become the incredible power he is today."

"And Abel," muttered the Inspector, "Abel's been paying back his debt of gratitude."

"Exactly. Abel was unconscious when he was pulled out; he didn't see who rescued him. He was a young child, and of course he believed the story his big brother-hero told. So Abel has come through these past forty years believing he owes his life to King. And so devoting his life to his savior.

"And Judah," said Ellery, "Judah was cuffed and cowed into keeping his mouth shut—Judah, who had reached the age of twelve scarred by the weight of his Judas cross and the cruelty of his schoolmates, not to mention that of his father. Judah couldn't fight his husky big brother. Judah didn't dare tell the truth. Judah could only watch the credit that belonged to him showered on the unscrupulous bully who had stolen it. There could be only one place for Judah to go, and that was still further into his shell. To complicate matters—the evidence is in these notes—Judah's always been something of a masochist. Deep down he enjoyed his martyr's role. . . .

"There could be only one port for a man like that—and that's where Judah has landed. At the business end of a bottle. He drinks for the reason most alcoholics drink. It's a way of enduring his unhappiness."

"I wonder how Abel found out . . ."

"The wonder isn't so much that he found out as that it's taken him so long. It seems incredible that Abel could have lived and worked by King's side for so many years and remained ignorant of such a simple fact as his brother's not knowing how to swim. But it's not as incredible as it seems. Abel's had a blind spot on the subject. From the age of seven he's *known*—impressed into his brain by a traumatic experience of great force—that King could swim. And King threw up a clever smoke screen. What did Karla tell us? That except for a bit of wrestling and boxing with Max, *King never takes any exercise*. They've led unbelievably crowded lives, and Abel himself is hardly the sports-loving type."

"Then Abel found out—"

"Or Judah, more than usually drunk, told him," nodded Ellery. "Then all Abel would have to do was manufacture a test, as I did today . . . and everything would curdle in Abel. Instantly. To worship your brother for forty years, to dedicate your life to him, and suddenly to find that you've been worshipping a fraud—worse, a cheat. . . . It would be a devastating experience. If Abel's worship of King had blinded him to King's faults, this knowledge would clear his eyes in a flash.

"So Abel drew up a new set of plans. The first plans of which his brother King had no knowledge."

Ellery fell silent, and for some time they sat without speaking, continuing to watch what was going on below them. The launches streaked back and forth, the ships loaded, the cars and trucks continued to stream down from the cliffs, vessels plunged out to sea, planes landed empty and took off full. . . .

"What the devil *is* he up to?" Ellery said at last. "Dad, this looks like a wholesale evacuation of the island."

"I wonder where he is. . . ."

"Who?"

"His Majesty. Do you suppose he's alone?"

"Why?"

"If he is," said the Inspector, "he's not exactly safe."

"He's safe," said Ellery gloomily. "You saw Max go after him. He hasn't let King out of his sight since the night of the attempt. They'd have to kill Max first."

"Well?" said the Inspector.

Ellery stared at him. Then he snapped on the ignition and kicked the starter.

XVII

THE GUARDS were gone from the foyer of the family's apartments.

The corridors were deserted.

"They're probably at the Home Office," said the Inspector.

"No," said Ellery, "no. If anything's happened, it took place here!"

They pushed open the door and went in. There were no flunkies about. Everything was in disorder.

"Max?" roared the Inspector.

Ellery was already racing toward King Bendigo's private suite. When the Inspector caught up with him he was at the doorway to a great bedchamber, looking in.

"Isn't Max—" began the Inspector.

Then he stopped.

King Bendigo was lying neatly on his bed, his head on the bolster and his open eyes staring up at the canopy.

There was no sign of Max.

The master of Bendigo Island was dressed as they had last seen him, with still-damp slacks and soaked sports shoes, his torso naked. Three trails of blood snaked diagonally down the right side of his face. They led from a hole in his right temple. The hole looked burned; around it the flesh was tattooed with powder.

A revolver with a nickel finish was gripped in the right hand, which lay on the bed parallel with the body.

King's forefinger was still on the trigger.

"S & W .22/32 kit gun," said the Inspector, turning it over in his hands. "One shot fired. Suicide, all right—"

"You think so?" muttered Ellery.

"—if you're blind. Look at the angle of the wound, from point of entry to point of exit, Ellery. The course of the bullet was sharply downward. If King had committed suicide, he'd have had to hold the gun *pointing* sharply downward—which means from above his head. To pull the trigger from such a position and make such a wound, he'd have to hook his right *thumb* around it. With the forefinger it's a physical impossibility."

Ellery nodded, but not as if he had been listening. "So after everything that's happened—all the planning, all the eyewash—something's gone wrong again," he murmured. "In Abel's hurry he forgot to take into account the angle of the shot. I wonder how he got Max."

"Let's go ask him," said the Inspector.

THEY found Abel in King Bendigo's office. Abel and Judah, and Karla, still together.

Colonel Spring was there, too. The Colonel was in mufti. Stripped of his beautiful uniform, in a wrinkled and badly fitting suit, he fooled them for a moment. But only for a moment. His hand came up with a brown cigaret, and he said something with a lazy sting in it. He was directing the feverish activities of a group of men, also in ordinary clothes. These men were hurrying in and out of the safe vault near the great black desk, empty-handed going in, coming out laden with documents, money boxes, and what might have been precious gems in sealed cases.

The safe was almost empty.

Judah was bundled up in a coat; he looked cold. Karla was in a suit and a long wool coat. Her face was swollen and red.

Abel Bendigo was at his dead brother's desk, going through drawers. A man stood silently by, holding a grip open. Abel was dropping papers into it.

The Colonel and his men paid no attention to the interruption, but the wife and the brothers looked up sharply. Then Abel rose from the desk and made a sign to the man beside him, and the man shut and locked the grip and put the key in his pocket and carried the grip out, past the Queens.

"We're about through," said Colonel Spring to the Prime Minister.

"All right, Spring."

The men went out under their last burdens. Colonel Spring followed them, lighting a fresh *cigarillo*. As he approached the Queens he looked up, smiled, spread his hands in a charming gesture, shrugged, and passed on.

"Getaway?" said Ellery.

"Yes," said Abel.

"You seem to be doing it on a wholesale basis, Mr. Bendigo. Who gets left holding the bag?" the Inspector asked.

"You'd better get ready, too," said Abel. "We're leaving in a very few minutes."

"Not before you answer a question or two, Mr. Bendigo! Where is Max?"

"Max'l?" Abel sounded preoccupied. "I really don't know, Inspector. When the evacuation started, he disappeared. Search parties are looking for him now. I'm hoping, of course, that he'll be found before we leave the island."

The Inspector's jaws worked.

Ellery stood by in silence.

"And where," rasped the Inspector, "have you and Mrs. Bendigo and your brother Judah been since you left us at the pool?"

Abel's stare did not falter. "The three of us—I repeat, Inspector, the three of us—went directly to the Home Office, and we've been here, together, ever since. Isn't that so, Karla?"

"Yes," said Karla.

"Isn't that so, Judah?

"Yes," said Judah.

"You haven't left this room, I suppose," said the Inspector, "not one of you?"

The three shook their heads.

"When did Colonel Spring and his men get here?"

"Only a few minutes ago," said Abel with a faint smile. "But that's of no importance, is it, Inspector Queen? Since the three of us vouch for one another?"

Now the Inspector was silent. But then he said, "No. No, if you vouch for one another, I don't suppose it is. By the way, my condolences."

"Condolences?" said Abel.

"I'm sorry, Mr. Bendigo. I thought you knew that your brother King is dead."

Karla turned away. She faced the wall, and she remained facing it.

Judah took a flask from his coat and unscrewed the cap.

"We know," said Abel. "I wasn't sure you did. My brother's death was reported to us—a few minutes ago. I'm told he took his own life."

"He was murdered," said Ellery.

They stared at each other for a long time.

At last Abel said, "If there were time to go into it . . . But of course there isn't, Mr. Queen. You understand that?"

Ellery did not reply.

Abel came around King Bendigo's desk and took his sister-in-law's arm gently. "Come, Judah."

"But are you going to leave him lying there—" began the Inspector.

"My brother," said Abel, and before his stare the Inspector felt himself tighten all over, "will be buried in a fitting manner."

A HALF-HOUR later the father and the son were in a launch, with their luggage, roaring up the bay. Ahead of them sped another launch, a larger one, with the two Bendigos and Karla.

The Queens said nothing to each other. The Inspector was sunk in something remote from launches and islands and people who did murder in such a way as to confuse and defeat a man, and Ellery was taking in the fantastic scene on shore and in the bay. He had never seen so many ships, such a variety. This is what Dunkirk must have been like, he thought, minus the bombs. The whole island seemed on the move, converging in its thousands on the little harbor. Far out to sea scores of other ships lying low in the water were hove to, as if awaiting something—a signal, or nightfall. Overhead, the planes screamed and streaked, most of them leaving the island, some of them still coming in. *He must have put in a call for every seagoing vessel and aircraft in the Bendigo empire. . . .*

When they climbed aboard the big cruiser, a seaman saluted and conducted them to the chartroom. There they found the Bendigos and Karla, looking back at the harbor through glasses. Two pairs of glasses were waiting for them. In silence Ellery and his father each picked one up. In silence the five kept their eyes on the island.

The activity had noticeably slackened. The gush of vehicles down the cliff roads had dwindled to a trickle. Most of the bay spread clear; the piers were still crowded, but things were coming to the end.

The end came ninety minutes later.

The last ship edged away from the dock and headed up the bay.

The roads, the piers were deserted. From one cusp of the harbor to the other, nothing moved.

The last flight of planes rose from the heart of the island, circled once, gaining altitude, then straightened out and skimmed off into the remote skies.

A REDFACED man in a brass-buttoned blue uniform and a cap visored with gold came in.

He said to Abel: "All ready, sir. There is no one left on the island."

"There's at least one," said Inspector Queen. "King Bendigo."

The officer looked at Abel Bendigo, startled.

"My brother," said Abel steadily, "is dead. I'm in charge now, Captain. You have your orders."

Ellery put his hand on Abel's arm. "Dr. Akst?" he asked.

"On board. Safe and well."

THE *Bendigo* got under way slowly. Slowly the cruiser headed out to sea.

They were all at the railing in the stern now, watching Bendigo Island shrink and lose color and definition.

Gradually the cruiser picked up speed. The sea was calm; the air was mild.

The armada of small ships and medium-sized ships and large ships was at full steam. Most of them had already vanished over the horizon.

Through the strong glasses Ellery kept watching the island. Nothing on it anywhere moved. Nothing lived.

Five miles from the island the cruiser's speed slackened, the seas churning. Gradually they subsided and the vessel lifted and fell gently in the swells.

And suddenly, very suddenly, the whole island rose in the air and spread itself against the sky. Or so it seemed.

A great puff of smoke rose swiftly from the place where the island had lain. It mushroomed like a genie.

The cruiser trembled. A blast of sound struck the vessel, staggered them.

And then there was another explosion, and another. And still another.

And another. . . .

They had no consciousness of time.

Eventually the smoke pall drifted clear, and the débris sank and vanished.

And a sheet of flame stood out of the sea from one end of what had been Bendigo Island to the other. The entire island was burning—the ruins of the exploded buildings, the trees, the roads, the very sands. When it should burn itself out, in the course of days, or weeks, there would be nothing left but a flat black cinder on the surface of the sea.

Ellery turned, and Abel Bendigo turned, and their glances met. And Abel's glance seemed to say: *Trust me.*

Ellery's remained opaque. He was deeply troubled.

But the Inspector said with bitterness, aloud: "And

what difference will this make? Nothing has changed. It's one king or another!"

"Something has changed," said Abel.

"Yes? What?"

"It's me now, not him."

"And will that make a difference?" cried the Inspector.

"Yes. There's nothing wrong with power. The world needs power. The world needs power more today than ever before in history. Enlightened power—if you won't laugh. Power directed toward the good. Instead of the other way." Abel spoke awkwardly. His eyes were on the flames now.

"Do you think I believe that?" said the Inspector scornfully. "That the leopard can change his spots? You were in it up to your neck for twenty-seven years."

"My brother always spoke to me of a dream he had," murmured Abel. "A dream of a glorious world, a dream that could come true only if power were absolute. I believed his dream. I convinced myself that the end justified the means."

Abel stared at the flames, one hand over Judah's on the rail, the other over Karla's. "But then I discovered that my brother was a liar and a cheat and that there was no good in him at all. And I saw how a man can fool others with 'ends' while he plays with rotten means. Because, when you get right down to it, no end is worth a damn that isn't the sum total of all the means used to reach it. And I knew that if the power ever passed into my hands, I'd use it differently. And Judah and Karla," he pressed their hands, "agreed with me."

Abel turned then and glanced up at the bridge.

He raised his arm.

The seas churned and ran white again.

The *Bendigo* moved.

Judah Bendigo stirred. His hand went up to cup his eyes as he stared back at the burning island.

Karla turned from the rail. Her eyes were full of tears. She walked away, looking down at the deck.

Abel Bendigo put his coat collar up. His lips were compressed, as if he were making some great effort.

"So the King is dead," said Ellery in a bleak voice. "The King is dead, long live the King. Point of information: Now who keeps an eye on the incumbent?"

Judah Bendigo looked over his shoulder. One eye was visible, and it was fixed on his brother Abel. It was a bleary eye, but it held remarkably steady.

"I do," said Judah.